HAWAIIAN SUN

M.D. NEU

For my husband, family, and friends.

HAWAIIAN SUN

1

FREDRICK SHUT THE BEIGE PINK DOOR, pushing the image of the two men out of his mind—or at least trying to. The low hum of the ship's engines had almost masked the noise but not the sight of Wilhelm on his knees before Gerhard in a state of undress and full arousal. Wilhelm should have been alone changing, so Fredrick didn't bother announcing his presence. He didn't think he would have to after everything they had been through.

I should've given him warning. No. Gerhard would have seen me.

Why would Wilhelm do such a thing? Fredrick and Wilhelm had plans. They were going to get off the airship, meet his aunt and uncle in New Jersey, and never look back, leaving Germany and the Nazis behind. The Frankfurt to New Jersey trip would be their final journey and now everything before him lay a jumbled mess. The airship was less than twenty-four hours away from New Jersey and their freedom.

Would America be any better than Germany? From the bits of information coming out of Germany and the rest of the world, who could say, but at least he wouldn't be rounded up in one of the raids. The last letter from his mother told him more of their neighbors had been taken away and that Gerhard had to report for military service.

His sister's youth might shield her, but his mother didn't sound hopeful.

If all goes well, I should be able to send for my sister and my parents.

Fredrick glanced down, taking in his white stewards uniform, ready for the dinner service. He pulled at a loose string and allowed the thread to fall to the floor. The smells of beef broth with marrow filled his nose as he moved closer to the kitchens. The sounds of the engines and the kitchen blocked out the banging of his heart as his fists unclenched. His face and neck remained warm. He would need to calm down. He couldn't be red-faced. Chief Steward Kubis didn't like to see any of the stewards in less than perfect order. And he didn't fancy a conversation with the airship's doctor, Dr. Rudiger.

Fredrick peeked over his shoulder toward the crew space, which wasn't nearly as nice as the guest's space, but this hall had been decorated in the same beige and pinks as the rest of the living space in case guests made their way down here. Nothing of interest would greet the visitors as the area had been built for function and nothing more.

As he inhaled more of the aromas from dinner, his heart slowed and his face cooled. Wilhelm's actions shouldn't surprise him—the man tended to be as bold as he was handsome. Wilhelm had no fear, unlike Fredrick, who always had to check over his shoulder, worrying someone would learn his secret. And then what? What would the Nazis do with someone like him? He had heard the stories, but who knew for certain? Information was always hard to come by.

He inhaled as deeply as his lungs allowed, notes of chocolate sauce and coffee that Chief made now filling his nose. His stomach gave a slight rumble as a hint of a grin tugged at his lips.

Dinner for the guests smells wonderful—hopefully our dinner will be as nice.

"I wouldn't mind some of that chocolate sauce," he whispered to no one, trying to replace the earlier images from his mind with something more pleasant. At least his duties would keep his mind busy.

Adjusting his black tie, he checked for any more errant pieces of lint, and took a few forward steps, pushing the image of Wilhelm and Gerhard from his mind. After all, he still had a job to do. Hurried footsteps approached him from behind on the gangway, finally reaching him as a hand landed on his shoulder.

"Will you wait?" Wilhelm pleaded. The words were soft but intense enough for Fredrick to stop and listen, despite his nose telling him he needed to report to the kitchen to begin his shift.

"What?" he snapped as he faced Wilhelm. His blue eyes and soft brown hair were only mildly messy from his dalliance. A pink tint colored his cheeks and his lips gave his earlier actions away.

Wilhelm's pleasant expression shifted to an icy glare as his brows narrowed. "You didn't see anything."

Fredrick laughed, but no merriment played through the tone.

"I'm serious, Fredrick. You saw nothing." Wilhelm quickly glanced over his shoulder and pulled him off the main walkway. "You weren't seen, only heard. Lucky for the both of us, the ship's engines masked all our noise."

"I may not know much," Fredrick started, the words oozing with as much venom as he could muster, "but I recognized what you were doing. We've done that very thing enough times."

Wilhelm pulled them along the corridor to the crew shower and bath. This area resembled the rest of this part of the deck, all built for the functions the locale served, but the crew accommodations were nothing compared to the guest showers. They knew this location would be empty this time of day as everyone was seeing to their duties.

Like we're supposed to be.

"Fredrick, it's not like that ..." Wilhelm paused, glancing over his shoulder and down the corridor of the giant flying machine. The drone of the engines and the gentle movements of the ship hopefully keeping their conversation quiet. He wasn't in his dinner uniform yet and would need to change, but he had the second seating, not the first.

He better not want me to cover for him ... again.

"Gerhard found out." The words dropped like ice in a scotch on the rocks.

Fredrick's set jaw and puffed out shoulders deflated and he rubbed his brow. Sweat built up on his forehead as his stomach plummeted to the floor. "What? How?"

"I don't know," Wilhelm countered, peeking over his shoulder before quickly meeting Fredrick's gaze again. This time his eyes were filled with worry and fear. "This is a small ship and you know the walls are thin. Perhaps he heard us, or intercepted a message from my father. I don't know. I think he only knows about me ..."

"Not us?"

Wilhelm bit at his lower lip. "I don't think he knows anything about ... that ..."

"Are you sure?" Fredrick's heart sank—he didn't want either of them to be found out. His family wasn't as connected as Wilhelm's and they couldn't protect him, but still, he didn't want anything to happen to Wilhelm. They had plans together.

"I don't know, but I didn't have a lot of opportunity to ask." Wilhelm ran a hand through his hair. "I think you're safe ... no, I know you're safe. Gerhard's stupid and would've said something."

"Why didn't he report you?" Fredrick glanced both up and down the passageway. So far no one was present, but the clock was ticking and soon they would need to report to duty. Most of the guests were up on A Deck in the writing room or lounge. Perhaps a few men remained in the smoking room or at the bar, so he wasn't worried about being seen by the guests. Those not there would be getting ready for the dinner service, but he couldn't be certain. Wilhelm was correct; the *Hindenburg*, despite her overall size, was not a big ship and even he couldn't account for all 97 people on board at the moment.

Fredrick's gaze narrowed. "Instead he had you on your knees before him." He wanted the words to sting and hurt, but as they came out the malice he intended came out as worry.

"I did what I had to do." He rubbed his lips. "I won't be shamed for that."

"And what about me?" Fredrick lowered his voice. "What about us?"

Wilhelm remained silent but the way his stare bounced around, unable to meet Fredrick's gaze, told him what he needed to know. Things had ended.

"I see." Fredrick shook his head. "I have work to do before dinner. I have my duties for the rest of the afternoon and supper. I won't be free again until later tonight."

"Are you mad?" Wilhelm extended out a hand.

"Yes. No. I don't know." Fredrick glanced around the space. "I thought this airship was the most glamorous place I'd ever been and I imagined you were one of the most amazing people I'd ever met. Now ..." Fredrick held out a hand and stopped himself, hearing voices from down the passage. "Go change. I'll tell the Chief Steward and the Chief you had a headache and will be a few minutes late."

Wilhelm squeezed Fredrick's arm before rushing off.

Fredrick closed his eyes and took as deep a breath as his lungs would allow before he headed to the kitchen. He needed to check in and see to his duties for dinner service.

• • •

Fredrick examined the mirror, meeting his reflection. The darkness under his eyes was inevitable after how he slept, or didn't sleep, the night before. Every part of him ached with exhaustion from yesterday and the poor rest he had. Even the gentle motion of the airship did nothing to help him sleep. As he continued his personal examination, he thought back to lying in his berth. He found the ceiling above his bunk more interesting than the back of his eyelids. When he laid his head on his pillow, a hum, or more like a growl, seemed to grow around him and continued, not appearing to take a break.

That noise is probably what kept me awake. The winds around these ships can cause many strange sounds.

He pushed the night's thoughts from his mind his lips pinched together. He didn't get the opportunity to speak with Wilhelm, but what more was there to say? Now they have a busy day ahead. The weather reports out of New Jersey were not in their favor if the officers were to be believed. If anything would hinder the airship's arrival, bad weather would be the offender, despite the advances. The *Hindenburg* now had some of the most advanced equipment available thanks to their refresh in Frankfurt.

He didn't envy the engineers or the pilot. Because of the potential delays, there would be no slacking off. Plenty of work needed to be done. He had cabins to tend to, luggage to account for and the guests still needed, and expected, the quality of service the *Hindenburg* provided.

The pride of the German Reich and the Führer.

However, the delays meant they would have a whole day of service in the air. Breakfast, dinner, cocktails, and light supper were on the schedule, depending on when the high landing, or flying moor, would take place. The last he heard, they would moor around 1900 local time. He glanced at his timepiece.

"I have a lot to do."

He pushed the growing growling or moaning out of his mind. Somehow the noise had swelled, not loud enough to keep him from doing his job, but an annoying background level that seemed to follow him around the ship.

As the morning turned into the afternoon and the afternoon met the evening, everyone grew anxious for the arrival. His enthusiasm to see his aunt and uncle grew, and now that he had the time to clear his head, he wasn't angry at Wilhelm any longer. Fredrick supposed he understood. He wished he had a moment to speak with him, but the universe was against them. They saw each other as they rushed about their duties, but they never had a moment alone to speak. They were able to share a smile now and again throughout the day. And a lot can be conveyed in a grin—at least that's what he had read.

As the ship moved into position for its mooring, Fredrick finally had a few moments to go over his and Wilhelm's plans. He had received written approval to see his aunt and uncle from Kubis and their Commanding Officer. He would need to keep it with his travel documents, in case there were any issues. Fredrick would leave everything on the ship with the exception of the one hundred and fifty dollars he had managed to save over the last two years, and a couple of photos of his parents, brother and sister. The rest, his clothes and everything else, could be replaced. He patted his pocket, feeling the coins and his billfold. He knew his aunt and uncle would have clothes for him and Wilhelm so he wasn't worried about that.

"Hey," Wilhelm called from behind him.

"Hello." Fredrick turned, pushing the continuing background noise away and planting what he hoped to be a pleasant expression on his face. "I haven't had a chance to talk to you all day. Sorry."

Wilhelm shrugged, delicious in his dress uniform. If he were honest, Wilhelm looked good in anything, but somehow this uniform genuinely made Wilhelm stand out. "It's a busy day. You ready? I heard we'll be mooring ..."

The noise plaguing him all day grew and for a moment Fredrick imagined a great beast might be attacking the ship. "Do you hear that?"

"Hear what? The ship?" Wilhelm asked, looking around.

"No ... it's like a groan or whine, perhaps even a growl. I've been hearing it since last night and the sound's getting louder."

Wilhelm beamed. "You and your super hearing. It's probably ship noises and the weather outside."

Fredrick's gaze narrowed as he glanced up and down the corridor. Yes, he agreed, he was probably hearing things, so he pushed the racket away and softly set his hand on Wilhelm's shoulder. "About yesterday ..."

Wilhelm held up a hand. "Don't worry, I took care of him last night after my final rounds. I told Gerhard that if he says anything, I would report him to the Chief Steward or our Commanding Officer. Perhaps both. I asked him who were they going to believe, him or me, especially with who my father is in Berlin. That took the wind out of his sails." His lips pulled up in a grin, enhancing the dimple in his chin.

"You think that'll work?"

"Well, when I saw him this afternoon, he wouldn't look at me, so I think we're in the clear. I wish I would've considered that before, but he caught me off guard and I panicked."

"I can't wait to get off this ship." Fredrick laughed with a glance to his timepiece: 19:20. "It'll be nice to feel the earth under my feet again."

"You say that every time we arrive at our destination."

"I suppose ..."

The ship listed backward as Fredrick stumbled to hold on, howls and screams filling his ears as he tried to regain his footing. An explosion rocked the ship yet again. Wilhelm lay on the floor and Fredrick knelt down to help his friend, trying to pull him up, blood dripping from a spot on his head where he must have gotten hit. "What's happening?" he yelled, trying to bring Wilhelm to consciousness by patting his face. "Wilhelm!" A rush of hot air engulfed him. Heat built around him as he tugged Wilhelm along the gangway to the airship's exit or one of the windows. "Wilhelm!" he yelled again. "Someone help! Please!" he called out, but was met with more screams and bellows for assistance from all over the ship. The moan he had been hearing was now a full-blown growl like someone had released all the dragons from hell to attack. Fredrick glanced up as a flood of reds, oranges and yellows came for him. A beast of flames rushed toward him as all senses seemed to vanish. "Oh my ..."

2

F REDRICK BLINKED SEVERAL TIMES as his eyes adjusted. The day was no longer windy or rainy, but warm and clear, not a cloud in the sky. The air filling his lungs was clean and fresh, no longer burning. Birds hung in the bright blue sky as he scanned his surroundings, taking stock of his new environment. There was a concrete platform under his feet and a trolley car behind him that slowly moved off with a hiss of electrics. It was followed quickly by all the people vacating the platform, moving off in different directions. Above him a sign flashed with the time: 5:45p.m.

That can't be right—we're not supposed to be in New Jersey until 1930.

Traces of the ocean with harsher salt aromas tickled his nose. "What?" He continued to take in his new environment. This platform had walkways leading off to a building with a sign above the entrance, people rushed in and out some with luggage. The building was unlike any he'd seen before—the structure appeared odd and the design felt wrong and off-putting, but it had a grandness about it, like one of the hotels he saw in New York, or Rio de Janeiro. Adjacent to what he assumed to be a hotel stood a much plainer, more utilitarian type of building of glass, maybe a sort of office or commercial building, he couldn't be sure.

Behind these structures was an airfield with a mighty airship unlike any design Fredrick had witnessed floating barely ten feet above the Earth moored at its docking platform. People buzzed about, tending to the vessel with vehicles rushing to-and-fro as crew supervised the fueling and other maintenance of the monster ship. Everyone stirred with a purpose familiar to Fredrick. Despite his new location, the work of an airship remained the same, from what he observed. However, this airship had dual sections seemingly fused together and the shape wasn't oval. The vessel was contorted and more flattened. Regardless, the *Hindenburg* would have been dwarfed in size, should the ship be here.

Where was the *Hindenburg*? Where's Wilhelm? More importantly, where was he? What happened with the fire and the bellowing of the beastly sounds of the ship? All the people? His crewmates and the passengers?

He scanned his body, taking inventory. He didn't appear injured, but he now wore civilian clothes: dark pants, polished black shoes, and a crisp blue long-sleeve button-down shirt. The crisp late afternoon air continued to fill his senses as a slight breeze kissed his cheeks, he dug into his pocket, fumbling with his billfold and the photos he still possessed.

"Hey," a chipper voice called out. "You must be my new guy. Fredrick, right?"

"Was?" Fredrick responded in his native German. The man before him was in an unfamiliar uniform with a leather satchel draped across his chest, not military, definitely not Nazi or American. The bars on his shoulders signified some sort of rank, perhaps an officer if he had to take a guess. The officer had short brown hair and hazel eyes. His slim frame offset his shorter height. A bright toothy grin dazzled Fredrick's eyes; he had never seen teeth so white.

He pulled his thoughts away from the man. Fredrick couldn't afford to be distracted by his appearance. *"Wo bin ich? Wo ist die Hindenburg?"* Fredrick asked, barely noticing the man before him any longer.

"Oh crap." The English words rushed from the Officer's mouth, waking Fredrick from his trance. "I'm sorry man, I don't speak German."

He pulled out some kind of a device from his satchel and tapped away. "Wait. Didn't your file mention you spoke English and French?"

"Yes, sorry." Noises of the various vehicles echoed around him, but not all the hullabaloo could be coming from the few vehicles he saw. There must be a large road nearby—what was happening? There were more buildings all around them with more voices speaking in English and other languages. It reminded him of being in Berlin, or New York, or even Rio de Janeiro. All this commotion and noise, how can anyone hear themselves think.

He pushed the foreign racket from his mind and focused. He'd need to calm himself if he didn't want to be found out. Off to what he assumed to be the north lay the huge ship, and beyond the airship, water—a bay, perhaps. This might be a new American Airship hanger. He had seen the one in New York, connecting to the Empire State building, but that wasn't a field or zeppelin yard.

A roar above him caused him to duck his head and glance up toward the sky.

"What?" Fredrick pointed at the tail end of a plane rushing off. Never in his life had he seen a plane of that size and configuration. Had America been planning for war and building all these huge machines? Germany and the Nazis had no chance of winning against such things.

The man followed Fredrick's gaze. "It's just a plane. Loud, I know—we're in the flight path. Annoying, really. Anyway ..." The man before Fredrick studied him, a look of uncertainty on his face. "If you don't speak English, we're gonna have an issue. And I really don't need any *issues* today. We'll have to hold off on your contract until we get this sorted. I understand wanting a transfer and the *Hawaiian Sun* is—"

"English, yes. Apologies. *Hawaiian Sun*?" Fredrick asked, the words coming easily to him as the sounds were not foreign to him. He was in America and he needed to speak English. And given how this man studied him, he needed to keep hold of himself.

I can't afford trouble, especially since I don't know what is happening.

The man gestured to the airship. "Tri-cylindrical airship design with a mix of rigid and non-rigid inflatable hull made from some of the toughest nonflammable composite flexible structural material around, including a mix of Kevlar, polyethylene, and polycarbonates. The lift is a hydrogen and helium dual-use system, with all the latest and greatest safety features." He laughed. "I sound like a total nerd, I know, but man, someday, hopefully I'm gonna fly her. Well, maybe. There's a lot to it and I … well … there's a lot. But airships are so much better than those metal death traps that zoom everyone around the world. Where's the elegance? The style?" He faced Fredrick. "So, you speak English?"

"*Ja* …I mean yes."

There was a buzz from the device the man held.

A frown quickly spread over the man's face as he pulled out the machine, tapped it, and inhaled as he closed his eyes. "I don't need this … not today." He tucked the device he had been using under his jacketed arm. "Sorry, where were we? Right. I'm Leo—well, Leopold, but everyone calls me Leo. I'm the Concierge and Butler Trainer." He presented his hand to shake. "I'm one of the youngest Concierges in the fleet, but I can assure you, I know what I'm doing." A grin replaced the frown on his face, brightening his hazel eyes.

Out of habit and the internal voice of his mother, Fredrick automatically took the man's hand and they shook. "Fredrick Rudolf."

"Where's your luggage?" Leo asked, glancing around Fredrick's feet.

"Luggage?" Fredrick asked, browsing down at the platform.

"Let me guess, the airlines lost everything? Shit. Just one more headache for me today." He pulled off his leather satchel and dug around inside. "Don't I have enough to deal with?" He stopped and leaned his head back, facing the sky. "Sorry, it's been a long day. See, this is why I don't fly in airplanes. They're nothing more than a bus in the sky and no amount of marketing or PR will ever change my mind. I don't care how cheap the tickets are. Or how quickly they can get you to places." He pointed to the empty ground next to Fredrick. "So, no luggage?"

"No. No bags," Fredrick confirmed as he scanned the ground around his feet. He remembered everything he had still housed on the *Hindenburg*.

"You still have your passport, right?"

Fredrick felt his pocket and pulled out his travel documents, but they weren't what he had before. He had a red book written all in German and it looked official but not what the Nazi Government had issued, and where were his other travel documents, including his leave paperwork? "This is what I have." Fredrick held the booklet out.

"Oh, I don't need to see the documents." Leo held up a hand, "I have copies in your file, so long as you didn't lose your passport."

Leo felt his jacket pockets. "Where did I put it?" He shook his head. "Well, we've got uniforms for you and all that... hold on." Leo lowered the bag to between his feet. He fussed with his machine. "Ugh. Here, do you mind?" He handed Fredrick the device.

Fredrick took the machine. The cool materials resting in his hands were unlike the metal of the devices he used on the *Hindenburg*. The smooth texture made him think this device had been crafted out of aluminum and some kind of glass, but he couldn't be sure. An image appeared as he shifted the machine, a view of a coastal town or resort with a sunset behind. The image appeared to be taken from an airship based on the angle and the shadow.

Leo dug into his back pocket and pulled out a rectangular green slab similar, but smaller, than what Fredrick now held. "Gotcha." He beamed and tapped the green box, then stopped. "Jesus Christ." He shook his head. "Bastard, can you just ..." He said nothing more as he tapped at the device and held the thing to his ear. "Tammy, hi," Leo began into the device. "The airlines did it again..." He paused before laughing, but no merriment echoed his mirth; frustration or possibly annoyance seemed the correct tone. "Right, and they wonder why people choose to travel by zep. Yep, I got the new guy, Fredrick ..." Leo scanned Fredrick up and down as he spoke.

Fredrick observed all the fuss about him, unsure what to say or do. Standing quietly seemed the least impertinent option. He didn't want to bring any more attention to himself than there already was.

"Yes, no, he's fine, but he's got nothing ... I don't know if he filed a claim." Leo glanced at Fredrick, finally addressing him. "Did you file a claim with the airline?"

"What?" Fredrick asked.

'File a claim'—what does this mean? File a claim for what?

Leo's lips pinched together. "No, doesn't sound like it. Probably not enough time—you know how the airlines are." Leo shook his head. "Okay, can you send Ollie or Tomas ..." Leo turned away from Fredrick, lowering his voice. "I've got a ton of stuff to do, and you-know-who has been blowing up my phone. I wanted ..." He turned back to Fredrick after a moment. "Yep, I'll take him, but ..." Leo glanced at his outfit, running a hand over his white uniform jacket and brass buttons. "While I'm out, can you please ask Aurora to take care of some of the details for the Captain's Gala and the welcome reception? I'll figure out the rest later … good. Thanks." Leo picked at some lint on his jacket. "Do you have any cash?" He faced Fredrick again.

Fredrick's hand made its way to his pocket. Finally, a question that made sense to him. "I have …" Fredrick pulled out his billfold, but didn't open the leather pouch. Everything he had in the world was now housed in his pockets and wallet and he didn't want to flash that kind of money around.

"Great …" Leo spoke back to the box. "I don't think it's right that he has to pay for this; it's not his fault." Leo adjusted the radio device to his other ear. "I'm sure I do, give me a sec." He patted his pocket with his free hand and pulled out his own wallet and fumbled with the leather, flipping a panel open. "Yep, I got the card. We'll sort him out. If I don't see you, enjoy your shore leave. Tell the rest of my team to get out as well—no point in hanging around, since I won't be returning for a while. Otherwise, see you later. Can you let security know?" He glanced around and up at the bright blue sky, a frown crossing his lips. "Thanks, Tammy." He tapped the machine. "Fucking hell, I really don't need this today."

"I'm sorry I'm such trouble." Fredrick's words were soft as he spoke, his shoulders dropping. He didn't want to be in this position and it sounded like this was the last thing that Leo needed. If he was anything like the Chief Steward on the *Hindenburg*, he did not want to cause trouble or be victim of his ire.

"Oh, hey." Leo shook his head. "It's not you. There's a lot happening and … look, you know how these layover days are. I was hoping to get you settled and … it doesn't matter. Here we are." Leo offered Fredrick a smile. "So, that was Tammy, Ms. Lam, and she said I'm to take you to the mall and get you some new clothes and other stuff like that. United Airships has an employee assistance plan to cover these sorts of things." He chuckled. "I doubt you've had these kinds of issues with the European zeps. Anyway, it's gonna be tight, but we can't have you walking around naked when you aren't in uniform. You can file a claim in the morning and reimburse the company when you get the check from the airline."

Fredrick bit at his lower lip, unsure what to say or do. Everything here seemed to be moving quickly, faster than he was used to. Plus, his English was good, but not perfect and so he had a mental lag as his brain translated the English words into his native German.

"We good?" Leo beamed at him.

Fredrick nodded. This man, Leo, appeared to be nothing like his former Chief Steward. He seemed to care for Fredrick's welfare and wanted to help, even with as frustrated and annoyed as he had been. He had concern for Fredrick, adding to the friendly and cheerful nature Americans were known to have. However, this level of concern seemed a bit much. The two men didn't even know each other.

I need to be grateful, but what happened?

"What happened to ... what happened to the *Hindenburg*?" Fredrick finally asked. "Are we in New Jersey?"

Leo barely glanced up from his little box. He tapped away as he shuffled to what Fredrick thought might be a ticket machine. Leo punched a few buttons on the machine then waved his radio box in front of the machine. A typing, like a telegraph noise, hit Fredrick's ears and a moment later Leo reached down and pulled out two small pieces of paper, handing one to Fredrick to take with his free hand.

An automated ticket machine that uses some kind of radio frequency. Incredible.

Fredrick barely noticed the words on the paper as he fumbled with it before slipping the ticket into his shirt pocket.

Stepping away from the ticket machine, Leo mused. "Oh man, jetlag must be a bitch. I'm surprised you didn't fly in a couple of days sooner to get accustomed to the time zone. I know the cost wouldn't have been covered by the company, which sucks, but I think the personal cost is worth it. Still better than dealing with..." He waved his hand in front of Fredrick. "And you would've been able to hit Santana Row...oh, or the Los Altos Beaux Vêtements instead of the Great Mall, where we'll be heading..." Leo slipped the small machine with his own ticket in his pocket and took the device Fredrick held for him. "Still, our setup is so much better than the cruise lines. Those poor bastards. I guess it helps that we don't fly under a flag of convenience."

What is he talking about? He speaks so quickly.

"I'm sorry, yes, the jet ... lag ..." Fredrick tried the new word on his tongue, keeping as neutral an expression as possible. "May I ask what the date is?"

Leo glanced at him, confusion filling his face. "Are we gonna need to do a drug test as well?" He laughed as he picked up the leather satchel from between his legs, before slipping his head and an arm through so the bag rested at the side of his midriff.

Fredrick remained silent—*drug test*—and his eyes narrowed as a frown stretched over his lips.

"Sorry, not funny." Leo adjusted the bag. "Today's Saturday May 10th, and we take to the air tomorrow. We only have a twenty-four hour turn-around, which sucks. I wish we had forty-eight hours like they did back in the day. Anyway, as for the *Hindenburg 2000*, that's the ship you're moving from ... right? I'm not sure if you're downgrading or upgrading. What a legacy and what a zep. I'm kind of jealous." He tapped the device again.

Fredrick licked his lips. "The year? Please?"

Leo huffed with a raised eyebrow, glancing up from the machine. "Are you messing with me? Come on, I know the time zones can mess you up and losing your luggage doesn't help but seriously man, what's up with you?" He shook his head, tension and disbelief filling his words as he met Fredrick's gaze. "Today's May 10, 2025." He shook his head and returned to scanning the thing while flicking his fingers over the machine.

Every part of Fredrick wanted to collapse or run as his heart dropped to his stomach and all the moisture in his mouth vanished. He steadied himself and searched for his billfold and photos—they were all he had left, and there wasn't even a picture of Wilhelm. His ship was gone, and he was in a new place, with almost ninety years separating him from what he knew.

How is any of this possible? I need to watch what I say and how I act. I need to play along as best I can.

Leo continued to focus on the machine in his hand. "Ah, okay, I see all your files from the *Hindenburg 2000* have been uploaded into our system, along with your work visa. Even with all our tech, sometimes these things still get messed up. Now—sorry, are we good? Or do you still want to play twenty questions?" Leo bit at his lower lip as he continued to review the files. "No wonder you're out of sorts; Frankfurt to New York, New York to Salt Lake City, Salt Lake City to San Jose. Ugh. You poor bastard."

Luckily for Fredrick, Leo's focus remained on the cool metal device, paying no attention to Fredrick as he tried to figure out what happened to him. The more Leo played with that machine, the faster

Fredrick's heart beat and the more the perspiration seemed to drench him. "Yes, but I don't know this place."

"San Jose?" Leo asked. "You've never been here before?"

"No. I was supposed to be in New Jersey," Fredrick confirmed; at least that much he knew for certain.

"Gotcha." Leo tapped away. "Right, for your layover, but I thought—wait … it says here New York."

"I'm very confused." Fredrick ran a hand through his hair.

"The airlines really messed you up. Or that going away party must have been the event of the year. I hope we won't see any evidence on social media. That can get you in a world of trouble. Especially if they can make out the ship you were on." Again Leo adjusted his satchel, fiddling with the flap. "I've heard stories from some of the other crew about those lower deck parties in Europe. Ollie has some great stories. And all the German guys I know love to party … if you know what I mean." Leo smiled up at Fredrick, their gaze meeting.

"I don't typically drink. A beer on occasion."

"Really … wow. Well, that's good I guess. I have a cocktail every so often. But I like to keep my wits about me and I don't want to get written up. I don't want to do anything to jeopardize my career, not now. Let's head to the mall, and afterwards we'll get you on the ship."

"Mall?" Fredrick asked.

"Store. You know, get some clothes and all that. Like we talked about." Leo's eyes narrowed. "You don't want to buy this stuff on the ship—it's crazy expensive and there's only so much branded merch one person should own."

Fredrick glanced around the station, not sure what to focus on.

"We leave tomorrow at 1600 and we have the welcome at 1900, so you'll have a day to get used to things and to get settled …" Leo reached out a hand. "Hey, I get it's not easy leaving what you know. But it's all the same, really. You have to keep the guests happy, you know, keep the illusion in place, and ensure they keep their hands off you— unless you want it, especially for this cruise … it's gonna be insane."

Fredrick pushed his hands into his pockets, unsure what to say or do.

This must be a dream, or a night terror.

"The *Hindenburg 2000.*" Leo whistled. "You Germans sure know how to make a zep, and what a legacy. You know, when I was a kid, I read up on the first *Hindenburg* and all its travels, how they used the ship for troop movements and as a command center during the war in Africa. I'd loved to have seen that beast in her heyday ... I understand the 2000 holds, what, four hundred guests? That must be wild. These airships are getting to be like the cruise ships out there." Leo glanced at the airship behind them before slipping the device into his bag, ensuring the machine was secure. "People love the ocean cruises, but give me the sky cruises any day. The elegance and the style ... there's something to seeing the world from the air and traveling in the clouds. Sure, they cost more, but what a way to travel. More relaxed ..."

This comment resonated with Fredrick. And he found himself agreeing. "I've never enjoyed traveling by sea."

"Right, and who can forget the image of Fred Astaire and Ginger Rogers dancing and singing their way across the Atlantic Ocean in the PanAm North American Splendor in *Flying High*?" Leo pined as a grin bloomed across his face. "Did you ever see *The Battle in the Skies* with Gregory Peck and ... oh ... Dorothy Dandridge? What a movie. The sky battles between the Nazis and the Allied Forces in those battle zeppelins, how they managed to make the scenes look so real ... crazy ... especially without CGI."

Fredrick watched as Leo's lips moved—he heard the words but nothing made sense. What war? He recognized some of the names Leo shared, but not the movies. Who were the *Allied Forces* he mentioned? Instead of bombarding the man with questions and coming off as insane, Fredrick remained quiet, keeping a pleasant expression on his face, or trying to. He didn't know what was happening around him, and maybe this was a trap to get him in trouble, so he needed to keep playing along for now.

"I've never been to Germany. I want to get there," Leo started chatting again, the words flowing from his mouth like a rushing river. "I hear some of the European airship cruises are incredible, but there're so many places to see here that I can hold off for a while. Maybe when I move up a bit more I'll transfer to one of the European zeps, switch to piloting or engineering. It'd be a big change but ..." His grin faltered. "Anyway, I like working for United Airships. Plus, we get paid better and are protected by US laws and regulations. And knowing the hospitality side of things is important no matter what." He laughed. "I really hoped we could get your paperwork done tonight, but I doubt it."

Fredrick gestured toward the hanger. "What about the ship?"

"It'll still be here. I'll give you the tour when we return, plus our tram'll be here shortly. I don't know if you'll be able to meet the rest of our team tonight, but we'll see." Leo pulled out his talking and listening radio and tapped the screen.

Fredrick watched as several chatty loud people joined them on the platform waiting for, what he assumed, to be the next train. Only an older couple paid them any notice, glancing both men up and down.

3

LEO DIDN'T MIND BABYSITTING his new staff, but this particular new guy seemed lost and out of sorts. What was up with him? And the strange questions. He really hoped Fredrick wouldn't give him any trouble. He had fought hard to get the guy and now ... well, now he wasn't so sure it was a good call.

Ollie had been a little off too, at first—must be a European thing. He hoped Fredrick would work out. He didn't need a problem child to deal with, given everything he had been through the last few months—months and the last few hours. Creating work plans and reprimanding staff were not a part of his job he enjoyed.

He squinted over at his new charge. Something seemed off about him, like he didn't belong here, but he had all the paperwork and everything was in order. He didn't get 'troublemaker' vibes from him, and given all this guy had been through: lost luggage, long travel day, and having to do three different flights to get to San Jose. He couldn't blame him for being a bit of a mess.

I doubt I'd be any better. And there's the whole language difference.
Leo bit back his smile.
I'd probably be a lot worse.

He nonchalantly glanced over at his quiet companion staring straight ahead as they rumbled and bounced along the tracks to the mall. Typically, the guys who came from Europe were outgoing and ready for anything. None of them ever came off as high-strung and reserved. Fredrick's demeanor might be part of being from a small town, but he'd worked in travel before, so ... Leo didn't know. How he acted at the moment didn't matter as long as the guy did a good job and kept the guests happy.

Or he's dealing with some personal shit, like everyone. Or exhaustion.

Squinting as the afternoon sun hit his face, his cheerful expression, or what he hoped his reflection showed, dropped. *So much personal shit.* The call with his ex before Fredrick arrived didn't help matters. Then all the messages from him. The guy was a jerk and it took all Leo had to not go apeshit all over his ass. He didn't need the added stress before his next trip, so once he was off the phone, he promised himself he would not talk to Barron again until he returned from this tour. He inhaled, refocusing his thoughts. Anyway, they can't all be your best friend. Some people work and leave their personal lives at home and don't get wrapped up in shipboard drama.

Or romance.

Leo cracked his neck as he studied the condos, storefronts, and vehicles zooming past. He scanned the rest of the tram's cabin. Different people from all walks of life occupied the rest of the tram car. Sniffing the air, he was now grateful for the few blasts of cool air from the ventilation system. There was nothing worse than being in a stuffy light rail car with people whose hygiene tended to be questionable.

Or someone who overdoes the perfume or cologne.

Crinkling his nose at the thought, he focused on Fredrick, giving him a real onceover. He hoped his new crewmate would work out and stick around longer than Jordan, the last Butler, did, jumping ship the minute another offer came.

Regardless, Leo couldn't deal with any additional drama, images of his messy break up filled his mind. *Nope.* He pushed the thoughts away he needed to focus on this next trip. He adjusted how he sat, doing his best to stay off his phone in case Fredrick wanted to chat ... though so far, nothing. He wasn't even distracted by his own phone ... did he have one? He sighed. Not everyone did.

God knows there are times I wish I didn't have one.

A buzz from his satchel caught his ear and he huffed out his irritation—case in point. He supposed the call might be work-related but he doubted it. Tammy'd cover for him while he was out with Fredrick. Still, he should check. He pulled out his tablet and quickly scanned his messenger system. An email from Barron. "Ugh." He tapped delete.

I have too much going on to deal with his bullshit drama.

Leo put the tablet away, securing the case. "Have you done a lot of cruises?" Leo, finally unable to stand the lack of conversation, asked, needing a better distraction than the scenery outside the window or the two goth teens glaring at everyone in between scanning their phones.

"I've been with the *Hindenburg ... Hindenburg 2000* since I started my career." Fredrick bit at his lower lip as his German accent bounced around the words.

Leo laughed. "That had to be a great zep to learn on." His lips pulled his cheeks up as he spoke.

"Yes," Fredrick answered.

Leo cleared his throat. "Anyway, I heard those cruises are out of this world."

Fredrick shifted in his seat before turning and facing Leo. "Yes, sorry, my English is good but I still get mixed up a bit. I believed I would be better at my words."

Leo leaned in as he spoke. "No worries."

"Thank you. I wish you spoke German." Fredrick worked his jaw, showcasing his dimpled cheeks.

Leo shrugged. "If I spoke German, I'd still be speaking English with you right now. One, so you can practice and two, so all these people around us didn't feel like we're talking trash about them ..." He glanced about the tram's cabin, seeing the two teens on their phones. The one with dark makeup and dark clothes was seemingly not paying attention to them, but Leo caught their expression shift as he spoke.

"On the *Hindenburg*"—Fredrick adjusted how he sat so he faced Leo—"we had guests from both Germany and the Americas. We always had to ensure they were comfortable."

Resting his hands on his bag, Leo added, "You know, I've spent my whole life being forgotten and ignored. Not only for who I am but for what I say and how I speak, so I won't do that to someone else by intentionally making conversation impossible for them to participate in."

"I understand; good customer relations are important," Fredrick responded, a thoughtful expression filling his face.

"I must sound ridiculous." Leo huffed, dropping his shoulders.

"Not at all." Fredrick scanned the passengers they shared the tram's cabin with. Leo noted Fredrick's accent seemingly grew less the more he spoke. "Here in this space and location, seeing all these different people around us," Fredrick continued, "I can see how feeling left out and excluded might be a concern. I guess I never saw that much where I'm from."

"Growing up in a small town in Germany, how was it?" Leo wanted to keep the conversation as light as possible and get off anything heavy or controversial.

The pleasant expression on Fredrick's face dropped and his gaze shifted as his shoulders sank and he worked his jaw back and forth. "I ... well ..."

Oh, great. I've made him uncomfortable. He must've had issues at home and growing up in a small town sucked.

"Look, I'm sorry," Leo rushed through his apology. "I didn't mean to bring up a sore subject."

Fredrick pulled at the sleeves of his shirt as he faced the front of the tram, not speaking.

Great. Good job, idiot.

Leo decided to keep to the silence for the time being. Maybe once they were at the mall, the conversation would pick up and flow more naturally. Everyone loved to shop and buy new things, right? He stared out the window as the tram rose along the elevated track, zipping by the correctional facility.

•   •   •

Once in the department store, Leo rushed them along to the men's section so Fredrick could replenish his wardrobe. "Let's get what we need and get out of here."

"There is so much." Fredrick pointed. "It's all so incredible."

Leo laughed. "You didn't get out much, did you?"

Fredrick bit his lip.

Leo pulled out his phone and checked the time. "Look, we need to boogie."

"Boogie?" Fredrick asked, his brows narrowing at the word.

"Move." Leo mimed with his hands. "We don't have a lot of time and I don't want to be stuck here all evening."

"Oh ... yes ... of course. I will not delay."

Leo was tempted to pull out his phone, but he stopped himself. *I need to be present.*

"I ..." Fredrick took as deep a breath as Leo had ever seen. "Clothes, yes. What should I buy?"

Leo smiled. "Let's grab the basics: socks, underwear, pants, shirts, and go from there."

"Yes. That sounds good." Fredrick nodded and appeared to relax.

Leo took the lead and they found different items for Fredrick to try on. His German companion had a classic style—if anything, Fredrick's choices in clothing reminded him of outfits his grandfather would wear. Leo did a lot of pushing to get Fredrick to look at a pair of jeans and grab a couple of fun t-shirts, but eventually they got there. He also did his level best to steer Fredrick away from the boxers and into colored briefs and boxer briefs.

Boxers are so gross. You might as well go commando.

Soon, Fredrick got into the swing of things and even smiled seeing his reflection in the mirror in his new clothes.

"Oh, look at this." Fredrick ran a hand over a black leather bomber jacket.

The coat was a lightweight bomber jacket probably made of lamb or manmade materials, but the cut was great and would look amazing on Fredrick, or Leo for that matter, but he didn't need another jacket. "Okay, that I approve of, but it's outside my spending limit." Leo pointed to the price—even on sale, the coat was over what he could spend, especially since the clothing item wasn't considered necessary.

Fredrick squinted at the red sale tag, staring at the numbers. Feeling his pocket, he exhaled and frowned. "I don't need anything that fancy or pricey. It reminds me of something a friend of mine once wore." He moved on to the shirts behind them.

Leo glanced at the price and the jacket. The cost wasn't out of line. If Fredrick wanted the coat, he should get it.

"You can buy the jacket," Leo suggested. "Unfortunately, I can't get it with the company card—it's not a 'necessity'." He made air quotes with his fingers.

"No. I don't need to spend that kind of money. I'll go without." Fredrick didn't look back and continued to browse the shirts he stood in front of.

Leo's brows lowered.

I bet he can't afford the coat. No cell phone either. He must send all his money to family. Poor bastard. Living for others.

"What do you think of this?" Fredrick held up a green fine-stripe long-sleeve shirt with a pointed collar.

"God. No. That's like something from the 40s. No way." Leo rushed over and plucked clothes off the racks. He would not allow this handsome man to buy anything that made him look like a ninety-year-old grandpa.

Making short work of pulling clothing, Leo sent Fredrick to the changing rooms again to try the new items he selected.

"See, I told you to trust me." Leo beamed as Fredrick appeared in front of him. He wore a pair of fitted dark denim jeans, black belt, and a printed tee-shirt. He looked like a model on a Paris runway, showing off the latest styles.

"I'm not used to these types of clothes." Fredrick gestured to himself. "These are garments my parents would never allow."

"Well, your folks aren't here." Leo forced a grin. "You look great."

Again, Fredrick's grin broke and he headed to the changing room.

Ah fuck, I did it again. I can't imagine the awful relationship Fredrick had with his family. I've been lucky.

"Hey, I'll be right back," Leo called. He needed to make this right.

"Alright," Fredrick answered from behind the dressing room door.

"Try on the other stuff, make sure the clothes fit, then we can get out of here," Leo proposed. "Sound good?"

"Yes."

Leo rushed over to where the jackets were, where a sales associate was busily rehanging the clothes and putting everything back into their sizes.

"Is there something I can assist you with?" The man turned around and Leo nearly gasped. The guy had short-trimmed black hair, and some of the brightest green eyes Leo had ever seen, which contrasted his flawless dark skin. There was an angelic glow about him and if Leo didn't know any better he would have sworn the man dropped from heaven with how handsome he was. He donned a black t-shirt and tan pants. His name tag read: Tad.

"I ... I ... um ..." Leo cleared this throat. "Sorry. I wanted to grab that jacket for my friend."

"Sure." Tad pulled out the jacket and handed it over. "He really looked good in this and I know it'll brighten his day."

"You think?"

"Trust me, I know." Tad beamed. "You need to look out for him," he added with a warm smile.

"What?"

"I heard his accent and based on your uniform, I'm guessing he works for you." He shook his head. "And since you're here, I can't imagine you've had a good day." He chuckled.

"Well no, but ..."

"There isn't enough kindness or understanding in our world." Tad tidied up the rack of jackets as he spoke. "I see it day in and day out—people can be cruel and so ... well, unpleasant." Tad glanced at Leo. "I'm sure you've seen it."

Leo couldn't help but nod his agreement—he had seen it all too often.

"All I'm saying is keep your eye out for him. It can't be easy uplifting your whole life and moving to a new place. I bet it feels like he's on a whole different planet." Tad smiled. "We all need someone who's on our side, no matter how strange or different we might be or act." Tad pointed. "Looks like he's about done."

Leo turned toward the changing room and saw the top of Fredrick's head emerge.

"Thanks." Leo turned around, but the sales guy was gone.

Must have had to take his break, but boy was that guy beautiful.

With the jacket tucked in under a few other items Fredrick had already approved, Leo made his way over to Fredrick. The shopping experience had brightened Fredrick's mood. Leo had done his best to keep the jacket hidden amongst the other items he held and would be buying. Luckily Fredrick seemed exhausted, or perhaps shell-shocked, and didn't notice the big black jacket.

I think that guy was right. I need to look after Fredrick and push away any misgivings I might have.

"Okay, let me pay for all this." Leo pointed to the big glass doors. "Why don't you go outside and take in all the sights and get some fresh air? I'll only be a few minutes."

"I would like to see more of the buildings outside," Fredrick agreed. "But I can wait, I don't want to leave you with all this."

"I'll be fine." Leo gestured. "Now go." He pointed with his chin. "Go out and enjoy the early evening."

"Thank you." Fredrick glanced toward the doors and back at Leo before making his way to the doors.

4

FREDRICK'S LASHES PRESSED TOGETHER as his eyes adjusted to the sun, which had continued to lower behind the rows of buildings across the sea of vehicles and the elevated train line. He couldn't believe what he'd witnessed and learned in such a short amount of time. The world had changed so much and yet there were things that felt familiar to him. Shops filled with people rushing about, an airship bigger than any he had seen before, names of American actors that he remembered from his youth. Well, he didn't think the last one was so odd—Fred Astaire & Ginger Rogers may have been Americans, but their talent for dance and the films they were in had appeared in Germany, although Fredrick had never heard of any movie filmed or set in an airship, and as far as he knew PanAm didn't have any airships. The *Hindenburg*, his *Hindenburg*, was one of a limited number and none were American or British for that matter.

"This place and time must be different ... somehow," he muttered in German as several young people rushed by him, heads focused on the small devices that seemed to be connected to everyone and everything.

So many mechanical marvels.

He looked up in time to have a couple run right into him, an older man and woman who appeared to be from one of the Asian countries of the Far East.

"Excuse me." Fredrick stepped to the side.

The couple didn't speak to him and rushed off, chattering in their own language.

Perhaps Leo had a point about the various languages. So many different kinds of people. Wunderbar.

Digging into his pocket, Fredrick pulled out his timepiece, running a finger over the device. A reminder of his world. His home. As he continued to watch the people, he didn't believe the Führer would approve of all these different races mixing together. Opening the timepiece, a memory of his father giving him the watch rushed to the front of his memories. He closed his eyes, picturing his mother and father on the day he got the position as Steward on the *Hindenburg*. They congratulated him and told him they were proud, but there was no fuss. All restrained. All normal, not like here where everyone seemed so emotional ... was that the right word? He wasn't sure. He focused on the memory of his folks and wondered what they thought had happened to him.

They probably think I burned up in the fire.

He shuddered. Assuming Leo was correct and the year they now occupied was indeed 2025, by all rights his parents, aunt and uncle, and everyone he knew would be long dead including his brother and sister.

I'm alone.

He pondered if there were ways for him to find out what happened to his family and his friends. From what Leo shared with him, the *Hindenburg* must have somehow survived the fire he witnessed as he tried to get himself and Wilhelm to safety, but fires typically spelled disaster for an airship, which is why they were so careful. So, if the *Hindenburg* didn't have a fire and went on as Leo told him, something changed.

"Hey-ya," Leo called, holding several bags in his hands. "You ready to boogie on out of here?"

"What?" Fredrick's lips pinched together.

Leo laughed. "Sorry, I'm all set, and we should get back. Here, take some of these." He held out a couple of the bags for Fredrick to accept.

Fredrick fiddled with the pocket watch in his hands.

"Oh wow." Leo gestured. "What a great antique—I haven't seen anything like your pocket watch in a long time. A gift from your grandparents or great-grandparents?"

Fredrick held the clock in his hands as he studied the machine ticking away in his hand. "Yes, a gift."

"Well, it's cool." Leo pointed to the elevated rails. "Let's get walking."

Fredrick took two of the presented bags and they made their way to the station. "Thank you for your ... help and your kindness today."

Leo's smile blossomed over his lips. "My pleasure, but don't thank me too much. United AirShips will want to get reimbursed when you get your airline settlement, and if the airlines don't cover the full costs, you'll be expected to pay the money back. All the details are in the employee emergency assistance program. Pretty typical stuff."

"I see." Fredrick bit at his lower lip. He had seen the prices of everything in the shop and the money he had saved to bring to America wouldn't cover half of what Leo and he spent this afternoon. "I had no idea things here would cost so much."

"Welcome to Silicon Valley, one of the most expensive places in the US, if not the world, to live. Everything here costs a freaking fortune, but I guess with all the high-tech companies and the engineers, they can afford the prices." He huffed. "I don't think I would have been able to stay here if my folks didn't help me out by letting me stay at home, but I'm saving my pennies"—he laughed—"as my grandmother would say. Hopefully, I'll be able to buy a place in a year or two." He shifted the bags as they walked.

Fredrick didn't speak as they continued through the fields of vehicles. He had never seen so many automobiles and how different they all appeared. The smooth lines, smaller sizes, and the colors were not what he was used to. This place had no resemblance to the movie *Megalopolis* that his parents took him and his brother and sister to see when they were younger. A world of the future, but nothing like this future. That future was dark and bleak compared to what he witnessed today. Although in fairness he did see some parallels to the film.

"Hey," Leo called for Fredrick's attention. "You okay? You've seemed off this entire time. If you're worried about money and all your stuff, don't. Everything will get sorted out. I even got you something." He beamed. "Check your bag."

They stopped at the corner and Fredrick's gaze narrowed as he dug through the bag. At first he didn't find anything but undergarments and the two pairs of pants; however, at the bottom he noticed the black and stopped. Quickly, he pulled out the black jacket he tried on in the store. "You shouldn't have … I don't know how I'll afford this."

"It's a gift," Leo stated as they waited for the light to change to cross the street. Automobiles blazed past them like ants on the march, some closer than others, which always made Leo wince. "I saw how much you adored the coat and given the day you had …" He shrugged, but redder tones filled his neck and cheeks.

"This is kind, thank you." Fredrick ran a hand over the coat, the cool leather soft under his touch. He glanced at the street and the vehicles and quickly pulled on the jacket, feeling the smooth leather and tugging at the sleeves. His cheeks twinged from his grin.

Leo's head bobbed up and down with approval. "Yep, looks great on you."

"I'll pay you back," Fredrick stated as a matter of fact.

"Like I said, the jacket's a gift, but don't say anything to the others. I have a reputation to uphold as a *hardass.* I don't want everyone to think that if they bat their lashes at me and show off their dimples, I'll shower them with presents." He closed out the statement with a chuckle.

"Well, I thank you and I won't say anything to anyone." Fredrick glanced up. "Oh, the train."

"Crap." Leo adjusted the bags he held. "Come on, we need to run if we're gonna catch it."

Fredrick and Leo started to rush with bags in hand. As they dodged the people, for the first time since arriving in this new time and place, Fredrick mused that he might like this brave new world.

•   •   •

Once at the airship terminal, Leo took Fredrick through the station shops to pick up hygiene products. Again, they all seemed familiar, but the materials and sizes were different. Plastic seemed to be used for everything and nothing seemed designed to last. In his mind, these products seemed wasteful, but since he didn't have his own self-care items, he appreciated getting the few things he needed. Even better to pay for them all himself.

Fredrick pulled out his billfold and the cash he had.

Leo adjusted his satchel and the bags he held. As he watched Fredrick, Leo suddenly focused and studied the money in Fredrick's hands. "Where did you get that cash from? Those bills are old, you sure you want to use them?" he ultimately asked.

"Is there something wrong with my money?" Fredrick examined the bills. "This is all I—"

"Your money's fine," the female clerk interjected. She beamed and quickly snatched the presented bills and hurriedly handed Fredrick his change, receipt, and new items housed in a paper bag.

Leo bit at his lower lip as they moved out of the shop. "Well, I'm pretty sure the bills you have are worth a lot more than face value, especially with how quickly that clerk seized them. Did some old couple tip you with them?"

"Yessss ..." Fredrick extended the word, unable to hide the hesitation in his tone as he answered, continuing to walk. He examined the new coins in his hand.

Even the money is different here—how can that be?

"When we get to Hilo, I know a store where you can have the rest of your bills checked and coins if you got'um. I'll send a text and let Uncle Billie know to expect us." Leo pulled out the small device again and tapped away. "You might be holding a fortune and not know. I understand American dollars are odd compared to the Euro, but still it'll be good to have your currency checked out so you don't get screwed over." He slipped the device into his pocket. "Do you have a lot? Do you have any Euros? We can exchange those on the ship."

"No. No Euros." Fredrick pocketed the change. "Everything I have is American, or older American I guess, but as you've noticed I'm not used to your currency."

What's a Euro?

Fredrick wanted to ask but decided he better not, so he gestured his agreement.

Leo continued to grin as he spoke. "I've gotten a few gold coins as tips before, that were worth $500 at the time, which amazed me." He chuckled, adding, "That's how I found the shop. Anyhoo, it was odd, but nice and thankfully the guest didn't expect anything *extra*.

As I'm sure you know, there're some eccentric people who travel the skies. And think they can buy anything." Again, he laughed as they made their way to the gangway and the airship.

Glimmers of recognition around the airship almost fooled Fredrick into thinking he was home: the gondola, the landing wheels and equipment, the landing pad and hanger, the guest passageways and the staircase. Much of the exterior mechanics of the ship were as they were on the *Hindenburg*, but the similarities stopped there. As they cleared the ship's security, placing their bags through a separate machine and crossing under a small arch with lights, they ended up in the main gallery of the airship. The security for the *Hindenburg* was nothing compared to this.

The left door stood open showing the ship's lifts and to the right a grand staircase going up to the above decks. This was the main entrance for passengers and crew. However, Leo explained, there were additional gangways for crew use at the forward and aft of the ship, as well as a service elevator for crew use outside of guest areas. All could be used in case of emergency, along with a mixture of fire-retardant emergency access areas and exits.

Leo pulled Fredrick past the empty foyer and up the first flight of stairs. "Welcome to 'A' Deck; this is pretty much our part of the ship. Guests are only allowed in the gallery here or the medical facility through that door." Leo pointed with his free hand to the door labeled 'medical office'. "Come on."

Leo scanned a badge and moved them through a set of doors. They were in a small hall with doors running down the passage. "Welcome to our world." He waved his free hand around the space. "This is where most of the crew sleeps. We have our own stairs that take us up to the Promenade where we can access our dining and rec areas. It's not bad—they did a pretty good job ensuring we have our own space away from the guests ..."

"Hiya Leo," a dark-skinned man greeted him.

"Tommy," Leo announced. "Tommy, this is Fredrick, he's my new Butler."

"Pleasure. Welcome," Tommy acknowledged with a thick accent Fredrick wasn't familiar with. "You ready for a crazy week? Some of the people on this *fairy flight* can be—"

"Tommy is one of our primo room attendants," Leo cut Tommy off.

"Thank you." Fredrick tried not to stare at the man—he wasn't used to seeing men like him around. "But what is a *fairy flight*?"

Tommy laughed.

"Never mind." Leo pinched his lips together. "You gonna have everything ready for tomorrow?"

"Yep, I'm heading up to Deck 3 to check on the suites, make sure they're all done so you *important* people won't have to mess your hair or nails." Tommy pulled out his own small device and looked at it. "I'll tell ya, man, getting everyone off the ship and turning this baby over for tomorrow's embarkation is always crazy. I can't wait till we lift off."

"You're preaching to the choir, my guy." Leo raised a hand to the sky.

Tommy stuffed his machine in his pocket. "Well, have fun. It's good to have you with us, Fredrick." He waved and headed off.

"Nice to meet …" Fredrick didn't finish as Tommy had already vanished through another door.

"He's a good guy, a bit mouthy. I hope he didn't offend you." Leo adjusted the bags again. "But the guests love him and he's got one of the highest ratings on the ship. Come on, let's get you to our cabin."

"Our cabin?" Fredrick switched the bags he held. The thin woven handle had begun to dig into his fingers and hand.

"Oh right, you're probably used to your own space. Sadly here, we have to share, and you're bunking with me. Hope that's okay." Leo's cheeks rose in a hopeful smile.

Fredrick nodded as he moved with Leo, passing a few other folks rushing about in various forms of dress. Some wore uniforms, some wore civilian outfits like him, and others had on officer or engineering garb. Despite the rushing around, several people stopped and spoke to Leo and introduced themselves to Fredrick. The diversity on board was unlike anything Fredrick had experienced. So many different faces, and unlike the *Hindenburg*, there was a mix of everyone you could imagine.

So much has changed. How will I not get found out?

The passage design appeared to be nothing special: a white smooth material posted with notice boards and safety and security posters in multiple languages, none German. The halls definitely had more room than on the *Hindenburg*. You could stand shoulder to shoulder with four grown men. The space gleamed with cleanliness and wasn't nearly as loud or as cold as the *Hindenburg*, which astonished him. A fresh scent also seemed to linger in the space, though Fredrick couldn't quite figure out what the smell was.

It's not offensive at least.

"Well ..." Leo stopped in front of a door marked A-37. He pulled out the card he used earlier and swiped the pass in front of the door handle. The light turned green and the door unlocked. "Welcome home." He pushed the door open to allow Fredrick entry. "I have a card for you."

"What is this space?" Fredrick asked, his mouth open in a gasp. Two bunks were mounted on the wall directly in front of him, and to the left of the bunks sat an empty maple color desk and chair in front of a small window to look out of. To his right was a separate desk area and chair, and on that desk was a bigger version of the machine that Leo used earlier set up on a stand, as well as files and other items spread about. A subtle scent of eucalyptus made its way to Fredrick's nose. The bags dropped from Fredrick's hands as he walked in, taking in the space. A sink and mirror with several shelves half-filled with items showed Leo had been here for quite some time using the space. An empty cupboard caught Fredrick's attention, housing hangers and shelves for clothing and other items.

So much more room than anything on the Hindenburg.

"I'm sure you're used to bigger spaces—I hope this'll work." Leo walked the rest of the way in, the door shutting behind him. Once inside, he tossed his satchel onto his desk. "We have our own mini fridge and microwave." Leo opened up the fridge, showing a few items in there already. "I keep a few sodas and milk as well as some fruit in here in case I miss a meal." He closed the door, "There's a few other snacks and stuff here, nothing fancy, munchies mostly." Leo pointed to a shelf filled with a couple of boxes and bags. "But feel free to rearrange and put things in here as well, especially if there're special snacks or treats you want, but don't buy them in the commissary or here on ship. If you want snacks, we can pick up stuff in Hawaii at the big box stores, and it'll be cheaper ... well, comparably."

Fredrick examined his fingers and fingernails unsure how to respond.

"If the Lani Club and Lounge aren't filled with guests, we can get a few treats up there as well ..." Leo added. "Easier than rushing to the mess to grab lunch or dinner." He unbuttoned his uniform jacket.

Fredrick scrutinized the two machines and the cabinet space Leo pointed to. He knew the mini fridge was a cooler, they had those on the *Hindenburg*, but a microwave was something new, and he assumed the machine heated or cooked, based on context, but he wasn't sure and would have to figure it out later when he was unaccompanied.

"The men's locker is down the hall with the bathrooms. If you want to get in there before everyone, you'll have to get up early. What I tend to do is take a shower at night before bed, and shave here in the room in the morning. It's not ideal, but ..."

Fredrick turned and met Leo's gaze. "So different."

Leo blinked several times. "Oh right, the *Hindenburg 2000* has huge crew spaces and the Butlers get their own cabins with bathrooms."

Fredrick bit back his frown and quickly tried to recover. "Well, this is still quite spacious and I was only a Steward."

A ding or buzz caused Fredrick to glance around the space. He hadn't touched anything, but with all these fancy technological marvels who knew what he might have set off.

Leo pulled out his phone, huffing, "Ugh, I should have left this thing silenced." He scanned the device. "Bastard. Nope, not gonna deal with you." He tapped the machine and stuffed the green box in his pocket.

"Is everything okay?" Fredrick couldn't help but notice the shift in Leo's face and the color change on his neck, not to mention the tone of his voice.

"Nothing. My ex." Leo inhaled and cracked his neck. "Anyway, I hope you don't mind that I have the upper bunk."

"I'm happy on the lower." Fredrick picked up the bags and placed them on the bed. "Easier to get in and out."

Leo nodded his agreement. "There's more storage under the beds. I keep my suitcase there, but there's space for yours ... Sorry."

Fredrick laughed. "Not to worry."

Leo snapped his fingers. "Right, before I forget, we each have our own safes." He pointed to two metal boxes each with a keypad of some sort. "You'll need to create your own code. But you can keep things like your money, wallet, passport, other important documents there." He shrugged. "Pretty standard stuff."

They didn't have anything like this on the Hindenburg. Nothing was private—well, not for the crew.

"Thank you."

"Once you get settled here, we'll go and get your duty clothes checked out, go eat in the mess, and I'll give you a tour of the ship. If we run into them, I'll introduce you to the rest of our team. Are you good with a needle and thread?"

"What?" Fredrick asked, not sure he understood the importance of the question.

"If you are, it'll save you money," Leo explained. "If you need to make minor repairs to your uniform and you can do them yourself, it's a cost-saving method. If not, you'll have to pay out of pocket for our Laundry Service. I'm pretty handy, I can help you if you need it." Leo pulled open a drawer. "Basic sewing kit here …"

"I've had to mend and darn some of my uniforms in the past." Fredrick huffed out a chuckle. "My mother taught me. My father wasn't pleased, but when he learned it would help with my posting he …" Fredrick trailed off.

"Well, I'm glad you're handy. Occasionally a guest might ask us for help with a button or whatever, and you don't have to say yes, but it's good customer service. Ollie and Tomas are both good with a needle and thread as well. Nuwa has a mini sewing machine with her and can sew. I had her do some tailoring on some my civvies when I lost weight, but she'll charge you. Still, it was worth it. Aurora refuses to learn anything more than sewing on buttons." He laughed. "I guess it reminds her too much of home. Anyhoo, get yourself sorted and we'll grab some food."

Fredrick tried to make a mental note of each of the names that Leo threw at him. "Okay." As if on cue, Fredrick's stomach moaned in protest.

"Unless you want to go get food now?" Leo asked, clearly hearing Fredrick's stomach gripe at the holdup.

"Excuse me." Fredrick's cheeks and neck warmed. "No, let me get this sorted."

"Okey dokey." Leo moved to his desk and started going through his satchel, pulling out folders and what looked like paperwork.

Fredrick rubbed his stomach before going through his bags and putting his clothes and hygiene items away. He might organize everything better later, but right now he wanted to get all the tags off and everything hung up. Nothing made him feel more settled than having himself and his personal effects sorted. Even though he didn't have much space on the *Hindenburg*, he always made sure his locker was organized. He couldn't understand how people lived out of a suitcase or duffel bag.

He peeked over his shoulder at Leo, now sitting at his desk typing away on his machine.

At least he appears organized and has good hygiene. He also seems quite dapper.

Fredrick smirked at the idea. Wilhelm would have definitely fancied Leo. Then he frowned a bit at the memory. He would never see Wilhelm again and of all the shocks he'd gotten today, that one was the one that hurt his heart the most. It didn't matter what had happened with Gerhard; Wilhelm would always hold a special place in his memories. That was something no one could ever take from him ... not even the Führer himself.

5

T HE CREW LOCKER ROOMS of the airship rivaled that of the *Hindenburg* guest areas as did the mess hall where Fredrick and Leo ate. Leo explained that on these staging days, the whole crew got to enjoy the dining venue and entertainment areas that were typically off-limits to all but the Officers and Suite Staff. However, the upper deck was open to all the staff.

An outside deck on an airship. I can't wait to see that.

Stomach full, Fredrick grew more and more curious to see the rest of the ship that would be his new home. Once they arrived at the Promenade Deck, the space opened to a grand atrium vaulted all the way to deck two. The dark blues of the floors reminded Fredrick of the ocean and the cream colors of the furniture were a perfect compliment. In the ceiling were mounted lights that sparkled, matching the night sky. He had never witnessed anything like this before in any kind of ship design.

"This is beautiful." The words dropped from Fredrick's mouth as he glanced every which way.

Leo stopped and looked around. "I'm so used to the space I don't even notice anymore, but yep, she's a glamorous ship. The designers did a great job on the refresh, and they didn't dive too heavy into the Polynesian theme, or it would feel gaudy and tasteless." He laughed. "When I was being trained on the American Eagle, I'm pretty sure I reacted the same way."

"American Eagle?"

"One of our sister zeps. She's older and smaller, but still nice." Leo started, "In our fleet we have eleven zeps. The Inland Sun is being refitted, since it's her turn." He chuckled. "And I believe she's getting some single cabins, which I wish we had …" He shook his head. "Maybe next time."

"I see." Fredrick continued taking in all the space and how open the gallery seemed. There was an unfamiliar warmth to the space and the air seemed fresh and clean. A slight hum caught his ears. In a way he missed the chill of the air in the *Hindenburg*. A small tug on his elbow caught his attention.

"Come on." Leo directed them as his gaze moved to an open seating area. "Over there is the *Kapua* Bar." Leo pointed to a lounge area with an open bar housing a mirrored wall for spirits, yet to be stocked. In front of the bar, several comfortable chairs and smaller tables for people to sit and chat had been arranged. "This bar, the Kapua Bar here on Deck 1, and the *Honua* Lounge on the *Pali* Deck are open pretty much all day for guests. They close at 0200 and open at 0800."

Fredrick continued browsing around. "Steward's Desk?" He pointed.

With a chuckle, Leo responded, "Sure. We call it Guest Services, for non-suite guests. We'll be coming by and checking in, but we'll be up in the Lani Club and Lounge most of the time. It's our version of a ship within a ship."

"Okay."

"Anyway, to the aft of the ship"—Leo pointed—"is where the Officers' cabins are and where we had dinner and the rest of the crew areas we passed coming here. Come on, I'll show you the Promenade Dining Room."

Fredrick's body tingled as he grew more excited to learn more of the ship.

Leo glanced around. "I love these layover nights. Everyone is out enjoying the night off, even the Captain and a bunch of the officers. We're lucky to have an Officer of the Watch right now."

"Really?"

"Sure, once the work's done and stations are secured for the night, everyone gets leave."

"And I messed up your leave?"

"No, I saw my parents last time we were in town. They knew I had a new Butler starting this trip."

Fredrick considered for a moment. They had a similar setup on the *Hindenburg*—that was how he and Wilhelm were going to run away. "As long as I'm not keeping you."

"You're not. Now come on." Leo shot a warm smile at him. Despite what appeared to be genuine cordiality, something lingered behind Leo's gaze, almost like he was avoiding something or trying to distract himself. Maybe convincing himself there was more work to do than there genuinely was.

Something to do about his ex.

Fredrick pushed the thought away. It was none of his business.

As they moved through the carpeted halls, passing several viewing windows showing the outside world, the gallery reminded Fredrick of the *Hindenburg*'s observation gallery. Simple design with railings and windows allowing guests to see out, but keeping them from being able to jump out or fall while keeping the weather at bay.

"The main dining room takes the entire forward of the ship and has some amazing views all around." Leo walked through the double open doors. "There are two seatings of 100 guests. First seating is 1745 and Second seating is 2000."

"Do we serve at breakfast or lunch?" Fredrick asked as he absorbed the space. There were staging stations and walls that didn't have windows but beautiful murals of the Hawaiian Islands and some of the associated gods. He couldn't imagine how much work went into the design of the space to make the location as warm and welcoming as the scene was. He appreciated how the dark blue carpet with motion in the pattern giving hints of the ocean that they would be crossing continued here as well. If only the designers of the *Hindenburg* were still around to see this amazing vessel.

"There are split shifts for breakfast and lunch which are buffet for the guests, unless folks are dining in the *Lani* Steakhouse, on deck 3 Forward, but the steakhouse only offers brunch and dinner. Unless the Captain is hosting a special event. And they have a dedicated wait staff, Dejan works there …"

Such a unique name. In fact, several of the names he had heard were odd to him. Fredrick took another peek around the dining room. Again, the contrast to the *Hindenburg* was unimaginable. He wished Wilhelm could have seen this ship. His heart ached as a memory of the fire and the smell of burning found him again. He pinched his nose, forcing the memory and the scent away. If he were honest, he longed for all his coworkers to have seen this place. He ran a hand over one of the chairs.

Unlike anything the Hindenburg had.

Moving through the double doors to the atrium and up the main staircase to the next deck up, the color scheme of the ship followed them. On Deck 1, Leo moved them forward to the Kona Lounge, which had a similar layout as the Kapua Bar on the lower deck. However, this lounge was bigger and had a small stage where performers might entertain guests. In front of the stage a small dance floor also occupied the space.

"I can't get over how different this ship is."

"I hope that's a good thing." Leo pulled them toward the midship. "On this side is the *Pii Aku* Shop, where guests will pay outrageous amounts of money for memorabilia of their trip. It also has things like Aspirin, condoms, toothpaste, and sewing kits; basically all the things people forget at home." He ran a hand along the railing of the window into the closed shop. "Over there is the *Nānā* Gallery with artwork for sale and photos that are taken on the trip by the ship's photographers."

Fredrick walked to the railing and glanced out. These were by far some of the largest windows and provided some of the best views of the outside. "*Wunderbar,*" he commented under his breath.

"Now that is a word I know." Leo beamed down at the view. "Once we're over the water, the view gets even better. On occasion we'll see whales and dolphins messing about. There are some great zep trips heading to Alaska. The ocean life you get to see, plus the glaciers, are incredible; they can't be beat. Not even by the Cruise Ships. They try, but we got them beat by a mile."

"I can imagine."

"We've got the passenger cabins aft of here." Leo pointed with raised brows. "Shall we continue? Unless you want to check out the guest cabins?"

Fredrick reflected for a moment. He would've loved to see a guest room or two, but Leo seemed to only offer to be polite, plus he didn't see the need to go traipsing through a room that was already set for the coming guests. He didn't like that when people did that to a cabin he had recently tidied up.

"Lead the way." Fredrick gestured in the direction away from the guest rooms.

Another time.

They moved to the atrium and headed up the grand staircase. Leo led them through another set of double doors. "This is the *Luau* Theater and Night Club. When there isn't a show going on, we have a DJ and this is where guests play games—you know, the silly stuff like trivia and game shows. It's a lot of fun."

"It's all so lovely," Fredrick offered.

Leo beamed as he faced Fredrick. "I'm sure the *Hindenburg* is nicer, and if I remember correctly, doesn't the 2000 have a Beer Garden open to the outside of the ship? That'd be great to see—I'd love to see the engineering behind that." Leo's words sped up as he spoke.

Beer Garden ... open to the elements ... how?

Fredrick held his own questions at bay. "I'm sorry, I don't know the details of such things."

"Right. Yeah. Of course." Leo chuckled, but there was a hint of suspicion hovering around his expression.

I will need to look up the Hindenburg 2000 so I can answer questions for people should they ask.

Fredrick sighed as he stepped toward the center of the room where the raised stage lay. This was the location for the games that would take place.

"Don't worry about the entertainment." Leo moved closer to Fredrick. "We won't make you get up on stage and sing and dance."

"Good," Fredrick commented, not relishing the idea of being an entertainer. He had heard stories about those types of people.

"Oh, except for the Captain's Gala." Leo's voice rose. "The gala is our zep's formal night. The event is a big deal, and the party starts at 1700 and goes till midnight," he proclaimed. "Do you know how to waltz? What about a swing or jive?"

"What?" Fredrick asked.

"For the formal night, we're expected to take people out to the dance floor and, yes, I know, dance." Leo shrugged.

"I ... well, I can waltz ..."

"Good. Most of the guests have no clue, but we need to help keep the event fun and ensure everyone, even the wallflowers, have a good time. We can practice together tomorrow night after we get off. The Lani Club and Lounge won't be offering any of its nightly services on gala night, but we'll keep one staff person there on duty. Probably Aurora, since she's my Assistant Concierge and doesn't enjoy all the hoopla."

"Okay."

"Come on ..."

Fredrick fumbled with his hands. When was the last time he danced? That wasn't something he did often. The last time he waltzed had to be when he was on leave and his baby sister Else wanted him to teach her.

She was so young and full of life. What happened to her? What happened to all of them? She'd be 106 now.

His heart sank at the memory of the two of them dancing around their parents' kitchen. The image was almost too much to bear.

"Hey, the gala and the dancing won't be too bad. We get to wear our formals." Leo beamed. "I want to show you the Lani Steakhouse and Club, and the Pali Deck before it gets too late."

Fredrick pushed the sadness and the memories away. There would be time to deal with that later. He inhaled as much as his lungs would allow. "No more on this deck?"

Leo pointed. "Aft is passenger cabins and some crew service areas."

They moved to the atrium and the bank of elevators. "Deck three is the upper passenger deck. We can use the crew stairs, but the elevator's quicker."

The lift wasn't anything special, except they were on a lift in an airship. There wasn't a lot of room, maybe enough for eight people and some bags. The cabin of the lift was well-lit and ventilated, a big plus. A soft ding announced the doors closing, and with a slight jolt the lift moved up. With another ding the doors opened on Deck 3 and they arrived in a lobby space similar to A Deck. Greeting them was a passage leading down the midship all the way to the aft.

"More passenger cabins?" Fredrick asked, pointing in the direction of the hall.

"Yep," Leo confirmed. "Forward's where we'll find the suites, the Lani Steakhouse, and our office, the Lani Club and Lounge. If we get a chance, I'll see about us having dinner at the steakhouse one night. David owes me a favor—he's the Head Chef."

Fredrick heard the pronunciation of the name *David*. Leo had used the French pronunciation of the name: *David* with its soft 'a' and hard 'e' sound. He would need to remember that for when he met the man. He hated to mispronounce people's names.

"Shall we?" Leo gestured, moving them down the forward hall to a waiting area opening into a built-in banquette for seating. Leo guided them through the foyer of the restaurant and into a large space with an open kitchen and several tables and chairs all placed in front of large picture windows. "They have the best views on the ship ... of course."

The Lani Steakhouse had 180-degree views of the outside. No wonder the design team picked this location for the restaurant. They sat forward and at, what Fredrick believed to be, the middle of the ship so the windows looked straight out to the night sky. Lights off in the distance twinkled, bouncing off the water and all around the bay, showing the mountains to both their left and to their right.

"Incredible." Fredrick scanned the grand space.

Leo shrugged. "You mean to tell me that the *Hindenburg* isn't as glam or as decked out? I've seen the pics, so I know you're messing with me."

Fredrick's heart pinched and the room blurred. He grabbed onto one of the chairs, digging his fingers into the soft wood and material.

How is any of this possible?

"Hey, you alright? You look pale." Leo patted Fredrick's arm. "Do we need to take you to the doc?"

"Sorry. Tired." Fredrick's grip on the chair loosened.

"It's been a long day, I know. Let's check out the Lani Club and Lounge. Our tour won't be too much longer."

This place, and this ship, are beyond words.

Fredrick and Leo moved out of the reception area. To their left were double doors that had an etched stained-glass window effect with the words Lani Club and Lounge embedded in the window, and above the words an image of the *Hawaiian Sun* hung in front of some clouds. The craftsmanship was impressive. Leo pulled out his plastic card and tapped the device next to the door. With a click and green light, they walked through the now unlocked door.

Greeting them was a large reception desk with two of the bigger devices he had seen Leo use, as well as what he judged to be two black telephones. If not for the futuristic technology, the space seemed like a familiar work environment that Fredrick had seen hundreds of times. Windows behind the desk revealed more views, not as grand as the steakhouse, but still impressive.

"Welcome to our office." Leo chuckled as he moved in deeper, showing off the space with his arms risen. "I think it's a pretty amazing place to work, if you ask me."

Fredrick took in the grand space. "Indeed." Mostly what caught his attention were the richer colors and more refined furniture. The wall to the left housed a long buffet, empty now, but he noted all the open shelving with serving items and clear glass, or plastic, above. Underneath the buffet housed more storage. Everything in the space was elegant but still built for form and function. At the end of the buffet lay a bar filled with glassware and various spirits. The space reminded him of the bar on the *Hindenburg*, a compact space but enough room for one, maybe two people to work comfortably.

"A full bar?"

Leo looked in the direction of the small station. "Yep, but this one is complimentary for our guests. You see the door there?" He pointed to a door that blended in with the wall and sat between the buffet and bar, that Fredrick had missed at first. "That's a door that leads to the back kitchen and bar for the Lani Steakhouse."

"I see."

"That way the waiters and bartender, as well as the service team, can easily move about."

"Makes sense." Fredrick moved forward past all the chairs and tables. He focused on the back wall and a huge mounted rectangular screen showed works of art that shifted every few minutes. "How many paintings does this machine hold?" he asked.

Leo laughed. "The TV? Probably a thousand or so, but most of the time we use it to show sporting events or news. Typically, it'll hold cruise details: location, altitude, weather, map of our trip, you know, stuff like that."

"I have no words."

"Oh, come on, it's not that impressive." Leo grinned. "See, I know you're messing with me, 'cause I know the old *Hindenburg 2000* has similar features in her suites section. All zeps do."

Fredrick deliberated a moment and decided to agree. "Yes ... yes. I didn't want to be a braggard." He forced a pleasant expression to his face and gave what he hoped to be a good-natured chuckle. "However, the style here is so different, so much fresher and pleasing. Very comfortable. Even these sofas seem more welcoming." He sniffed the air. "And do I smell the ocean and ... coconuts?"

"Hopefully the scents don't bother you. We use them to help keep the tropical vibe." He shrugged.

"No." Fredrick breathed in deeper. "It's nice."

"I think so as well." Leo's grin grew across his lips. "And in the corner there"—he pointed—"is a small stage with a piano, and connections for other instruments. It's nice for the ambiance and the guests seem to like it. Margo is good. I think you'll enjoy her playing; she's never overly loud and tends to hit a perfect balance."

"When we had the piano on the *Hindenburg*, people enjoyed the music," Fredrick offered, leaving off that they removed the piano later because of the weight as well as the two chandeliers.

"We only offer live music in the evenings. Occasionally we'll have a musician during afternoon tea, depends on if we're in port or not."

"This will be a lovely place to work."

"Good, glad to hear you're excited. Now come on, we still have one place to get to: the Pali Deck. Afterward we can go and you can get some sleep or we can hang out with everyone else for drinks, seeing who's still on the ship."

"Maybe," Fredrick responded, taking in the view of the club/lounge one more time. Nothing he had seen on the *Hindenburg* compared to any part of the *Hawaiian Sun*. "It has been a long day."

I must find out what happened to my ship. Somehow.

As the two men returned to the lift, Fredrick replayed all he had seen in these last few hours. He wondered, however briefly, if he survived the fire on the *Hindenburg*, and was now laying in a hospital dreaming, trying to recover from his injuries. He realized a more reasonable explanation had to be out there somehow; nothing he'd seen this afternoon could be real.

It's not possible to travel to the future. There has to be another explanation. This must all be a dream.

With another ding, the doors of the lift opened onto an outdoor deck. The warm night sky brushed his cheeks as a million stars twinkled above them. The moon hung in the darkening sky, showering them in moonbeams, and illuminating their surroundings. Several of the crew lounged about and sat chatting to each other, relaxing and enjoying the evening. Some waved to Leo and Fredrick, others focused on their conversations and their refreshments.

"The crown jewel of the *Hawaiian Sun*. The Pali Deck." Leo walked around, his arms outstretched. "During the day, the chairs are laid out for guests to enjoy and the hot tubs will be running, but not tonight. The tubs have been drained, sanitized, and cleaned, and they won't refill them until the morning. Same with the *Hoomaha* Spa and Gym. Well it's being cleaned, not drained." Leo's gaze met Fredrick's. "Anyway, we can come up and check them out in the morning. I want you familiar when our guests ask."

Fredrick's gaze wandered over to the closed doors. "What is the *Ka Makani* Teen Club?"

"Oh, that's for the kids, a place to go and hang out, away from the adults. They have video games, TVs, stuff like that. Luckily, we don't have to deal with them. The Ka Makani Counselors get to hang out with them, but we're not expecting many kids this trip and none in the suites. They might open the club up for the adults …" He shrugged.

"What's that?" Fredrick pointed to the edge of the airship's walls. The deck was located lower on the inside of the airship, providing a windbreak and protection from the elements when the *Hawaiian Sun* was in the air, but something rested on either side of the giant opening to the sky.

"Those are the retractable transparent ceilings. Oh right, the *Hindenburg 2000* doesn't have those. Too cold over in Europe, right? Hey, something we have up on your old *Hindenburg* … go us." Leo smirked.

Fredrick remained silent.

"If the weather gets bad, we close the ceiling so people can enjoy the deck and the amenities. I like this feature of the ship, and I wish more of the zeps would do this, but … I don't know." Leo pulled out his device. "Well, that's the ship. I'm sure there's a lot more you'll need to see, but for now we covered the big stuff. In the morning I'll show you around the service areas, go over emergency procedures, where all the dirty work is taken care of, and I'll take you to the kitchen and introduce you to the galley crew in the Lani Steakhouse. They're a good lot and really helpful."

Fredrick exhaled. "What an amazing airship."

"I like her," Leo extended his agreement. "Come on, let's head down and meet up with Tommy and some of the others. See if Aurora, Nuwa, Tomas, and Ollie have returned. Today's been a whirlwind, but we have to have at least one drink to welcome you on board." Leo waved to some of the crew as he moved them to the lifts.

"One drink won't hurt." Fredrick glanced around again, taking in the sights of the upper deck one more time.

I could probably use several drinks after all I've seen and experienced today.

Fredrick stole another peek of the moon and stars. Everything seemed calm up here … almost normal. Inhaling deeply, he allowed the warm night air to fill his lungs, before they headed to the lifts again. If this was a dream or some kind of a fantasy, Fredrick wasn't so sure he wanted to wake up.

6

S TARTLING AWAKE, LEO MOANED and felt around for his phone to stop the incessant shrieking. He would never get used to the sound of his phone's alarm. Matters weren't helped with the knowledge that one drink turned into two, and three. He wasn't a big drinker and stopped after drink number three as did Fredrick, but still the booze impeded his sleeping.

He rested back onto his pillow, stretching out his feet and legs and trying to bring his body to life. His hand ran down the dip in his stomach to the soft lump between his legs and he started to rub himself. Images of Barron ran across his mind, the two of them kissing and the first time they fooled around. Their lips felt so good together. His body stirred at the memories. His member arose and woke up.

He huffed out a sigh.

What's the point? Why bother?

Leo removed his hand from his crotch as his eyes fluttered open. He scanned the cabin. The space remained dark which he appreciated. As he dropped his legs over the edge of his bunk, a beep echoed from the door light slowly pushed back the darkness as the opened. He quickly pulled the blanket over his chest to cover himself. He had to stop from protesting at the intrusion, remembering that he once again shared the room. Slowly, the door revealed Fredrick dressed in his new uniform, all brushed and polished. He looked like he had walked right off the covers of a magazine and every part of him sparkled and shined.

"Morning person?" Leo grumbled the words out with a yawn.

"I'm sorry, I hope I didn't wake you." Fredrick slipped the rest of the way in, closing the door and minimizing the amount of light infiltrating the space. "I wanted to bathe and be ready for work before you got up."

Leo's eyes adjusted to the lower level of light in the room. He hopped down from his bunk and rubbed a hand over his mouth and eyes before scratching his arm and bare stomach. Then he pushed open the curtain to the outside window so the only light coming from their shared cabin came from the outdoors. "Trying to make the boss look bad?" Leo tried to tease, hoping the words were as cheery as possible for this hour of the day.

Fredrick hardly acknowledged Leo, instead crossing to his cupboard and putting his grooming and bathing items away. Freezing, his heart stopped and stomach dropped, Leo felt around his hips to ensure he had something on. Typically, when he was alone he slept *au naturel*, and this would be awkward if he was nude. The soft cotton fabric of his briefs met his fingertips. And he exhaled. "How was the locker room?"

"A few people there when I left, so you might be able to take a shower if you want while the water is still hot."

"Hot water is the least of my concerns." Leo moved to his closet and pulled out his shower kit. He slipped on some shorts, t-shirt and his flipflops. "Why don't I meet you at breakfast, then we can get started?"

Fredrick took a quick peek over his shoulder. "I don't mind waiting if that's okay. I don't—"

Leo's laugh cut him off. "I get it, I don't like eating alone either. Give me ten minutes."

Leo felt Fredrick's gaze following him as he rushed out their cabin door and headed to the showers. The hot water would feel good and help wake him up. Some food and hot tea were in order as well. Today was embarkation and these were always the busiest days of any trip.

• • •

Leo didn't need to rush, but since Fredrick waited for him he didn't want to dawdle and ogle the eye candy always willing to show off in the locker room. Plus, he had seen almost everything that was on offer, and by now it was all old hat. He smirked as he bathed himself—for a bunch of straight guys, some of them sure didn't mind giving you an eyeful from time to time. Not to mention how Leo caught several of them checking out the other guys when they figured no one was watching. But among crewmates, an unspoken rule of not saying anything or lingering your gaze seemed to be the norm, at least on this airship.

A quick shit, shower, and shave later Leo was now dressed, and sat with Fredrick in the crew mess. The food and warm earl grey tea hit all the right spots, getting him ready for the busy day ahead of them.

Still would have been nice to have a lay in and relax, but that won't be happening for another couple of months.

"There are so many people," Fredrick commented over the last of his scone.

"A lot different than last night." Leo glanced around the dining space. The number of folks seemed normal to him. Although Fredrick hailed from a different country and a different line, so maybe the larger airships had more facilities for the crew and spread everyone out.

Fredrick sipped his coffee as his eyes darted around the space. "So different."

"The coffee or our dining room?" Leo laughed. "You know, if I didn't know any better, I'd swear this was your first time on a zep ..." He narrowed his gaze on Fredrick. "Have you been messing with me? Are you playing the shy, quiet novice, so once we get to work, you're gonna blow me and the others away?"

Fredrick sat back, his eyes growing large and a frown rushing across his lips. "No. Sorry. I ... this ship ... you ... everyone ... so ..."

Leo barked out a laugh, "Dude, I'm messing with you." He stuffed the last of his strawberries into his mouth, chewing then swallowing the partially macerated chunks down. "Come on, let's get going. You have some paperwork to finish up, and procedures to go over, a meeting with the rest of the team, and we need to prepare to fly." Leo chugged down the rest of his tea before wiping his lips with his napkin.

After breakfast, the rest of the morning had been filled with paperwork, introductions, basic safety trainings, policy and procedure reviews, tours of the crew work areas, and getting final sign offs for Fredrick and Leo's shopping trip. No matter how quickly Leo rushed them through each of these steps, they seemed to fall further and further behind. Luckily Fredrick was a quick study which helped, giving him the opportunity to review the day's schedule, however briefly, for his team meeting.

Leo's team occupied the empty and quiet Lani Club and Lounge. The space was set and cleaned for the new guests, but when the club wasn't open, he used the space as their conference room. Often Leo would do some of his work here, so he wasn't always stuck in his cabin with his paperwork or planning everyone's schedules.

Plus, it's a nice spot to work, when it's quiet.

Leo observed Fredrick as he addressed his team, instructing them on embarkation duties and barely necessitating the use of his tablet. None of this seemed to show any concern on Fredrick's face. Clearly, Fredrick was comfortable with the embarkation process. *Good.* Leo quickly reviewed his agenda items on his tablet, noting a message that there had been some changes on the guest list. He could worry about that later.

When aren't there last-minute updates and changes?

He would stay on the ship with Fredrick and continue his onboarding process. They could go around and meet their guests later. Aurora and the others would be able to handle the welcome and escorting of their club guests. After going through where everyone was to be stationed for embarkation, Leo licked his lips and took a deep breath. The last thing on his agenda for the morning was to have Fredrick do a quick introduction of himself.

Fredrick's voice was quieter than it had been when they were alone. "As Leo mentioned, I'm from Germany and I worked on the *Hindenburg* as a Steward, so this is going to be a change for me." Fredrick managed to make eye contact with everyone, but from the color in his cheeks, Leo noted he wasn't comfortable. "I grew up in a town south of Frankfurt called Seligenstadt, which feels farther away over the last few days ..." He paused to inhale, and a smile filled his face and he showed off his dimple again. "However, I'm happy to be here." He ended with a nod.

"Welcome," Aurora greeted. Her dark long hair combed softly in the middle falling right below her shoulders. "It'll be nice to have you here. If you want to know what happens here on ship, you come talk to me." She winked over at Leo, her smile growing.

"Funny," Leo countered with a slight shake of his head.

"Welcome aboard, mate." Hints of Ollie's British accent dusted his words and his expression was warm as usual, and he smiled but not nearly as much as the rest of them.

"We're looking forward to working with you. Sorry we missed you last night." Nuwa adjusted her glasses as she spoke.

"No, I'm glad you enjoyed your time off," Fredrick acknowledged. "I'm sorry I took up Leo's night."

"Leo, are you kidding? He's always working." Tomas beamed, his usual aura of mischief running over his face. "That's why he's the boss."

"Okay. Okay. Thank you, Fredrick." Leo didn't want to make Fredrick suffer in the spotlight anymore than he needed too. "As a final reminder, we're adjusting the clocks again tonight and tomorrow, so when we arrive at Hilo we'll be on Hawaiian Standard time. Make sure you remind the guests as you greet them and escort them to their cabins."

There were several moans from the group. "I know, it's a pain. An hour back every night till we get to Hilo, and an hour forward starting in Nawiliwili till we arrive in San Jose."

"Lame," Tomas grumbled.

"Hey, it's part of the itinerary, it's nothing new. No whining; we're here for the guests," Aurora reminded the team.

"That's the worst part about the trip." Nuwa pulled off her glasses to give them a wipe with a cloth. "I hate all the time changes."

"We didn't usually have these issues in Europe and the UK only has one time zone," Ollie added with a yawn before fussing with his strawberry-blond hair. "We stayed on one time, airship time, and it was brilliant." More of his accent followed his words.

"Anyway," Leo brought them all to focus, "we're gonna have a full Club this trip. We're expecting 30 guests, and the arrival times are staggered so you should have enough time to greet them and get them settled before the next group arrives."

"You and Fredrick won't be there, so if we need to double up will that be fine?" Aurora flicked her long dark hair over her shoulder. "In case folks are early … or late. Or do you want us to keep them in the airfield's club lounge?"

"Whatever works best is fine; I trust you all to use your best judgment." Leo picked up his tablet and scanned the device to ensure he hadn't forgotten anything. "Remember, it's all about the fantasy and the experience." He waved his hands around and wiggled his fingers as he glanced at his team. The *Hawaiian Sun* had a small Suite Staff on board, a five-to-one ratio which wasn't bad, but with Fredrick being new, things might not be up to scratch. Still, he knew his team could adapt and the guests would have a great time.

I wish I could get one more Butler or perhaps two Assistant Butlers like on some of the other airships. That would be great.

"Any kids?" Aurora asked as she sat deeper in her chair.

"Nope." Leo smiled, checking his tablet. "At least not in the club."

"Thank fuck." Ollie exhaled. "They can be a right pain in the arse. Little buggers feel entitled when they get a taste of the suite life."

"Oh, come on, Ollie, you know you love'um." Nuwa laughed, running a hand through her thick black hair. "Being from that big family of yours."

Tomas smirked as he watched the banter.

"Not bloody likely," Ollie countered.

"Let's give Fredrick one day where we're on our A-game, before he learns the messy truth, shall we?" Leo beamed at his team, trying to cut off the banter. They still had a lot to do before lunch and the passengers' arrival.

"Sorry." Ollie extended a nod to Fredrick.

"Busted," Tomas whispered loud enough for everyone to hear.

"It's fine." Fredrick still had a pleasant expression on his face—Leo figured the face was a default expression of his. "If I may, will there be many children on this trip?"

Leo tapped his tablet to check the guest numbers. "Looks like twenty-four ranging in ages. So not too bad."

"Better than the holiday trips where the ship seems like almost 50% of the guests are kids." Aurora clasped her hands together, resting them on the table.

"At least we won't have to bother with them." Ollie ran a hand under his chin.

"Well, not in the club," Tomas added.

"Don't you like children?" Fredrick faced Ollie.

Everyone laughed with the exception of Ollie and Fredrick.

"Never mind that. Unless there's anything else"—Leo glanced at his staff—"we all have places to go and things to do. Tomas, you're working the desk here and I'll have Fredrick shadowing me. Aurora, you'll be in the terminal lounge with Ollie and Nuwa wrangling our guests and showing them where to go. If you need backup, call me and I'll have Tammy come man the lounge and we'll send Tomas out with you. She knows Fredrick will be with me. If there're any issues, call me. Questions?"

No one spoke up.

"You know how to find me if anything comes up. Let's get to it. Don't forget we have the welcome reception tonight, so wear your dress uniforms," Leo added as a way to end the meeting.

With the staff meeting finished, Leo and Fredrick continued to race through the rest of the morning, still not able to catch up despite Leo cutting his staff meeting short. Happily, they all knew what they were doing. Still, they had precious little time for lunch before the passengers started to arrive and the real work began. They would greet guests and ensure everyone had what they needed and got to where they were supposed to go. Embarkations were a dance, sometimes graceful and elegant and other times a mass of bodies not making any rhyme or reason. Today was the former.

Hanging up with Aurora, Leo inhaled, taking in as deep a breath as possible. He wouldn't let any new passenger issues get to him; these things happened and there was no need to make anyone else panic.

It'll all be fine.

He glanced over at Fredrick, who watched a couple of the Guest Services team chat and address guest issues. He could have left Fredrick to them, to give him a good understanding of how things worked here, but that wasn't the job of guest services. That was his job.

Adjusting his uniform jacket, he slipped his phone in his pocket and moved over to Fredrick, meeting his gaze. Leo walked over to the desk and slipped behind the counter through the side door. "How's Fredrick doing?" he asked Raven, the Guest Services Manager.

"Good." They met Leo's gaze. "Everything okay?"

"Nothing I can't handle." He pointed to one of the vacant workstations. "Do you mind?"

"Be my guest." Raven gestured to the computer.

As he typed away, he kept one eye on Fredrick, taking note of how he was doing. He clearly wanted to learn. He watched everything Raven and their team did. Fredrick appeared to be a sponge.

And that will help him a great deal.

There weren't a lot of issues yet from what he saw, mostly the usual: questions about guest rooms, guest accounts, and the odd request for dinner seating changes and reservations.

That's good. Don't want poor Fredrick to get sucked into any drama. At least for the moment.

Leo printed out a few documents, folded them and put the items into a *Hawaiian Sun*-branded envelope, and sent a note to room service to bring a bottle of Champagne and plate of chocolate-covered strawberries to the guest room early tonight. With a tilt of his head, he signaled Fredrick to join him.

"Thanks Raven." Leo waved.

"Glad to help." They turned to the guest they were now assisting.

Fredrick thanked the folks he shadowed and moved over to Leo.

"Getting your wings?" Leo asked as they moved from Guest Services. He stuffed the envelope in his closed tablet. They walked to the main Promenade area, guests rushing about and chatting, some stopping to take pictures, others pushing past them to get to one of the bars or the upper deck. A gay couple with two younger kids stopped and asked if Leo would mind taking a photo of them. He obliged, snapping a couple of pics with one of the dad's phones before they rushed off. There was a quick pang in Leo's heart—they looked so happy. Music filled the ship, though nothing loud or obnoxious, more fun and energizing.

Embarkation days are the best. All the energy. All the excitement.

Leo noted how Fredrick watched the family. His new employee continued to scan the space and the guests. Leo wasn't quite sure how to decipher the expression on Fredrick's face.

"Why are there so many men?" Fredrick asked in a hushed voice so only Leo heard.

"Oh, there'll be others on board, not as many, you know how these specialty—"

"There you are," a strong polite voice called out. "You haven't returned my calls and after our short conversation yesterday ..."

Leo froze and the pit of his stomach dropped out. He knew the voice in an instant. He swallowed deep and put on his best expression.

"Hello, Barron." Leo turned so his green-eyed gaze burrowed into ex. The man stood in front of him in dark blue jeans and a silk tan-colored Tommy Bahama button-down Disney shirt, opened at the neck to reveal a white gold necklace mocking him.

So handsome and so freaking annoying.

Leo scanned the Promenade and all the oncoming passengers, as well as the other crew. The main gallery was not the place for a scene and he certainly didn't want to drag poor Fredrick into his mess.

"I'm glad you're here; I wasn't sure I'd see you." Barron shared no trace of malice or hurt, but why would there be?

"Well, I work on the ship, so …" Leo forced a bright look, doing his level best to sound neutral and pleasant. "Is there something I can assist you with, *Sir?*"

"Come on, Leo." Barron's voice lowered. "Don't be like that. I had to think of something since you refused to speak to me … for how many months now?"

"Barron, I'd like to introduce you to my new trainee, Fredrick. Fredrick, this is one of our more frequent guests, Barron Hillchild."

Barron extended a hand in greeting to Fredrick. "Nice to meet you, Fredrick. I'm sure Leo will take good care of you."

Fredrick took the outstretched hand and shook, glancing between Leo and Barron. "Thank you. Welcome onboard." He beamed, showing off his dimpled cheeks.

"Can we please talk?" Barron asked as he focused his attention on Leo.

"Barron, I have work to do and embarkation is not a good time. If you'll excuse us, we have a guest to attend to."

"You won't be able to dodge me for the next ten days. I'm one of your suite guests," Barron countered, his gaze blazing into Leo.

Why isn't one of my team attending to you? Bastard knows our operations, probably already got settled and came to find me. Fuck!

"Maybe not, but now is not the time. I'm sure you know where your cabin is, and if not, one of the stewards can assist you. Now please excuse us." Leo gave a terse nod and ushered Fredrick off to the grand staircase.

Leo remained quiet as they moved up the stairs and thank goodness Fredrick didn't speak or ask questions. On the deck three landing, Leo promptly took a breath and turned to Fredrick. "Sorry about that."

"He seemed keen on speaking with you," Fredrick stated, not a question, which Leo appreciated but open-ended enough so if Leo wanted to share he could.

"I won't bore you with the details, but suffice to say Barron and I are not on good terms right now. And clearly, I missed that he would be on this trip. In a suite as well. I bet it's under his buddy Elijah, he's all about the drama." He shook his head. "I should have checked the roster better. Idiot."

"Understood." Fredrick ended the conversation and greeted a couple of older men as they passed.

Leo smiled as well. They were clearly a couple, but from a different time as they weren't as touchy as the gay family he took a photo of. However, they shared an unmistakable closeness.

Leo checked his tablet, tapping away. "The gods have been in our favor today ... mostly. Come on." He moved them down the hallway on Deck 3 to the suites.

"Why are we heading to the suites?" Fredrick asked.

"We have to make nice with an Evaluation Auditor, from United Airships." Leo shook his head in irritation. "Typically, these things don't happen, but when they do we get to deal with the situation. He wasn't supposed to be here for two more trips, but surprise. Aurora gave me a heads up when she called—he caused a bit of a situation in the terminal. It'll be fine." Leo faced the hall as they walked. "I hope."

With Barron and now with this surprise evaluation, things may not be as smooth for us as I hoped.

"Sorry."

And Barron ambushing me doesn't help.

Leo cracked his neck as they walked. "Ready?"

Leo and Fredrick stopped at one of the cabin doors. Leo checked his tablet again, ensuring the room number matched what he had on file. "Before we go in, Mr. Sherman wasn't on our passenger roster until this morning, a huge mix-up I missed. He's a suite guest who paid full price, though he's a contractor for United Airships and technically works for the company. He'll be evaluating everything from ship services, crew interactions, ship appearance, even us. Most of the time we don't know when they're going to be on the zep, but with the mix-up this morning, with his arrival, we found out. We're here to make nice and assure him these things don't happen … You know."

Fredrick smiled. "I understand. We are here to ensure the guest is happy and doesn't give us a poor rating."

"And to keep the fantasy in full effect."

"Right." Fredrick understood customer service is key.

"Aurora already spoke with the guests who had to be relocated, but luckily they weren't upset and said as long as they had access to all the suite benefits, they didn't care about what room they're in … thank goodness," Leo added.

Fredrick's head bobbed up and down in acknowledgement.

"Good, but everything we do has to be by the book and per our policies with this guy." Leo huffed out a chuckle, "It wouldn't surprise me if this wasn't part of his M.O. A way to throw us off our game." Leo tapped on the door. "Hello. Mr. Sherman." Leo's voice filled with warmth as he put on his best customer service face.

The door slid open and a guy in his late twenties or early thirties greeted them. His brown hair was perfectly styled, complementing his hazel eyes. Mr. Sherman's slender frame was flattered by the cut of his blue polo shirt, dark jeans, and polished brown shoes. The man was striking as almost all the other men on this cruise.

"Can I help you?" Mr. Sherman asked, perusing both Leo and Fredrick.

"I'm your Concierge Leopold Asher, and this is one of my Butlers Fredrick Rudolf, we're here—"

"Ah." Mr. Sherman examined both men. "I know why you're here. The Officers sent you up to make nice so I don't complain anymore. Come in and let's get this over with." He moved to the side, allowing them access to his cabin.

Leo glanced at Fredrick who wore a beautiful bright expression showing off his killer dimples.

The guy knows how to work that smile.

"At least they sent you two and not a couple of *'uggos'*. Or, that other person … what was her name; Aurora?" Mr. Sherman snipped as the door slid closed behind Fredrick.

"'Uggos'?" Fredrick whispered.

Leo shook off the comment as they entered the cabin. He always loved the suites—they were some of the roomiest cabins on the zep, even nicer than what most of the officers had, except the captain and a few others.

The suite opened to a sitting area with a sofa, two small ottomans that doubled as a coffee table, two side chairs, a built-in desk by the door, and a cabinet with TV mounted above. Ahead of them were large floor to ceiling windows that looked out at the airship terminal at the moment, but would have an amazing vista of the sky once they left the landing pad. Next to the cabinet and TV, a door lay open to the bedroom holding a king bed, end tables with built in lights, and out of sight were the ample closet and bathroom. The suites were designed for four people; however, Mr. Sherman had reserved the room for himself.

Clearly this Auditor had money and would expect everything to go perfectly.

"Let's get this over with." Mr. Sherman pointed to the sofa as he took a seat in one of the side chairs.

Leo gestured to the couch for him and Fredrick to sit down.

"On behalf of Captain Danielle Monroe and Head Steward Tammy Lam, we want to apologize for the difficulty you experienced with your arrival today and we—"

Mr. Sherman waved off Leo's remarks. "Look, Mr. Asher and Mr. Rudolf, let me save you the time and trouble." He crossed his right leg over his left. "I'm here to do a job for United Airships; however, foremost I'm here to enjoy myself. I took this contract to spend time with my community, since most of my audits occur on family cruises with lots of kids underfoot. Which I can assure you is not my favorite, but it's my job, one I'm quite good at. That all said, I'm not here to cause trouble and I apologize for my frustration earlier. I'm glad the other group who were booked in my suite were accommodated, with no disturbance to them or their vacation, showing favorable customer service on your part. I'm here now and I would like to enjoy my trip and do my evaluation." He forced a grin as he focused on Fredrick. "I promise you won't have any issues with me. I'm here to work, enjoy, and ... maybe get laid." He pushed an agreeable expression to his lips.

Leo followed Mr. Sherman's gaze and bit away his frown—clearly the face was for Fredrick.

Well, that may be an issue.

"I'm sure there are plenty of guests for you to meet and mingle with," Leo suggested, taking the focus off Fredrick.

"I suppose." Mr. Sherman directed his comments to Leo, resting his hands in front of him with his fingers drumming together forming a triangle. "As it is, I'm sure word will get out for everyone to be on their best behavior since I'm aboard, which will skew my report, but it's too late to cancel and change."

"I've been advised to assure you, that other than the Captain, the Head Steward, myself, Aurora, and Mr. Rudolf, the rest of the crew will not be made aware of your presence. We would like to ensure a fair report. And since Aurora, Fredrick, and I are part of the Lani Club and Lounge service team, there should be no additional contamination."

Mr. Sherman laughed. "We'll see about that. What about my room attendant?"

"They will not be informed," Leo assured.

"Fine, is there anything else?"

Leo's body relaxed as he tried not to roll his eyes at the power move. Sometimes these conversations didn't go well. Considering what he heard about Mr. Sherman's interaction with the gate agents, Leo wasn't sure what they were going to come across. So far, the man seemed as reasonable as described and not nearly as frightening as warned about. The guest who yelled, screamed and called you names was easy to deal with; you kicked them off the zep, no matter if they were an Auditor or not, before you depart. It's the polite forceful ones that often caused the trouble and that's who Leo deemed they would be up against. But he seemed more calculating, knowing what to say and how to say it to get exactly what he wants, which meant a lot of this might have been for show, a test, to see how they dealt with difficult guests.

An arrogant fuck trying his powerplay on us to trip us up, to see what he can get out of us.

"As with all our guests, we're here to ensure your comfort, that you're satisfied with your suite, and to apologize for the mix-up earlier."

Mr. Sherman stood. "Thank you."

Leo stood, followed quickly by Fredrick.

"Also ..." Leo held out the envelope he had prepared at Guest Services before they ran into Barron. "We'd like to offer you and a guest a complimentary dinner at Lani Steakhouse, for any night of your choosing this cruise, and a four-hundred-dollar credit for the Hoomaha Spa for use on this cruise."

"And my position has nothing to do with your offer?" Mr. Sherman watched the two of them.

"As I'm sure you're familiar, this is a standard offer, as outlined by company policy. We would make this gesture to any guest who had a similar incident as you did today. We've made the same offer to the people who were moved to another room to accommodate your stay. And I've arranged for a personal apology gift to be sent to both your rooms later this evening."

There's no point in keeping the sweet treat a secret, at least from Mr. Sherman.

Mr. Sherman's firm expression softened. "In that case, that's kind of you." He took the envelope. "Now if you don't mind, I'd like to get unpacked and settled. I hear there's a not to be missed deck party up on the Pali Deck as we depart, hosted by our local legend Krystal Chandelier."

"It'll be something and the views will be impressive, I can assure you." Leo adjusted his jacket as he moved to the suite door. "As a reminder, we'll be setting the clocks back an hour tonight. The clock in your bedroom should automatically adjust, but if there's an issue, please let us know."

Mr. Sherman moved with them to the door. "I don't suppose you're free to join me for dinner at the steakhouse, Mr. Rudolf? I hate to eat alone. Or is that against policy?"

"I ..." Fredrick stumbled over his words. "That is kind of you, Mr. Sherman ..."

"Please, call me Martin."

"I don't think that would be suitable given the nature of your position with the company," Fredrick cautiously spoke, "But I appreciate the offer."

"Hmm." Martin beamed. "We'll see. Either way, thank you both for stopping by. I'm sure I'll be seeing you around the ship."

Fredrick and Leo left the room as quickly as possible. Once out of earshot and away from any of the other guests, Fredrick halted and reached out a hand to stop Leo. "What was that all about? Was that man making a pass at me? Is he a *pansy*?"

"A what?" Leo smirked. "And yes, probably, but no one uses that word. Listen, you'll need to get used to it, especially on this cruise, and with your good looks."

"I don't understand." Fredrick bit at his lower lip. "Doesn't he have a job to do, and how is that appropriate?"

Leo peeked up and down the hall. "You do know this is a queer cruise, right? All our guests are queer and it would seem our auditor is as well."

"You mean this is a homosexual cruise?" Fredrick's cheeks pinkened as his words sped up. "How can that be? What will people say? What about the government? Clearly—"

Leo watched Fredrick through a narrowed gaze as what can only be described as panic filled his words and his expression.

"Wow." Leo touched Fredrick's shoulder. "It's fine. We do these cruises all the time, twice a year now for the last eight years. As for everything else, no one cares. Not anymore. This isn't the 80s or 90s."

"But ... all these people are homosexual? Even Mr. Hillchild, the man you spoke with earlier?"

"Especially Barron. I can tell you stories about how gay he is." Leo continued to glance down the corridors, though no one appeared to be around. "Look, Fredrick, Barron's my ex, we were together six months. I'm gay." He bit at his burgeoning frown. "That won't be an issue for you, will it? Cause the next ten days we're going to be surrounded by the queer community all here to have a good time, and you, my friend, have caught the eye of Mr. Martin Sherman, one of our company's Auditors, and that should be interesting for us all. However, if you're uncomfortable or you have personal feelings about being around queer people, I need to know, so we can deal with this before we take to the sky."

"But ... how ... I ... we ..." Fredrick licked his lips and a laugh escaped him, betraying the worry on his face. "That won't be a problem. I'm sorry. I'm not used to ..." He waved a hand around him as if to wave off an unpleasant aroma.

"I'd have supposed you'd be used to all this, given you're from Europe."

"I'm from Germany," Fredrick corrected.

"Same thing." Leo shrugged off the comment. "I mean, the EU

and all, right? They all but pushed the US on gay rights. Plus, I've heard about all the clubs in Berlin."

"Yes. Gay rights," Fredrick echoed as the color returned to his cheeks. "The clubs in Berlin. Yes, gay. All very gay."

"Look, it's none of my business if you're straight, gay, bi, pan, asexual, demisexual, or whatever, but if you want to talk, I'm here. And our job is to ensure the guests have a good time and don't get out of line or take things too far."

Fredrick studied his hands, then rubbed his palms on his pants. "What about the offer from Mr. Sherman? Should we report his query to Ms. Lam?"

Leo snorted. "Why? He didn't say or do anything crossing any lines. That's why there're two of us when we go and speak to guests in their cabins. However, if he does say or do something and you don't feel comfortable, you certainly can report him, but I don't think he'll push anything. Now, if you want to have dinner with him, you unquestionably can. There aren't any rules against crew fraternizing with other crew, even Auditors, but be respectful and understand 'no' means 'no'. What you do on your off time is up to you." Leo sighed and adjusted his uniform jacket, before leaning closer to Fredrick. "A word of advice, don't expect anything more than a fling. Especially with someone like Mr. Sherman. I wouldn't be surprised one bit if he turned out to be married with kids and a wife. Got it?"

Fredrick bit at his lower lip. "Ah, one of those."

"Good. Now come on, you'll be fine. Honestly, people like Martin will lose interest the minute they run into some drunk twink in a Speedo with an overstuffed basket up on deck at the party."

"I don't understand."

Leo laughed as he walked again. "You will. Now we should make our rounds, go to all the suite guests and check in on them, say 'hello'. Ensure they know they can contact us if they need anything and to remind them about the welcome reception tonight in the Lani Club."

The two started off again, and Leo gave Fredrick a quick scan up and down. The poor guy couldn't be that clueless and unaware. And who used the word pansy anymore? Fredrick seemed to be a proper fish out of water. Then they had Martin Sherman—something about him tickled Leo's brain. The man seemed too focused on Fredrick, and the fuss he made earlier didn't add up with his flirty behavior a few minutes ago.

I hope the guy isn't a troublemaker, and doesn't become a problem, not only for the ship but for Fredrick.

7

F REDRICK REFLECTED ON the encounter with Mr. Sherman. Thankfully, that incident had been the only confrontation of the sort the rest of the afternoon. Fredrick and Leo made their way around introducing themselves to the other Suite guests, all of whom were either friends or couples, and all homosexual. And sure enough, they ran into Mr. Hillchild's friends, which did not please Leo, but you wouldn't have known by how he treated them. They appeared to be surprised that Leo was here on the ship, which Fredrick didn't feel was sincere.

Regardless, the idea of being on a cruise with so many gay people excited and terrified Fredrick. None of the incredible things Fredrick witnessed to this point had compared to being around so many people like him. All happy and enjoying life, not living in fear. Back in Germany he had heard stories of all the homosexual clubs in Berlin, before the Reich came to power, but they were closed by the time he got there and no one spoke of such things any longer. Now to be here and witness so much gaiety. He felt normal, like a real person and all the fear and weight seemed to leave his body the more interactions he had with all the different and wonderful people.

Who knew there were this many homosexual people? Amazing.

Leo had kept Fredrick busy, as did the guests; he had much to learn and figure out. Some things where familiar: finding misplaced luggage, assisting guests who were lost, and tidying up the club when the guests stepped away. Leo introduced him to the airship's computer system he'd be using, another miracle of science. One he fortunately only had to observe while playing the language barrier for his lack of understanding, for now. He would have to practice and figure the machine out, as much of his new job entailed a lot of work on various versions of this sort of machine, especially when he would be at the Concierge Desk in the Lani Club.

Privately, Leo informed Fredrick they would work on his laptop in their quarters which would help to get Fredrick up to speed. And Leo assured Fredrick he understood not everyone was *tech savvy*.

At first, Fredrick assumed the machine was a modified typewriter, but he quickly learned there was much more to the electric beast, intimidating him for sure. Still, he found himself more and more giddy to try all these new gadgets.

One device working similar to a telegraph, radio, typewriter, balance sheet, and ship's log. Fantastisch. Perhaps, if I understand the machine correctly, it might help me find out what happened to my family and the Hindenburg.

Easier aspects of his job included getting to know the many different people on board. He quickly fell back into his customer service skills with ease. He learned there were several different parties and events he hoped to see and learn about, including several drag performances, dance parties, a nonbinary fashion show, cabaret acts, and deck parties. Those were the affairs he noted on the schedule (add calendar and diary to the list of services the computer provided); Leo informed him that guests hosted several 'off book' parties which were a lot more intimidating and risqué.

There's a lot for me to see and learn in this new world.

However, unlike on the *Hindenburg* where the Stewards did everything, here on the *Hawaiian Sun*, the Concierge and Butlers had a lot to do, but focused on the 30—well, now 31—Lani Club Suite guests. Expectations included working the Welcome Reception tonight, but that wouldn't be an issue except for the late night. However, since he wasn't on duty until later tomorrow, he would get to sleep in a bit, assuming he could sleep, given he still wasn't used to the hours yet. In general, while on duty they would tend to the suite guest's needs and make themselves available when required. However, at 2200 they were off the clock, until the next morning.

After setting to the skies, Fredrick and Leo took their break, before they had to be back in the club at 1700 to relieve Oliver and Nuwa. Fredrick and Leo needed to be dressed in their formal uniforms by 1645. Now, they had time to rest up. As much as Fredrick wanted to see the first launch party, he wanted to practice on the laptop and learn the computer systems. Stopping by their cabin, the two picked up Leo's laptop and made their way to the crew leisure area and lounge, near the rear of the airship. Here they could watch as the airship flew over the bay, making their way to the Pacific Ocean. According to Leo, they needed to see them flying over the Golden Gate Bridge. San Francisco glimmered as the lights from the city filled the growing darkness. The buildings shot to the sky, causing Fredrick to wonder how tall the buildings were in places like New York, or Frankfurt or even Berlin.

The world has grown up.

Leo walked Fredrick through the basics of the computer system, which Fredrick found almost intuitive. As he worked, he picked up snippets of conversations from other crew members as they enjoyed their time off. Fredrick learned the world of the 2020s had become a wonderous place. Nothing he might have dreamed matched what he learned. His new time wasn't perfect, as fighting in various parts of the world continued, some locations sounding familiar while some didn't. China, Russia, and the United States seemed to be at each other's necks all the time. Homelessness and immigration came across as huge concerns and topics people didn't want to talk about, but still did. There were terrorist groups in the Middle East which didn't surprise Fredrick given all the trouble that region was in during his time.

How can there still be these issues? How can we have all these marvels and still face so many troubles?

Fredrick noted two women, one in officers' garb while the other wore a Guest Services uniform, sitting together in an embrace watching out one of the large windows enjoying the moment and the view. His mind flashed to the conversation he and Leo had about the ship being filled with homosexuals. The knowledge that there were so many gay people around filled him with wonder. Gays able to live in a world so open, not afraid to be caught or jailed; the concept liberated him in ways he never knew possible. The weight he always seemed to carry in his shoulders had slowly lessened over the afternoon, leaving him feeling lighter than the ship they traveled in. Witnessing some of the people on the airship, what they wore, how they acted, how they made no bones about flirting and showing affection toward each other, impressed him. The private parties Leo mentioned, that would be going on throughout the trip, Fredrick had gathered were sexual parties. He wouldn't lie, the idea reminded him a bit about the Pansy Craze he heard about and reckoned might be fun.

I wonder what Wilhelm would've considered about all this, this time. He would have loved it. I'm sure.

"You've been quiet," Leo mused from across the table as he picked at his plate of food. "Are you okay? You feeling more comfortable with our systems? I know learning new software in a language not your own can be a pain in the butt."

Fredrick glanced at the screen before him, populated with words and numbers that showed various reports on the guests and the ship. So much to learn and understand. He huffed and picked up his glass of soda—the drink was sickeningly sweet and nothing he cared to finish. The pop even smelled syrupy. But he wanted to try new things and needed something to give him a moment to think. He glanced at his empty plate.

At least my meal was good.

Returning the drink to the table, he noted how negligible the vibration was even in the crew area. The ship must have an amazing team of Elevatormen. "There's a lot I'm not used too," Fredrick spoke, no word of it a lie.

"Well, you've been catching on and I think in a couple of days you'll have your feet about you." Leo smiled, but the sparkle didn't carry to his eyes.

"Thank you." Fredrick leaned forward, thinking about Leo's conversation with Barron from earlier, and the reaction of Barron's friends. Dejection was something Fredrick understood all too well. "I'm sorry if I seem off. I too, left someone I assumed cared about me, before I came here."

Leo's brows rose as he leaned toward Fredrick.

Fredrick's palms started to sweat. He felt unsure if he should speak of such things. No one liked listening to someone complain and speak of their misfortunes, but Leo didn't seem like that. Leo may be someone for him to talk to … on some matters; after all, they had heartache in common.

Leo gazed out the window. "Not a good break-up?" he spoke before facing Fredrick again.

Fredrick's head shook in the negative as he licked his lips, a knot tightening in the pit of his stomach. "I found them in a …"

"Oh wow. You caught'um cheating," Leo stated as a matter of fact, not a question.

"Wilhelm …" Fredrick paused, waiting to see how Leo responded before continuing. Seeing no reaction other than concern, he continued. "He … he was with someone else. Told me he had no choice …"

"They always have a choice, but men can be pigs." Leo frowned, pulling the laptop away from Fredrick. Shifting his half-eaten plate of food, he tapped on the machine before focusing all his attention on Fredrick again. "I'm sorry this happened before you got here. What a messed up thing to have transpired. I'm sure it sucked."

"Yes." Fredrick peered toward the ceiling of the crew's common area. "I'm sorry, I shouldn't tell you such things." He wiped his hands on his pants. "No one wants to hear of these matters. My parents raised me not to complain—there's nothing more tiresome than listening to someone else's misery." The knot in his stomach tightened.

"Hey." Leo reached out a hand. "It's fine. I sympathize, and honestly this explains a lot about how you've been so lost and out of sorts. No wonder you freaked out when that guy hit on you."

"Mr. Sherman?" Warmth built up in Fredrick's chest and continued rising to his neck and cheeks, countering the growing tightness in his gut.

Leo closed the machine, putting it next to him as he shifted his plate in front of him. "Maybe you should have dinner with him, work this Wilhelm guy out of your system."

"I don't understand."

"You know, play the field. Go out and get laid, get the old German Sausage taken care of." Leo chuckled.

"Oh." Fredrick's face and neck burned. He still wasn't used to how freely people seemed to speak nowadays.

"If anything," Leo continued, "I bet the Mighty Mister Martin Sherman is good in bed—probably has lots of experience."

"Um ..."

"Oh, sorry." Leo cleared his throat. "I shouldn't have said that. I apologize if my remarks made you uncomfortable." He inhaled, taking a moment. "Sometimes my mouth moves faster than my brain can stop."

"No, it's fine ..." Fredrick pasted a smile on. He didn't want Leo to think he had been offended—in truth he was only a bit red-faced and as he recalled, Wilhelm loved to make Fredrick blush. Teasing him with bawdy humor was almost a sport with him, see how flustered he could get him.

"Okay." Leo's brows rose as his chin dropped. "Well, tell me to hush if I cross a line."

Fredrick grabbed for his soda before stopping. He didn't want any more of it and he wasn't going to choke it down. The image of him pulling an unconscious Wilhelm rushed to the front of his mind, the fire racing toward them. Fredrick felt sick.

"Anyway," Leo started, not seeming to notice as he glanced out the window again, "there's a swimsuit contest tomorrow, right after lunch during our break. We can go. Or I can arrange for us to be judges—you'll get an eyeful and it'll make you forget all your troubles."

"I don't think so." Fredrick forced the words out, the knot in his stomach taking over his whole torso. The stink of acid burning filled his nostrils. He waved a hand in front of him to clear the imagined stench.

"Why not?"

"I think Wilhelm died, but I don't know." The words burst out of him with the knot engulfing him.

"What? Bloody hell." Leo's head snapped as he glanced around the room seeing who, if anyone, was paying them any attention. "What happened?"

Fredrick didn't mean to take the conversation here, but he had and now what was he going to say? He quickly scanned the space and ensured his voice was low. "An accident ... I think. I don't know. I'm sorry, I shouldn't have said this, it's too much."

Leo remained quiet, finishing off the rest of his drink before turning to his leftover plate of food previously ignored. "Fuck me! Jesus! Okay, I get it, I'm sorry. That's all kinds of messed up, but the offer stands, if you want to talk."

"Thank you." Fredrick sighed, the weight in his shoulders again seeming less so after sharing his troubles with Leo. "Do we need to get going and prepare for the reception?"

I need to refocus and push these thoughts away.

Leo pulled out his smartphone. Fredrick heard the name a couple more times, and eventually remembered what to call the device.

"Probably." Leo stuffed the machine away. "Doesn't hurt to show up early and go over what David has planned for the reception. The extra time will give you a chance to sample the food, so you know what you're talking about, and find where all our supplies are."

"I'll be assisting you, correct?" Fredrick pointed to the machine next to Leo. "And no computer?"

A grin blossomed on Leo's face. "Yep, but you might need to deal with issues on your own … I think we'll be fine."

Fredrick stood, picking up his tray with his used utensils and the last of his sugary sweet drink. Leo joined him, slipping his laptop under his own tray as they made their way over to dispose of their used items, and out of the crew galley and off to their quarters to change and drop off the laptop.

Fredrick did his best to give Leo privacy as they got into their dress uniforms. Leo didn't seem uneasy about changing in front of Fredrick, but Fredrick was not so comfortable. He tried to never look at his fellow stewards and he did his best to keep his eyes to himself; one couldn't be sure who would notice and how they'd react. Getting caught might cost him his job, or worse.

"Do you need assistance with your tie?" Leo asked. "I wish they'd allow us to use clip-ons …"

Fredrick turned around after finishing off his bowtie. He was used to tying a tie and a bowtie. It was an artform learned from his father. "No, I think I have it. My father made sure my brother and I could do such things. He always believed a man was only as good as the dress knots he created." Fredrick peeked in the mirror behind Leo.

Leo for his part stood with his pants still not buttoned and his shirt barely tugged on, revealing a smooth chest, a contrast to

Fredrick's. "Well, you look great." Leo beamed at him.

Fredrick did his level best not to gander at Leo's bare chest or *schwanz*.

At least everything is covered. Well, mostly covered.

Fredrick adjusted his jacket as Leo pulled himself together.

Clearly Leo's done this a few times.

Leo moved toward the mirror and stuffed a hand down his front, adjusting himself before tucking in his shirt and buttoning his pants.

Fredrick turned away as heat filled his face and neck.

Leo finished making his last-minute adjustments while Fredrick busied himself with invisible pieces of lint he dusted from his jacket.

"Do I look okay?" Leo asked as he walked over to the sink to wash his hands.

Fredrick cleared his throat, turning around and seeing the man with his arms straight, everything he wore impeccable and well-tailored. "You look nice."

"Thanks." Leo pointed to the door. "Let's boogie."

•　　　•　　　•

The lounge had appeared much the same as earlier; comfortable chairs and couches, tables adorned with what Fredrick guessed might be real candles, but discovered they were small mechanical devices to resemble actual candlelight. The air hung with smells of hot food tickling Fredrick's nose and making his stomach grumble. Unlike earlier, there were guests milling about getting ready to head off to dinner, some holding drinks while others enjoyed the small bites that were set out the whole day. In the corner by the piano, a woman fussed around, getting herself set up to entertain the guests. Fredrick figured that had to be Margo—he would need to say hello at some point. Oliver and Nuwa were at the concierge desk, the latter assisting a couple of guests with dinner reservations at the Lani Steakhouse. Oliver got up from the desk and made his way over to Leo and Fredrick.

"Leo, do you mind if I head out?" Oliver asked. "I want to have a bit of a lie down, before the reception. I've got a headache." He peeked over his shoulder, ensuring no one listened.

"How's the day been?"

"Fine, the usual. I've been asked to set up a private tea for 1500 tomorrow for one of the suites; it's been added to the calendar. I made a few reservations at the spa, but all is well. Oh, and I added a few guests to some of the excursions for Maui and Nawiliwili."

"Sounds good. Go on and take off." Leo pointed toward the doors. "With the three of us here, we'll be fine. Most of the guests will be heading off to dinner soon, so we can cover."

"Thanks." Oliver headed out of the lounge.

"Let's check on everyone, then we can head in and go through tonight's event."

"Okay," Fredrick acknowledged as he adjusted his bowtie, loving the heavier weight of the materials in his dress uniform—so much sturdier than the uniform he wore earlier in the day.

They made their way around greeting guests, ensuring everyone had everything they needed and reminding folks that the first dinner seating would be at 1745, or 5:45pm for some folks who weren't familiar with the 24-hour clock. Leo had Fredrick refill some of the guests' drinks while the servers were busy setting up the space. He took a moment to remember where things came from and were placed, but had no issues otherwise.

At least serving drinks hasn't changed in ninety years.

Once he and Leo made their rounds and Fredrick finished pouring a couple of glasses of Prosecco, they headed to the prep galley. Leo instructed him to taste each of the hors d'œuvres that David and his team prepared for the reception. Fredrick found he preferred the bacon wrapped date and mini beef wellingtons—the chicken skewer and the vegetarian canapé were fine, but not to his personal taste.

While Fredrick assisted the serving team with the final preparation, basically doing as he was told, Leo hurriedly pulled Fredrick to the side seemingly out of nowhere. "Looks like our friends are here and might be skipping out on dinner tonight."

"What? Our friends?" Fredrick moved over to the buffet to see who Leo spoke of.

"Look." Leo focused toward the club's entry. Walking in were Barron and Martin.

"Mr. Hillchild and Mr. Sherman." Fredrick's lips almost pinched together before he caught himself. He relaxed his face and his shoulders—he had a job to do. "I'm surprised they're going to miss dinner in the dining room and stay here at the reception the whole evening. Maybe they have the second seating?"

"Nope, I checked. They're both first seating which'll begin in ten minutes." Leo sneered, not bothering to hide his annoyance. "This is so typical of Barron. At least his buddies aren't here."

"Why? Why would they do this?" Fredrick wiped his hands on a napkin, then stuffed the used item in his pocket.

"Barron wants to be a jerk."

"But …"

"Gentlemen." A polite professional voice belonging to Aurora filled Fredrick's ears. "Is there a problem I need to know about?"

Fredrick noted her formal uniform, not quite as tailored as Leo's, but she was equally as polished as him, probably more so. Instead of the simple part in the middle of her head, her hair was slicked up into a neat bun.

"Aurora, did you see our guests?" Leo asked with a quick glance toward Mr. Sherman and Mr. Hillchild.

"Yes, I'm a bit surprised to see Mr. Sherman again." Aurora's grin didn't leave her face as she spoke. "At least he appears to have softened since we got everything cleared up this afternoon. Which I'm pleased to see."

"And he has the hots for Fredrick," Leo added through pinched lips.

Fredrick's gaze dropped to the dark blue carpet.

"That would explain our conversation." Aurora shifted how she stood. "He wanted to ensure you would be here tonight. I told him we all would be. Also he asked if missing dinner would be a problem, since he wants to be here for the full reception." Aurora's tone softened. "Who's the other man?"

"Barron."

"Oh." Aurora frowned. "I'm sorry. That has to be frustrating. Is there something I can do?"

Leo's lips pinched together in a manner reminding Fredrick of his mother when she wanted to reprimand him and his siblings but couldn't. The look usually meant there would be hell to pay later.

"No, thank you." Leo's shoulders dropped.

"What about you, Fredrick, anything I can do?" Aurora asked.

"No." Fredrick faced Leo and Aurora, keeping as bright an expression on his face as possible. "I've dealt with flirty guests before."

"I'm sure you have." Aurora patted his arm; her jacket sleeves were a bit too long for her arms. "We can always talk to Tammy—she's good about these things. Leo, will she be stopping by tonight?"

"Not until later," Leo answered tightly, but his expression softened a bit as he spoke. "This is why I've asked for additional staff, so we don't have difficult situations of this nature. Our jobs are hard enough." He inhaled as he closed his eyes, taking a moment. "Sorry."

"Hey, we've got this." Aurora rested a hand on Leo's arm. "Let me know what I can do. I'm happy to run interference for you." She glanced between them. "For both of you."

"Thank you." Fredrick stiffened his shoulders, continuing with what he hoped to be a polite smile on his lips. He hated drawing attention to himself, and he loathed appearing weak. In his world having attention on you was never a good thing.

This is a new place. A new time. I don't have to be afraid anymore.

"We got this." Leo's tone stiffened as he glanced over at the table the two men now occupied. "And our guests are waiting."

"Yes." Fredrick adjusted his bowtie, inhaling a lungful of air.

The two men worked the tables, greeting the arriving guests, checking in on how everyone was doing, and how they were enjoying their first day. Aurora managed the desk as Nuwa left to go take a break before the reception.

"Good evening everyone," Leo greeted the table with Mr. Sherman and Mr. Hillchild. "As you may remember, I'm Leo your Concierge and this is Fredrick, our newest Butler."

"Good evening," Fredrick greeted the table.

"Oh, a fellow German," The middle-aged person sitting to the right of Mr. Sherman expressed. She wore a patterned shirt framing her neck and short dark hair. "I recognize that accent—what part of Germany are you from? I don't think we got to chat earlier. I'm Sandra by the way, and this is my wife Teresa."

"Nice to meet you," Fredrick greeted them. "I'm from a small town near Frankfurt, Seligenstadt."

Teresa laughed. "Oh, that's funny." She sat adorned in what Fredrick supposed to be a kind of sundress. The attire was much more casual than he had been used to seeing on the *Hindenburg*.

"What?" one of the others at the table asked.

"I was there," Teresa started. "As an exchange student. Well, not there, but the town south, Mainhausen."

"What are the odds?" Martin asked the table. He sat in a tan-colored short-sleeved shirt that had next to no give and stretched across his chest and arms.

"It's a beautiful area," Sandra spoke to the table. "I love the lake there. If I remember I think that's where I got stung by a bee, found out I wasn't allergic. Thank God." She sipped her drink. "Anyway, I have no doubt Fredrick, here, will take good care of us."

"Oh, I have no doubt either," Martin added, a perfect grin filling his face, but not meeting his eyes.

"Well, I'm looking forward to this trip," Barron commented. "It should be a lot of fun." He wore the same clothes he was in when Fredrick had been introduced this afternoon. The simple necklace, Fredrick couldn't help but notice, around his neck continued to catch the overhead lighting. However, this time he now knew more about the man and the shirt he wore. He had heard of a movie called *Snow White and the Seven Dwarfs,* by a man named Walt Disney, which had won some big award in the United States when it came out. Fredrick had no idea Mr. Disney would later create a global empire based on animated films that people continued to enjoy today.

Leo gave Fredrick a pensive look. "Shall I tell you all what we have going on tonight?" He smiled through each of his words.

This reset of the conversation got everyone focused on the reception and allowed both Fredrick and Leo to focus on their duties. Once Leo finished his overview, Fredrick gestured to the servers to get drink orders. They made their way to the desk where they might take a moment to regroup, continue chatting up the other guests, and ensure everything ran smoothly. As with all events, they moved quickly and neither Leo nor Fredrick had time to focus on anything other than the job at hand.

Once the live music from the airship's band began, conversation became challenging, forcing the guests to enjoy the entertainment and giving Fredrick and the other Butlers time to deal with any situations that came up. His ears caught what he guessed might be American Jazz, something not allowed in Germany, but he managed to hear the music on his travels on the *Hindenburg*, and this music he enjoyed. Not quite as good as what Margo played, but she played the piano and sang alone.

As the event continued, Fredrick learned that Sandra, Teresa, Marco, and Rick had all been friends for years, and were in the habit of going on these airship cruises every year. They understood what to expect and were easy to deal with. Sandra, Teresa and Marco all shared a bottle of red wine, while Rick enjoyed his soda. The two couples were pleasant and recognized when to make conversation with Leo and Fredrick and when to leave them to their work. Martin had been polite and didn't drink, instead enjoying water and tea. While Barron had a Lemon Drop Martini followed by water, he too remained polite but all his attention focused on Leo, and if Fredrick had to guess, the reception had been harder to get through for Leo.

Many of the other guests in attendance were much the same; they all seemed to know the routine, which made Fredrick's job easier. The older couple Fredrick had noticed earlier in the day were polite and easy to talk with. It fascinated Fredrick that two men from different races would end up together and for so long.

But why not? Who cares. I've seen plenty of mixed couples today.

As the fates would play havoc, the friendly foursome had the second seating for dinner and needed to rush off. They also had plans to go to the drag cabaret act that night. So, they wouldn't be back. Even the older couple had vanished. Which left Barron and Martin alone as the reception continued, but with fewer guests.

Luckily Tammy had arrived to welcome everyone and have an obligatory glass of Champagne, which she only took a few sips off of. But during her welcome address she kept there from being any additional awkward moments between Fredrick and Mr. Sherman or Leo and Mr. Hillchild.

"How's your first day been?" Tammy moved over to Fredrick after chatting with some of the guests.

"Good, thank you, ma'am." Fredrick glanced around. "Everyone has been helpful, especially Leo—I mean, Mr. Asher."

"Well, I know Leo's been excited to get a new Butler in place." She scanned the lounge. "And the guests?"

"The guests have all been lovely and very gracious." Fredrick couldn't help but beam.

"So long as we keep the fantasy alive." Tammy took one last sip of her Champagne. "I'm going to give this to you before I drink it all."

"Yes, ma'am." Fredrick took the half-filled glass from Tammy. "If you need anything, please let me or Leo know."

"Thank you. Now, if you'll excuse me." Tammy headed over to Aurora and Leo.

Fredrick picked up another abandoned glass from the table next to him, before he moved over to make another round with the remaining guests.

"This was an excellent evening," Martin said. "Who needs a full dinner when you have all this? Thank you." He adjusted the pillows on the seat after he stood. "Fredrick, I do hope to see you again and the offer for a meal stands." He glanced at Mr. Hillchild and Leo. "Gentlemen," he stated as a farewell.

"See you around." Barron waved.

Fredrick picked up the empty plates from their table. "Have a pleasant evening."

No longer needing to make idle chitchat with Fredrick, Barron stood. "Have a nice night, Fredrick."

Fredrick quickly excused himself and busied himself as best he could. He checked on the remaining guests, and spoke with the Lani Steakhouse serving team, finding out what else he might do to assist them. They appreciated the assistance Fredrick offered and the additional work kept him out of Leo and Barron's way. He didn't want to push in on Barron who seemed to drag out staying in order to force conversation with Leo, so Fredrick left them to it.

By the time Leo returned to the concierge desk, his face burned scarlet with either embarrassment or anger.

"Can I do anything?" Fredrick looked from the machine to Leo.

"No," Leo snapped, his cheeks crimson. "I'm sorry. No, thank you."

Fredrick tapped on the keyboard of the computer, making a few notes on the calendar for tomorrow. "Please check this; I want to ensure I entered everything correctly. I made a reservation at the Lani Steakhouse for tomorrow night and a spa reservation for a massage."

Leo glanced at the machine, clicked the mouse a couple times, and nodded. "Seems good to me."

"Good. Everyone seemed nice," Fredrick tried to change the subject. "I think tonight's event was lovely. I wish I was a part of this on the *Hindenburg*."

From everything I've learned today, I'm sure this type of event would have been even grander there.

"Barron wants to talk tomorrow morning and I had to agree or he'd keep after me," Leo huffed, not acknowledging Fredrick's comments. "But talking won't change things. It's over. Nothing will change." He dragged his hand over his face. "He doesn't get it …"

"Perhaps there's hope." Fredrick licked his lips. "He seems to care a great—"

"Fredrick, you don't know what you're talking about, so please …" Leo headed off to the kitchen, leaving Fredrick alone at the desk.

Aurora made her way over. "That situation …" She shook her head. "Anyway, I'll help you out." She sat next to Fredrick. "His relationship with Barron is complicated, so don't take it personal." She typed on the keyboard, pulling up the next day's schedule with Fredrick. They still had to finish up the prep work for the next morning as Nuwa and Oliver were free to leave once the event wound down.

And at first, I figured this would be easy.

Fredrick pulled out his timepiece. Leo still hadn't returned as a few guests managed to arrive before the end of the night to pick up drinks and treats before heading off to the late-night entertainment. As with most of the guests, they were pleasant enough, several folks dressed in something called "High Drag", and Fredrick marveled in amazement at their appearance. These people were a lot of fun and enjoyed teasing him, which he didn't mind and took in good fun.

With thanks to Aurora and his own initiative, Fredrick remained busy and by the time Leo returned, he wasn't the same man as earlier. In fact, Fredrick and Leo hardly spoke. Fortunately, if the last few guests had any clue to the underlying tension, they kept their knowledge to themselves. Fredrick was impressed as Aurora did her best to keep things as light and fun as possible for everyone. By the time the reception finished and clean up concluded, Leo made an excuse about needing to get additional work sorted for the rest of the trip, leaving Fredrick to his own devices for the remainder of the night.

8

F REDRICK WRAPPED UP the last of his duties for the night by
2300. Despite the busy day, he wasn't ready to vanish to the
cabin given the mood Leo had been in. He would have asked
Aurora if she wanted to chat, but she told him before he got a
chance to say anything that she wanted to get some rest, since she
would be opening the Lani Club in the morning. He heard about a
DJ dance party up on the Pali Deck, figuring he might make his way
there and see what all the fuss was about, plus seeing such an
event might be entertaining.

Instead of taking the guest lift, he made his way aft and took the
service elevator up and snuck out by the Honua Lounge, which
pulsated with bodies in all manner of dress and undress. Unknown
music assaulted his ears and overwhelmed his thoughts. The music
banged around the deck, sounding more like noise than any kind of
composition he ever heard. He couldn't say he was impressed. The
guests cheered, blew whistles, and waved glowing sticks in the air
moving in time with the melody. Clearly, they enjoyed the noise,
which he conceded was all that mattered.

Perhaps this music will grow on me.

Celebrating under the moon and stars, the guests were all over the bar and out on the main deck. Many of the guests had changed from their dining clothes to more revealing, colorful, and festive outfits. Various Drag Queens danced and sang along with the music, almost as if performing. Leo had not lied about the fashions—many showed off as much skin as when people frolicked in the hot tubs or as they laid out during the day. Everyone appeared in a festive mood, and why not? Tonight was the first night of a ten-day voyage.

Memories flashed to the *Hindenburg* and how excited everyone was the first night of the journey, and how impossible those nights were to get any rest. Why should this night be any different?

But it is different. It's all different. All these homosexuals. All this merriment. This is amazing.

His cheeks ached from smiling and his mood lifted. He wondered if the clubs in Berlin were once like this before the Reich took over. He would have loved to have seen those bars and clubs filled with other gay people. He wanted to believe they would have been similar, possibly with better music and more clothing.

He wasn't a prude, but seeing all these scantily-clad people was something he wasn't used to. A majority of the guests didn't feel the need to wear a lot of clothing, at least here on the upper deck for the party. Not that he was complaining—there were some handsome men that didn't mind flaunting their bodies.

But where's the mystery? Where's the specialness of sharing your body with someone if you've both already seen everything? Where was the excitement?

"Enjoying the scenery?" a voice from behind him called over the loud music.

Turning, he saw Tommy with a few other folks who must be crew, though they were out of uniform and dressed in their normal clothes. A mix of jeans, slacks, and casual short-sleeved shirts, much more conservative than what the guests wore.

I suddenly feel overdressed in my uniform. But I'm comfortable. I should make note of how they dress so I can imitate them, especially if I want to fit in and not get discovered.

"Where's Leo?" a shorter man with dark hair, eyes, and slacks asked. He appeared Asian, but not Japanese or Chinese. Fredrick didn't remember his name. He sported dark slacks and a short sleeved blue shirt.

"He mentioned he had paperwork to finish," Fredrick responded, trying not to yell, so he leaned in to be heard.

"That guy is always busy," a female crewmate countered, she wore tight blue jeans and a yellow pullover short sleeved shirt. "Guess that's why he's one of the bosses."

"Not yet," the male guy in the dark pants responded. "I don't think Tammy's ready to give up her post … yet."

"His sights are a lot higher than Head Steward. He's going after the Captain's job," the female crew member announced. "But I don't know. I don't see it."

"You don't think he can do it?" Fredrick's brows lifted, surprised by the comment.

"Oh, he can, but …" She shook her head and chuckled. "I think he likes hospitality more than he'll admit. Seeing him with the guests, that's where he shines." She stuffed her hands in her pockets. Plus, he has a big ladder to climb to reach the Captain's chair."

"And more education," the shorter guy added.

"Have you met Marco, Dallas, and Jemma?" Tommy gestured to each of his compatriots.

"I don't think so." Fredrick presented each of them a nod of his head.

"Fredrick is our newest Butler, working under Leo in the Suites," Tommy continued making the introductions, he stood adorned in faded jeans and a multicolored blue and purple short sleeved shirt. "Dallas and Jemma are room attendants and Marco is a Junior Helmsmen who works the mid shift."

"I got off a bit early tonight," Marco shared, with hints of a Spanish accent. "Tina owed me a favor." He beamed at the crowd of guests out dancing, his head moving in time with the music. "And I had to see the party tonight. This event is always over the top. I love it!"

"You love coming out and scoping out all the boys." Dallas, the dark-haired guy, jabbed Marco's side. He stood donned in cream-colored shirt and gray slacks.

"Nothing wrong with looking." Marco continued to scan the group of party goers.

"I heard there were several guys up in the spa trying to get in for a body trim and bleaching." Jemma chuckled. "You would think they'd do all that before they arrive."

"Why? Hey, they want to look their best for the next ten days ... and tonight," Tommy added.

"The grooming you can do in your cabin, God knows we clean up enough pubic hair and other trimmed hair, but the bleaching ..." Dallas shook his head.

"Grooming? Bleaching?" Fredrick questioned, his brows scrunched together.

His group of coworkers laughed.

"Oh, right you German boys are all natural," Tommy teased. "Some of our guests get their buttholes bleached. No idea why. I guess they think the bleaching makes them look better, and the 'grooming' ..." Tommy made finger movements with both his hands for some kind of emphasis. "You know, trim up the old twig and berries, so things *look* bigger."

"And you would know all about needing to make things look bigger, don't'cha." Jemma elbowed Tommy.

"I've never had any complaints." Tommy's lips pinched together.

Fredrick watched the exchange, unsure what to say. He had noticed several of the guest's chests appeared shaved or trimmed. Few men had body hair, so from what he gathered of the conversation, they also trimmed their pubic area. The smoothness all seemed odd to him, but this was a different time and people here seemed conscious of their appearance and how they looked. Another thing for him to make note of in the new place and time. Not that people didn't do their best to always look good and not stink, but nothing compared to what he'd witnessed today.

Perhaps I need to trim my body hair to fit in better.

"Not everyone is into that whole *twink* look. You know we have a bunch of bears on board, and they take pride in their body hair." Marco shrugged as he spoke.

"And their bellies, chests, thighs, arms—" Jemma gestured to several larger barrel-chested men who were covered in body hair.

"Anyway," Dallas continued, "there're a lot of handsome people on this cruise ..."

"And others." Jemma nodded in the direction of several women enjoying the music as they danced. "Personally, I'm looking forward to seeing the Bear Den event tomorrow—should be interesting."

"Bear Den?" Fredrick asked.

The three laughed again.

"Oh, you're in for a treat, if you get a chance to see it … do you like hairy guys, Fredrick?" Tommy asked. "If so, you'll want to check out the Bear Den event tomorrow for sure."

"There's someone for everyone on this zep," Marco added. "You see anyone you fancy, Fredrick?"

"Me? No." Fredrick scanned the people out dancing and having a good time as the music pounded through his head all the way to his feet. There was one man, but he didn't see him at the moment. If Leo was correct about Martin, he probably already found someone, and was enjoying their company privately given how quickly he left the welcome reception. "Plus, we aren't supposed to fraternize with the guests."

"Says who? I mean, technically that's true," Tommy agreed with a glance to the guests out on the dance floor, "but this isn't like the ocean liners with all their rules. Things are more …"

"Lax," Jemma finished. "Speaking of, can we have a cocktail or two tonight or no?"

"Not out here with the guests. We'd have to go to the crew cantina." Tommy frowned.

"Cheaper anyway." Jemma peeked over to the bar.

"Hey, don't forget I'm an officer, so be careful." Marco's expression hardened.

"A Junior Officer and you're a bigger slut than anyone here. How often have you done the walk of shame?" Jemma crossed her arms in front of her chest.

Marco's eyes grew wide but the flush of his skin betrayed him.

"What they mean to say"—Dallas cleared his throat—"is don't get caught and don't do anything stupid, cause it'll get you in trouble and you can end up getting fired. You can interact with the guests socially as long as you aren't on duty or in uniform, but it's best to keep your sausage in your pants; you don't want to risk your job. Still, you can always have some fun." He raised his eyebrows up and down.

Fredrick peeked down at his outfit.

I should have changed out of my uniform before coming up here.

"So, if you meet someone, be careful and only spend time with them when you're not in uniform, but since you're a Butler ..." Tommy ended with a wave of his hand.

"Hey, listen, are we gonna stand around all night or go and dance?" Jemma grabbed Marco's arm. "It's not every night we get to come out and party with the guests, and I don't want to waste a minute. Plus, this is a great song. I love Lady Gaga."

"Fine. Fine," Dallas conceded as they moved to the dance floor, but off to the edges as to not interfere with the guests or their fun.

"You coming, Fredrick?" Tommy gestured with a hand. "Loosen up and dance off the stress of the day."

"No. I'm good." He waved them off.

"See ya later." Tommy waved and vanished with the others.

Fredrick watched as the music played.

What and who is Lady Gaga?

As Fredrick leaned against one of the pillars of the bar as he watched and listened to the music, the bartender asked if he wanted anything. Fredrick asked for a glass of water. As he sipped his drink, he paid more attention to the music playing. This song wasn't bad and not nearly as loud as some of the others. People danced, sang, drank and continued to have a good time. The more he listened to the songs, the more he discovered the melodies had a way of drilling into one's skull.

He had almost had his fill when Martin appeared next to him. "Enjoying the party?" Martin leaned in, still in the same outfit he wore at the welcome reception.

"Mr. Sherman, good evening," Fredrick started. He finished his water and returned the glass to the bar next to him. "I was about ready to leave; the music can be a bit loud and it's been a long day. Are you having a good time?"

"I can imagine." Martin checked out the dance floor and all the people partying. "And please call me Martin."

"Yes, of course, Martin." Fredrick's cheeks lifted in what he hoped to be a warm expression. He caught a few whiffs of Martin's cologne. There were hints of the ocean, but with something warmer enhancing the smell.

He smells wonderful.

"Have you met anyone yet?" Fredrick asked.

Martin's smile grew and a twinkle of moonlight hit his eyes as he focused his gaze on Fredrick. "No, but I have my sights set on someone."

"I see. Well ..." Fredrick scanned the deck, then looked up at the night sky to see all the stars twinkling. "What a view."

Martin peered up. "It's a beautiful night. I forget how relaxing a night like tonight can be."

"It amazes me how some things never change," Fredrick commented.

"Meaning?"

Fredrick pointed up. "All these stars, the night sky ... all the same."

"Well, technically, they change all the time, and the stars we're seeing tonight are distant images from the past. These stars probably died out millions of years ago with their light only now reaching us. A visitor from the past."

"Oh ... um ..." Fredrick didn't know what to say. Was Martin hinting at knowing that Fredrick wasn't from this time? Or was his comment only about the stars? Is that how the stars in the night sky worked? Like the music and the clothing, there was a lot that had changed and been figured out in the last almost ninety years.

"Sorry." Martin chuckled as he moved out a hand before quickly retracting it and stuffing it into his pocket. "I ..." He waved off whatever he was about to say with his other hand.

"No. It's fine."

"Have you thought any more about my offer?" Martin changed the topic by way of his question.

"I ...well ..." Fredrick stammered. "Technically you're a guest ..."

"I'm a contractor." He spoke in hushed tones and his eyebrows rose. "I work for the company, but you're not supposed to know that."

"Either way, I should probably say no. I don't want to influence your work, one way or the other."

"A 'probably no' isn't a 'no'."

"My schedule is hectic and this is my first contract, so saying yes might not be the most responsible choice," Fredrick elaborated. "Either way, I would want to clear it with both Leo and Ms. Lam." He glanced around, catching sight of Tommy and the others enjoying themselves.

Why can't I have some fun? Maybe I'll wake up and be home. This might be my chance to live in a reality that isn't my own.

"I wouldn't worry about that or them," Martin suggested. "I'm the one asking you and I assure you I have no intentions of getting you into trouble."

Fredrick deliberated a moment as he took a lungful of the warm night air. "Only a meal ... nothing more."

Martin's grin bloomed like a field of flowers waking to the morning light. "When is your next evening off?"

"Perhaps I can do brunch with you tomorrow before my shift or the next day before the Captain's Gala."

Martin pulled his smartphone out of his pocket, tapped away, then put the device back in his pocket. "Excellent." He placed his hand on Fredrick's arm. "I'll make all the arrangements."

"It's brunch, nothing more." Fredrick reminded, glancing at the hand on his arm. "And if Leo and Ms. Lam say no, I can't go."

Martin beamed. "I'm looking forward to it."

9

L EO GUARANTEED he remained busy the rest of the night, so he didn't have to speak to Barron or Fredrick. Anger and hurt filled every one of his cells and they were all stuck on this zep with nowhere to go for the next couple of days, so he stayed away until he cooled down.

And that's what Barron wanted: us stuck, so we'd have to talk.

By the time Leo got to the cabin, he had calmed down and wanted to apologize to Fredrick for his behavior. Especially after Fredrick shared with him his recent breakup, including the potential death of the guy he cared about. As angry and hurt as Leo was at Barron, he would be devastated if anything happened to him. Their breakup wasn't all on him, but still. No matter what happened between Barron and him, he wouldn't know what he would do if Barron died, or was killed.

As he entered the cabin, the space was dark and the sound of soft breathing was the only sound over the hum of the zep. Fredrick was asleep and Leo didn't want to bother him now.

It'll wait till morning.

Sleep didn't come easily. Once slumber found Leo, he shifted in the bed searching with his hand to find the warm skin of Barron next to him. He inhaled as a vibrant spicy dark woodsy smell with hints of vanilla filled his nose. After a moment, his gaze cleared, revealing floor to ceiling windows, the wall-mounted TV, and the shadowed colors of the Eyvind Earle painting next to the highboy dresser. Leo shifted again, rubbing his hand along Barron's naked body, heat emanating from him. Every part of Leo basked in the warmth and comfort of the bed and down comforter.

"Babe, I still don't know how the contractor managed to get around all the building codes and height restrictions in the city," Leo found himself saying.

Barron's condo sat on the nineteenth floor of The Heights in downtown San Jose. The views out the window showed a wakening city in the cool morning light, the sun hidden over the hills out of sight from the room. A bright morning golden glow was slowly creeping into the space. The condo tower was the tallest building in San Jose. Leo sighed as he stretched his legs and feet, waking up his muscles.

Barron shifted and faced Leo, the gaze of his green eyes boring into Leo, a slight frown on his lips. "I think he lives here, up in the penthouse, but ..." He brushed some of his mussed dirty blond hair out of his eyes and off his forehead. "Some people say he's a witch or vampire and used some kind of magic on them." He huffed out a chuckle but there was no mirth.

"Ridiculous." Leo continued to force a pleased look, wanting to stay in this moment. He rubbed a hand on Barron's slightly fuzzy chest, making Barron breathe deeply and his heart quicken. These last six months have been everything to him. The happiest he'd been. He wanted to postpone the inevitable for as long as possible. "I love this view and your chest," Leo purred, pushing away the coming turbulence.

"So, we're not going to talk about what happened?" Barron's frown continued to grow. "You're going to pretend everything is fine?"

Too good to last. Why can't we stay like this without speaking?
"Can't we ... no. Why?"

"Because ... because its the first time something like that happened and I think it's important." Barron's tone remained soft despite his expression, or perhaps his exasperation.

"You freaked out before you laughed!"

"I ... I didn't know what to do or say ... it's not—"

"Don't say 'it's not important' because it clearly it is. And your reaction last night didn't help. Look, I don't want to talk about it." Leo's tone soured, the view no longer magical for him, this moment no longer a pleasant memory.

"I didn't freak out, and I laughed because you surprised me and I ..." Barron huffed out a breath. "How am I supposed to react, or respond? I figured if we slept the night off, we might talk about—"

"I can tell you for sure you're not supposed to laugh." Leo threw his legs over the side of the bed and stood up, his naked form shimmering in the twinkle of the city's morning light. "Staying last night was a bad idea."

"Wait." Barron leaned up on his elbows, brushing a hand over his face, pushing the falling hair out of his eyes again. "Don't. It's fine."

"Clearly not." Leo shook his head. "I don't think we should see each other anymore." He started to pull on his clothes, and searched for his missing sock and belt.

"Come on, you're being silly."

"I'm being silly. Wow!" Leo's tone and volume grew. "Okay. Thanks." He continued to bang around as he got dressed.

"Leo, what's this all about? Come on, talk to me." Barron moved from the bed.

"Just don't." Leo held up his hand to halt Barron, his naked body silhouetted in front of the large tinted glass window. The gleam of the gold necklace that Leo gave him hung around his neck, catching the morning light. "I have to go. We're continuing the trip in the afternoon after we finish with our layover here in San Jose."

"I thought—"

"I won't be on the *Hawaiian Sun* for a couple of months. I need to train as Concierge before they'll bump me up." Leo finished getting dressed. "Two more months and I'll be promoted off the American Eagle and to the *Hawaiian Sun*, as a Concierge and Trainer."

"Can we please talk about what happened, Leo? Why don't I make some breakfast and we'll have a real conversation?" Barron pleaded. "Don't go."

"There's nothing more to say. We had some fun and now it's over."

Barron crossed the empty space between Leo and him. "A little fun? We shared more than that it's been six months."

"Was it? I don't think so."

"So, I was a *fuck* to you? What the hell, Leo? We talked all the time. We—"

"Wasn't that all I was to you? Isn't that why you want to talk? Our *fucking*?"

"No. Yes. No …" Barron ran a hand over his face. "Look, it's more than that. If something's wrong—"

"Nothing's wrong. Everything's fine." Leo snatched his phone from the bedside table. "Bye, Barron." Leo marched to the bedroom door, through the living room and out the main door.

Leo woke with a start as the door slammed in his dream.

Six months.

Leo glanced around the cabin and found his shared space empty and cleaned up with no Fredrick to be found. The only sound was the hum of the airship.

Well, he knows how to steer clear and give people their space if need be.

By morning light, the world always seemed different and, in most cases, better. He knew he would have to have the conversation with Barron today, but he wasn't going to let their pending confrontation eat at him or interfere with his training of Fredrick. Not anymore than it already had. As it turned out they had the morning off, and didn't come on duty until after lunch, so there was no telling what Fredrick would be up to. Luckily, there were only so many places to be on an airship, so they would see each other.

Once showered and dressed, he made his way to the crew galley for breakfast. Off to the side, by one of the exterior windows, Fredrick sat reading a book—an actual, physical book. Leo grabbed his breakfast and walked over to his Butler in Training. "Hey."

"Good morning." Fredrick put a napkin in the book as a page marker before closing the novel.

"Where did you find the book? What is it?"

"The crew commissary." Fredrick held up the book to show off the cover. "This morning. It's called *Life after the Fall*."

"Is the story any good?" Leo asked, placing his tray down.

"So far." Fredrick's tone was level and conversational. "I like the idea and the author is a good storyteller. The dialogue has been stilted, but that might be me."

"About last night—"

Fredrick held up his hand. "You don't owe me any explanation."

"No, I do." Leo placed his napkin on his lap and grabbed his fork, moving his eggs and potatoes around. "I shouldn't have taken things out on you. The whole situation with Barron is frustrating and annoying and ..."

"Relationships are never easy, no matter where you are." Fredrick sighed with a glance to his book, pushing the paperback farther away from his bowl. "I ran into Martin last night at the dance party up on deck. I told him perhaps brunch today might be nice, if he was sincere about the offer and you and Ms. Lam were okay with us meeting socially."

"What? Really?" Leo beamed over at Fredrick. "It's not too soon ... you know." He glanced around the mess, seeing who might be listening to them.

No one cared, but sometimes people liked to gossip. Especially if folks heard them talking about Fredrick's ex.

Fredrick shrugged. "I don't know." He lowered his voice and leaned in. "But I figure a meal can't hurt, and given the man is here to evaluate the ship and the crew, there's no harm in ensuring he has a good time."

Leo moved in closer, scanning the space again, his voice also lowering. "I hope you're not planning on sleeping with him to ensure we pass."

Fredrick's cheeks pinkened as he shook his head. "No." The word was barely a whisper coming from his mouth. "That's not who I am."

"I didn't think so." Leo smiled and leaned back in his seat. "What made you change your mind?"

"You." Fredrick picked up his glass of what appeared to be cranberry juice.

"Me? Why me?" Leo continued poking at his breakfast.

"Because I watched how you studied Barron and how you would sneak peaks at him. I never had that with anyone, and I imagined maybe ..."

"That's sweet, but Fredrick, guys on these cruises, guys like Martin, are only after one thing. Afterward, they'll go home and go to their wives or boyfriends or whatever and forget all about you."

"I don't know. It's possible ... but maybe not." Fredrick huffed. "Who knows? That might be what I need. Something brief and ..."

Leo didn't know what to say to Fredrick. This wasn't going to be good and every part of him told him so. Something was off about this Sherman guy—maybe he's here to evaluate the ship, or maybe something else. But who was he to tell Fredrick what he could and couldn't do? This was a lesson they all had to learn on their own. All he can do is be here for Fredrick when this all fell to shit.

Assuming it did indeed fall to shit.

"Okay, I don't have any issues with you having a date with Martin, and I'll make sure Tammy is okay too." Leo put down his fork. "But please be careful. There's something about that guy I don't like."

"And what about you?" Fredrick waved a hand at Leo. "What are you going to do about ... well ..."

"I agreed to meet up with him later this morning, before my shift starts." He took a forkful of his eggs and began to chew.

•   •   •

Leo checked his breath in his hand as he made his way to the Kapua Bar, where there were no activities scheduled so the bar should be quiet with all the guests either still in bed, having breakfast, up in the gym, or on deck. The first morning on ship was usually quiet. As with everything, there was no guarantee others wouldn't be around, but meeting in a public space was the safest option—*at least for me; it'll keep me and my emotions in check.* Hopefully being in civilian clothes would offer him a bit of anonymity. Luckily, most guests noticed the uniform and not the person inside.

As he arrived he noted that the space was devoid of guests, and he saw only Jamal and Femi on duty at the moment.

Thank goodness.

Finding a seat away from the bar and the walkway, Leo checked his smartphone for the time.

Barron should be here momentarily.

"Morning, Leo. Bit early for you, isn't it?" Jamal smiled.

"I'm meeting a guest."

"Oh ... sorry." Jamal's expression changed at once. "Did you want something from the bar?"

Leo shook his head. "Nah … Wait—yes, get me a cranberry and orange. Thanks, Jamal." Leo tugged at his shirt and dusted off his lap, seeing a few random crumbs from his breakfast.

"You got it." Jamal headed over to the bar.

Taking in the lounge for the first time in quite a while, he reflected on Fredrick's wonder at the space. He never gave the interior much thought; the area was a lounge and seating area. It was a spot for the zep to make money selling drinks, while providing guests with a spot to enjoy and relax. He appreciated the soft-sided seating and the cream colors all designed to be soothing and comfortable. While the tables a simple dark tone to offset all the colors of the lounge. He ran a hand over his seat.

"Making sure the fabric meets with your approval?" Barron's chipper voice called his attention as he sat next to him.

Jamal appeared, placing Leo's drink down. "Is there something I can get you?"

"Whatever Leo's having."

"Cranberry and orange it is." Barron handed over his room card so that Jamal could charge Barron's account accordingly, though suite guests had all their specialty drinks, with the exception of top shelf alcohol, included. "How's your morning going so far?"

Leo waited for Jamal to exit out of earshot. "Cut the crap, Barron. You wanted to talk, let's talk. I'm here. Under duress, I might add."

Barron's lips pinched together as his head tilted. "Fine. Why did you freak out on me? Why did you bail on us without even talking to me?"

"You know why."

"I know?" He barked out a laugh. "I don't know anything. All I knew is one day everything we had was great and the next you shut me out. You headed off on your airship." He leaned in as the white gold chain Leo gave Barron peeked out from his shirt. "Do you have any idea how upset I was?"

I can't believe he's still wearing that chain.

"You? Upset?" Leo glanced at the bar where Jamal and Femi were chatting as Femi put together Barron's drink. His voice lowered. "That's funny, coming from you."

Barron sat taller as Jamal returned with his drink and the bamboo wood check holder.

"Please, let me know if you need anything else," Jamal remarked before leaving them to continue their conversation.

"Yes, I was disturbed." Barron shifted deeper into the chair. "I didn't understand."

"I'm not doing this again." Leo's heart pounded from his toes to his ears. His hands trembled so much that he moved them to his sides so they wouldn't show.

"Talk. To. Me." Barron emphasized each word despite his neutral tone. "Tell me what's happening with you. If it's your health, I want to know."

Leo's face, his whole body, burned with heat. "I suffer from retrograde ejaculation and I'm sterile. So, I don't come and you laughed at me." Leo's voice was now barely a whisper.

Barron had to lean in to hear him. "That's why nothing ... happened ... well, nothing appeared?"

Leo massaged his head. "Yes," he snarled.

"Are you okay?" Barron's gaze grew larger, worry filled every corner of his face. "You don't look sick. You're not sick or dying, 'cause I don't think—"

"It's from some of the medication I take for my heart," Leo huffed. "I've been to my cardiologist and the urologist and everything's fine, except for that. I've tried other medications, but they don't work as well, so ..."

"But you're not sick, right? I mean, you're okay otherwise?" Barron's words rushed out. "You never told me anything about your heart." He reached out a hand, before taking it back. "Are you going to be—"

"My blood pressure's high and I have an abnormal heart rhythm, and otherwise nothing's wrong with my heart. I don't talk about my health stuff, because I don't want people to treat me differently. So ..."

"Soooo, you can't have kids." Barron bit back a growing grin.

Leo couldn't be sure it wasn't from relief or to mock him. "And this is why I left. You laughed and made fun—" He stood.

"Wait. Please." Barron held out his hand to grasp for Leo. "I don't care about that. I mean, as long as everything works. And you're healthy and don't have some awful disease. Big deal ... so, you're not a shooter." He moved closer. "Listen, to make you feel better, I've been known to pop off from making out, and not only when I was younger. I can be premature sometimes especially if I haven't done anything in a while or if I'm incredibly turned on ..." The skin on his neck and cheeks were a bright pink color. "And you know about my mouth guard and how sexy that makes me feel."

"It's not the same thing. At least you can still ..." Leo waved his hand. "Anyway, do you have any idea how difficult this is for me? It's like I'm not a real guy anymore. I can barely face this, let alone share this with anyone, especially you. I mean I used to ... you know. There was a lot and now ..." Leo ran a hand through his hair. "I feel like something important to me was taken away."

"I shouldn't have laughed." Barron ran a hand over his mouth. "And I'm sorry. I didn't understand and you didn't explain—you shut down and shut me out. I thought maybe you were faking things with me and when I saw ..." He shrugged.

"I wasn't faking ..." He sat down again.

"How was I to know ... you didn't say anything. And we mostly used condoms so ..." Barron glanced over at the bar to ensure they were still free to speak so candidly. "So, you can still ... you know ..."

"Yes, of course, it only affects ... the ending."

Barron picked up his drink and took a sip, then rolled the glass between his hands. "I apologize for making you feel badly about yourself. That wasn't kind of me."

"Well, now you know." Leo found it difficult to meet Barron's gaze. His tone lowered. "I figured ... well, I figured you wouldn't want to be with me anymore. I'm not a real man, and I'll never be one. I'm defective—"

"What?" Barron's voice and tone elevated as his brows rose and his mouth dropped open.

"I know what you think." Leo sighed. "I know how people respond to things like this. You aren't the first person who's found out." The pain in Leo's words poured out of him. He wanted to crawl into his bed and sleep. Or find a nice hole to hide in and never come out.

Barron put down his drink and grabbed both Leo's hands. "Dammit, Leo, how shallow do you think I am? I love you, not your dick. Well, not only your dick." He let go of Leo's hands, his face now an even brighter shade of scarlet.

Leo's heart dropped along with his stomach as he heard the words coming out of Barron's mouth. "You love me?" He picked up his drink and took a large sip to finish it off.

I wish this had alcohol in it.

Barron's expression faltered and he cleared his throat, grabbing for his empty drink and frowning. "Why else would I be here? I could've moved on when you left, but I … I …" His gaze dropped.

A deafening silence filled the space between Leo and Barron so the clink of glass echoed around the lounge like an avalanche, the hum of the ship blared like a siren through every corner, and Femi laughing at something Jamal said was akin to nails on a chalkboard. Leo's mind bounced to everywhere and nowhere at the same time.

"Don't feel like you have to say anything. I … well …" Barron stood and the action pulled Leo out of his daze. "I should … I need to … um—" Barron rushed off.

Leo watched Barron hurry off, frozen in the softness of the chair.

I should've said something. I should've stopped him. Barron told me he loved me and I let him run off. What am I doing? Do I love him? I like him. But do I love him? Why didn't I say I love you? What's wrong with me? I really am defective.

"Are you okay?" Jamal asked as he picked up the empty glasses on the table.

"I think …" Leo's voice shuddered. "I think I fucked up." He ran a hand through his hair before glancing in the direction of where Barron disappeared.

10

F REDRICK DUSTED OFF the lint from his new long-sleeved light blue shirt that he spent too long ironing. He wanted to look shipshape for his brunch with Martin. His dark slacks, black belt and polished black shoes were as shiny as he could make them. Leo told him he'd look fine, and not to fuss, but Fredrick understood how important first impressions were. Even though this wasn't his and Martin's first meeting, brunch today was their first meal together, in a social setting, and he didn't have the structure of his uniform to rely on.

Impressions are everything.

"Right on time." Martin crossed over to the banquet seating were Fredrick stood and took in the sight of him. "You look ... well ... you make quite the picture."

Fredrick's neck warmed slightly under Martin's gaze. He took a slow level breath, forcing himself to relax. "Thank you." Martin wore dark denim, with gray socks, brown suede shoes, a white and deep burgundy striped shirt with gray lightweight sweater, and a rich burgundy blazer. He looked absolutely stunning and Fredrick instantly felt underdressed. "I feel a bit ... well ... you look great."

"I think you look perfect. Shall we?" Martin ushered them to the host stand.

Fredrick noted an open book sitting on the stand, it appeared to be some kind of memory book, where guests were invited to sign and share their impression of the restaurant. Giving guests the chance to share their memories seemed like a nice touch. The host arrived and greeted them, checking them in. Both Martin and Fredrick lingered in comfortable silence, allowing the dull roar of the ship and conversation breeze past them.

In short order, they were escorted through the restaurant and Fredrick noted all the couples and groups seated, enjoying their meals. Their host seated them at their white linen covered table, which had a stunning view of the outside. He could easily see the ocean below and the clear blue sky laying out ahead of them. A smattering of clouds filled out the picture.

It's a beautiful day.

"These sights are amazing," Fredrick commented, gazing out the window.

"You're not jaded by the view?"

Fredrick's stare narrowed on Martin. "Never. How can anyone not love these views? This is why we fly; this is why our airships draw so many people." He huffed out a laugh. "This is as close to the heavens as I think we can truly get."

"Quite the poet," Martin commented as he adjusted the cream-colored plate with the *Hawaiian Sun*'s logo painted in gold.

"I don't know about that," Fredrick paused and glanced at the table. A small vase filled with white roses sat centered between their plates. He gave a small laugh as he picked up the vase. "I love white roses; they remind me of home."

"In Germany?"

Images of his mother and her garden filled Fredrick's mind. "My mom grew them, so whenever I see them I think of her. It's my connection to her and the rest of my family." He put the vase down. "I think that's the hardest part about all this. But I've always loved airships."

"I suppose that's why you work on zeppelins," Martin commented as the waiter came to their table.

"Good morning, I'm Dejan and I'll be taking care of you today.

Have you dined with us before?" he greeted them as he filled their glasses with water.

"This is my first time," Martin scanned the restaurant. "On this ship."

"I work with Leo, here in the Suites area," Fredrick explained.

"Of course. Fredrick, right?" Dejan stopped and placed the bottle of water on the decorative built-in counter separating Fredrick and Martin from the table next to them. "I'm sorry about that, we spoke the night before embarkation." He shook his head.

"It's fine." Fredrick put on his most pleasant expression for Dejan. "There're so many people on the ship, it's hard to remember everyone."

"Too true. How are you getting on? You enjoying the ship so far?" Dejan glanced between both men, his smile broadening.

"Yes, there's a lot to learn, but I'm enjoying it."

So much for keeping anything private. I guess there're worse things for him, or the rest of the crew, to find out.

"Excellent." Dejan picked up the custom plates in front of each man and placed them on the built-in, then picked up the menus. "We're offering our welcome mimosa with Champagne or Prosecco. The first one's on me."

"I'd love a mimosa with Champagne please." Martin reached into his jacket pocket, pulling out his room card and handing the plastic card to Dejan. "And anything Mr. Rudolf would like."

"I'll have the orange juice and I'm good with water." Fredrick didn't want to drink while on duty.

"Very good." He placed the menus down on the table in front of each man. "Shall I show you the buffet before I get you your drinks? Or would you like to enjoy the view while I get the drinks? That way you have time to review the menu."

Fredrick glanced at Martin, figuring it was best for Martin to decide for them since he was the host.

"What do you think?" Martin asked Fredrick.

Guess he wants me to decide.

Fredrick glanced over at the buffet. "Let's take the tour."

"Wonderful." Dejan stepped to the side, allowing both Fredrick and Martin to stand. The three made their way over to the built-in buffet display and Dejan gave them an overview of everything on offer. Fredrick had never seen a display of so many different types of food before. The buffet had everything: crab legs, caviar, shrimp, oysters, fruit, fresh baked pastries, bagels, smoked salmon, cheeses, cured meats; basically everything that anyone might ever want.

If only Chief Cook Maier saw all this.

Memories of Maier's wonderful cooking on the *Hindenburg* came to Fredrick. Maier's beef broth with marrow was unmatched.

Dejan told them about the menu they may order from as well: eggs benedict with either ham or crab cake, various frittatas, soups, waffles and pancakes, veal, sirloin, mushroom ravioli, parmesan-crusted chicken breast, lasagna Bolognese, and sirloin steak. And that didn't even begin to cover the many desserts on offer, one of which was a chocolate soufflé Dejan told them was a must get.

By the time Dejan left them to their own devices at the buffet, Fredrick wasn't sure how anyone can eat all this food. The setup here was unlike anything on the *Hindenburg*. He was sure Maier would be joyfully jealous to see something like this.

Amazing.

They returned to their table where their drinks sat waiting, plates filled with some of the selections from the buffet.

"I'm glad I went to the gym this morning." Martin placed his napkin on his lap.

"I can't believe they have all this on offer." Fredrick sipped his orange juice.

Freshly squeezed. Yum.

"Really?" Martin glanced at him over his plate of food and his drink. "I'd have supposed you'd be used to all this, given you worked in Europe. And those airships are huge."

Fredrick extended his sip, giving him a moment to think of something to say. "I only worked in the main dining room, so the menu wasn't quite as extensive. Still, we put on a good show."

Martin studied him a moment. "I can only imagine working on something like the *Hindenburg*. What a ship. I hear the Beer Garden is something to be seen."

"Yes, the Beer Garden is quite impressive, especially with its inside and outside feature." He forced a polite chuckle. "I wish I understood the mechanics behind its design. The *Hindenburg 2000* is a magnificent ship, a fitting legacy to her namesake."

Fredrick paused a moment as he watched Martin, the man focused on him and every word he spoke. The way Martin's eyes studied him almost reminded him of how some of the Nazi officers talked to them when they were in Germany, scrutinizing each of their words to ensure they weren't hiding anything.

I'm being ridiculous. He's making polite conversation.

"What're you going to have?" Fredrick asked, not giving Martin a chance to ask a follow-up question.

Martin picked up his menu. "I think the eggs benedict sound good, but I'm wondering if I can get them with smoked salmon."

"That sounds good." Fredrick glanced at the menu resting on the table next to him. "I know it might be a bit heavy, but I would love to try the veal. I haven't had it in a long time. My mother used to make veal for us when I was young."

"Are you close with your family?" Martin asked over his sip of mimosa.

"My parents have passed on, but we were close, yes. Well, at one time." Fredrick picked up his biscuit with a spread of caviar and took a bite. His heart sunk at verbalizing his loss. He didn't know anything for sure, but given all the years ... he pushed the sadness down with his bite.

Fredrick needed to figure out what happened to his family. Were they his family? Was this place his home? Or did he belong somewhere else? He played around a bit with the computer, using some of the search aspects that he heard mentioned, but he wasn't able to find anything. Well, at least nothing on his family. The technology was all new and he didn't fully understand how to find out such things.

What he did learn horrified him. He discovered there were concentration camps scattered throughout countries Germany invaded and Germany itself, even one not too far from where he grew up, where millions of people were murdered. Six million Jewish people were killed in what they now call the Holocaust and that wasn't counting the other people killed, people like him and the rest of the homosexuals on the airship. How could the people he grew up allow such a thing? It was beyond upsetting and disgusting. He never thought the situation in Germany could get worse than they were in 1937. He thought of the conversation he had with his father learning about some of the Jewish doctors not being allowed to treat non-Jews. Kicked out of the hospitals they worked in. Some losing their businesses altogether. And for what? None of it made sense to Fredrick. He hated it. He hated the Nazis, was he the only one back then that did?

Then there was the awful propaganda. How many good people died? Fredrick thought of his family, did they support this? Did they sit back and say nothing like so many others? Fredrick learned that Frankfurt had been devastated during World War II, as the war was now referred as. But there was nothing about Seligenstadt.

Perhaps I have relatives still out there. But what will I learn about them. Can I even look at them knowing what I know now?

"I'm sorry about your parents." Martin pulled Fredrick from his thoughts.

"Thank you." Fredrick finished his caviar bite and before he needed to elaborate any further, Dejan arrived to take their orders. Once their selections were placed, Fredrick took a moment to collect his thoughts. He found the view outside a great distraction and a good way to clear his mind and calm his pounding heart. After a few beats, he turned to spot Martin watching him. "Are you close with your family?" Fredrick ensured his smile landed in place.

No one wants to hear of other's misfortunes.

"Not since I moved out to the West Coast." He sighed as he pushed the fruit on his plate around. "I don't get to see them nearly as much as I'd like." He speared a strawberry and took a bite before continuing. "I have two sisters, both married. And my parents are very much the doting grandparents."

"You have nephews and nieces?" The shift in conversation to Martin and his family assisted Fredrick in finding his center again. He picked up one of the shrimp he had on his plate, took a bite, and savored the chilled sweet meat.

"Three. Caleb, he's the eldest at seven." Martin paused, continuing to poke at the food on his plate. "There's Eliana, she's five, and Aviv, she just turned two ... no, three," Martin corrected before returning to picking at the berries still on his plate. "What about you?"

"No." Fredrick blurted out, much shorter than he wanted to be. For now, he was alone here and he had no idea if he had any other relatives, but he didn't think so, especially given how brutal the Nazis truly were.

I wish I knew more. I wish I had something definite. I hope my family fought those monsters or died trying.

And would they be *his* relatives, since he possibly didn't belong here?

"Only child?" Martin examined Fredrick.

"I suppose so," Fredrick lied as a knot tightened in his stomach. "Either way, I'm no longer close with my family. They wouldn't approve of all …" He trailed off, focusing on the food in front of him. He hated lying and talking so much about himself. How had Martin gotten him to open up so quickly?

Maybe I want to share, so I don't feel alone.

"Oh, I see." Martin glanced down at the table and cleared his throat. "They don't approve of you being gay."

Fredrick forced a bright expression on his face. He needed to change the topic. "What about your family? Do they know you're a homosexual?"

Martin laughed. "Wow. That's a five-dollar word. Yes, I told them when I was thirteen, the day of my Bar Mitzvah. They weren't happy with my timing, but—"

"You're Jewish?" The words dropped from Fredrick's mouth quicker than he could stop them.

"Yes, is that a problem?" The tone in Martin's words held a bite.

"No. I just … well … you don't look Jewish." Fredrick tried to recover but regretted each word as he spoke. Wasn't that what his contemporaries would say to dehumanize his Jewish country men? Isn't this how everything started. You start to see people as different then you and then you no longer see them as human making it easier to hate them and hurt them … kill them. A cold chill ran through him.

Isn't that why Wilhelm and I were running away? We saw what was happening and fled and what I just said? Am I no better?

"And how do Jewish people look?" Martin's words struck as sharp as a knife. "Big noses with dark beady eyes? Isn't that what the Nazis taught?"

"I'm not a Nazi." Fredrick rushed to stand his chair hit the half-wall behind him. He hated the Nazis. Yes, he was German, but he wasn't a Nazi.

But I played along and didn't say anything because I wanted to keep my job. I should have said something. We should have done something. I was complacent. I'm no better than those I claim to hate.

Still, wasn't that why he and Wilhelm wanted to escape? And because of the Nazis, there was a good chance everyone he ever cared about was gone. "They are monsters."

Martin slid from the table, "Wait! Please. That comment about looking Jewish ..." He pointed to the chair Fredrick vacated. "Please."

Out of nowhere Dejan appeared. "How's everything?" His voice shook, and the pleasing expression on his face couldn't hide his concern. "Your meals should be up shortly. Is there anything more you'd like from the buffet?" Dejan filled their glasses of water, despite them not needing the refresher.

Fredrick quickly scanned the dining room as several people watched the two of them. He took a breath.

"Very good, thank you." Martin's voice ran smooth as butter as he addressed their server. "I think I'm good for now. Fredrick?" He instantly had a toothy grin on his face, as if everything was perfectly fine and they were having a jolly good time.

"Yes." Fredrick inhaled. "Will you excuse me? I need to use the restroom." He placed his napkin on the table and relaxed his shoulders as he made his way to the exit, where the bathrooms were located.

Once in the restroom and after peeing, he stood at the mirror, washing his hands and focusing on his reflection. Replaying their conversation and his comments.

Does he know? How can he know? Do others know? Can he be from 1937 too? He's not from the Hindenburg, that's for certain. Maybe someone from the ground crew. But how? How is any of this possible?

"You're being ridiculous." He pointed at his reflection. The conversation about his family had upset him. And his comments upset Martin. The remark about him not looking— "Ugh. Ignorant. I'm Ignorant."

"I wish I spoke up more. I wish I knew what happened to my family. I wish I found something." He closed his eyes and took a deep breath. The Nazis were gone and the world was a better place.

Well, comparatively.

"I need to apologize for my behavior. For what I said." Fredrick opened his eyes and focused on his appearance. He adjusted the collar of his shirt and his shirtsleeves.

With a warm expression once again on his face, Fredrick made his way out of the head and returned to Martin and their table. He passed several happy travelers enjoying their day, none of them looking at him, which was good. The scene was hopefully already forgotten. A plate covered with a cloche waited for him as he sat down.

Dejan appeared. "Allow me." He removed the cloche. "Please enjoy."

The Veal Cotoletta alla Milanese sat in front of Fredrick, a picture of perfection. The breading appeared to be toasted to a flawless brown and the bits of fried basil on top were an excellent accompaniment.

"This looks delicious." The aroma of cooked veal and the seasoning made their way to Fredrick's nose, causing his mouth to salivate.

"Bon appétit," Dejan said before vanishing.

"I'd like to apologize." Fredrick returned his napkin on his lap. He needed to make this right and offer up some kind of explanation that wasn't a lie.

"Let's just eat," Martin countered.

"No please. I was out of line and wrong." Fredrick inhaled a shaky breath. "Knowing what those monsters did and all the people they killed. People like you and like me. I should have known better. I shouldn't have said what I said. Several of my parents' friends and co-workers were taken by them, and I ..."

Martin raised an eyebrow.

"Sorry. I'm still getting my English confused with my German." Fredrick tried to recover. "What I meant is several of my grandparents' friends and co-workers were taken by the Reich and we never saw them again. So many people died because of them and because of people not standing up and fighting back. So many people watched and did nothing." He trailed off.

"We lost family during the Holocaust." Martin sighed. "None of it is easy and given all that is happening in the world these days it's like we're watching everything on repeat."

Fredrick had seen many news reports and newsfeeds about the state of the world and Martin was correct, a lot of what was happening now could have been pulled right from the media of 1937.

Perhaps we'll do better this time. Stand up and fight back, before we repeat the past.

"Still, I'm sorry," Fredrick acknowledged. "So much loss, and for what? Talk of the Nazis set me on edge." He did his best to keep a pleasant expression on his face and his voice calm and level. "At least your family is okay."

There, not a word of a lie.

"Not all, unfortunately." Martin inhaled. "My great-grandfather had six siblings and he was the only one to make it out of the camps." His voice softened.

"I see." Fredrick picked up his water and took a deep swallow, no longer hungry for the veal sitting in front of him.

Perhaps brunch was a bad idea.

•　　　•　　　•

After a less than picture perfect brunch with Martin, Fredrick needed to get ready for work. Their brunch hadn't been all bad, especially once they got past their rocky beginning. Overall the food had been excellent and helped to bridge the gaps of the awkward conversation. Fredrick did everything he could to steer the conversation away from him and his past, or World War II and the Holocaust, to learn more about Martin. For the remainder of the brunch, what should have been a delightful conversation seemed to be a sparring match. Either way the *date* was over and now he made his way to his cabin. With a click, he opened the door and was surprised to see Leo lounging on his bunk, tapping away on his computer device.

"How's brunch?" Leo looked up at Fredrick, his tone soft and his expression void of any happiness.

Oh no. Things must have not gone well with Barron.

"What happened? Are you okay?" Fredrick closed the door and moving over to Leo, who appeared utterly defeated and any joy he once had now vanished. "The talk with Barron—"

"I screwed up." Leo put his device down next to him. "Barron told me he loved me and I didn't say anything. I sat there. Silent."

"What? How wonderful for you!"

"No. Didn't you hear me?" Leo faced Fredrick, his eyes as red as roses. "I didn't say anything and when I didn't respond Barron rushed off ..." He shook his head. "I messed this up."

Fredrick deliberated a moment, not believing what he heard. He'd never known two men to tell each other they loved one another. Such things were never spoken aloud, no matter how you felt about another fella. "Well, surely you can speak with him now, let him know how you feel?" Fredrick suggested.

"That's the thing." Leo raked a hand through his hair. "I don't know how I feel."

"Oh." Fredrick pulled over his desk chair and sat. "I'm sorry."

Leo sighed. "It's not your fault, it's mine. I ... what was I supposed to say? We talked about all this other stuff and he told me he loved me. I had no idea those words would come out ... I don't want to talk about this right now. How was brunch?"

Fredrick ran a hand over his face. "I'm glad I went, but ..."

"No sparks?" Leo adjusted to his side to watch Fredrick.

Fredrick glanced around the cabin, buying himself some time. "It didn't go badly, but brunch wasn't what I had made the encounter out to be in my head."

"That sucks." Leo kicked his feet over the edge of his bunk. Sounds like we both had a rough morning," He stood with his computer in hand, then moved to his desk to put the machine away. "On the bright side, we can go and see the 'Hunks in Trunks' and 'Babes in Bikinis' contest up on deck. Maybe we'll see Mr. Sherman up there."

"I don't think so. He mentioned he had work to catch up on ..." Fredrick frowned. "But I would have figured he would want to evaluate the ship's special events too."

"I would think so as well." Leo shrugged. "Anyway, it'll be a good way for us to clear our heads before our shift. And this contest is always a blast. Plus, we'll inevitably be getting an eyeful."

"An eyeful?"

"Given what these guys wear, I think they are as close to naked as they can be."

Fredrick chuckled, heat filling his cheeks. "Sounds fun."

"Okay, well, let's get dressed and head up. I can't wait to see all the guys in their teeny tiny speedos." He laughed as he started to pull off his shirt.

"If you say so," Fredrick commented as he turned to the door, giving Leo privacy. He took off his shoes and got himself into his duty uniform. He afforded a glance at Leo and saw the frown peek through on his face. Clearly, he was putting on a show.

Aren't we all? I guess we're keeping the fantasy going even for ourselves.

T HE PALI DECK WAS SLAMMED with bodies and everyone chatted and drank. Inhaling the warm ocean air, Leo was reminded of why he loved flying over the ocean in the *Hawaiian Sun*. Observing how the deck sat on the inside of the zep, he wished they could figure out a way to have the whole deck open so guests might go to the edge and look down at the water. The views here were amazing, but how much better would they be if they could see down and out, not just up?

Oh well, maybe someday.

Leo grabbed Fredrick by the arm and they moved toward the front where folks where yakking away. Standing near the bar, Krystal Chandelier fussed with her outfit. The statuesque drag queen had on her jet-black hair, large bronze dangling ear rings, and dark makeup. Her bronze and brown outfit with a stylized captain's hat atop her head looked brilliant. The outfit she wore took Leo a moment to figure out, but ultimately he placed the outfit: she was an Airship Pirate. The Victorian clothing, accented with gears, swords, and even a fake flintlock pistol were a dead giveaway.

He caught sight of Dapper Dave looking like a toddler standing next to Krystal. His darker skin worked well with his pencil thin mustache. His gold pocket watch and pinstriped suit played right into the whole gangster vibe.

"Who are they?"

Leo glanced to where Fredrick watched and chuckled. "Those are the hosts, Krystal Chandelier and Dapper Dave III. I love their outfits. Krystal always goes all out. I love the whole Steam Punk Pirate look; it's brilliant. DD always plays up the 40s gangster look and does a great job."

"They're impressive," Fredrick agreed. "I like Dapper Dave's suit."

"Now before we start"—Krystal adjusted the microphone in front of her—"I've been asked by Head Steward Tammy Lam to remind you all that the clocks get moved back tonight."

At once, a deep sultry voice filled the air all around the deck. "If I could turn back time ..."

Leo pushed down his delight. It didn't matter how many times he heard this joke—the image of Cher singing this song always made him happy.

"I don't understand ..." Fredrick glanced around as the crowd roared with laughter.

"Because of the time change, tonight and tomorrow night." Leo watched Fredrick's face for any sign of recognition. "The song. Cher."

Fredrick smiled and turned to the entertainers.

How can anyone not know this joke? It must lose something in translation.

"Okay. Okay." Krystal waved her hands. "Big D, we ready to do this bitch?" she spoke into a microphone.

"Waiting on you, Doll Face." Dapper Dave adjusted his hat.

"*Hawaiian Sun*, you ready to see some hunky boys and bountiful babes in their swimsuits?"

There were cheers and clapping from the crowd, which Leo and Fredrick joined in. Leo even whistled, which caught Fredrick off guard.

"Sorry." Leo chuckled.

"I wasn't expecting that."

"This is gonna be a fair contest." Dapper Dave's voice was artificially deep, but given he was a performer, it worked for the character. "Oh, right—another reminder, this is an adults only event, so if you have young ones around, you might want to take them to the silent dance party down in the Luau Theater," Dave announced. "Seeing any kiddies about, Doll Face?"

Krystal held a hand to her forehead as she scanned the crowd. "All clear."

"Excellent." Dave continued. "You all know how this works. We'll bring out our contestants ..."

"I figured I'd find you both up here." Tammy joined Leo and Fredrick.

"We couldn't have Fredrick miss out on this event."

"Definitely not." Tammy glanced at Fredrick and smiled at him. "But are you sure he can handle it?"

"Oh, I'm made of tougher stuff than you might think ... ma'am," Fredrick added.

"I'm sure." She pointed to where Krystal and Dapper Dave were finishing up their instructions to the crowd.

"Now, we expect you all to behave and treat our wonderful contestants with all the respect and dignity they deserve." Krystal pulled out her pistol and waved it around. "I promised Captain Monroe I wouldn't use this again, so don't make me go back on my promise."

There were chuckles from the crowd.

"And I got these." Dapper Dave pulled out a pair of brass knuckles and slipped them on his hand.

"Those props almost got taken by security," Tammy said as she leaned in.

"I can see why," Fredrick agreed. "For a moment I imagined they were real and not toys."

"Fredrick, check out his pocket watch." Leo pointed. "Kind of like the one you have."

Fredrick's stare moved to the pocket watch. "Similar, I think."

"Maybe." Tammy eyed Fredrick. "If Dapper Dave doesn't work out, we can send Fredrick up there to co-host."

"I think I'm good where I am, ma'am." Fredrick smiled.

"Save your strength for tomorrow night's Gala." She laughed.

"Okay, Doll Face"—Dapper Dave turned to Krystal—"are we starting with them Mugs or them Dames?"

"Well, I would say ladies first, but we're all about equality here, so let's bring on the basket brigade."

"And who am I to question a dame like you?"

"Darn right, Big D." Krystal pointed the toy pistol toward Dave. "Let's have our gentlemen come on down—and a reminder you have to keep your suits on; we don't want to have a repeat of last time."

There was a collection of laughs, boos, and ahs from the crowd as all kinds of different shapes and sizes of men moved to the front of the stage. There were so many bodies it was hard to see as Dapper Dave worked on getting the men all lined up.

"Each of our gentlemen will take to the stage and it's up to you to cheer for your favorite."

"What the hell?" Leo's stomach dropped as the familiar face of Barron appeared amongst the crowd of men.

"What?" Fredrick glanced to where Leo stared. "That's ..."

"Barron," Tammy finished.

Barron stood with the rest of the men, smiling and chatting. The only thing covering him was a tiny white swimsuit that barely hid anything and the white gold chain glistening on his bare chest.

"Bastard," Leo snarled under his breath.

This was not where Leo expected to see Barron, and what the hell? Barron just that morning told him he loved him and now he was up here showing off his dick and ass to the whole fucking zep.

"Well, I haven't seen this many large baskets since I shopped at Costco last week," Dapper Dave announced as everyone laughed and whooped.

"Jealous?" Krystal commented.

"You know it," Dapper Dave agreed. "I've told you I'm a grower, not a shower."

There were more laughs.

"Who'd love to see Big D up here with our boys?"

There were more cheers from the crowd.

"Sorry, the hosts can't participate." Dapper Dave frowned. "Them the rules and you know this mug always plays by the rules—he don't want to deal with any coppers."

"I can't believe he's doing this." Leo shook his head, trying to keep his voice and emotions in check as he spoke to Fredrick and Tammy. However, his heart was about ready to burst from his chest and he wanted to throw up. "He hates these sorts of things. Calls them demeaning. I'm going to talk to him—"

"No, you're not," Tammy interjected and held up a hand to stop him.

"But he—and I—and this morning—"

"None of that matters." Tammy's words came out in a neutral tone. "He's a guest here to have fun, and you're in uniform."

Leo looked down at his clothing, frowning.

"It's okay, Leo. I doubt anyone will notice him. Look at all the other men up there. I don't think I've seen such an interesting mix of men," Fredrick volunteered.

Leo crossed his arms over his chest and said nothing more as his heart pounded all the way to his head. He was going to have one hell of a headache.

Krystal Chandelier and Dapper Dave III moved the men through, each one accompanied by the old song *I'm Too Sexy*. The crowd cheered and laughed as each man went up and spun around, showing off. The guy with the loudest cheering would be deemed the winner and get dinner in the Lani Steakhouse. Leo didn't think the prize was worth all the embarrassment of being up on stage making a fool of yourself.

I can't believe Barron is doing this. I should leave.

Barron appeared on the stage, and when he and Barron's gaze met, locking eyes for a second, was when Leo's temper bubbled over. Leo moved forward but was stopped by Fredrick and Tammy. Barron started down the catwalk, his eyes narrowed. He grabbed a bottle of water from some random person in the crowd and poured the liquid on his stomach and swimsuit, instantly making the material transparent, and what once had been covered by the fabric was now visible for everyone to see.

What ... the absolute fuck.

Leo burned from head to toe. At least Fredrick showed some respect and looked away as quickly as his eyes would allow. But Leo doubted anyone else was as considerate. The crowd erupted into cheers.

"You cheeky devil," Krystal Chandelier commented, pulling out a fan to fan herself. "My goodness, if you assumed that basket was packed, we can certainly see why. An ample supply of meat and potatoes. What a wonderful meal—someone call David to get this served up."

"Now we've seen it all," Dapper Dave responded. "Literally."

The crowd continued to whoop it up and cheer.

Leo shook his head, releasing himself from both Fredrick's and Tammy's grip.

Barron smiled and snatched another bottle of water, then poured the fluid over his hair and the rest of him. He turned and wiggled his butt in time with the music, getting more cheers and shouts from the crowd.

With that Leo had had enough and headed to the elevators, Fredrick on his heels.

•   •   •

By the time Leo returned to the Lani Club, he had time to partially cool off. He wondered if Barron planned this all from the beginning, to make a spectacle of himself. But Leo didn't think Barron owned a white thong. Not that he couldn't have bought one for the trip, but still, that didn't jive with the man he knew.

Thought I knew.

Taking as deep a breath as he could and releasing air with as much of his frustration as possible, he fumbled for the sensor with his keycard.

"Are you okay?" Fredrick's concerned voice gently pulled Leo's focus from the door.

"No, but I'll be fine." Leo faced Fredrick. "As Tammy reminded me, he's a guest and I'm in uniform so there's nothing for me to do or say at the moment." He touched Fredrick's arm. "Thank you for asking."

"If there's anything I can do?" A deep smile filled Fredrick's whole face, not only showing off his dimples but how truly handsome he was.

This must be his real smile.

"I appreciate the offer." Leo pulled out his smartphone tapping the device. "Shall we get to work?"

"Yes."

Leo reengaged the door and the two men entered an empty club. Ready to greet them were Aurora and Oliver at the desk. "How's everyone?" Leo's tone was as bright and chipper as he could make it.

Aurora glanced down at her computer. "We weren't expecting to see you for another half hour. As you can see, we're slammed here.

Figured you'd be up watching the Hunks in Trunks and Babes in Bikinis competition."

Leo didn't say anything so Fredrick jumped in. "We were, but there were a lot of folks up there, so Leo suggested we make our way here before things wrap up. Didn't want to get held up at the lifts."

"Right." Leo moved over to the desk and leaned against it.

"Smart move. This place emptied out as guests headed up on deck for a good view or to get ready." Hints of Oliver's British accent peppered his words. I can only imagine what you guys saw up there." Oliver tapped his console. Once finished, he stood and offered Leo his spot.

Leo took the station vacated by Oliver. "Thanks."

"You have no idea." Fredrick's expression was as pleasant as always, but now Leo had seen the sincere Fredrick. Leo now knew there was a difference. Either way, you'd swear nothing ever phased that man.

At least not outwardly.

"What time is your afternoon tea?" Leo asked Oliver as he scanned the schedule for the rest of the afternoon and evening, not seeing anything that would be too unmanageable.

"I waited for you or Tomas to arrive so I might get everything sorted with David and his team."

"Well, we're here." Leo looked up from the monitor. "Go ahead; we probably won't have a crowd until the event upstairs is over."

"Cheers, Leo." Oliver adjusted his uniform jacket. "I'm off."

"Hey, wait a sec." Leo's head shot up.

"What's up?"

"Once Tomas arrives for his shift, I'll send Fredrick over and have him shadow and assist you with the tea. I'd like for him to see how we do things here, and given how rambunctious folks can be after some of these events, it's probably a good idea."

"Sure, I'm always game to have an extra set of hands." Oliver beamed.

"That okay with you, Fredrick?"

Fredrick stood taller and his shoulders straightened. "Absolutely. I'm happy to help and I'd love to see an American tea service."

"Great." Leo updated the notes on Oliver's scheduled event.

Aurora, Leo and Fredrick watched as Oliver headed off. Once they were alone, Aurora narrowed her gaze on Leo. "Now, care to tell me what's happening?"

Leo slumped into his chair, running a hand over his face. It took him several minutes, but he relayed what Barron had done up on deck and how he let it bother him.

"Well, I'm glad Tammy and Fredrick were there to keep you from doing something stupid," Aurora spoke through pinched lips. "Still, we can always have Tommy or Jemma go to his cabin and accidently lose all his clothes so he only has his white thong to prance around in."

Leo laughed.

"Thong?" Fredrick asked.

"The swimsuit, or lack thereof, that he wore up on deck." Leo's gaze narrowed. "Oh, right, you call them swim briefs, or something like that. Do they even use swimsuits in Germany?" He couldn't help but poke fun. Fredrick seemed to be out of touch at times, which made teasing him easy and the guy needed the levity now.

"Those were not swim briefs." Fredrick shook his head.

"Anyway," Aurora continued, picking up the desk phone, "should I call Tommy? He's always game for a little mischief."

Leo puffed out his lips and moved them side to side. "No ... as funny as it would be, nah. I'm not that upset anymore." Despite how intuitive Aurora was, Leo didn't see the need to tell her about his and Barron's conversation in the morning that, if he had to guess, was the reason for the display up on deck. Plus, there was no reason to muddy the waters farther with her.

"Well, that's good," Fredrick said.

"Still, I'm sorry he did that." Aurora tapped her console. "I know how much you liked, or like, him despite what happened between you."

Fredrick's gaze moved between him and Aurora. Leo hoped he wouldn't say anything. Fredrick continued his discretion, which Leo appreciated.

"I have to ask, was the view at least worth all the hassle?"

Leo bit at his smile as he snuck a look at Fredrick.

"I didn't notice." Fredrick straightened his shirt as he spoke.

"You didn't notice?" Aurora leaned forward. "Is it really that small?"

Leo's brows rose. "Care to elaborate, Fredrick?"

"No, not in the least." Fredrick moved over to the buffet and started tidying the food station and organizing the chairs and tables.

"You know there's a story there."

"Or he's trying to be nice, for my sake." Leo watched Fredrick. "He strikes me as quite the gentleman, so his response doesn't surprise me."

"I suppose." Aurora glanced at the door as it opened.

"Hey all." Tomas entered, buttoning up his uniform jacket. "I had to take the stairs—the elevators are getting busy."

"Looks like we're on." Aurora cracked her neck.

"Tomas, go and let Fredrick know he can head up and meet Oliver for his tea. I think he's in the service corridor."

"Gotcha."

The club door opened again, new conversations and laughing filling the space.

Leo motioned at Aurora and they put forward their professional smiles as a group of guests walked in. It was going to be a busy afternoon and night. Given how chipper this crowd was, they were in for a lively group, but most of the time the guests in the club were always pretty good no matter how much mischief of their own they have been up to.

12

FREDRICK TRIED TO FOCUS on his work and not the display he witnessed up on deck. Not even the aromas of the various teas helped clear his mind. Images flashed to the front of his mind reviewing all the beautiful men, and he loved seeing all the different shapes and sizes of the participants. All the confidence each of the fellas displayed impressed him. More importantly, he noted that there was a mix of men with not only smooth but hairy chests and everything in between. His earlier worry about his own chest hair was now a moot point. In general, people were so much freer here and, in a way, he found the idea liberating. He doubted he would ever do anything like participate in a swimsuit contest, showing off his body in such a way. No. Plus, he doubted his attributes would measure up. Not that Wilhelm ever spoke of such things.

I guess that's a downside to seeing so many men in a state of undress; you question and worry about your own body.

Exhaling, he thought about Mr. Hillchild and his performance, how hurt his presence made Leo. As much as he enjoyed witnessing the men in their *altogethers*, there was something about the whole situation that bothered him.

How would I have reacted if Wilhelm did something like that? I have a contradiction of emotions around the whole affair. Still, there were several attractive men and I wouldn't have minded seeing more. Even Mr. Hillchild looked good. Not that I'll say anything.

The rattle of the cart caught his attention. He checked the list as he and Oliver verified everything on the trolley for the tea service. "Teas: Earl Grey, Darjeeling and English Breakfast." Fredrick glanced up, waiting for Oliver to confirm.

"Yes, and I've added peppermint and turmeric in case they want something at the end of the tea for digestion."

"Is that common?" Fredrick caught a whiff of the peppermint tea and inhaled deeper, the minty scent reminding him of the peppermint candies he had as a youth. He smiled at the memory as he watched Oliver shift the plates, utensils, and other serving items.

"No, but I like to include them." Oliver grinned at Fredrick. "Better to have them and not need them, than to need them and not have them. It's all about anticipating the guests' needs." He lifted one of the small creamers. "I have both cream and dairy-free as well as sugar and sweetener."

"Okay, that makes sense. We'd do the same thing; I hated being caught off-guard." Fredrick made a note before he continued to review the list from David and his team. "Sandwiches: smoked salmon, cucumber, egg, coronation chicken, and prawn."

"Yes, and we have enough for six people," Oliver added. "Oh, did you bring your white gloves?"

"I'll put them on when we serve—I didn't think wearing them now was a good idea."

"Brilliant."

"How many people are we serving today?"

"Four, but we have food for six."

"Just in case." Fredrick glanced over to Oliver, his cheeks lifted in what he hoped to be a good-natured expression.

"You're learning." Oliver beamed over at Fredrick. "Some people eat up at these teas and forgo dinner or they've skipped lunch. We'll leave all the extras with them." He moved to the cabinet and pulled down a couple of larger serving plates and put them under the smaller tea plates. "These are for any leftovers. Americans love their big portions and their take-away bags."

"Good to know." Fredrick chuckled.

"Also, Ainsley, one of the guests at the tea, uses they/them pronouns. I know this can bugger people up, but we're here to provide a service and everyone has to feel welcome and respected."

Fredrick agreed. "I saw the note. Frankly, I don't understand all the fuss—call people what they want to be called and treat them with respect. That isn't difficult."

Oliver smiled. "Agreed."

"Now saying that, watch me make a mistake." Fredrick glanced at the clipboard with the work order and all the details for the event.

"You'll be fine." Oliver knelt down to check the lower cart, "Right, we've got plain and cheese scones with our house-made preserves and lemon curd, clotted cream, plain and whipped butter, and honey, of course." He moved some of the trays out of the way.

"That leaves the cakes and pastries."

"Let's see." Oliver checked the last tray. "Victoria sponge, bakewell tart, carrot cake, Battenberg, chocolate eclairs, and crème brulée tarts." He stood up. "I think we're set. If these blokes go through all this, or need more treats, I'll have you come pick up some additional items from the club, but I think we'll be good."

"Will it matter if we don't provide them the same things?"

"Hopefully not, but I don't think we'll have any issues. This is a load of food and if I know David he probably has some extras put away in case they are needed."

Fredrick made a mental note. "So, I'll check with David or his team if we need more?"

"Yes. If he doesn't have anything left, we'll grab from the club." Oliver dusted off his jacket. "Have you done a private tea before?"

"No. I'm familiar with the process, but not in a small setting." Fredrick folded up the order sheet and stuffed it in his coat pocket, then put the clipboard on its hanging spot. "Where will we set up? The suites don't have tables."

"We unload the trolley and the trolley can be set up as a table, if they want it. However, I try to steer them into using the living space as is." Oliver buttoned up his jacket. "It's more comfortable for everyone and a bit easier on us."

"Understood."

"Basically, once we get it all set up, we are there to make sure the water is hot." Oliver pointed to the large electric kettle they would be using for water. "You'll serve everything in order, sandwiches first, scones, followed by pastries. I'll serve the tea throughout. You can take your cue from me and between us, we'll take good care of our guests."

"Thanks for letting me come with you." Fredrick checked his jacket and felt for his gloves to ensure he had them. "I appreciate the opportunity to see how this is done."

"It's not hard, and they can be pretty fun. Most of our guests do a private tea for the experience. They may or may not know what to do or how to act, but we're there to ensure they have fun and enjoy." He chuckled. "I think they like us there to fuss over them and give them that whole *Downton Abbey* or *The Gilded Age* television experience."

"I don't know what that is." Fredrick pinched his lips together. He'd heard of movies, but television was something new—from what he gathered, television was a smaller movie screen that people watched instead of listening to the radio for entertainment. He'd only watched a few things when he was in the crew mess. *Another wonder of this time.*

"Bloody hell, where did you grow up?" Oliver laughed.

Fredrick fell quiet as his face warmed, not sure what to say.

"Hey, mate, I'm taking the piss out of you." Oliver grinned, his accent growing stronger and less formal. It was something he noticed Oliver do quite a lot. When Oliver was dealing with guests, he spoke more polished like some of the folks who Fredrick ran into before he *appeared* here.

"You okay?" Oliver asked, his voice lowering as he studied Fredrick.

"Yes. Sorry. I'm still getting used to things. We didn't have television when I grew up, so there's a lot I'm sure I missed."

"Oh, sorry." Oliver fumbled over his words. "You didn't miss anything. My mum loved *Downton Abbey*—well, to be honest, so did I. It's a great period piece about an Earl and his family in the early 1900s. Maybe some night we can give it a go. Might be fun." Oliver tapped the kettle. "Anyway, shall we get this going? We have to be set and ready by 1500 and I want to make sure the water is piping hot. That's the key to good tea: the water. Some people'll say a tea is all about the food, but a proper tea comes down to the hot water and don't let anyone ever tell you differently."

Fredrick's brows pushed together as did his lips. "Water … hmm … I'm not so sure about that."

"Shows what you know—you're not English." Oliver put forth a firm nod of his head. He arrived at the service door and tapped the button, opening the door for them. He gestured for Fredrick to go out first so he could guide the trolley while he pushed from behind.

As the two men moved down the passageway, they had the corridor to themselves, making the journey easy.

Everyone must be out enjoying the deck or one of the private parties. Or they might be fussing over the men and women who were part of the swimwear competition.

Once they arrived at the suite, Oliver knocked on the door. "Tea service," he called out. Voices from inside the cabin chattered as someone walked to the entrance and opened the door. "Mr. Masson. I'm Oliver and this is Fredrick; we're here to provide your afternoon tea. May we come in?"

"Hey, I know you," Mr. Masson greeted. The man's hair was an unmovable sculpture, perfectly crafted to his desired effect, Fredrick supposed the look complemented his puffier cheeks and his larger frame. "You're Leo's new boy … Frank … no, Fredrick, right?"

Fredrick studied the man for a moment. His short sleeved red shirt hung loose around him, not hugging his body like so many men wore here on the ship. His dark gray, or perhaps black, pants seemed less form fitting then what Fredrick had become accustomed to. Recognition came slower than he hoped, but he placed the face and the man: Mr. Hillchild's friend, Elijah. His heart sank. They were providing a tea service for four people, so if Elijah, Mr. Masson, was one of them, that meant that Barron must be one as well.

Sure enough, Barron came out of the bedroom, a bright expression planted across his face. He donned a lavender long-sleeve shirt and gray slacks, a stark contrast to what he wore earlier; however, he still had on the necklace that seemed to find the light no matter where he was. The outfit flattered Barron's body. "Mr. Masson and Mr. Hillchild, good to see you both," Fredrick managed to say by way of greeting.

"Fredrick is our newest team member," Oliver announced. "He's here to assist me with the service today."

"Well, what a treat." Elijah clapped his hands, appearing somewhat childish. "Ainsley and Minh will be back shortly, but please come in and do whatever you need to do. I've been looking forward to this for months. We don't really have any teahouses in San Jo. Well, none that aren't filled with a bunch of girls playing dress up." He laughed.

"Given we're all going to be here, you might need to take back that statement." Barron grinned, standing by the bedroom door.

Fredrick shifted his stance as he watched the two banter.

"Bitch! Still you're probably right." Elijah laughed. "Anyway, wait till you see the outfits Ainsley put together for the couple's drag competition and the non-binary fashion show. Beautiful." Elijah stepped closer to Barron. "You should have them design something fun for you, get you out of your stuffy business clothes all the time."

Fredrick wasn't sure how to take their closeness. Given all he had seen the last couple of days, something about how Elijah eyed Barron, focusing more attention on him than anything else going on in the room at the moment, struck him as off-putting. *Aren't they cozy?*

Oliver and Fredrick moved the service cart nearer the desk so they had space to work. The suite was similar to Martin's in that there was a main room which they would set things up in and beyond the door were two beds instead of one.

Well, it doesn't seem that Barron is fooling around with Elijah, so that's something.

Fredrick pulled the serving items off the trolley and placed them on the desk as he assisted Oliver in the setup. True to his word, the first thing Oliver did was plug in the large kettle on the desk to keep the water hot. Once the water was plugged in, they moved to empty out the rest of the cart, setting everything on the desk so the items were out of the way. Once emptied, Oliver shifted the trolley.

"Would you like us to set up the table, or would you enjoy keeping the setting more informal, so you can relax and enjoy?"

"Please, keep it simple." Barron motioned to the sitting area. "No point in going through all the fuss."

"But ..." Elijah whined. "Fine, I guess we can sit around the sofa and the chairs."

"Excellent." Oliver didn't miss a beat and pointed to Fredrick to help him over at the small sitting area. They would adjust the two chairs around the built-in sofa, which when pulled out and down doubled as a bed where two people slept. They moved the ottomans and arranged the seating for conversation. Oliver pulled out a cover for the ottomans, which once set in place held them together and provided a larger flat surface for a linen table cloth, which Fredrick placed.

By the time the door clicked opened and Ainsley and Minh arrived, the living room was set and everything was ready. Fredrick had his white gloves on and took up his station by the food while Oliver stood ready to pour their tea, once their guests were ready.

Fredrick already caught whiffs of the Earl Grey tea Oliver had ready and waiting. Earl Grey wasn't Fredrick's favorite—he preferred the one called English Breakfast. The tea reminded him of being in a freshly cut field, the gentle fragrance brought out even more by adding milk.

I think mom would've liked that tea, if we had it when I was growing up.

"Oh, this looks fun," Minh sang out, and inhaled deeply. "Yummy." He was the shortest of the group with a deep tannish complexion. There was something on his forehead that Fredrick couldn't quite see as Minh had his hair set to cover it up. "I knew I should have brought my hat and gloves." He fussed with his flowing blouse and puffy pants, or shorts, Fredrick wasn't sure. The outfit didn't look like anything Barron or Elijah wore, and from what he saw had to be something Ainsley had created.

"I think we brought enough clothes," Ainsley countered as they adjusted their belt, which did all the work to hold up their dark jeans. The person appeared so thin despite the bulk of their long-sleeved shirt over an undershirt. Ainsley didn't look sick, simply slender, and again well-put together. It was clear both Ainsley and Minh's outfits were designed to complement each other. If Fredrick was honest, the clothes were absolutely stunning.

Clearly Ainsley is very creative.

The group made their way to the seating area and began gossiping away. Oliver signaled to Fredrick to bring the sandwiches, beginning their service.

The group worked their way through the sandwiches, scones and tea. Fredrick and Oliver melted into the background as their guests continued yakking. Fredrick tried to ignore the conversation about the people they had already met and how many more folks there were for them to spend time with. Their conversation dove into the swimsuit contest and how good everyone looked, but they hadn't mentioned anything about Barron … at least not yet. Which Fredrick appreciated. Honestly, none of what they talked about interested Fredrick. Their chatter was like most conversations he heard on the *Hindenburg*—people seemed to talk about nothing and say nothing of importance. Especially if others were hovering around on the fringes of the room able to hear them. So, it surprised him when they started talking about Leo and Barron.

"I'm glad you spoke to him." Ainsley motioned to Barron using their plate. "You need to get that man out of your system." They sipped their tea. "At least now you can have a good time. I hated seeing you all bound up like that."

"No man is worth that," Elijah added before sipping his tea. "Especially, no man that looks as good as you in a thong." He smirked.

"Well, what did he have to say for himself anyway?" Minh took a bite of his scone with clotted cream, seemingly ignoring Elijah's comment.

"It doesn't matter." Barron noted that Oliver and Fredrick were still in the room, though clearly the others didn't seem to care. "We talked. I told him what I needed. He said what he wanted and now …" His gaze dropped to the floor, trying to avoid everyone.

"If your display today says anything, I'm sorry." Minh touched Barron's leg, then pulled back and smiled. "However, I'm not complaining. It's nice to see you out there having fun. It's been what, five months? Plus, you got a lot of attention."

"Six," Barron corrected. "And I shouldn't have … it was stupid …"

"Six what?" Ainsley asked raising his cup to his lips.

"Six months." Barron took up his tea, which Oliver was over to refresh with the hot liquid. Fredrick noted that Barron, Minh, and Ainsley all preferred the Earl Grey while Elijah drank the English Breakfast. "Thanks." Barron gave a slight nod of his head.

Oliver didn't say anything, moving away and observing, trying to anticipate the guest's needs. It wasn't for them to comment or join the conversation. It was for them to provide a pleasant experience and ensure the guests wanted for nothing.

Minh cleared his throat. "Hmm, well, I don't think my thong will ever be the same … which you know you can keep. Who knew your egg roll and dumplings were so … ample?" He laughed as he went for one of the mini sandwiches.

"I could have told you that," Elijah stated. Everyone looked at him, including Fredrick and Oliver. "Oh please, we've all been to the gym."

Fredrick bit at his grin and from the look on Oliver's face he did the same as everyone laughed, including Barron, even if his chuckle appeared to be halfhearted.

Minh finished his sandwich and wiped his mouth before speaking. "But I have to know"—he leaned in and picked up his cup of tea—"was the water cold or warm? Cause that makes a difference." Ainsley and Elijah chuckled as Minh sipped his tea, looking over the cup with his brows risen.

"Being up there today in that stupid contest was a bad idea." Barron shook his head. "I can't believe I let you talk me into doing that." He looked at Elijah, who shrugged.

"Why? You won" Ainsley laughed, and took a bite of one of the scones, savoring the flavor before continuing. "Even though you wore white, you should've let me zhuzh the thong up for you, make those assets pop. Anyway, now you can take us all to dinner at the steakhouse."

"We'll see." A hint of mischief grew ever so slightly on Barron's face. He sat deeper in the chair holding one of the small plates, where a half-eaten smoked salmon sandwich and an untouched cheese scone rested.

Elijah leaned in, offering to take Barron's hand. "Hon, listen to me. He hurt you, and—"

"I don't think Fredrick or Oliver need to hear us talk about their coworker." Barron glanced at Oliver before he met Fredrick's gaze placing his plate on the table. Fredrick's neck warmed.

"Oh, please, they don't care," Elijah countered, not even acknowledging Fredrick or Oliver.

"It's being catty and bitchy and it's not right." Barron's tone had more of an edge.

"I don't give a rat's ass what gets to Leo," Elijah huffed out, wiping his mouth with his linen napkin. "He's a prick for how he treated you. I'm sorry if his coworkers learn that their boss, or coworker, or whatever, is a dick that goes around crushing people's hearts." He didn't bother to look at Fredrick or Oliver. "You can do better and everyone agrees. You need someone who isn't off flying back and forth to Hawaii for three months at a time."

"Wait." Barron's face pinkened. "Is this why you planned this tea event?"

"What? No." Elijah's voice broke as color filled his cheeks and forehead. He quickly picked up his tea, taking a long drink from his cup.

"It is." Barron leaned back in his chair. "I told you the other day I was going to talk to Leo this morning and you set this up. So you can what?" Barron glanced up at Fredrick. "When did Elijah contact you about this tea?"

"He didn't contact me," Fredrick responded, trying to keep his tone and face as neutral as possible. Leo told him they were to provide the guests with a wonderful illusion and it was up to them to keep the fantasy in place, as much as possible.

"Fine." Barron twisted and faced Oliver. "Oliver, when was this set up?"

"I'm not sure, Mr. Hillchild," Oliver responded without missing a beat. "I'd have to check the paperwork."

The paperwork that's sitting in my pocket.

Fredrick tried to keep as neutral an expression as possible, shifting from one foot to another, before steadying himself.

Barron laughed and gestured to both Oliver and Fredrick. "See, that's being polite. They don't know. We all know that's a lie, but they have enough decency to conveniently not know." He shook his head. "And I bet that's why you pushed me to do the competition today. You figured Leo would be there."

"That wasn't—" Elijah started.

"In all fairness"—Ainsley's voice softened as they put down their own plate of sandwiches—"we kind of all pushed you into doing the contest. I mean, I figured you'd have a bit of fun."

Minh bit into his sandwich, his brows risen as he swallowed hard.

"Still." Barron's face grew red with fury.

Elijah peered around the suite before focusing on Barron. "Barron, I only wanted to provide you a comfortable spot for you to be with your friends. So, you can speak freely in a safe space."

"But this isn't a safe space. It's a tea service with two of the staff, who happen to report to Leo." He ran a hand through his hair. "You wanted all this to get back to him. And we all know you love an audience."

"Come on, Elijah, you didn't do that. Did you?" Minh put his cup and plate on the table.

"That's not cool," Ainsley added.

"What? Oh, come on." Elijah flushed with ... well, Fredrick wasn't so sure. "I planned this tea so we can all sit around and talk. So Barron felt comfortable and supported by his friends. I had no idea they—"

"That's BS." Barron's voice shook. "You've done plenty of teas before—you know the staff always sticks around to serve. That's one of your favorite things about a private afternoon tea: people get to dote all over you."

Elijah licked his lips. "Fine, maybe I did set this up so they might hear, but I did it for you. You need this. When are you going to see that Leo is no good for you? When're you going to see that we don't need him? I can take care of you."

"You know what, Elijah? You're an ass." Barron stood. "You don't give a damn about anyone's feelings as long as you get to have a front row seat to the drama. I can't do this right now." He walked over to Fredrick. "I didn't know about this and I'm sorry. Leo is a good man and a great guy; that's all that matters. He's one in a million and you're both lucky to work with such an amazing person. I'm sorry." He walked to the cabin door and left the room.

"I think I'm done here." Ainsley stood, adjusting their outfit. "Thank you both and sorry you had to witness all this." They waved their hand. "I'm going to check out the shop so these two gentlemen can clean up in peace. Minh, you want to join me?"

Minh stood, a slight frown crossing his lips. "You know, El, I've known you a long time and I've seen you do some shitty stuff, but this tops everything. You know Barron has never felt anything for you and yet you keep beating that drum. There are 200 people on this ship—I have no doubt you can find someone, but you have to open your eyes and stop treating people like toys."

Ainsley stopped and placed a hand on Elijah's shoulder. "I know you don't mean to do the things you do, and I know there's a good person in there. Be that person. Don't be this guy."

Ainsley and Minh both made a hasty retreat from the cabin, leaving Fredrick, Oliver, and Elijah alone. Elijah watched them go, then glanced at Fredrick and Oliver. "Well, there's no point in continuing. If you'll excuse me." He got up and walked to the bedroom. "Don't worry about me saying anything; thanks for playing dumb about the reservation." He closed the bedroom door behind him.

Fredrick looked at Oliver, unsure what to say or do. Oliver paused for a moment before starting to pull the tea service apart. The two men worked in silence condensing the leftover scones and uneaten pastries onto one of the serving plates Oliver brought so they might leave them in the room, but everything else was cleared up and removed. Fredrick had never moved so quickly to get out of a cabin in his entire career and he didn't think Oliver had either.

Once in the service pantry next to the club, they continued to unload the trolley. Oliver stopped and focused on Fredrick. "That's not how these things typically go."

"I know," Fredrick responded as he put the last of the dirty dishes in the bin to be cleaned. "I don't think we should say anything. Do you?"

"Absolutely not; however, I'm going to have to speak with Leo despite it not being our place. You'll have to be there, but please let me do all the talking." Oliver pulled off his gloves. "In all my years I've heard plenty, and a lot of what we hear is catty and nasty, but never about someone I work with and respect." Oliver sighed as he tucked his gloves into his pocket.

"I feel so bad for all of them." Fredrick's heart sank.

"You're a better person than I am. I think Mr. Masson is a right prat, and deserved everything he got."

"I suppose." Fredrick wasn't so sure about any of that. No one warranted being disregarded in that fashion; clearly Elijah wasn't a good person—well, not in this regard—but if all they said was true and he was in love with Barron, his actions explained a lot. Unrequited love can push people to do things they wouldn't normally do.

"Come on, we have to get things cleaned up. We'll chat with Leo before our desk duty." Oliver motioned to the few remaining items they had on the trolley as they made quick work of securing the serving items and trolley away.

13

L EO TAPPED AWAY at his terminal. He reviewed the excursion list for their upcoming ports of call, seeing a new private tea set up by Nuwa for the next day, and updated his reports, revised the guest numbers, kept track of the ins and outs of the guests, ensuring that the ship's amenities were being used, and processed guest comments. He also noted a message from the spa staff that they were considering offering suite guests a discount at the spa, but nothing had been confirmed yet. The data entry was busy work, but providing feedback was important to all their jobs.

Hopefully they'll see we need more support here.

The club had several guests milling about relaxing as Margo, the pianist, played. If Leo was correct, she was playing *Piano Man*, but giving the song her own twist, which was nice. She impressed him with her talent—not only could she play the piano but she had an impressive voice, which she wasn't using at the moment. She would probably be singing later.

Tomas engaged the Montgomery-Clarks, two older men, one white and one black, in conversation. The couple seemed sweet and charming. They never seemed to miss an opportunity to come to the lounge and enjoy David's fair and Margo's playing.

He quickly pulled up their guest profile and noted that this was their twenty-sixth cruise with United Airships. He would arrange for something special to be sent to them in their room. He would also check and have Captain Monroe prepare a card for them.

He watched them for a moment and wondered if he would ever have a relationship like theirs. He frowned as his mind jumped to his interaction with Barron earlier. Taking a deep breath, he refused to go down that path. With a nod at the older couple, he reminded himself guests like them made these voyages enjoyable. They also proved to him and everyone else that anything was possible.

"Looks like Ollie and Fredrick finished their tea service," Aurora commented as the door by the service area opened and the two slipped in.

Leo cocked his head, switching screens to pull up the staff calendar. "Hmm, they're not supposed to be out until 1730."

The desk phone buzzed. "Maybe the group finished early." Aurora picked up the phone. "Lani Club and Lounge, this is Aurora. How may I assist you?"

"Welcome gentlemen," Leo greeted his staff. "I trust everything went well with the private afternoon tea." He noted the lack of smiles on each of their faces.

"Yes, I can assist you with setting up an excursion on Hilo, did you have something in mind?" Aurora asked on the phone, beginning to tap away on her computer.

"About that," Oliver started through pinched lips, "we need to talk to you. In private."

Oh shit, what happened? How bad is it going to be?

"I see." Leo stood and buttoned his jacket. He glanced at Aurora; she waved them off. He gestured toward Tomas who acknowledged the signal, before quickly excusing himself from the guests he was currently engaged with and heading over.

"Hey, guys. What's up?" Tomas asked, fussing with his uniform. "You wouldn't believe the stories—"

"I need to speak with Oliver and Fredrick," Leo cut Tomas off, keeping his tone as neutral as possible, but he didn't want to be regaled with a story at this time. "It's only going to be you and Aurora."

"Sure. Sounds good." Tomas beamed, seemingly understanding the situation. "Don't worry—we'll keep things flying smooth."

"When we return, if there's time, you can share the story." Leo motioned to the entrance of the club and the three made their way out. "Do we need to call Tammy?"

Oliver rubbed his chin. "Probably."

Leo glanced between Fredrick and Ollie. "Well, I can't wait to hear what this is all about." Leo pulled out his phone and called Tammy.

"Afternoon, Leo," Tammy's voice rang out.

"Tammy, we have a situation." Leo didn't rush his words or raise his voice, keeping himself even keel in case someone overheard him. News, especially drama, traveled like fire on zeps. "I'm bringing Fredrick and Oliver to your office for a chat."

"Sounds like a good time, see you soon." Tammy hung up the phone.

The trip to Tammy's office and quarters on the Prominade deck was quick. Despite the three's silence as they moved through the passageways, they managed to pleasantly greet guests they passed. Leo knew something had happened and it couldn't have been good. He hated these situations, but it was better to get ahead of any bad news before the guests came after him and started to complain.

Assuming they are going to complain. Who am I fooling? Some of our guests enjoy nothing more than to fuss about something.

At Tammy's door, Leo knocked.

"Enter," Tammy called out.

Leo opened the door and allowed Fredrick and Ollie entrance first. Tammy's cabin was bigger than the suites, but not by much. The extra space was because the Officers' cabins doubled as their offices. As the door closed, the group entered into what would have been a living room. Instead there was a large meeting table, a desk, and a built-in sofa along with a mounted television and several built-in cabinets and storage areas. To the right a closed door lead to Tammy's bedroom, closet, and bathroom. The private closet and bathroom were the big perk that Leo couldn't wait to have when he became Head Steward.

Is that something I want?

Tammy pointed to the table. "Have a seat." She joined the three at the table, pulling out a tablet and tapping away. "So how bad?"

Leo glanced at Oliver, waiting for him to begin.

Oliver huffed out a breath and recounted what happened at the tea service.

Leo raked a hand through his hair. The news didn't please him, and if he had paid more attention to the reservation for the tea service, he would have known to not send Fredrick. Though Ollie would've been there on his own, and given how nasty Elijah clearly tried to be, having both men there was probably for the best. In case of an investigation, having two witnesses seeing all that transpired made it a lot harder to discount them and their stories.

If I can get additional help in the club, I think I'm going to insist on having two staff at all private in-room dining events.

"I'm sorry, Leo," Oliver ended his report on the incident.

Tammy made a few notes on her tablet. "At least it doesn't sound like they're going to say anything, or take the event any farther." Tammy leaned away from the table. "Still, I'm not happy with this kind of behavior from the guests, especially ..."

"Especially what?" Oliver asked, glancing between Leo and Tammy.

"Especially with this being Fredrick's first time out with us. It's not a good look," Tammy continued. "I'm sorry you had to experience this, Fredrick."

Leo knew she had almost made a slip about the Auditor, but hopefully Fredrick would play along.

"It's fine, Ms. Lam. As you can imagine, I've experienced worse," Fredrick replied, the first words he spoke since returning from the tea service. Thankfully, they were perfectly executed. "Unfortunately, these things happen, even in Europe."

"Well, knowing Elijah ..." Leo tried to keep his voice level. He wanted to track Elijah down and confront him, but he knew that wouldn't make the situation any better. And in reality, doing so would feed into Elijah's love of drama. "I agree with Barron—this was a setup for Elijah's enjoyment." Leo's lips pinched tighter into what he knew was a frown. The man loves drama, especially if he can facilitate maximum tension.

If I could throw his ass out the window, I'd so do it.

"I'm sorry to ask"—Tammy leaned forward, glancing at Leo— "but what did you and Barron speak about?"

Leo shook his head and took several breaths, trying to lessen the tension in his neck and shoulders, as well as release the knot in his stomach.

There is no way I'm telling any of them the whole thing, not unless I absolutely have to. Fredrick knows a little so I might as well tell them the minimum I have to.

"As you all know, we broke up a few months back and he's been trying to talk to me about our relationship, and … well, I didn't want to discuss it," Leo grumbled. "Anyway, he took this cruise knowing we would have to talk and we did. He expressed his feelings for me and I … I didn't say anything."

"I see." Tammy studied Leo. "Well, I'm not going to pry anymore. What happened between the two of you sounds like it's a personal matter, so I think we can all go about our duties. But if Mr. Masson or Mr. Hillchild do anything that cross a line, you let me know. We can take them off in Hawaii if we need to."

"If I may?" Fredrick shifted in his seat.

"Go ahead."

"Mr. Hillchild was quite respectful the entire time and honorable toward Leo's good name. The dressing down he gave Mr. Masson in front of us seemed sincere and genuine. I don't think there'll be any issues with him." Fredrick maintained eye contact with both Leo and Tammy.

"That's good to hear—that only leaves Mr. Masson." Tammy tapped on her tablet.

"Regarding Mr. Masson," Fredrick started, "I think we've all been in situations like this, and once we get put to task, we don't want to risk any more embarrassment. Mr. Masson might have wanted to embarrass Leo and us, but instead it backfired on him. I don't see him causing any more trouble."

"I agree with Fredrick's assessment," Oliver added. "The man seemed gutted."

Well, shit. I don't like Elijah, but if he got whammied like that, no one deserves that. Not even him.

"Sounds like we'll have to trust your judgement." Tammy placed her tablet down before standing. "Still, I've flagged both their accounts in case there is another situation. Now, shall we get to work? We have jobs to do, despite the real world breaking into our perfectly crafted bubble of indulgence and adventure. We can't let this incident destroy the illusion we create for our guests. Thank you."

Leo stood as did Fredrick and Oliver. He wasn't happy about what happened at the afternoon tea, but Tammy was right—they had duties to attend to. As long as Elijah behaved himself, there was nothing more to do. But what about Barron?

Poor Barron; that had to be awful for him. Should I text him?

As the threesome left Tammy's office, Leo came to the realization that Barron never betrayed their conversation. He refused to provide his friends the laughable details of Leo's … infirmity. Including why they broke up in the first place. Which spoke more to the kind of man Barron truly was. The idea made his heart drop and a pang of guilt filtered up through his body.

He must love me.

Something in that thought made the rest of the day fly by.

14

AFTER FINISHING the computer paperwork that Leo asked him to work on, Fredrick played around with the computer getting more familiar with the new technology. There was a lot to learn, but it wasn't as difficult as he assumed it would be. Running into dead ends, Fredrick gave up on searching for any information on his family or Wilhelm. The computer and technology were incredible, better than anything he may have imagined. However, trying to dig up materials on people who weren't historical figures and lived before photography was commonplace had proven to be almost impossible.

He deliberated asking Oliver and Tomas for assistance, but didn't want to bother them and wasn't sure how he might explain his fascination in trying to find people whom he shouldn't know, even if they were family and Wilhelm. Plus, if they were family, why would he need to look them up? Wouldn't his parents be able to tell him all about them? No, doing everything on his own had been easier and safer.

As he navigated the computer, he learned of a couple of ancestry places that promised to help you trace your genealogy, but they wanted him to sign up and create accounts. Fredrick had no interest in doing anything like that … at least not now. And unfortunately, he didn't have a credit card or any kind of online money.

Switching from investigating information on his family and Wilhelm, he decided to search out details on airships and their history. So much of the zeppelin technology had changed since he was on the original *Hindenburg*. Airships were not only being used for luxury travel, but provided cargo service, emergency, and relief services. Some were dedicated for education and exploration endeavors. The airships could go to the jungles of the world or other hard to access places. They allowed scientists to research areas like the Savanna, Antarctica, the Arctic, and hard to reach mountain locations in relative comfort, all without disturbing the natural environment. It was truly incredible.

Fredrick also discovered there were giant medical airships, like the US Mercy and HMS Compassion. He was thrilled to learn that Germany had one, named after the 1914 FGS Ophelia that had been lost to the British in The Great War. These great airships would travel to wherever help was needed, even to war zones aiding civilians and taking care of the wounded. The images left him with a lump in his throat, knowing all the people these ships saved around the world. All of it was marvelous.

Lounging on his bunk, he decided to move from the history of airships and search the *Hindenburg 2000*. The airship was huge, even larger than the *Hawaiian Sun*, though he wasn't sure how that was possible. Unlike the *Hawaiian Sun*, the airship had no upper outdoor deck, but there were several mixed venues that were both inside and outside. He assumed they were able to close off these sections in case the weather changed. Even when sealed off from the outside elements, all these locations had amazing views.

Incredible.

The cabin door clicked and slowly opened. Fredrick closed down the images and returned to going over the software he was still learning.

"Good, you're practicing—or are you watching porn?" Leo laughed as he stripped out of his jacket and hung it up.

"There's pornography on here?" Fredrick quickly closed down the files he was working on and snapped the computer closed. *Those dirty French and English 'art magazines' that some of the guys on the Hindenburg had can be seen on computers?* Warmth filled his cheeks.

Leo laughed. "Only if you know where to look. I'm not saying you should look up images of Mike O'Toole, but I'm not *not* saying you should. He's a bit of a silver fox, but sexy as hell, and his name should tell you all you need to know." His eyebrows rose and a bright smile bloomed across his lips and cheeks. "But stay off the pay sites!"

Heat continued rushing to Fredrick's cheeks and neck as his eyes bounced around the cabin, not sure where to look. Fredrick had seen some of the images: nude and semi-nude photographs of women, though none of it appealed to him. He didn't know that there were similar images of men ...

"Oh, Fredrick—what are we going to do with you?" Leo laughed. "I feel like you're an innocent babe plucked out of a different world and dropped here."

If you only knew.

"Thank you for giving me this afternoon to work on the computer." Fredrick tugged at his shirt collar, trying to cool off his face and neck. "I believe I got everything sorted. I don't think I'm going to get anywhere with the airline ..." He hated lying, but there was no point in contacting the airlines. Plus, he didn't know where to start with the air company, so he decided he would find a way to pay for all his clothes another way.

"Don't worry about it." Leo unbuttoned his shirt. "I didn't figure you would; they are pretty bad. Did you get the assistance paperwork filled out and submitted?"

"I believe so—the computer said you would be sent the documents for approval."

"Excellent. I'll check it later." He pulled off his shirt and draped it over his chair. "Right, now we need to check your dancing skills."

"What?" Fredrick's stomach dropped and his skin warmed again.

"Remember I told you we'd practice today, before the Gala tonight?" Leo rolled his shoulders and cracked his neck. "The Captain and Tammy are adamant that we all ensure the guests have a good time and that means dancing with them. Stand up."

Fredrick rose slowly from his bunk. He'd never danced with another man before. And his awkwardness didn't help as Leo stood in front of him only in slacks and a bright white t-shirt, seemingly a bit tight, showing off more of Leo's firm frame than Fredrick was comfortable with.

Not that I'm interested in Leo, but still. How does this even work? Do I lead? Does Leo?

Leo held out his hands to Fredrick. "I'll lead, you follow, and afterward we'll switch."

"I typically lead," Fredrick commented, still unsure.

Leo chuckled. "Of course you do." He snapped his fingers. "Hold on." He pulled out his smartphone and tapped the device. In short order, jazz music filled the cabin. "Shall we?" Leo held up his hands again.

With a deep breath, Fredrick moved toward Leo.

"Come on, don't be shy. I don't bite ... unless you ask nicely." Leo moved his arms into the proper position around Fredrick, pulling him closer, until their bodies touched.

Fredrick tensed under Leo's touch. He had never been this close to another man that wasn't Wilhelm. It was both terrifying and exhilarating. His heart pounded like a drum, rushing blood to every part of his body.

"Relax. It'll be fun." Leo smiled as they started to move around the cabin in time to the music.

Feeling Leo's hand on his shoulder blade and resting his left hand on Leo's shoulder felt incredible; he'd never been held like this. Their bodies touched ever so softly and moved together as one. Feeling Leo's breath as they brushed against each other, Fredrick thought there was something so intimate yet relaxed about the hold.

This is amazing. Wonderful. It's everything and more.

"Well, if you lead as well as you follow, our guests are in for a treat." Leo smiled as he met Fredrick's gaze.

Heat filled Fredrick's neck and cheeks as they moved. Parts of his body stirred to life as they continued dancing. Leo moved in closer, stepping in and spinning Fredrick. Fredrick bumped Leo's desk chair. "Oops, sorry about that."

"Why, Mr. Rudolf, I do believe you're blushing."

Fredrick broke their hold and stepped away, trying to gain control over his body and his emotions. "Sorry. I ..."

Leo stopped and stepped away. "You okay?"

"No ... I mean, yes," Fredrick stammered as he fanned his face, pulling at his collar again. "I've never danced with another man before."

"Never? Not even in the clubs?"

Fredrick shook his head, taking a breath before running a hand over his hair, smoothing it down. "Sorry."

Leo sat down on the chair. "Don't worry about it. I get it. Well, I don't get it, but I understand. Dancing with someone can be intimidating, but it'll be fine." Leo scanned their cabin before standing and extending out a hand. "Dancing should be fun—that's what tonight is all about. Here." Leo waved his hand for Fredrick to take. "We don't have to dance so close. Let me show you."

I'm being ridiculous. This is silly.

Fredrick pushed his awkwardness down and his professionalness forward and moved closer to Leo.

We're just dancing.

This time Leo's hold was farther apart. "In school one of my teachers insisted that when we danced together we left enough space for the 'Holy Spirit'." He chuckled. "At the time that was fine with me, cause I didn't like dancing with the girls, but what're you gonna do, right?"

Fredrick smiled as they started moving around the room again, Leo still leading them. If Fredrick was honest, he missed the sensation of Leo being so close to him—feeling that intimacy was unlike anything.

"Better?"

"For now." Fredrick beamed as they continued to move in time with the music. "Should we switch now? I think I have a feel for following."

"You got it." He stopped and they changed stances. "I can show you some basic swing steps as well and maybe a bit of the jive—it's a lot more fun."

"Okay, if you don't think it'll be too much?" Fredrick grew more excited at the idea of dancing with another man, perhaps even dancing with Mr. Sherman.

It's going to be incredible.

•　　•　　•

Despite Fredrick's trepidation at first, Leo found Fredrick to be a quick study and light on his feet. Some folks didn't take to dancing, but Fredrick wasn't one of them, as long as he didn't get too flustered. The more time he got to spend with Fredrick, the more unlike everyone else Fredrick seemed to be. He hadn't lied when he told Fredrick he seemed to be an innocent babe plucked out of a different world. The odd behavior, the confusion with so many things that Leo, and everyone, took for granted all made him wonder about the kind of sheltered life Fredrick must have had back home. Were there Amish people in Germany? But how would that explain his knowledge of the airship's operations? In some areas, Fredrick's work was on par, if not exceeding his colleagues' work, but there were moments.

He doesn't quite seem to fit here.

As they finished up their dance lesson, Leo turned off the music. They had worked their way through the waltz and moved on to some basic swing dancing, but he saw Fredrick getting anxious when he suggested going over the jive, so they stopped. "Well done. I think tonight's gonna be fun."

"I hope so; I don't want to embarrass myself or anyone else." Fredrick bent over to catch his breath.

"You'll be fine." Leo chuckled as he raked a hand through his hair. He was glad they went over the dance moves so he would be loosened up for tonight. "Hey, let's have a chat."

"Sure." Fredrick plopped down on his bunk, fanning his face.

Leo nabbed his shirt and hung the article of clothing up, before grabbing the desk chair, sitting. "I know we haven't talked about what happened yesterday. I wanted to see—"

"These things happen," Fredrick interrupted, a pleasant expression showing off his dimple. "I don't—"

"Please." Leo held up his hand. "I mean, I'm glad you didn't let it bother you, but I wanted to talk to you more like friends."

"Oh." Fredrick's head bobbed up and down, as he moved Leo's laptop out of his way. Shifting on his bunk to meet Leo's gaze.

"Do you think I fucked up with Barron?" There was no way to easily ask the question. Why dance around the subject? "I mean, him telling me he loved me ... is a big deal, and I froze. I sat there dumbstruck, not speaking, and his whole display up on deck ..." He wiped his damp palms on his pants.

"I'm not good with matters of the heart," Fredrick eventually commented. "I've only known one love in my life and that ... well, that ..." Fredrick's gaze faltered as he looked off toward the wall. Was he searching for the words or were the memories too painful?

I wish I knew what was going on in his mind.

"While you were out," Fredrick eventually started, "I looked to see if there was news about Wilhelm on your computer, but there's nothing."

"Well, that's a good thing." Leo perked up as he spoke. "Did you check his social media?"

Fredrick shook his head. "Neither of us use the social medias. But that's not important—what I mean to say about this is Wilhelm and I never talked about our emotions. That wasn't done ... back home." His voice softened as he met Leo's gaze.

How is this guy keeping it all together, and still trying to listen to all my drama?

"I don't know if he loved me," Fredrick continued. "Seeing the people here on this ship and hearing how you talk about Barron, even your reaction during the meeting yesterday, told me all I needed. Well, at least to me. If you love him, you need to tell him. Tomorrow isn't guaranteed and you don't want him to end up like me: wondering. I would rather know than not. I think the not knowing is the worst, so much more than anything else."

Leo leaned forward in his chair, letting Fredrick's words wash over him. He was, of course, making sense.

"Even if you don't feel the same, tell him. Be honest," Fredrick added, raising his brows.

Leo huffed out a single laugh. "I'm not sure how I feel."

"I'd bet you know." Fredrick stood, dusting off his pants. "But if not, perhaps use this time to figure it out." He pointed to the laptop on his bunk. "May I use this again?"

"Sure." Leo waved his hand. "I'm not going to use it right now."

Fredrick took the machine and crossed to their cabin door.

"Where're you going?" Leo perked up as he watched Fredrick.

"I'm going to work more on the computer and give you time to think," Fredrick proposed with a sincere look lighting up his entire face. "We have a few hours before the Gala tonight and I want to see if I can find ..."

"Sure." Leo's tone was soft.

"I'll be in the crew rec room, if you need me." Fredrick turned and exited their cabin.

Leo watched as the door clicked closed before glancing up to the ceiling. "He's right. I need to tell Barron."

Let the chips fall where they will.

15

AFTER THEIR AFTERNOON dance lessons, Fredrick became more comfortable with the coming Captain's Gala. And giving Leo time with his thoughts seemed like a good thing to do, especially since he saw the love Leo had for Barron, even if Leo didn't. *But he will, I'm sure.* The time alone gave Fredrick the opportunity to think about his situation here and what he left behind.

Given all he'd learned, the war with the Nazis had been awful with so many good people lost in Holocaust and the war itself. Perhaps he was lucky to have missed all the conflict. *Maybe I could have done something, helped to have saved people or at least died trying.* He shook the thought away, none of that mattered now, what he wanted now was to know what happened to his family and to Wilhelm. As he dug deeper into the war's history, he learned that Wilhelm's father died (he had become a low-level Nazi officer). *He always was a monster.* His death occurred during the liberation of Berlin, near the end of the war. Unfortunately, Fredrick couldn't find any other mention of the rest of Wilhelm's family or Wilhelm.

As for his own parents, brother, and sister, he uncovered nothing. He hoped finding something on Wilhelm's dad would have given him a way to find out something about his relations. But he came up empty-handed. He prayed they lived long lives, but his heart told him differently.

Not knowing is the worst. There're still the genealogy websites. Maybe I should look into those.

"Hey, you got this," Leo whispered to Fredrick. "You'll do great out there." He pulled at his formal jacket's sleeves to adjust them.

Fredrick glanced at Leo and put on a smile. "Thank you." He shoved the thoughts of life before the *Hawaiian Sun* away and focused on his current surroundings. Since he was comfortable with the waltz, he and Leo spent more time on the swing, which wasn't too difficult and Fredrick found to be a lot of fun. However, when Leo suggested the jive, that was too much for Fredrick to wrap his mind and body around. Leo said they'd have more time to practice, and by the time he was ready to renew his contract, he'd be a proper dancer.

A six-month contract. At least I have a home for six months. Hopefully, I'll be able to figure out what happened to me.

With another glance around, Fredrick went over the details for the night. Instead of the two seatings for dinner, a buffet had been set up in the main dining room and additional food stations were set up at all the bars, allowing guests to grab their dinner whenever they wanted and enjoy the reception at their leisure. Specialty cocktails would be served by the wait and bar staff throughout the night, but if guests wanted something different they could order and pay for the libation at the bar. The jazz music that Fredrick was growing used to played throughout the ship. From everything Fredrick saw, the ship and the crew went all out for the reception. All guest-facing crewmembers were dressed in their formal attire. Guests were dressed in gowns, tuxedos, or a combination of both.

Fredrick caught sight of Minh and Ainsley, their outfits once again designed to go together. Ainsley's attire was a tuxedo top opened at the neck, showing off their upper chest, while the lower part of the outfit was a floor length gown. In their hand, they held a glittering gold clutch. Minh wore a tuxedo made of the same fabric as Ainsley's outfit. The sight of the two of them together was impressive, as were so many other people—everyone looked incredible.

The photographers will be busy tonight.

Fredrick's outfit wasn't as snazzy as Minh's or Ainsley's but he still reckoned he looked good. As he adjusted his stance, he glanced at Leo and the other Butlers off to one side of the Luau Theater, which buzzed with guests chatting and enjoying the night's offerings. Fredrick hadn't seen Martin Sherman yet, but he was sure the man would be here. In fact, Fredrick was positive there wasn't going to be a person missing from the event.

Of course it doesn't hurt that the Lani Club and the Lani Steakhouse are both closed for the night.

The music lowered as the lights on the main stage rose. Standing in full dress uniform, the captain beamed with a warm expression of greeting. Fredrick couldn't believe that a woman was the captain of an airship. On the *Hindenburg*, only one female crewmember was onboard and she was a steward, like him, so seeing Captain Danielle Monroe standing in full regalia was a sight to behold.

What a wonderful world to be a part of.

"I want to take a moment to welcome you all," Captain Monroe started as the crowd quieted. "Thank you for joining us on our cruise to Hawaii." Applause filled the chamber. "I hope my crew has been taking good care of you." She smiled and there were more cheers and clapping, which Fredrick appreciated, even if he hadn't had a chance to interact with all the guests.

"Tonight, the *Hawaiian Sun* celebrates her eighth year, hosting the unflappable Queer Community on this specialty cruise to Hawaii ..."

The room erupted into more roars and the vivacious noise bounced around the space.

"No, please." She waved her free hand. "It's we who should be applauding you." She stopped and clapped for the guests. Quickly all the crew applauded as well, including Fredrick.

"Now, I don't want to hold up this beautiful night any longer." A waiter arrived with a glass of Champagne resting on a silver serving tray for the Captain. "Here's to all of you and to the *Hawaiian Sun*. Enjoy your evening, everyone." She took the Champagne and raised the glass to the assembly. "Cheers," she toasted before sipping her drink. She was followed by a round of cheers and glasses clinking from all those in attendance. "Now if the lovely Miss Krystal Chandelier would join me on the dance floor, let's get this party started." She handed off her microphone.

Fredrick's cheeks ached from the grin he had on his face, watching the Captain and Miss Chandelier commence dancing. Between the heels and the big hair the performer wore, she towered above the Captain. As the music began the two took to the floor and started dancing.

They look so cute.

"That's our cue." Leo tapped Fredrick's elbow. The others in their department had already moved off.

"Okay. Who should I dance with?"

"I see Sandra, Teresa, Marco and Rick, some of our club guests. I'll dance with Marco and you can dance with Rick," Leo suggested as he moved toward the foursome.

Fredrick inhaled as he noted Aurora had already pulled one of the guests to the floor. Nuwa and Oliver were moving in on a couple of other guests. Tomas had found the cute Montgomery-Clark couple he'd spoken with the day before, asking the shorter of the two men to dance.

"I hope you're all having a good evening." Leo beamed at the group.

"I can't believe we've been doing this for eight years," Marco volunteered. He wore black pants and a cream dinner jacket with black tie.

"We've been having a great time," Rick added, brushing off the sleeve of his jacket. He sported a simple black tuxedo with bowtie and a gold paisley vest, and the combination was striking.

"In that case, we must share a dance." Leo extended his hand to Marco.

"Would you like to dance?" Fredrick asked Rick, smiling as brightly as possible.

"And what are we, chopped liver?" Teresa's voice was lighthearted as she smiled. She stood donned in a lavender gown with thin shoulder straps, and around her neck hung a white gold necklace with a large purple stone.

"I didn't come here to dance with a guy." Sandra's hint of a German accent peeked through her words as she took Teresa's hand. "Plus, you're the only one I want to dance with." She had on a black tuxedo with lavender tie and pocket square.

Leo chuckled. "Well, I expect at least one dance tonight, Sandra."

"We'll see," Sandra teased through her white toothy grin.

"Well, I'll happily give you a spin around the dance floor. It's not every day a handsome man asks me to dance." Rick took Fredrick's hand as they moved to the floor.

"Hey, we danced at our wedding," Marco countered as he and Leo joined the others on the dance floor.

"And how long ago was that?" Rick asked with raised brows.

Before Marco responded, Leo spun him around on the floor and they danced.

Rick laughed. "Your boss is light on his feet, and knows how to mediate a discussion."

"He's quite the dancer," Fredrick agreed.

"And you're not bad either."

The two moved in time with the music. Fredrick noted how many of the crew had partnered with guests to ensure the dance floor was full. There were So many same-sex couples dancing together and enjoying the event. This was something that Fredrick would have never deemed possible, and yet here he was, in the middle of this beautiful event in an airship flying to Hawaii.

Perhaps everything before this trip was a bad dream.

After their spin around the floor, Marco and Rick continued on dancing, as Leo got his waltz with Sandra. Fredrick's heart fluttered as he witnessed everyone moving in time with the music. He would have been twirling around with Teresa, but she confessed that she didn't wear heels often enough and she didn't want to end up with blisters on her feet. With a nod, Fredrick excused himself and found a glass of sparkling water. After his drink, he considered asking Ainsley to dance. Or maybe Minh. He might even ask Elijah, to show that there was no awkwardness between them.

Ensure they all feel like nothing happened and that they can still enjoy their trip.

"You're quite the dancer," Martin's voice caught Fredrick's attention as he appeared, glass of Champagne in hand.

"It's good to see you here, Mr. Shermin—Martin." Fredrick offered and took a sip of his drink.

"Unfortunately, I had some reports to send off, and I had some research to do." His eyebrows rose. "Did you miss me?"

Fredrick cleared his throat. "It's our job to ensure you're having a good time … and I planned on saving you a dance."

Martin finished his Champagne and placed the glass on the table next to him. "In that case, how about it?"

Fredrick stood taller as he finished off his fizzy water. "It would be my pleasure."

The two moved to the dance floor and Martin pulled Fredrick close, their bodies closer than he and Leo were earlier in the day. "I hope you don't mind, but I like to lead."

Being this close to Martin felt incredible and Fredrick's heart skipped several beats at their closeness. He wasn't sure if the butterflies in his stomach were excited or terrified. Either way, he reveled in being joined to Martin in this manner.

This is so nice. So much more intimate. Unglaublich.

"Lead away," Fredrick responded as Martin moved them around the floor. As they danced, Fredrick found himself getting lost in the rhythm of the music and their movements. There was something magical about Martin's firm grip, holding Fredrick in place as they moved, their bodies oscillating together. Fredrick had never felt so safe and so unnerved before. How can this man have this kind of influence on him? How can any man have this kind of impact on any single person?

Martin held him closer and tighter as the melody moved them. Fredrick wanted to melt in Martin's arms, and to stay like this, the two of them dancing amongst the clouds, no one else around. Only him, Martin, and the music, their motion inseparable and exhilarating. This was life; this was living. This was the closeness he and Wilhelm never had when they were together. The blood in his veins and the air in his lungs kept time with their movements. Every part of his body was enthusiastic for what came next under Martin's touch and control.

Martin met Fredrick's gaze. Fredrick was completely adrift in Martin's ravishing hazel eyes. Continuing to move them in and around the other dancers on the floor, Martin's smile widened. "I don't think my dancing has had this kind of effect on anyone in a long time. If ever."

Fredrick inhaled Martin's deep warm oceany scent. "What do you mean?" His own voice was soft and wispy as they continued to sway.

I could stay this way forever.

The grin on Martin's face continued to bloom as he leaned in closer to Fredrick's ear, whispering, "I can feel you ... I mean, I can *feel* you."

"We're dancing," Fredrick cooed. "I can feel you and you can feel me."

"Yes, but I can feel you against my leg." The amusement in Martin's voice was hardly restrained.

As Martin continued to move them, pressing his leg slightly more into Fredrick. Instantly Fredrick felt what Martin was referencing as his stomach dropped. His neck and face blazed.

An angry image of Wilhelm jumped to the forefront of his mind, a scowl filling his otherwise handsome face, his gaze boring deep into Fredrick. "Look at you now. At least I had no choice in the matter. You left me to die. *Hure!*" Wilhelm's words overtook the music and the conversations all around them.

I didn't leave him. I tried to get help. I'm not a whore.

Fredrick would have bolted from the dance floor but that would draw more attention to an already awkward situation. "I'm sorry." His face burned as Wilhelm faded, but the word endured.

Martin's gaze lingered as he guided them in their waltz. "I'm not complaining in the least. In fact, I'm flattered. It's nice knowing I still affect a handsome man in this way."

"We should ... I should ... perhaps we should finish." Fredrick tried to step away, but Martin held him firm.

This can't be happening. I need to get some air.

"You're referring to our dancing, or are you indicating we take care of something else?" He pushed closer to Fredrick, feeling his quickly diminishing state of arousal.

Fredrick cleared his throat. Martin's teasing wasn't helping. He needed to get control of himself. "Our dancing. Yes, I mean our dancing. Now please, if you don't mind."

"Certainly." Martin moved them back toward the table they'd been standing at.

Fredrick took stock of himself and his body. His uniform jacket should cover any embarrassment until he fully softened, which given Wilhelm's accusation, wasn't taking long. "Thank you for the dance." Fredrick forced his voice to be as neutral as possible, the heat still fresh on his face and neck. "Now if you'll excuse me, I should see to the other guests."

Martin didn't take his eyes off Fredrick. A polite, and knowing, expression filled his face. "The dance was my pleasure ... I enjoyed our closeness—all of it."

•　　　•　　　•

Leo made good on his promise to dance with as many of the club-level guests as possible. He caught sight of Fredrick and Martin dancing and he couldn't deny the two made a handsome pair. They both seemed lost in their own world. Fredrick was still new to the *Hawaiian Sun*, but Leo did hope he wouldn't need to remind Fredrick that he should dance with the other guests.

Meh, I'll let them dance at least for a little while longer. Let Fredrick enjoy himself. And Martin.

"Did you save a dance for me?" Leo turned, meeting the bright-eyed gaze of Barron. He stood before Leo in all black tone-on-tone attire, which made his green eyes pop.

"You ... well, you look fantastic," Leo stammered as he scanned the sleeve of his jacket wiping away a piece of lint.

"I bet you say that to all the guests." Barron's tone was good natured and polite, which Leo was grateful for.

"No. Not all." Leo forced what he hoped to be a warm expression as he met Barron's gaze. A flutter of butterflies made their presence known in Leo's stomach and the theater suddenly felt warmer. He cleared his throat.

"About yesterday." Barron's face grew pink. "The tea service, which I'm sure you heard about—"

"Stop, you don't have to." Leo raised a hand, cutting off Barron. "I get it. But you have nothing to apologize for." Leo quickly scanned the Luau Theater; the music helped to mask and alter what was being discussed so no one would hear them. "I'm the one who needs to say sorry." He sipped his almost forgotten soda. "You caught me off-guard."

I'm messing this up. Come on, Leo. Say it. You know you want to. You've wanted to for a long time.

"Leo, you don't have to say anything." Barron's hand shook as he tried to rest his hand on Leo's arm. "if you're not ready. I shouldn't have—"

"Will you please hush?" Leo rested his empty glass on the table next to him. "I'm trying to tell you I think I'm in love with you too." The words rushed from Leo's mouth.

"You think?" Barron questioned with a toothy smirk.

Leo shook his head. "No, I mean I know." He raked a hand through his hair. "Babe, these things aren't easy for me to say." He took a deep breath, catching hints of Barron's spicy sandalwood cologne.

He always smells so good.

"And you think me coming here to tell you how I feel about you is?" Barron shifted his weight from one foot to another. "I've been a wreck, and with Elijah—"

"I don't want to talk about him." Leo's shoulders stiffened as he found himself standing taller. "Fredrick told me what you said to him. Thank you."

Barron snorted. "He's been walking on eggshells since everything went down. I guess Ainsley and Minh tore into him."

"Good," Leo grumbled.

"You don't mean that." Barron's tone softened as he squeezed Leo's arm, before pulling his hand away.

"No, but I wish I did." Leo glanced around and saw Elijah dancing with a bigger guy with brownish red hair and beard.

Looks like he found someone to occupy his time.

"To be clear"—Barron stopped fidgeting, calling Leo's attention to him— "I meant everything I told you. I don't care about that whole other thing as long as you're healthy and we can still enjoy each other."

Leo chuckled as his cheeks warmed. "Thank you, and so we're both on the same page, I do love you, Barron. It took me a minute to realize. Also, I can't wait for us to have"—he lowered his voice—"some sexy time again." His heart beat fast as his chest and shoulders lightened. The tension he didn't know he held in his neck slowly vaporized.

Barron's face brightened and a hint of pink kissed his cheeks and lips. "I know I can't kiss you, but I want to."

Leo peeked around to see if anyone watched them, but he saw no one. He leaned in and kissed Barron's lips softly. "For you, babe, I think I can break the rule this one time. But only this once."

"Thank you for doing that." Barron beamed at him, his stance and voice relaxing at the same time. "Now, can I have my dance? I've been waiting all night to get you alone."

"Absolutely." Leo reached out his hand to Barron, pulling him in for a hug, and took them out on the dance floor.

Leo watched the others dance as music filled the air. Before he gave himself completely over to Barron and their dance, he caught sight of each of his team. They were all dancing with various guests, including Fredrick, who danced and chatted with Barron's friend, Minh. He spun Barron, gazing into Barron's dazzling green eyes as they moved around the dance floor. This was only the second night of the trip. What else did this cruise have in store for him and the others?

I'm so happy. This is going to be an unforgettable trip.

16

F REDRICK RELAXED HIS HEAD on the bulkhead as he stared out the window of the airship. The first rays of the morning light had begun to replace the night sky as the ship moved through the air, the airship's interior lights dimming. Over the last couple of days, he grew more amazed at the grace and speed of the ship. So many advances since the *Hindenburg* flew—he can see why Leo wanted to become a Captain. They approached Hilo, and from everything he'd learned from the other crew members, the Hilo International Airport also doubled as a zeppelin terminal for the giant airships, boasting three landing strips.

I wonder if we'll see any other airships?

As the island continued to fill more of his view, Fredrick's thoughts replayed the prior night's events. Was Wilhelm right? How can he even think of another man given what happened? Wilhelm and he were going to run away together and now he found himself attracted to another man. However, Martin seemed to take great pleasure in the lift in his pants.

Does that make me a whore? Is Wilhelm right? But I caught him and Gerhard together. Did Wilhelm care for me, or was he only using me to get free? And all Martin and I did was dance.

Huge planes landed and took off as more of the morning light woke up the island. Off to the side, Fredrick caught sight of another airship. The airship was huge with a giant logo painted on the side, though he couldn't quite make out the name under the logo. The ship didn't look like a luxury ship, but something for freight. Platforms rose and lowered, holding large cargo containers as big trucks waited for the new shipments to be loaded so they could go off and deliver their wares.

Absolutely incredible.

Along the coast, large hotels coated in bright tropical colors came into focus. The city wasn't nearly as large as he imagined, based on the way his fellow crewmates spoke. Hilo looked more like a large town—tropical, yes, but nothing as large as he pictured in his head.

A clatter of trays caught his attention and he glanced over his shoulder in the direction of the noise, half-expecting to see Wilhelm glaring at him.

"Sorry." One of the crew he didn't know waved. "Still waking up."

Fredrick nodded without a word as he turned to the window, leaving the team member to get their breakfast so she could carry on with her day. He had the morning and afternoon off, as most of the guests would be ashore enjoying the sights. He didn't have to be on duty again until 1400. "I should be getting some sleep." The city, much like the ship, leisurely came to life. Peeking at his barely touched tray, he wasn't sure of the time. He might check his timepiece if he was curious, but that felt like too much effort at the moment. Sleep avoided him for most of the night—every time he closed his eyes, Wilhelm was there to accuse him. Instead of tossing and turning, he decided to get up, shower, and come sit here as the day came into being.

"There you are," Leo's voice interrupted Fredrick's quiet contemplation. "When I got up I didn't see you in your bunk." He placed his tray down. "I got worried."

"I didn't sleep well," Fredrick said no lie as he continued to monitor the happenings outside the ship.

"I hate when that happens." Leo sat across from Fredrick. "How'd you like the Captain's Gala last night? Looks like you had a good time." Leo shuffled items around before picking up what Fredrick assumed to be his glass to take a drink.

Fredrick's eyes closed, blocking out the activity outside and inside the ship. He sighed; this time Wilhelm didn't greet him.

"Fuck, what happened?" Leo asked. "Did someone get handsy?"

Fredrick shook his head. "No, everyone behaved themselves." In the end, he faced Leo, taking him in. He was dressed in civilian attire: dark jeans with fade marks (that seemed to be a fashion) and a short-sleeved pullover shirt in an orange color that flattered his natural coloring. He appeared ready to enjoy his morning and early afternoon off.

"Good." Leo took a bite of his bacon. "What happened?"

Fredrick wasn't sure how to explain. He wasn't even sure he wanted to discuss the matter. But Leo always seemed genuine in his offers. "I had a personal …" Fredrick lowered his voice and leaned in. "Well, something … something happened with Martin when we danced and it was rather embarrassing."

"For him or you?" Leo leaned closer and lowered his voice to mimic Fredrick's body language and volume.

"Me." The heat in Fredrick's cheeks and neck betrayed him much like his *schwanz* did last night.

"Oh." Leo shifted in his seat. "Well, whatever it is, you can tell me."

"It's childish." Fredrick studied his fingernails as he couldn't bear to meet Leo's gaze. "My manhood stiffened when Martin and I danced and he noticed …" He peeked at Leo to discern his reaction.

Have I made a mistake in telling him?

Leo cleared his throat. "I see." He rubbed his chin, hiding his mouth before meeting Fredrick's gaze. "These things happen. Look, it's no big deal … or it might be if Martin noticed …" A smirk filled his face.

Fredrick's lips dipped along with his shoulders. He didn't see the humor in this. What if Martin mentioned something? That wasn't acceptable. Fredrick doubted he would get in trouble, but still.

Leo sat taller after clearing his throat again. "Either way, good for you?" His voice rose at the end.

"That's not the worst of it," Fredrick huffed as he continued. "When Martin noticed and made a comment, I saw Wilhelm and he accused me of …" He shook his head. "He called me a whore,"

Fredrick blurted out before looking out the ship's window. The *Hawaiian Sun* appeared to be in a holding pattern off the coast. The groundcrew seemed to double around the carrier airship.

Perhaps that's why we're sitting here.

"Oh, Fredrick, I'm sorry." Leo rested a hand on Fredrick's. "That had to be awful."

"I know the image of Wilhelm was only in my mind, but still … it felt so real."

"Don't let that take away your light and sunshine." Leo's voice was firm as he squeezed Fredrick's hand. "Listen, if every guy who got caught being *bricked up* was a whore, well, every man on the planet would be wearing a giant 'A' on their clothes. You did nothing wrong."

"Haven't I? I'm not so sure."

Leo shook his head, his tone still soft. "Didn't you say Wilhelm cheated on you? That fact hasn't changed."

His eyes had started to sting, but he refused to shed any tears—not now and not in front of Leo. He inhaled as deeply as his lungs would allow before speaking. "But he's dead, and I'm here, and it all seems so fast."

Leo remained quiet as he took several bites of his meal before speaking. "I can't speak to what's too fast and what's not for you. But I will say, seeing you with Mr. Sherman dancing last night, your expression … well, the look wasn't your work default look. That has to mean something. What did Martin say?"

Fredrick pulled himself from the view, it seemed like the cargo airship was still a hive of activity. The distraction helped him focus his thoughts and keep his emotions in check. "I didn't tell him about Wilhelm, and as for the other matter, he seemed flattered."

"Okay." Leo continued to focus his attention on Fredrick, which he appreciated. Not many people cared enough to give you their whole attention.

He's a good man.

"I ended our dance quickly after that."

"I understand … getting a … well, having …" Leo had a sheepish expression. "I think we've all been there before. Sometimes our bodies have a mind of their own. As for the vision of Wilhelm, well, my guess is it's your uncertainty manifesting itself."

"Probably." Fredrick huffed. "It's so hard … you know."

"What?" Leo asked. "It's happening right now? You're insatiable."

Fredrick's brows narrowed before a chuckle escaped his mouth. "You know what I mean."

Leo grinned. "I do, but I needed to see you smile."

Fredrick closed his eyes and exhaled. Talking with Leo was making him feel better, despite the brash comments.

"I wouldn't let what happened last night ruin this trip," Leo added, his voice less flippant. "Or what may or may not happen between you and Martin." He took several bites of his breakfast. "Listen, after we finish eating, why don't we go down to the cockpit? We can watch them land our zep. I asked Captain Monroe if I could observe our landings in Hawaii, and I doubt she'll mind you tagging along."

"I wouldn't mind watching." Fredrick's neck and shoulders relaxed. "I never got to see the docking on my old ship. We were always too busy."

"Excellent. Once we get cleared by customs, we can head into town and check out your money. The fresh Hawaiian air and sun will do you some good. Help you clear your mind."

"Will we have enough time, before I'm on shift?"

I think the time away from the ship will do me some good.

"Yep." Leo pulled out his smartphone and looked at the time. "We've got about a half hour to finish up here." He ate the rest of his breakfast while Fredrick watched outside the ship, noting the few clouds huddling around the mountains off in the distance. The cargo airship in the foreground with the mountains and clouds in the background made for a beautiful photo.

If only I had a camera.

•   •   •

The cockpit was nothing like what Fredrick ever expected to see, where were the pullies, nobs, levers and steering wheels. All the instruments were mechanical, large screens showing display readouts and maps of the Island. Big monitors and buttons filled most of the stations. He did notice something akin to radar—the *Hindenburg* didn't have radar, but they were planning on adding the system once they returned to Germany. Several crew members manned different stations, some sitting, some standing. All were focused on the task at hand. The sheer space and marvels surrounding Fredrick made him take pause and stare.

"I love being in the cockpit." Leo leaned into Fredrick so they weren't talking loudly. "I try and get down here as often as I can, but it's not nearly as nice as the lounge, eh?"

"Gentlemen," Captain Monroe called both Fredrick and Leo to attention. "Welcome to the heart of the *Hawaiian Sun*."

"Captain." Leo gestured toward Fredrick. "I hope you don't mind, I brought Mr. Rudolph to watch, since this is his first cruise on our zep. I figured the experience might be informative."

"As long as you both stay out of the way." The Captain stood in her duty uniform, a contrast to her dress uniform the night before. "Our landing today should be relatively routine, since we don't have any weather to worry about."

"Thank you, Captain," Fredrick spoke as he continued to glance around the space. "I appreciate the opportunity."

"I understand you joined us from the *Hindenburg 2000*. She's a beautiful ship," Captain Monroe stated, eyeing Fredrick up and down.

This was the first time he'd met the Captain, and if he would have known, he would have worn his uniform, but instead he stood greeting his superior in light-colored jeans and a simple blue short-sleeved button-down shirt.

"How did you enjoy working under Captain Bauer? I had the pleasure of meeting him a few years ago—seems a bit of a stuffed shirt."

Fredrick pondered a moment before speaking. If Captain Bauer was anything like Captain Pruss or Chief Steward Kubis, the man was probably serious and focused on his duty. He remembered seeing the photo of him from the day before; the Captain did smile in some of the photos, but the expression didn't seem natural. "I never directly interacted with him," Fredrick started. "However, he always struck me as focused on his duty and doing his best by his zeppelin and crew."

Captain Monroe's grin filled her face. "Spoken like a true diplomat. I can see why Mr. Asher nabbed you up."

"He hasn't disappointed, and the guests seem to like him," Leo responded. He had moved over to one of the stations, watching a woman at her terminal. "Aisha, why are we still holding if the landing pad is clear?"

"The airport is stacked up with takeoffs and the air cargo ship is still floating about. So, we have to wait," a man said from his seated station. He had what Fredrick supposed to be a headset on but one of his ears was uncovered.

"And people question why I hate flying," Leo expressed through pinched lips.

"Well, it's not the planes. The cargo zep had some platform issues earlier, so they are trying to clear the landing pad of the work crews for us … guess they needed the extra space."

"Thank you, Mr. Johnson and Ms. Rossi," a tall man asserted. His uniform was as crisp as his words. He stood next to the Captain. "And not all flying is bad, Mr. Asher."

Clearly her First Officer.

Captain Monroe chuckled. "Don't forget, Mr. Asher, we nabbed First Officer Erikson from the airlines."

"Right. Sorry, sir." Leo swallowed as his skin pinkened.

"Which airline?" Fredrick asked the First Officer; the man's slight accent caught his attention. "If you don't mind my asking."

The tall man was German, there was no doubt about it. He recognized that same steadfast expression he saw on the officers of the *Hindenburg.* "German Airways."

"Not Lufthansa?" Fredrick asked, surprised. The only airline he knew was Lufthansa, so Germany having an additional airline filled him with pride.

"No." First Officer Erikson turned to the windows of the cockpit.

Leo leaned in. "Bet there's a story there," he whispered.

Fredrick's brows rose has he bobbed his head in agreement.

"Mr. Cruz, let's keep the Sun nice and level. We don't want any of our guests to fall out of their beds, or worse, slip in the shower."

"Aye Captain," Mr. Cruz responded. The Officer tapped at his station and moved a knobby handle thing. He must be one of the airship's elevator men—they had to keep the ship balanced and level.

I'm surprised they aren't able to do this mechanically by now.

"Ms. Rossi"—The Captain studied one of the screens in front of her— "if you don't mind, let's reduce our altitude to 200 meters so when we get our clearing from the tower, we can move into position."

"Aye Captain, changing altitude to 200 meters," Rossi confirmed.

"Captain, I've heard from the tower," Johnson relayed. "We're clear to proceed to pad two. I'm sending the heading and speed now."

"Understood," Captain Monroe acknowledged. "Well, everyone, time to land this bird."

"Here we go." Leo bounced on the balls of his feet.

The dance of the command crew reminded Fredrick of how he and the other stewards on the *Hindenburg* worked. They had a shorthand and would anticipate each other's actions. It was a talent that was typical of any team that had worked together for a long time. This was also something he noticed with Leo and his new crewmates.

As the airship moved closer to the landing pad, the crew, Leo, and Fredrick had 360-degree unobstructed views of Hilo and the airport. The cargo airship still hung at landing pad one, but the commotion on the ground seemed to not be the hive of activity as before. The officers didn't rely on sight alone, but had their screens and gauges to assist them. As the ship gradually moved closer, Fredrick spotted the ground crew rushing about, clearing their landing space.

"You feel that?" Leo whispered.

"What?"

"We're not quite level." Leo pointed to the horizon. "Look."

Fredrick barely registered a shift, but now that Leo pointed out the change, he saw and sensed the angle. He glanced over toward Mr. Cruz who was working his controls.

"Keep us steady, Mr. Cruz," The Captain instructed with not so much as a glance in his direction.

"Yes, Captain."

Some things never change. That is one challenging job.

Commands from the Captain batted around the cockpit as the officers and the ship responded in kind. As he glanced at Leo, the excitement that dripped off him was tangible.

He absolutely loves this. But is this where he belongs. He's so good at his job, and I can see him thriving as Head Steward. These officers seem so rigid and that isn't Leo.

"Forty meters," Ms. Rossi called out.

"Prepare all moorings and landing gear," Mr. Erickson, the First Officer, ordered.

Leo leaned in. "This is incredible. I mean, all these minor movements and adjustments and yet I bet none of the guests are feeling a thing."

"Touchdown," Ms. Rossi called out. "We have touchdown."

"Landing confirmed," Ms. Patel responded.

"All stations prepare for docking. Mr. Johnson, please contact Chief Hernandez and inform him he can begin refueling and other docking procedures as soon as we get clearance from ground control," Captain Monroe instructed. "Let's lock her up and prepare for our first day in Hawaii. Well done, everyone."

"All stations prepare for docking," Mr. Johnson spoke into his microphone. "Chief Hernandez, once we get clearance from ground control, you are good to go."

"And you're sure you want to do this?" Fredrick asked.

Leo considered a moment. "It can be a lot."

"Engineering has confirmed, Captain." Mr. Johnson tapped away.

Captain Monroe acknowledged, "Well, Mr. Asher, did our landing and docking meet your expectations? Are you going to be willing to make the move from guest services to ship's operations? You know you're going to have to give up your cushy position and begin at the bottom again."

Leo's expression shifted, his smile dropping slightly. "It's something to consider, and with a landing like that ..."

Captain Monroe looked at Fredrick. "What about you, Mr. Rudolph? Do I have another officer in the making?"

"I'm happy in guest services, Captain," Fredrick responded. As interesting as this was, he enjoyed working with the guests and interacting with people.

She laughed.

"Captain, thank you. This was incredible." The grin on Leo's face went from ear to ear. Fredrick didn't think he had seen him like this since they met.

"What'a'ya think, Mr. Erikson? Should we give Sofia an assistant when we arrive at Nawiliwili?"

The First Officer glanced from the Captain to Leo to Ms. Rossi, Sofia, at her station. "What do you think, Sofia?"

"I wouldn't mind having an extra set of eyes," Sofia proclaimed. "As long as he listens to my instructions and does as I say."

"Seriously?" Leo's gaze bounced from person to person in the cockpit.

"We'll see what the weather's like and if we have as good of conditions as today. If we're 100%, I don't see the harm as long as Tammy is okay with you starting your shift at 0400," The Captain continued. "Also, we wouldn't want to keep you from your trainee. Would it be okay with you, Mr. Rudolf?"

"I don't think I'm the one you need to check with." Fredrick smiled. "But I don't mind."

"Excellent."

"And Captain," Fredrick called her attention again, "thank you for letting me watch. Seeing the landing process is something I'll never forget."

Captain Monroe offered a slight tilt of her head in recognition. "Now let's finish up here." The Captain turned to her elevator man with a grin. "I believe, Mr. Cruz, we were half a degree off-pitch, which means you're buying the coffee."

"I'm never off-pitch, Captain." Mr. Cruz tried to hide his grin. "That had to be an air pocket."

"Are you arguing with your Captain?" Captain Monroe had a raised brow but it was countered by the grin on her face.

"Coffee it is," Cruz responded as the officers, Leo, and Fredrick all laughed.

17

L EO'S MIND BUZZED with excitement and anxiety as they crossed over to the airfield's ground transportation center. Being in the Cockpit of the *Hawaiian Sun* and watching the landing procedure was exhilarating. His heart banged like a drum in his chest and his cheeks ached from the expression he had on his face. Yes, if he wanted to make the change from hospitality to operations he would be at the bottom, but given that the company covered any additional education he might need, it might be worth it.

I love working with people and helping guests. If something happened and I couldn't become Captain, I'd still get to fly the zeps, but I wouldn't get to work with the guests anymore. Is that a change I want to make? So much to consider.

There was still one major step, and that was to get the endorsement of one of the senior officers.

It'd be great if Captain Monroe endorsed me, but any of the officers would do. Would they be willing to do that?

If he wasn't with Fredrick, he would have rushed and talked through making the change with Barron. Barron was great at weighing the pros and cons. How would this affect his future with

Barron? There would be a lot of changes and he'd be away for longer periods of time. Was that fair to Barron?

I can tell him later and we can talk about my career.

"Thank you for taking me to see the landing this morning; it was breathtaking. And the Captain was so nice. I didn't see a lot of that on the *Hindenburg*. I'm not saying they were awful—they weren't. They were different, more ..." Fredrick chuckled. "German. Can we walk to the store?"

As the warm mid-morning air swept over him, Leo glanced over his shoulder at the *Hawaiian Sun*. "Nah, I ordered a rideshare." Leo checked his phone; the guy should be here soon. He stuffed the phone in his pocket and dusted off his orange polo shirt. He would've been in shorts and a t-shirt if he had his druthers, but they were in the cockpit and he wanted to dress more professionally. He peeked over at Fredrick. Everything he wore, even his regular jeans and simple blue shirt looked fabulous on him. "It's too far to walk to Kamehameha Avenue. If you want, we can grab some lunch before we return." His lips curled. "And goodness knows, we don't want to mess with your perfect appearance."

"What?" Fredrick looked down at his outfit.

"All I'm saying is you're way too pretty to walk outside in this humidity." Leo laughed.

"You're teasing?" Fredrick asked.

"Yes. I'll admit, I'm jealous of how well you wear all your clothes ... It's not fair."

Fredrick shook his head, his dimples making an appearance. "Thank you, but you're incredibly handsome as well."

Leo hummed, not believing the comment, but appreciating the flattery.

"I can't believe any of the money I have is worth much," Fredrick commented as he glanced around the trellised shelter.

"That reminds me"—Leo pulled out his smartphone— "do you have any coins or is everything paper?"

Fredrick pulled out his wallet and drew out his cash. "Mostly bills, but I do have a few coins." He stuffed the money into his billfold, and dug into his pocket to remove the change he had with him. He held the coins out for Leo to examine.

There were pennies, nickels, three dimes, and seventy-five cents in quarters. "Wait. Are those silver dollars?" Leo reached over and picked up one of Fredrick's coins.

"I think so."

"Wow. No, that's a half-dollar." Leo scrutinized the coin, before giving it back to Fredrick. "Let me see the pennies."

Fredrick handed the pennies over. "Why?"

Leo turned the pennies over in his hand. "Well, these are Wheat Pennies: 1930, 1935, and 1936."

"I don't understand."

"These might be worth a lot of money." Leo handed the pennies back to Fredrick.

"You think so?"

Random conversations made their way to Leo, along with the rustling of backpacks, purses, and clothing. "Put these away." Leo gestured as more people, guests and some fellow crewmates, joined them in the waiting area. "Uncle Billie will know for sure."

Everyone's probably too excited to pay us any attention, but you can never be too sure.

"I didn't know you had family here." Fredrick stuffed the money back into his jeans pocket.

Leo chuckled. "I don't."

A white Subaru 4-door wagon pulled up in front of them and stopped. The passenger side window rolled down. A man with dark hair and puffy cheeks leaned over to the passenger window and called out, "Aloha—you Leo?"

"That's our ride," Leo told Fredrick. Pulling his phone back out, he checked the rideshare details, before waving to the driver. "Pika?" Leo responded.

"That'd be me, brah." Pika sat back.

Leo turned to Fredrick. "Let's boogie."

Fredrick's brows rose as he got in the backseat of the car. Leo opened the passenger door and plopped into the well-worn seat. The Subaru's tan and black interior gleamed and there wasn't a speck of dirt to be seen. Despite the lack of cushion in Leo's seat, Pika took pride in his car and kept it well-maintained, at least on the inside. Next to his door handle, in the door's storage bucket, were a couple of bottles of water.

As Leo glanced at the driver, he got hints of jasmine, but he wasn't sure if that was from the inside the car or from the Pīkake plants nearby. He had wonderfully tanned deep skin and tattoos were visible on his arms and neck. Leo loved the traditional Hawaiian markings and considered getting one, but doing so, somehow, seemed disrespectful, and the company policy dress code prohibited visible tattoos of any kind.

Pika glanced at his phone for their destination. "Uncle Billie's place?" He laughed as he glanced over his shoulder, checking for traffic. "Help yourselves to some water."

"Uncle Billie's a friend," Leo replied as the car started moving. He tugged on his seatbelt to click it into place.

"I hope so. How's the air back there, brah?"

Leo glanced over his shoulder and saw Fredrick was focused out the window. "*Vas?* Sorry, what?"

"Cousin, you need me to turn up the AC?" Pika asked again, pointing to the controls on the center console.

"Are you warm? Do you want more air?" Leo asked Fredrick, then to Pika he said, "He's from Germany, so ..."

"Ah, no worries, brah."

"No. I'm fine." Fredrick scanned the interior of the vehicle. "I've never ridden in an automobile like this before. It's wonderful." The window next to Fredrick started to go down and he jumped away from it.

Pika laughed. "Serious, brah?"

Fredrick smiled and watched as the window went down all the way, then back up. "Marvelous."

Such a little kid. And I imagined I was bad in the cockpit today.

Leo huffed out a bit of a chuckle as he yanked at the seatbelt so it didn't cut into his neck. "You know how Europeans are."

Pika raised a brow as he continued driving them down the road. "Whatever you say, brah."

•　　•　　•

Leo appreciated how Pika was able to easily move them around the traffic. The breeze with the car's windows down filled the cabin with more of the jasmine, and what Leo was sure had to be gardenia scents. He loved all the tropical smells of the Islands— that was something San Jose didn't have, that he wished it did.

As they turned off Kamehameha Avenue, Leo caught sight of their destination: Hilo Coin Trove was a small shop off the main street. The building was nothing special and typical of the other structures around it. Pika pulled the car to a stop in front of the Palace theater. "Here you go," he said. "Don't forget to rate me, brah—I've had a couple of bad Haoles."

Leo unbuckled his seatbelt. "I got you, cousin. Mahalo." He opened the car door with a click, stepped out, and inhaled the moist tropical Hilo air.

Gardenia, jasmine, plumeria, and hibiscus. Mmm.

Fredrick stepped out of the car and watched Pika drive off. "He has a nice vehicle. And it was so tidy." He sniffed the air. "The air smells so lovely ... if not warmer than I'm used to. Things are so different here." He unbuttoned the second to the top button of his blue shirt and tugged at it, revealing his upper chest and his untrimmed chest hair. He fanned his face with his hand.

Leo only gave Fredrick's chest a passing glance. "Let me guess— you don't own a car back home?" Leo pulled out his smartphone, checking the time.

"No." Fredrick moved under the awning of the theater, getting out of the sun.

"You'll get used to the heat, but the humidity can be the killer. Anyway, you'll find public transit here in the US is nothing like Europe." Leo pointed across the street. "That's Uncle Billie's place."

The old rust-stained building had dirt streaking the façade. However, they could still make out the stylized filigree inscription at the top of the building reading 1920, the year it was built. The art deco style seemed to substantiate the claim of the structure's age. The upkeep on the building left a lot to be desired. The shop needed a good pressure wash and the green painted concrete in front of the doors also required love and attention, as the color was all but faded.

Leo wasn't sure what the original use had been, but now the location had been divided into two separate stores. On the left was a dance studio and on the right was the coin shop. Bars covered the big picture windows and doors encouraging people to keep walking. In the corner of the building, a security camera with a glowing red light watched them.

Uncle Billie didn't mess around with security.

"There used to be a great restaurant next door, but the owner tore it down a few years ago. Probably hoping for something better." He shrugged.

Fredrick peered up and down the street. "Is this place safe?"

Leo took him by the arm. "Absolutely. Now come on, I don't want to keep Uncle Billie waiting."

Moving them out of the shade and into the *Hawaiian sun*, Leo got them across the street. As they walked into the shop, a buzzer sounded. "Aloha, Uncle!" he called out as they walked through the front door. The burst of cool air instantly sent a small shudder down Leo's spine. Disappointedly, all the wonderful scents from outside vanished as the door closed behind them.

That's always the tradeoff: cool air or the smells of the Island.

"Is that you, Leo?" a deep voice called from the rear of the store.

"It is, Uncle." Leo took in the shop—nothing ever changed, only getting older. The store had looked the same since the first time he came here, with its glass display cases holding different collectable items, and more security cameras scattered about. Billie carried some of everything that the tourist might want, including some high value items which warranted all the security. However, his bread and butter were his cases of coins. He mostly dealt with US money, but he had quite a bit of Japanese and other Asian countries' currency.

Leo never got into coin collecting, but since he traveled a lot, knowing about Billie had been a godsend.

You never know what, if anything, a guest is going to give you as a tip.

Uncle Billie appeared from the back room wearing a bright red Hawaiian shirt, shorts, and flipflops. His Hawaiian complexion and stature promised a warm welcome, but his face often countered any welcome his posture presented. Peeking out from under his left shirt sleeve was one of Uncle Billie's traditional tattoos, a collection of intricate shapes and shading in a beautiful tapestry. He also had a similar one on his left leg. Leo never asked about the meaning behind the markings, but he knew there was an important story there, one he would learn about one day. "How's Kiana doing? You keeping track of her like you promised?"

Leo smiled. "I spoke with her last week. She's doing well on the American Eagle, and she told me she's gonna be home in between her current contract and her next one."

"Good—she needs to see her mother." He moved over to one of the counters, brushing past a flowering yellow with orange flecks

Orchid, and took up a perch on his seat, next to the cash register. "Who's your *haole* friend? This the guy you texted me about?"

Leo gestured toward Fredrick. "Fredrick, this is William Kekoa."

Fredrick stepped forward with a bright smile and stuck out his hand.

Billie eyed him up and down, working his jaw back and forth, before taking Fredrick's hand. "You work on the *Hawaiian Sun* with Leo?" Billie asked, not releasing his grip.

"Yes, Mr. Kekoa."

"Bah, call me Uncle Billie." Billie released Fredrick's hand. "Any friend of Leo is a friend to me. Now show me what you have." He leaned back on his chair, resting his hands on his stomach. His salt and pepper dark hair had been cut short and his skin had a fresh glow to it. Once he smiled, the entire atmosphere changed in the shop.

Now this is the Uncle Billie I've come to know.

Fredrick reached into his pocket and dug out his wallet. He took out the various bills and placed them on the counter in numerical order. Then, he pulled out the change he had.

"I think Fredrick has a couple of Wheat Pennies that might be worth something."

"Do I come to your airship and tell you your business?" Uncle Billie's gaze bore into Leo, the agreeableness vanishing from his face.

Heat rose to Leo's neck and face in an instant. "No, Uncle."

"Let's see what you have here." Billie shifted on his perch and picked up the first bill, studying it a moment before putting it down. He scanned the change and the other US notes on the counter without saying a word. He picked up several of the coins and flipped them over and over again. He pulled out his pocket magnifying glass to review a coin. He then dropped the coin on the counter with the magnifying glass, stood and hurried to the front door of his shop, locking the door, and flipping the sign to 'closed'. "What is this, Leo? *Ho'opili 'oe i kēia malihini i ko'u hale kū'ai. He aha kēia e pili ana?*"

"Uncle?" Leo asked, confused. The Hawaiian rushed from Billie's mouth so quickly he wasn't sure if he caught it all. The big man stood to block the exit and glowered at both of them. "I didn't bring him here to cause trouble. I figured you'd help him."

"Jesus! How'd you get all that?" Billie turned to Fredrick, pointing to the money on the counter. "You can't bring stolen items here. I won't have it!" His voice grew louder as his face became red.

"I don't steal! I'm no *dieb*," Fredrick fired, stepping away from the larger man. "I worked hard for this money—they were tips. I saved—" He stopped speaking.

"Let's all take a breath." Leo needed to deescalate the situation. "Come on, Uncle."

Billie's gaze narrowed, but he finally took in a deep lungful of air.

Leo faced Fredrick, gesturing for Fredrick to breathe. They breathed together. Then Leo took up a position between both men. "Now, Uncle, why would you say that?"

Billie pointed to the counter. "If that's real, and I have no reason to doubt my eyes, what I've seen so far is worth ..." He ran a hand through his salt and pepper hair. "Lord." He moved past Leo and Fredrick to look at the money on his counter again. He held up one of the half silver dollars. "This coin. This one coin ..." He shook his head. "At least $4,000. I'll have to double check." He put the coin down and picked up one of the quarters. "$900, maybe more."

"For a coin?" Fredrick barked out a laugh. "This is some kind of joke. It's nothing. It's a quarter."

Billie eyed him up and down. "A unique US quarter. This is a 1927-S Standing Liberty Quarter. I've only ever seen one." He put the coin down. "And you swear you didn't get this in some unsavory way?"

"I did not!" Fredrick held firm. "I'm a hard worker and I would never sully myself to get money."

Leo touched Fredrick's arm, where there was a tremble.

He's upset.

"Many guests tip us for the work we do, or for better service. I had one couple offer me a lot of money to get them a motor before the other guests—they were in some sort of a hurry." Fredrick's words were strained, but he appeared to be calming down.

"He's not wrong," Leo added. "Remember when I got the gold coin? Uncle, when Fredrick arrived in San Jose, that was all the money he had. The airlines lost his baggage. It was a big mess. I assure you I have all the paperwork on Fredrick, and everything checks out:

background check, work visa, employment documentation, all of it. He's a good guy."

Billie stood quiet, examining both men as he drummed his fingers on the display case. "Okay, he would've had to come through Customs and Immigration."

"Of course," Leo agreed.

Thank God, he's starting to see reason and come around.

"And they didn't stop you or say anything about your *collection*?" His gaze narrowed on Fredrick.

"No," Fredrick spoke after taking a beat. "No one said anything. I didn't know anything until Leo pointed this all out."

"Customs only looks for large sums of cash." Billie shook his head. "*Lolo* fools. Okay, well, you've lucked out. Someone clearly didn't know what they gave you." He picked up a few of the notes and shook his head, picking up his glass again and putting the device to his eye. "Probably some stupid kid who raided his grandparents' sock drawer after they died."

"Uncle, do you think Fredrick's got something good here?"

Billie put down the glass and the money. "I'd say there's about $13,000 worth of coins and notes here, but I have to check a bit more."

"What?" Leo and Fredrick said in unison. The nerves Leo had been holding broke free as a laugh.

"But how?" Fredrick questioned. "How is this possible? It's just money."

"Old and rare money, though not all of it." He held up a five dollar note. "This is worth maybe $6.50. Not really worth much."

That made a lot more sense to Fredrick than the other numbers Uncle Billie had been giving him.

How did Fredrick get all this money? He'd gotten some odd tips in the past but nothing like this. Everything Fredrick has is from before the 1940s. Maybe his grandfather took it off a dead soldier during World War II.

Leo pushed the images from his mind. "What does he do?" he asked. "Will you buy any of it? Should he sell it?"

"Some, but not all." Uncle Billie looked up at Fredrick. "I'll only buy a few things if you want to sell them. I'd like to keep the sale under $7,500 for banking and tax purposes. It's better for you too, but since you're a foreign national, I'm not sure how that'll work. Either way, I'll ..." He moved the coins he was interested in, including the four half dollars. "These. I'll take these, and I'll give you $7,365 for it."

Leo had to bite back his threatening outburst.

Holy shit! Way to go, Fredrick. Lucky fucker.

Fredrick looked at Uncle Billie. "That is ... that is more money ... are you sure?"

Uncle Billie sat deeper and met Fredrick's gaze. "Listen, Fredrick, I'm not in this for charity, and since you're Leo's friend ... Leo's been watching after my niece. I'll be straight with you. Despite what I'm offering you, I can put this one coin ..." He picked up one of the half dollars. "I should be able to sell it for ... well, at least five grand, either here in my shop or online."

"Billie, are you serious?" *I'm going to need to pay more attention to the cash I get.*

"I never joke about my business, and there are always stupid *haoles* willing to part with good cash."

Any color Fredrick had in his face had drained. He placed a quivering hand on Leo's arm. "I ... I don't know. Leo, what do you think I should do?"

Leo huffed. How can he make this decision for Fredrick? He fussed with his orange shirt, suddenly finding the folds and wrinkles incredibly fascinating. Uncle Billie always treated him fairly and never took advantage of him. But how far would Leo's friendship with Billie's niece Kiana go? At last, Leo spoke. "Fredrick, I can't tell you what to do. There are other shops on Honolulu, if you want to go there. That said, I trust Billie. The choice is yours."

18

FREDRICK'S HEART POUNDED in his chest and in his head. This whole morning had been insane, and none of what happened to him felt real. Billie telling him he would give him almost $7,400 was laughable. From what he remembered, his father didn't make anywhere near that in a single year as a doctor. Fredrick glanced from Leo to Billie, trying to figure out what he should do.

So much money.

Fredrick's palms were moist and drips of sweat beaded on his neck. His mind continued to race. Watching the *Hawaiian Sun* land, being in Hilo, riding in that vehicle, and now this coin shop. His gaze dropped to the money on the counter. Fredrick almost wanted to leave the bills and coins and flee from this place. Forget he was ever here. Yes, he needed modern money to blend in. But he had a job, so he'd be earning. Still, with this money he could pay the company for his clothes, and maybe he could save the rest, keep the cash in case of an emergency.

I can buy anything. But what do I need?

Fredrick closed his eyes and took as deep a breath as his lungs would allow. "What do I do with the rest of it?" he eventually asked. "Do you want it? I … I … don't need all that money." He faced Billie. "You can have it."

"*E ka haku*. Why couldn't you be a tourist?" Billie shook his head, biting at his lower lip. "No, I wouldn't feel right with you giving your collection to me, but what we can do … how much time do you two have?"

Leo pulled out his smartphone. "We have a couple hours. Why?"

Mr. Kakoa ran a thick hand through his hair. "I can't believe this. What we'll do is go through what I'm not taking and I'll price it out for you. I'll even give you some holders." Billie pulled out a couple of books as he spoke. "We can get your collection organized. When we're done, I'll drive you to the airfield, make sure you get back nice and safe. I don't want you getting robbed." He shook his head clicking his tongue as he stood, "What do you say?"

Fredrick rubbed his damp hands on his pants, the incessant banging in his head and chest eventually shushing.

Why is this so difficult? It shouldn't be that hard. And he's being kind and very generous.

Fredrick nodded his head. "Thank you, Uncle."

"Let's get to it." Billie crossed through the doorway he had originally arrived from, leading to the back of his shop.

Fredrick turned to Leo. "I had no idea. I know I must look crazy to him and to you, but I … well, I didn't know. What am I going to do with all this?"

Leo rested his hand on Fredrick's arm as he smiled. "You're fine. It's a surprise, and a good one, but nothing to fret about. First thing, when we return, we'll put what Uncle Billie doesn't take in your safe in our room." Leo froze. "Why do I have a feeling you don't have an American Bank account?"

Fredrick shook his head. "I didn't think I would need one."

"And what about at home?"

"Yes, I have an account there …" Assuming the account still exists. "I don't have a lot of money back home. Plus, where I grew up, we didn't trust the bank." He remembered all the banks failing when the German economy collapsed, before the Fuhrer came to power.

When I got the job on the Hindenburg, I had to have an account in the Reichsbank. We all did, especially with the Fuhrer's proclamations this year—I mean, in 1937. At least the small amount of money I had there was safe … Is the money still there?

Billie returned with a handful of items. "Okay, will cash work for you?"

"Yes, I think cash will be best," Fredrick agreed.

Were there other options?

"I agree." Billie sat firmer on his perch. "Let's get this done. I don't want to keep the shop closed too long—people might miss me." He laughed.

"Mahalo," Leo remarked.

"Yeah, sure." Billie waved off the comment, opening one of his books and scanning another one of Fredrick's coins.

"I mean it, Uncle." Leo took the big man's hand. "Thank you for this. For what you're doing. You're a good man."

Hints of a grin broke across Billie's face, and he extended a brisk nod before returning to the book and the coin in front of him. "Make sure my niece comes to see her mother," he barked.

Leo watched as Fredrick moved closer to the counter. Fredrick was fascinated with the process. Billie explained the differences between the coins, how he would grade and price each one before moving on to the bills.

By the time Fredrick and Leo finished with Uncle Billie, as he insisted on Fredrick calling him, most of their morning off had vanished. They got to the airfield with only an hour to spare before their shift. Uncle Billie had suggested they stop so Leo and Fredrick might get some lunch, but they declined, knowing they could eat on the ship.

Fredrick couldn't believe what he had learned and how much money he had. Uncle Billie gave him the cash for the items he kept, and even after that, Fredrick still had over five thousand dollars in unsold coins and notes. Billie mentioned to Fredrick if he wanted to return on their next trip and sell more, he may be willing to buy additional items, assuming he recouped what he paid out to Fredrick on this first buy.

They walked to the airship with the rest of Fredrick's collection in a bag from a local merchant. The day had grown warmer and the humidity had bumped up, but the sun was the killer. It seemed so bright that it made his eyes hurt. He noted several people walking around with eyeshades, and considered getting something like that. The styles of sunglasses were different than he was used to seeing.

His eyes as well as his head appreciated the covered walkway. The lack of people and a breeze from the undercover fans helped to move the air around them. "Everyone must still be out."

Leo pulled out his phone. "We don't depart until 1900 tonight so it'll be quiet. Unless folks come for dinner."

"I guess that's good." Fredrick inhaled the tropical air. He didn't recognize all the scents, but they were lovely.

Leo stopped, peered around, and then grabbed Fredrick's arm. "Is there something you aren't telling me?" His tone was firm but there was a slight quiver to it.

Fredrick froze. "I don't understand."

"Look, since I picked you up at the light rail station, you've been nothing like any of the other Germans, or Europeans for that matter, that I've worked with." He lowered his voice. "And today with all your *stuff*. I just ... is there something I need to know? Is there something more about what happened to your friend? You're not in some kind of trouble, are you?"

What do I say? I can't tell him the truth. Can I?

"You mean about Wilhelm? No, there is nothing more." A lump built up in Fredrick's throat. He had so much he wanted to say, but how can he? It all sounded crazy even to him, and he lived through the experience. "I ... I don't know ... Things haven't been normal for me since I got here." He stumbled over his words. Mr. Kakoa had brought up a lot more questions than he could, or would, answer.

"Good afternoon. Mr. Asher. Fredrick," the smooth silky voice of Martin Sherman called out. The man had appeared out of nowhere, dressed in pressed white linen shorts and button-down powder green shirt, untucked to flow around his waist. The black slip-on shoes weren't something Fredrick was used to seeing, but they looked good.

Martin always looked good.

Leo released Fredrick's arm and exhaled before turning. "Mr. Sherman, back so soon?" Leo's face had transformed from concern and worry to his guest-facing expression.

"Good afternoon, Martin," Fredrick greeted with what he hoped to be a polite nod.

I never imagined I'd be happy to see Martin.

"I went into town for an early lunch and figured I'd relax on the ship. Unfortunately, I have some work to do." Martin fanned his face. "Plus, AC is my friend."

Leo chuckled. "Yes, it can get a bit muggy here." He adjusted the collar of his shirt.

"I'm still not used to it." Fredrick shifted the bag from his left hand to his right, the plastic handle digging into his fingers.

"Really? I would have assumed you'd be used to the warm air, traveling the Mediterranean and all that." Martin's gaze didn't leave Fredrick's face.

"Do you ever really get used to warm humid air?" Fredrick glanced around the airfield. "Still, I suppose it's better than the cold."

With no additional chatter, the three men made their way through security. Fredrick had to give over his bag to be scanned and had to remove his wallet and change for the security officer to examine. The female officer reviewed the images, but said nothing about their contents. As they stepped fully into the airship, the cool air brushed over Fredrick and a relaxing shudder ran down his spine. Leo fell in step behind him as they moved into the ship's gallery.

"I'll see you both later." Martin beamed as he took a few steps up the stairs before stopping and turning toward Fredrick. "When will you be on duty?"

"1400—Sorry, 2pm."

"Well, I'll see you later. Hope to see you as well, Mr. Asher." Martin headed up the stairs.

Leo waved. "Enjoy your afternoon."

They moved into the crew passage heading to their cabin. Luckily there wasn't a lot of time for them to finish their conversation. Fredrick punched in the combination to his personal safe, not worried about Leo seeing, since he was busy on his smartphone. Once everything was secured in his safe, he dropped onto his bunk and started taking off his shoes. They didn't have too much time to get ready for duty.

Fredrick turned and faced Leo as he buttoned up his uniform shirt. "Thank you for your help today. I've never had a friend like you ... who I can trust to help me." He glanced around their cabin. "Most people only want something from you and will toss you aside. Or when they find out who you are, they throw you out in the rubbish ... or worse."

Leo's expression softened as their gazes met.

"I know I seem lost and a bit odd. And I can't blame it all on how I grew up," Fredrick continued as he pulled himself together for his shift. "I promise I've not done anything wrong and I'm doing my best to fit in here ..." He couldn't finish his thought. He would like to tell Leo, but he didn't want to risk everything just so he can feel better. Sometimes keeping secrets was for the best for everyone.

Leo's jaw worked. "I get it. I know how hard change can be. Just ... you know, if I can help you with anything, please ask." He pulled on his uniform jacket, his pants not buttoned up and his shirt still untucked, showing off some of his slim frame. "You're a good man, Fredrick."

"Thank you." Fredrick dropped his gaze.

Will I ever get used to seeing how free Leo is with himself when he's getting dressed?

"Now let's move. I don't want to have Aurora complain that we're late." He laughed as he checked the time. "She has no give when it affects her downtime."

Fredrick inhaled. "You know, maybe I should get a smartphone ..." He shrugged on his jacket and pulled at his cuffs.

"I'm not sure, given you have a foreign bank account."

"Oh ... right." Fredrick pulled on his jacket and buttoned the buttons.

I'm going to need to figure out something.

19

LEO SCANNED THE LOUNGE; as he expected, the place was quiet, everyone off enjoying their day in Hilo, as they should be. Aurora all but ran out of the club once Leo and Fredrick arrived. He couldn't blame her—she wanted to get off the zep and enjoy her afternoon and evening off. That left Nuwa, Fredrick, and him for the rest of the day. Hopefully he'd be able to get caught up on his reports. He also wanted to dig into what it would take for him to cross over into operations, what he might lose, and what assistance United Airships provided.

I want to have all the details so when I talk with Barron, we can talk everything out.

"I'm going to check on this evening's food order." Nuwa stood and buttoned her duty jacket. "Unless there's something specific you need me to do right now."

"No, that sounds good." Leo glanced up from his monitor. "I checked the guest roster. We only have seven of the thirty-one club guests on ship right now, and I doubt we'll see a big jump before we leave." He glanced out the lounge window to see bits of the Island with the ocean beyond. "You might want to let David know, so he doesn't overprepare for the night."

Nuwa pushed her glasses into place. "Okay."

Leo checked his messages, seeing if there were any updates he needed to pay attention to.

There were always adjustments and updates on port days.

"Will it be this quiet on days we are in port?" Fredrick asked as he glanced around the empty club. Leo had him making rounds. He had been tidying up and keeping busy, ensuring everything was guest-ready should someone come in, but there wasn't much to do, and the phone hadn't rung once since they'd started their shift.

"No. Well, maybe. Kahului, tomorrow, will probably be busier since it's a small port of call. Honolulu will be empty like this, since that will be our largest port with so much to do. Nawiliwili will be quiet as well—that's our last port before we head home." He shifted deeper in his chair as he took in the quiet lounge. "But who can say?"

"Well, it's giving me more time to practice and learn the ship's systems." Fredrick took a seat at the station Nuwa vacated and woke the computer up.

"Are you enjoying yourself? On the ship, I mean?" Leo asked, turning to face Fredrick.

He looks so much more comfortable at the station now. He's working out, despite his eccentricities.

"It's similar to my old job. The people are nice enough which makes a world of difference. I find the time goes faster when there are guests to assist."

"True," Leo agreed, then he bit at his lower lip. "Can I ask you something?"

"Yes," Fredrick confirmed, but his shoulders noticeably stiffened.

"What do you think of Barron?"

Fredrick smiled as his body relaxed. "I like him. I didn't ask— did you see him at the Gala last night?"

Warmth filled Leo's face. "I did. We had a good talk and a nice dance, almost as nice as yours with Martin. But neither of us got bricked up." His words were filled with mischief. "Well, not for me at least ... but there was potential."

Fredrick's lips pinched together. "I'm glad you two made up."

Leo exhaled. "I told him I loved him."

"Was! Das ist unglaublich. Ich freue mich so für dich." Fredrick stopped and shook his head. "Sorry, my mouth moved faster than

my brain." He took a breath. "That's wonderful. I'm happy for the both of you."

Leo's heart skipped a beat and he felt lighter than the zep. He might float away. "I was thinking I might spend my afternoon off with him tomorrow, away from the zep and his friends."

"That sounds nice." Fredrick's sincerity filled his face. "You're so lucky."

"I think so," Leo agreed. "I mean, I don't know what's going to happen, but for the first time in a long time, I feel good. Hopeful. Ya know?" He spoke faster as he continued, "I mean, before, I only had my career to think about, and now—well, there's so much. I'm trying not to overthink about Barron, but who knows?"

Fredrick's gaze moved from Leo to the workstation.

Fuck. What'd I say?

"Hey, what's wrong?"

Fredrick shook his head. "Nothing. I'm happy for you." Fredrick still wasn't meeting his gaze. "I was thinking how nice it must be for someone to tell you they love you, and for you to feel the same way. How wonderful it must be to feel safe enough to reciprocate the gesture ..." He met Leo's gaze again. "I'm happy for you and I think you and Barron spending the time together will be nice."

I'm an idiot. Here I am gushing about Barron when Fredrick's been through it. What an ass.

"I'm sorry." Leo patted Fredrick's arm. "I wasn't thinking. I mean, I wasn't thinking about everything happening with ... well ... you know."

"No, don't apologize. Everything I've seen on this ship has given me hope. Hope for me and my future. I don't think Wilhelm would have ever said that to me." He pulled at some lint on his uniform jacket. "That wasn't him. He had many good qualities, but talking about feelings ..." He sighed. "I guess that is something he and I had in common."

"Well, there's still six nights left on our trip—who knows what'll happen?" Leo grinned. "And hey, there's always Martin. Maybe you can get him to give you a private wet speedo competition and see what's on offer."

Fredrick shook his head, a small chuckle escaping from his lips. He turned to the computer and resumed typing, but Leo noted Fredrick's cheeks and neck had pinkened.

Play shy all you want—I've seen how you look at him. Maybe I can play matchmaker and work out some kind of meeting for them. Give them some alone time.

The door by the bar opened as Nuwa returned from the steakhouse kitchen. Leo was about to say something, but was cut off as the main door to the club opened. Both Leo and Fredrick faced the door to greet the guests as they made their way into the lounge.

20

F REDRICK HARDLY NOTICED the hours move on as the club slowly filled with guests. After the ship disembarked from the Hilo airship terminal, the activity in the lounge picked up as the club guests shared stories about their adventures in Hilo. The buzz in the air from all the conversations was electric, filling the air with an excited charge as to what lay ahead for the next few days in Hawaii.

Fredrick had the opportunity to speak with Sandra, Teresa, Marco and Rick. They spent the day at Volcano National Park and went to some of the local caves to explore. The foursome ended their day by having dinner near Uncle Billie's store. The sweet older couple, Larry and Stan, told him all about the jewelry stores in town, and where he can find some excellent deals, if he was interested.

Fredrick did his best to make as many mental notes as possible so he'd have locations to check out when he returned to Hilo on their next trip. He garnered some suggestions for things to do in Kahului during his afternoon off, however he supposed a trip to a general store might better serve him. He wanted to pick up some pomade, assuming they still had it; he loved how the product held

195

his hair in place and gave him a polished look. He also planned on seeing if the store had some familiar treats he might enjoy.

Perhaps I should look into getting a smartphone as well, or at least see what I need to do to get one.

By the time Fredrick returned to his cabin, he was ready for some sleep. With the time change and all the excitement of the last few days, he needed the rest. He barely kept his eyes open as he changed from his duty uniform to his sleeping clothes, then at last got into his bunk, the pillow and bed absorbing him as the ships hum lulled him off to a dreamless slumber.

Once he awoke, he shifted in his bunk and listened for Leo's soft breathing. Not hearing anything, he opened his eyes and scanned the cabin, the early morning rays of light slowly filling the space. Fredrick tossed his feet over the side of his bunk, then stood and stretched. His tank top bunched at the waistband of his pajama bottoms. He glanced at Leo's bunk, but as with the day before, Leo was up early to observe the airship's mooring. He yawned, happy he decided to rest up since he would have a busy first shift, as guests took full advantage of the club's complimentary breakfast before heading out for the day. He picked up his pocket watch and checked the time.

Good—I have time for a shower and some breakfast.

He rushed through his morning routine and breakfast, wanting to get to the lounge before opening, so he can take his time setting himself and the computer up for his shift. Leo would be there, but still Fredrick wanted to show he could accomplish these basic tasks without the need of supervision.

After all, I didn't need anyone to watch over me on the Hindenburg. I'm getting used to being here.

Feeling good, Fredrick tapped his keycard to the Lounge's doors locking and unlocking mechanism. With a click, he pulled open the door. Instead of an empty lounge though, Captain Monroe, First Officer Erikson, Ms. Lam, Leo, and Martin were there. He froze as his heart dropped to the pit of his stomach. "Is everything okay?"

"Fredrick, have a seat." Captain Monroe pointed to one of the guest chairs. "Mr. Erikson, please see to the door and ensure we're not disturbed." She was dressed in her duty uniform, clearly having just come up from the cockpit.

"Yes, Captain." The First Officer moved to the club doors, and without even so much as a peek over his shoulder, exited the club, closing the door behind him as the click echoed around the space.

Fredrick's heart pounded as sweat broke out all over his body. He pushed his nerves down as he crossed to the chair pointed out by the Captain. As he sat, he scanned the remaining people in the room, unsure what to say or do. None met his gaze with the kindness he had grown used to. Fredrick's leg started to quake as his mouth grew dry.

This isn't good.

"Now will you please explain what's going on?" Leo demanded, glaring at Martin. "We have guests to see to before they go out for the day. And what about the rest of my team? Are you going to keep them out as well?"

"Agreed." Ms. Lam's arms were firmly crossed at her chest. "This is highly unusual."

Martin's face was a blank canvas—not a twinkle in his eyes, nothing.

"Did I do something wrong?" Fredrick stomach dropped as his heart thundered throughout his body.

I knew I shouldn't have had brunch with a guest. Especially Martin.

"No." Captain Monroe said. "And if it were—"

"Thank you, Captain," Martin interrupted, his voice filling the club with enough force to get all their attention. "I think I can take it from here." He pulled out a badge. "My name is Special Agent Martin Shaw. I'm from the FBI, and we've been watching you, Mr. Rudolf, for quite some time."

FBI, the American federal investigating department—he had heard about them.

"What?" Leo's voice roared. "This is some bullshit. What's he done? This can't be about the coins he sold at Uncle Billie's."

"Leo." Captain Monroe held up a hand.

"No, this has nothing to do with what Fredrick sold yesterday."

"You've been spying on me?" Fredrick's voice cracked, sounding broken and hollow to his ears. Memories of the brownshirts stopping and harassing people in Berlin pushed to the front of his mind, all before the Reich came to power. This is why he and Wilhelm wanted to run away. America was supposed to be better.

Instead it's just as bad, or worse.

Mr. Sherman—no, Mr. Shaw, wasn't that what he called himself now?—ignored his question. "I'll be taking you from the *Hawaiian Sun*. We'll take a chopper to Honolulu for questioning."

"Captain, you can't allow this." Leo's tone faltered as he continued. Fredrick noticed Leo avoiding him or his gaze as he spoke.

Fredrick's mind raced. *Wilhelm? No, how would anyone know about that? I haven't mentioned anything to anyone about him or how I ended up here. Leo was the only one I talked to about Wilhelm, and I didn't share anything to give myself away. Did I? And I've tried my best to fit in and not stand out, but there's so much to learn. Slipups were unavoidable.*

"Danielle, this isn't right," Ms. Lam insisted.

"Mr. Rudolf won't be going anywhere." Captain Monroe's tone was firmer and filled with more authority than Fredrick had ever heard. "He's a member of my crew, and the last I checked, the FBI doesn't have authority here." She clicked her radio, "Mr. Johnson, have you heard from the FBI in Honolulu? What about Corporate?"

"Not yet, Captain."

A sneer crossed Martin's face.

"You didn't think I'd take your word for it"—Captain Monroe squared off with him—"did you, Mr. Shaw?"

"Captain, let me remind you, the *Hawaiian Sun* is registered to the US which gives me and the FBI jurisdiction wherever you are, however as a courtesy and to ensure as little disruption to you, your crew and your guests I waited for the *Hawaiian Sun* to arrive here in Kahului. Now we can do this the easy way, or the hard way." He stepped closer to her. "That's something you do have control over."

"We'll see how much control and authority I have," Captain Monroe countered. "Mr. Rudolf won't be going anywhere, at least for the time being."

They're all standing up for me. They want to help.

Fredrick's spirits lifted hearing his Captain and Leo fighting for him. They barely knew him and they were willing to stand up and protect him. He would have hugged them both if he could.

Something that didn't happen back home. People were too scared. I was too scared. As more and more happened, by the time everyone woke up, there wasn't anything to be done. They were trapped.

It was a standoff of wills and all Fredrick could do is sit and watch. What authority did she or anyone have over this man from the FBI?

"That's why you were in the cockpit this morning," Leo snarled. "You weren't there to evaluate the mooring process." He shook his head. "I never trusted you, you fucking ass."

"Leo," Ms. Lam admonished.

"I'm sorry, Tammy," Leo started, "but this is wrong and we all know it. This man is a nothing with a badge who thinks he can walk all over everyone. And he all but sexually harassed Fredrick, fawning all over him."

"I beg your pardon?" Martin fired off a retort.

"Regardless, I don't think—" Ms. Lam was cut off.

"Captain Monroe," Officer Johnson's voice broke over her radio.

"What is it, Marcus?" The captain clicked her radio. "Did you get confirmation?"

"Yes, we've been informed by the FBI Office in Honolulu that we're to comply with Special Agent Shaw's orders, and provide him any support requested." There was a pause before Marcus continued, "And Captain, Corporate has confirmed we're not to get involved."

"There you go." Martin tilted his head. "Well, Captain, your move."

Captain Monroe bit her lip before clicking her radio. "Thank you, Marcus." Her gaze dropped to the floor. "We don't have a choice." She put a hand on Fredrick's shoulder. "I'm ... I'm sorry."

Fredrick didn't think his heart could sink any lower in his stomach, but here he was, a stranger in a strange land with no one.

I'm alone.

"That's bullshit—what has he done?" Leo demanded. "I've been with him the entire time and he's been nothing but an exemplary crew member and friend. You danced with him the other night, for Christ's sake."

"Mr. Asher, I appreciate the difficult position you're in," Martin began. "However, I assure you, you do not want to interfere, especially with how well things have been going between you and Mr. Hillchild."

"Asshole," Leo barked.

"You will not threaten any member of my crew or any guest on my ship." Captain Monroe's voice hardened, as did her expression. "I may not be able to stop you from taking Fredrick, but any threats veiled or otherwise will not be tolerated. By anyone."

All the talking was getting them nowhere. The food in his stomach threatened to come up and he wanted all this unpleasantness to be over. "It's fine," Fredrick's voice fell from his lips. "I'll go. I won't make a fuss. There's no point, but thank you Captain, Ms. Lam. Leo."

"Smart man." Martin adjusted his black suit jacket. "Now, Captain, I'd like to leave with as minimal a fuss as possible. It's still early enough—I trust you can hold off opening the gangways to the guests until myself and Fredrick are off the ship."

She extended a curt nod.

"What about his and your luggage? Your personal items?" Ms. Lam asked with her arms crossed and a scowl on her face.

"And what are we supposed to say to the guests and to the rest of the crew?" Leo's brows were risen as he spoke.

"Mr. Rudolf fell ill and had to leave the ship."

"And you think anyone is going to buy this?" Leo scoffed, red filling every part of his face and neck.

"As for the rest, when you get to Honolulu, I, or someone else, will meet you. Now, unless there are any additional questions or comments, we'll go." He glanced at Fredrick. "Do I need to use my cuffs or are you going to be the gentleman they all think you are?"

Fredrick shook his head. What was the point of trying to flee? There's nowhere to go, and everyone who might help him was dead and buried. He barely had the strength to stand. "I won't do anything." He faced the Captain and the rest of his crew. "Thank you all for being so nice to me. I'm sorry. I hope you'll forgive me."

"We're not giving up. I'm not giving up." Leo crossed his arms in front of his chest. "Wait until Corporate hears about this."

Martin turned and smiled. "How do you think I got on this cruise? You didn't think my reservation was a mix-up, did you?"

Leo's face dropped. "I don't care. I'm going to file so many complaints, you won't be able to find a job picking shit out of a septic tank. Trust me, this isn't over." There was no more fight in his voice, but the words still made Fredrick feel good.

Ms. Lam shook her head, defeated. "They knew?"

"They knew enough, but not the details," Martin admitted. "Now, Fredrick, shall we?" He faced Captain Monroe. "Thank you, Captain, for the lovely holiday."

"Get off my ship," the Captain barked.

Fredrick and Agent Martin Shaw walked to the club's door and exited the space.

•   •   •

Fredrick's mind raced, though he was aware enough to keep his practiced guest-facing expression on as they walked. There was no point in making any more of a fuss than had already been made. The two men made their way through the crew sections of the ship, running into very few staff as they made their way to the exit. The few crew members they did run into paid them no attention. For all they knew, Fredrick was assisting one of the Club guests.

His face was brushed with the warm morning air as he glanced back at the giant airship. Everything about the Zeppelin was a wonder to him—would he ever see it again? He knew all this had been too good to be true, seeing all the happy people and being off the *Hindenburg*. Meeting Leo and the others. Even meeting Martin Sherman— no, Shaw—had filled his head with so many wonderful possibilities of a better world.

If only there was a way for me to end things. What was the point of going on?

"Watch yourself with the helicopter," Special Agent Martin Shaw instructed. He needed to see this man not as Martin Sherman, who had been funny, kind, and an excellent dancer, but as an FBI man that wanted something from him and potentially wanted to hurt him. The Special Agent moved them into the waiting autogiro, another marvel of this world. Who would have imagined autogiros would change so much?

But everything has changed. Bigger, louder, faster. More affirmation that I don't belong here.

Silence filled the space between Agent Shaw and Fredrick. He couldn't stand Martin watching him like he was some animal in a circus. Fredrick peered out at the incredibly blue ocean.

I can jump out and they'd never find me.

The trip to Honolulu didn't take nearly as long as Fredrick assumed. They arrived at the metropolis and Fredrick noted all the tall towers. Honolulu was huge, unlike Hilo or Kahului.

Still not as large as Berlin. I wonder if I'll ever get to see my home again.

Instead of landing on the ground, the helicopter landed on the roof of one of the taller buildings.

"Come on." Agent Shaw helped Fredrick out of the helicopter, the air finding his exposed skin not nearly as warm as the environment they left.

"Are you going to tell me what's happening? And what you're doing with me?"

Agent Shaw remained silent as he maneuvered Fredrick into the building, the frigid air assaulting Fredrick's body. They moved down a flight of stairs before arriving at a landing with an elevator. The agent revealed an identification badge, tapping it to a reader, followed by entering a code on a keypad. A light turned on, followed by the hum of a motor. Fredrick caught a whiff of mechanical fluids and perhaps some kind of lubricant. Within a few moments, the metal doors opened and Agent Shaw gestured to the inside of the lift. Fredrick stepped in, followed by Martin. Once inside, the agent pushed one of the buttons on the wall panel.

"Are you going to speak to me?" Fredrick asked. "I thought you liked me, Special Agent Shaw, or was that all for show? Was it all to get close to me? Why?"

At least I'm going to try to get some answers.

Martin faced him, and for a brief moment, Fredrick caught a glimpse of sorrow in the agent's face. But instead of speaking, Agent Shaw only huffed.

As the doors to the lift opened, Fredrick saw an office filled with people rushing about. Several were sitting in short walled-off spaces and worked on their computers. None of them paid any notice to him or to Agent Shaw as they exited the elevator. Martin moved them down one of the halls before stopping at a solid wood door and opening it. "Have a seat."

Fredrick complied. The space was large enough for a utilitarian table and four chairs, two on each side. The lights were built into the ceiling but not near as nice as what was on the *Hawaiian Sun*.

"I'll be right back." Agent Shaw closed the door with a click.

If they were going to hurt him, wouldn't they have already done so? And if this had to do with him being German, what can he tell them? Everything he knew about Germany was ninety years old. Fredrick pulled out his pocket watch to fondle the small machine. This was his only link to his past and his real home. Everything else he had had been left on the *Hawaiian Sun* and the *Hindenburg* before that. As he waited, his legs quaked, his stomach grumbled, and his mouth grew dry.

We should have never made plans to leave the Hindenburg.

"I doubt that would have mattered," he blustered to himself.

Adjusting how he sat, he faced the ceiling to fixate on the white squares. They weren't interesting. In fact, nothing about this building was interesting. Whereas the *Hawaiian Sun* was full of color and beauty, this office was blank, as if intentionally designed and built to be completely unremarkable.

Probably so people aren't comfortable.

The door clicked open and Special Agent Shaw returned, holding two cups and a laptop under his arm. "I figured you might be thirsty." He offered him a cup. "It's water."

If they're trying to kill me, I doubt it would be by poison.

"Thank you, Special Agent."

"Don't." Martin shook his head. "Call me Martin, please."

Fredrick took the cup and had a sip. The cool water easily slid down his throat, washing away the desert that had built up in his throat and mouth. "Thank you ... Martin."

Martin sipped his water and sat across from Fredrick, before putting his cup and laptop down. "First, let me say I'm sorry. None of this should have happened the way it did."

The laugh dropped from Fredrick's mouth before he could stop himself. Heat built up from his stomach, not from nerves, but anger and frustration.

Now he wants to be friends and is sorry.

"As I told you on the *Hawaiian Sun*, my name is Martin Shaw. I work for the Department of Abnormal Affairs, a division of the FBI that deals with paranormal, supernatural, and occult phenomena. Specifically, I work on *Project Elysium*."

"What are you talking about? I don't know what any of that means."

"Most people don't," Martin acknowledged. "A little over a hundred years ago, a First Nations woman appeared out of nowhere. She caused quite a stir—folks weren't used to having a Wampanoag woman with no ID in traditional dress walking around in the middle of downtown Boston. Once the police were called and they found someone who could communicate with her, she told them about a growing rumbling like thunder she heard hours before she arrived. And she spoke about a fire. One minute she thought she was going to burn alive, and the next she was there."

That's what happened to me. This happened before? How? To whom? Maybe I can go home.

Fredrick leaned forward his mind racing with thoughts and theories, but he kept his comments to himself.

"Well, typically, they'd have locked her up with the other mentally ill at the time, but her clothing and jewelry were unlike anything seen before. No one could explain her sudden arrival. Either out of curiosity, or general human kindness, the authorities called in a few experts." Martin inhaled a deep breath. "Well, experts for their time, and they took samples of her clothing and jewelry. Sure enough, the materials matched what they knew about the Wampanoag people in the area. She was the first reported *Jumper* we knew about."

"Jumper?" Fredrick promptly asked. His annoyance, anger and frustration vanished, turning into confusion and questions.

"That's a term we use now." Martin opened the laptop. "The term we use for people like you."

"Me?"

"Don't play with me, Fredrick—I saw your reaction to the story." Martin's lips broke in a grin. "Never play poker. You wouldn't survive."

Fredrick's lips pinched together.

I assumed I did quite well given all I've been through.

"We know you're from 1937. And that you were on the *Hindenburg*, but not our *Hindenburg*. Our *Hindenburg* never caught fire in New Jersey. We think Jumpers have been ending up here on our Earth for years, affecting our world in small ways. Nothing major, small shifts, like here—airships have been a big part of our history, but in your world, not so much."

"How do you know this?" Fredrick asked, unable to believe his ears.

"From other Jumpers. You weren't the only one to come to our Earth from 1937 and from your *Hindenburg*." He tapped away before turning the screen to face Fredrick.

Fredrick's heart dropped as tears filled his eyes. He reached a hand toward the screen before quickly pulling away. He took a breath of air, another, and one more for good measure. "Wilhelm."

Martin's voice softened as he spoke. "He appeared at Moffett Field on January 7, 1942. He scared the hell out of the guards who saw him appear, and when they found out he was German … well, you can imagine."

"They killed him." Fredrick's voice shook. "Wilhelm … I'm …"

"No." Martin shook his head. "Once they reported the incident to their commander and brought Wilhelm in for questioning, the FBI was contacted and we collected him. He got lucky."

Fredrick pushed from the table and stood as everything bottled up burst out of him. "What did you do to him? Where is he? He didn't know anything—we were running away. We were going to leave and go to my aunt and uncle who were supposed to meet us that day. We hated the Nazis! He didn't hurt anyone. Please, please tell me."

Martin stood and pulled Fredrick into a hug. "We know." His tone was soft and gentle as his arms held him tight. "We know you both planned to leave. We never hurt Wilhelm—that's not what we do. I swear."

Fredrick's breath shook as he pulled back to meet Martin's gaze. "Please, what happened to him?"

"Have a seat." Martin returned to his chair, and rubbed his finger over the touchpad. He turned the screen toward Fredrick again. "This message is for you. Are you ready?"

Am I ready? No. But what choice is there if I want to learn what happened to me?

Fredrick rubbed his chin, extending a slight movement of his head to signal Martin to proceed, and Martin tapped the space bar.

Wilhelm's face appeared, though it had lines and seemed so much older. His once soft brown hair was now fully gray and his bright green eyes had faded. Age had been kind to him, but still, he had grown old. Fredrick's lips pulled up slightly—Wilhelm's chin dimple was a handsome feature not even the onslaught of time took from him.

His voice was mature, but much the same, as he spoke. "Fredrick, I'm sorry we didn't make it to your aunt and uncle's. If you're seeing this video, I died before giving you this message in person." Wilhelm smiled. "We had such dreams of starting over in America. Getting away from the brown shirts. I'm sorry about the night on the *Hindenburg*. You know the night I mean. I don't want you to be sad for me. I've been happy here and the work I do with Project Elysium has been fulfilling. I've learned so much about the universe and the world we live in." His grin grew. "I get to help people like us. There aren't many Jumpers, maybe a hundred or so since I got here, but I'll let the agent get into that. This work is not like our jobs on the *Hindenburg*." He laughed. "I think you liked your job more than I did." He inhaled, coughing before he continued, "Be happy for me. Live your life to its fullest. Find someone wonderful to love—we can do that now. Enjoy this world. I can only imagine the things you're going to see and experience." He held up a hand to touch the screen. "*Auf Wiedersehen, meine Liebe.*" The message ended.

"When?" Fredrick's voice shook, eyes still on the screen.

"He was 89." Martin's tone was soft and thoughtful. "He died in 2004. You missed him by over twenty years. I'm sorry."

Fredrick swiped at his eyes. "Was he happy? I mean, was he really happy? Wilhelm often tried to shelter me. Did he have someone who loved him?"

Martin turned the machine around, tapped on it, then swiveled the machine back to Fredrick. "He did. He and Phil met in 1977."

The image on the monitor showed a younger, but still older, Wilhelm. He had an arm wrapped around a man of similar height, but his build was heavier and his hair much thinner. They both seemed happy.

"Did you know him? Them?"

Martin laughed. "I'm not that old. No, I never had the pleasure. But when I was recruited for Project Elysium, we all knew about you. When Director Wilhelm Hoffmann took over Project Elysium, he left standing orders that we keep an eye out for you. He never gave up. We focused on the area that was once Moffett Field, since that was where Director Hoffman appeared. He knew you'd be one of the Jumpers."

"How'd he know?"

"He never heard the roar of thunder. All the Jumpers hear a growing groan, or thunder, or some think of the noise as a growl, including you. Typically, that happens twenty-four to forty-eight hours before the catalyst event. He remembered you telling him about the noises you'd been hearing the day before and the day of the fire."

"He wasn't supposed to jump?"

"I don't know, maybe not. He remembered the explosion and had vague images of you tugging him, not letting him go. You probably pulled him with you, but that's only a theory."

"I figured I left him. I assumed he died." Fredrick's limbs were weak; he wanted to crawl into bed and sleep.

"You probably ended up saving him." Martin turned the computer and typed some more. "I'm sorry you didn't get to see him again. There are more of his personal files for you if you want to go through them."

"Thank you." Fredrick raked a hand through his hair.

Martin turned the computer to face Fredrick again. "There's more. It's about your family. Well, the people here on this Earth that would have been your family."

"My family."

"Since our brunch date, I saw how much your family meant to you ..."

Fredrick pulled the computer to him and started scanning the details. He found out that indeed his family, or the people who would be his family here, had died. None of them had lived beyond World War II. His brother was executed for insubordination, when told to kill a fleeing Romani family, and he refused. His parents and sister were killed in a bombing in Frankfurt, as his father had been moved there to work in one of the military hospitals. But that wasn't all—after the bombing they found two families, ten people, also killed in the house; they were hidden behind a false wall in his parent's home.

"They fought back." Fredrick's heart lifted. "They weren't complacent, they tried to make a difference."

"Yes." Martin acknowledged.

Fredrick took a shaky breath as he continued to review the information. There was nothing on his aunt and uncle and there was nothing about him. A laugh escaped him as he saw some images of his brother and sister neither of them smiling. He was glad they fought back against the Nazis. If more people had, then maybe the Holocaust wouldn't have happened or the Nazis would have been defeated before they came to power. He saw another photo; his father and mother stood outside a house he didn't recognize and both wore stoic expressions.

These aren't the happy people I knew. The war took the joy from them long before the bombing took their lives.

Fredrick was both grateful and devastated by the discovery. Shifting the computer in front of him, he studied the document again. There wasn't a listing of him or Wilhelm as ever working on the *Hindenburg.*

"We never existed here?" Fredrick glanced up at Martin.

"We believe you're able to exist here because you never had a counterpart on this Earth," Martin explained. "But that's only a theory"—he huffed out a chuckle—"based on the research that Wilhelm provided when he tried to find you."

Fredrick rubbed a shaky hand over his lips. He now knew the truth. He irrefutably had some understanding of what happened to him and his family. Why didn't he feel any better? The pit of worry and unknowing was empty, leaving him a void that he didn't know how to fill.

"Now what am I supposed to do?" Fredrick peered around the bare office space. "Can you send me home?"

"No, we don't know how. Some of the team working on Project Elysium think that the universe, or God and the Angels, have this world set aside for something. Or perhaps it's the Fates. We don't know, and one explanation is as good as any other." His gaze dropped from Fredrick's. "Honestly, there's a lot we don't fully understand. Again, I'm sorry, but … well … you can stay here. Make a life for yourself like the others have."

Fredrick's hands and legs trembled. "So now what?"

"We have to run you by medical. You'll have some choices to make. But I'll be here to assist you and Wilhelm has made some arrangements to help you along."

"Arrangements?"

"Yes, but we can go over that later."

That's something, I guess.

Fredrick stood. "Okay, let's get started. I can't sit here any longer."

21

L EO COULDN'T FOCUS on his duties, and he found his temper growing shorter and shorter, not only with his team, but with several of the guests. How can Corporate do nothing? None of this made any sense. What did the FBI want with Fredrick? And why'd it take Special Agent Dickhead so long to do something?

He stared at the screen as he reworded and changed the email he wanted to fire off. Captain Monroe forbade him from firing off any messages that might bite him in the ass, but did make him a promise that she'd do everything she could to find out answers. And that was the only thing holding his temper. With no one to yell at, or tell off, he bubbled, waiting for something to cause him to boil over.

Poor Fredrick. He'd been charming, polite, and funny.

But he did seem odd. What if it was about his ex, Wilhelm? Did he have something to do with Wilhelm's death … or disappearance?

"No." Leo shook the idea from his mind as the single word crashed out of his mouth louder and harder than he'd intended.

"No what?" Ollie glanced at him from the workstation he sat at.

Leo shook his head. "Thanks for jumping in and helping today. I'm going to make it up to you … somehow."

"I can't believe Fredrick got sick enough to be taken off the ship. It's too bad the medical team couldn't help him."

"Better facilities in Honolulu." Leo's tone was flat with the practiced statement he, Tammy, and the Captain came up with. His stomach twisted around the lie, making him feel sick. The medical team had been advised that Fredrick suffered a medical emergency in the lounge, and since they were already moored, contacting the local fire safety and rescue made the most sense, or so they claimed.

The story was crap with more holes than Swiss cheese, and he couldn't imagine Dr. Young being the least bit happy about not being apprised of the situation, especially given she had overall responsibility for the health of the guests and the crew.

Leo rubbed his stomach. He hadn't eaten a thing and now he wasn't so sure if he'd be able to eat or if food would make him ill. He closed his eyes and took a deep breath, then peeked over at Ollie. Dealing with his team had been easier—he sent them a text letting them know, and Ollie jumped in to help for the day. He would need to do something special for the guy.

Perhaps a full day off in port.

The door to the club opened and Aurora and Tomas strolled in. "Hey." Tomas beamed, bright white toothy grin all pressed and polished. No one would know of any underlying drama—at least, not by their appearances. If Leo wasn't so damn annoyed he'd be proud. He loved his team.

And that's why they're all great at their jobs, no matter what's happening. They can put on a good face for guests and each other when needed.

"Me, Tomas, and Nuwa tonight?" Aurora asked, the comment more of a confirmation than a question as she looked around the empty club.

Leo closed out the file he was working on. "We'll do duals while we're in port and have threes for the evening."

"And what about the last two days at sea?" Tomas questioned, then quickly added, "Assuming Fredrick isn't well."

"Tammy volunteered to help us if we need her." Leo glanced at the door as Nuwa walked in. "But I think we'll be fine. We have a good group and no one has been too demanding."

"Except for Mr. Masson. Barron's friend. He's been ... a challenge since the afternoon tea." Ollie strained to keep his voice level.

Elijah was a piece of work, but they can deal with him.

Nuwa buttoned her jacket. "Sorry, security took a bit longer. More folks are returning early today."

Leo cracked his neck, trying to release the built-up tension in his body. "Like I was telling the others, we'll do duals during the days at the next two ports. If Fredrick isn't better and back onboard, Tammy will help us out on the sea days."

"I wish there was something we could do for Fredrick." Nuwa's lips curled in a frown, her glasses slipping down her nose slightly. "He's a good guy, and getting ill … that sucks."

"I hope it's nothing serious. When I had my appendix out, it took me three weeks, cause they had to cut me open." Tomas rubbed his side where the scar must have been. "That was no fun."

"Listen," Leo started, his voice hard, but he needed to continue before rumors got out of hand, "we don't know what happened with Fredrick. If I hear something, I'll let you know, but until we have any updates, we have a job to do. And I don't want to hear any rumors about Fredrick, or"—he inhaled—"Mr. Masson. I know he's a pain, but he's still a guest. Clear?"

There were nods from his team.

They're a good group and I can't imagine ever leaving them. However, right now, I need to be anywhere else.

"Now, unless there's something more"—he scanned his team, hoping they wouldn't have any more to ask or say—"Aurora, the club is yours. Ollie, have a good night off. If you need me, I'll have my cell." Leo grabbed his jacket and left the club and his team. He needed to get off the ship to get some air.

•   •   •

Leo pushed his mochiko chicken around the bowl. He didn't want to eat. His stomach continued doing flipflops, and even spending more time in the restroom trying to let his body work everything out didn't help. Now he sat at one of the best places to eat on Maui with Barron, and he couldn't bring himself to eat any of his meal. His skin prickled from the breeze and he had to remind himself to breathe evenly. Barron sat across from him, watching and waiting for him to say something.

What can I say? It's not like I know anything. I wish he'd stop staring at me.

Leo put his fork down and took another breath before speaking so he didn't bark at Barron. "I'm sorry. I know I'm not any fun."

"Is this about Fredrick?"

How did he know?

"Don't worry, no one knows anything." Barron leaned in. "We've all heard he's fallen ill and was taken off the ship early this morning. But …"

"You don't believe the story?"

Barron shook his head. "Seeing you like this, no. If Fredrick was sick, you wouldn't be so … I don't know … so angry, I guess. And you wouldn't be sitting here with me. You'd be with him, ensuring he not only has the best possible care, but making sure he doesn't want for anything. That's what makes you so good at your job. You care … maybe even a little too much."

He's not wrong.

Barron's gaze ran over Leo's face. "Did he not work out? He seemed like a good guy. He knew how to handle himself, especially with that Martin fellow. And the whole tea service. Everyone likes him and, as odd as this may sound, we're all worried about him. I wish you could say something."

"Babe, can we get out of here? Are you finished?" Leo gestured to Barron's half-eaten supper.

"Sure." Barron pulled his napkin from his lap to wipe his face before standing.

Leo stood and they made their way to the door, dropping off their bowls and utensils at the rubbish bin. Outside, the afternoon air washed over him. Off in the distance, the *Hawaiian Sun* hugged her moorings. Even from here, the floating zep was impressive, a true beauty.

Barron took Leo's hand. "You gonna tell me what happened?"

Different scenarios ran through Leo's head. What can he say? What should he say? No one told him not to say anything, but the confidentiality had been implied, wasn't it? And the whole FBI thing … Have you seen Martin Sherman today?" Leo asked as he glanced up and down the street.

Barron's gaze narrowed. "No. Why?"

"It's interesting that you haven't seen Martin today. And with Fredrick being under the weather, having to be taken from the ship." Leo chose his words carefully. "I bet there are people out there who would think it's some kind of conspiracy or something."

Barron's lips and brows scrunched with confusion. "What are you talking about ... a conspiracy ... that's ..."

Leo's brows rose as he looked at Barron, hoping he would catch on to what he was trying to tell him. "I'm saying a lot of people love conspiracies, and they can be a lot of fun to play out ... don't you think?"

"No ..."

Leo's lips dropped into a frown.

"Oh ... gotcha." A grin bloomed on Barron's face as he dragged out the words. "Yes, yes it would, but conspiracies are a joke. Hey, maybe Martin's some undercover agent and Fredrick was his partner ... that would be a fun theory."

"A better theory would be that Martin was an undercover agent and Fredrick was his mark. Can't you see it now? An undercover FBI agent on a gay zeppelin cruise, tracking down Fredrick, a German national, and pulling him off the zep for some unknown reason. I'm sure there's a book plot out there just like it."

Barron's focus moved from the *Hawaiian Sun* out to the ocean. His voice filled with a mix of worry and concern as he replied, "That ... that would be an interesting conspiracy theory. But why would the FBI, in this case, want Fredrick?"

"That's the million-dollar question." Leo exhaled as his shoulders dropped. "But we both agree that conspiracy theories are rubbish, and I'm sure there's a perfectly logical reason for you to not have seen Martin today. And poor Fredrick's in Honolulu all alone with some nasty bug."

"Wait, Honolulu?" Barron questioned. "He's been moved to ..." He covered his mouth with his hand, blocking his inhale.

"So many wild conspiracies ... right?" Leo added, watching Barron carefully. They were playing a dangerous game.

"You know, I guess in this scenario, or plot, you'd need someone to make a few calls to, say, the Honolulu FBI Field Office, and make some inquiries. With that info, we can really play the conspiracy theory out."

"That'd be convenient, wouldn't it?" Leo huffed. "As far as the conspiracy goes, I mean."

"Absolutely. By the way, did I ever mention that Elijah's mother is a detective for the San Jose Police Department? She's even worked with the FBI on some local cases."

"Really?" The pit in Leo's stomach was slowly releasing the more they spoke.

At the very least, telling Barron has helped my stress.

Barron's lips pulled up in a bright grin. "And she loves me."

"Who doesn't love you?" Leo leaned in and gently kissed Barron, before the comment fully soaked in. He pulled away and studied Barron. "Wait, seriously. Do you think she would make a few calls?"

"We're still talking about this fully made-up conspiracy, right?"

Leo remained quiet as his focus shifted to the ground, taking in the sandy dirt and uncut grasses. The knot in his stomach pulled tight again.

"Okay." Barron stepped away and pulled out his cell, then tapped the screen. "Elijah. Hey, where you at?" His voice was friendly but strained. He kicked at the dirt and earth under his feet as he spoke. "Yes, I'm still annoyed, but we're friends and I'll get over it." He paused and inhaled, his chest puffing out. "Plus, I need your help. Someone might be in trouble. So, where are you?" He frowned. "Fine ... fine ... You're the best person in the world and I should always listen to you. Can we move on now? This is important and I don't have time for your games."

Leo crossed his arms over his chest. He noted hints of pink moved up Barron's neck and into his cheeks.

Calling Elijah wasn't a good idea.

Barron exhaled as he ran a hand through his hair, glancing toward the zep. "Okay, I'll meet you on the ship in fifteen minutes. I'm bringing Leo. You're going to have to put your feelings aside." Barron's tone rose. "No, this isn't about me and Leo." He fell silent as a mumbled voice grew louder from his cell phone. "Thanks, we'll see you soon." He tapped the phone and slipped it in his pocket with a grumble. "He's not happy, but he'll help ... but you're going to need to tell him what's happening and it can't be hypothetical or a conspiracy. Are you willing to do that?"

Leo faced the ocean, the waves breaking on the beach, the people frolicking and enjoying the sun and the seaside. He turned from the coast toward the lush tropical mountains. The mix of the ocean and tropical plants perfumed the air all around them. Maui was beautiful and the way the zep sat there made for a perfect picture, if not for all the trouble that lay inside her rigid inflatable hull, and how he would shortly be adding to that drama.

If worst comes to worst, there are other airships and other companies.

"If it'll help Fredrick, yeah." Leo met Barron's gaze. "I have to."

The trip to the zep seemed to take forever and getting through security had been painful. *Now I know how the guests feel some days.* Leo and Barron made their way up to deck three, then rushed down the passageway to Elijah's cabin. Before pulling out his keycard, Barron glanced at Leo. "You sure about this?"

"Not in the least." Leo's hands trembled and his stomach swarmed with a rabble of butterflies.

Barron tapped the key reader and the door opened. Lounging on the built-in sofa, Elijah held a glass of wine, his other hand draped lazily over the edge of the sofa, one of his legs crossed over the other. "So now, you actually need me." His gaze narrowed on them. "How the tides have changed." He sipped his wine.

"Elijah, don't be a dick," Barron barked crossing the threshold. "We think Fredrick's in trouble and we need you to call your mother."

"Wait, the good-looking German guy from the club?" Elijah put his wine down on the coffee table and shifted how he sat, uncrossing his legs. "Fuck." He pulled out his phone to check the time. "San Jose two or three hours ahead of us? I forget."

"Three." Leo moved to one of the side chairs, sitting down and wiped his sweaty palms on his shorts. "For what it's worth, I never wanted to hurt you, Elijah."

Elijah chortled, glaring up from his phone. "I wish I could say the same, but that doesn't matter right now." He tapped the cell and held the device out for everyone to hear, waiting for the other end to pick up.

"Eli, this is a surprise," the soft voice of a woman answered. "How's your trip?"

"Mommy, I need your help for a friend." Elijah didn't waste any time.

"What did you do?" The woman's voice instantly grew firm, taking on a tone that was ready to chastise him, or someone.

"Nothing, Mommy. I swear." Elijah frowned.

"Uh-huh. Okay." She dragged out the words. "I'll see what I can do."

"Hi, Detective Masson," Barron greeted in what was his most charming voice.

"Mommy, I have Barron and Leo here with me. I'll let them explain." Elijah moved the phone closer to them. "Go ahead."

Leo took a breath, his heart finding a home in his throat. He needed to do this and nothing else mattered. He gulped down his fear and relayed the story. If he lost his job, he might as well go out in a blaze of glory.

22

FREDRICK HAD BEEN POKED and prodded for what seemed like hours. Martin told Fredrick the tests were to ensure that he didn't have any medical conditions or any diseases that this world didn't already know about. But the tests were also to ensure that this place didn't have anything that Fredrick's body couldn't fight off. The doctor gave Fredrick several shots, saying the drugs were vaccines for some of the various diseases they had overcome, like Smallpox, Diphtheria, Tetanus, Polio, Mumps, and a few others that Fredrick couldn't remember. All he was sure of was that both his arms and his butt were sore from the needles.

I feel like a pincushion.

Fredrick shifted in the passenger seat of the vehicle Martin now drove. Another marvel of engineering, there were so many buttons and nobs, and a center screen that either he or the driver might interact with. After the medical exam and getting cleared by the doctor, Martin informed him they were done for the day and he should go rest. Fredrick was glad to walk around on solid ground—he'd grown so used to floating around in the skies, he had almost forgotten how the ground felt. *Or maybe it's all the medicines they gave me.*

Fredrick closed his eyes, blocking out the glare until his eyes grew used to the light. He didn't realize how tired he was. So much had happened, and he had so much more information about his circumstances, but the new knowledge didn't make him feel any less alone or lost.

"Where are we going?" Fredrick asked.

"There's no reason to keep you at the office." Martin changed lanes, then checked over his shoulder as they drove down a ramp onto some kind of large boulevard. "And you're not a criminal, so I'm taking you to a safehouse, where you can rest."

"Safehouse?" Fredrick blinked a couple times, his eyes adjusting to the brightness.

"We have many safehouses all over the country. You'll be able to take a shower, eat, get some sleep."

"What about the stuff from Wilhelm?"

"We'll go over that too."

"How did you know?" Fredrick asked. "I mean, how did you find me? And how did I already have a job waiting for me on the *Hawaiian Sun*? Was that you?"

Martin smiled as he adjusted his grip on the steering wheel. "The first question is easier to answer." They got behind a long line of cars slowing down, speeding up, and slowing down again. "Honolulu traffic is no joke."

"Does everyone here have an automobile?"

"Seems like. To answer your question, in the 70s and 80s, Project Elysium, with the help of NASA, launched several satellites, so we can monitor not only the US, but other countries, for Jumpers."

"Satellites ... NASA ...?"

What are all these things?

"Oh, right." Martin glanced at Fredrick. "Well, our space agency is called the National Aeronautics and Space Administration, NASA, and satellites are minicomputers we have orbiting the planet."

Fredrick rubbed his forehead.

"I know it's a lot. Sorry."

"There's so much. So much has happened."

"If it helps, you've been adjusting quite well." Martin quickly smiled at him before turning his attention back to the road. "Some people have a harder time. The 1930s aren't that different from now, and I think Leo helped you, more so than I imagined."

"Leo—is he part of all this?"

"No." Martin chuckled. "No, he unfortunately got tangled up in this whole thing, more than others. Which is on me. I shouldn't have …" He shook his head; a pink tint touched his cheeks. "I should've taken you off the airship in Hilo."

"You found me with a satellite. But what about my passport and my job?"

"When a Jumper appears, there is a small electric static pulse that we're able to pick up on. The pulse gives us the area, and if we're lucky, we can tap into the area's security cameras and verify a Jumper has arrived. The San Jose Zeppelin Terminal has been under surveillance since Director Hoffmann took over. He knew you'd show up there. Anyway, most of the time we're able to get out to them, but sometimes, like with you, they are met by a local."

"Leo."

"Correct." Martin checked the mirrors of the vehicle. "Remember what I said earlier about the Universe and Fate?"

Fredrick pondered the idea of the universe and fate playing a part in all this. It was a stretch, but he didn't have any other theories, so …

Martin continue, "Well, we think the universe tries to self-correct to accommodate for the Jumper. We'll find they have current IDs, and some, like you, will have a job that knows all about them, typically a new hire—" The car decelerated quickly. "Idiot!" Martin shouted, honking the car's horn. "Sorry, the guy cut me off." He changed lanes.

"And that's what happened to me." Fredrick tried not to focus on all the automobiles around him. His pulse already raced through his veins; he didn't think his heart could handle any more, despite the doctor telling him he was perfectly healthy.

"Yep."

"How does it all work?" Fredrick rubbed his arm where he got one of the larger shots, massaging the spot.

Martin's head tilted and his lips pinched together. "That we still don't know, and we can't send you to 1937. We haven't figured any of it out. I'm sorry."

As they moved off the main road, they turned onto a small street with several houses. "Where are we?"

"Not too far from Diamond Head. No ocean views I'm afraid,

but the house is clean and well-stocked. We'll have to do our own cooking, but I'm not too bad."

"You're staying with me?" Fredrick's heart leaped as his stomach dropped; the flutter of butterflies returned.

"For the time being. I'm here to help your transition into our world." Martin pulled into the driveway of a pink house, under a covered parking space before stopping the vehicle. "We're here."

The house was a pale pink color and seemed small, but matched its surroundings. Much like the office building in the downtown, the house was neat and clean but uninteresting. Martin pushed open the car door, then opened the back door and pulled out a couple of duffel bags. After Fredrick got out of the vehicle, the car locked with a loud beep. Fredrick followed Martin into the house, and much like what he expected, the space had basic furnishings and no personal effects. "It's so sterile."

"That's the FBI for you." Martin pointed. "There's a bathroom down there with the two bedrooms—pick whatever room you want." He placed the duffels on the kitchen table and held out his arms. "And this is the kitchen and living space." He chuckled. "And it, too, can be yours for the low low price of 1.5 million dollars."

"What?" Fredrick's jaw dropped.

"Honolulu's expensive, like Silicon Valley. The price is cheap for this area." Martin pulled off his jacket and hung it on a chair. "Let me get the AC going. Try and cool this place off a bit."

Fredrick shook his head. "How can anyone afford such things?"

"A lot of people can't." Martin moved over to a window with a mounted box. He turned the machine on with a loud whoosh of air. "That'll help." He grabbed a laptop from the duffel bags and placed it on the table, then plugged it into a wall socket.

"Now what?" There wasn't much here and he doubted the Special Agent would let him go out and walk around.

"While you were with the medics, I put together this duffel bag for you. There's clothing and all the basics. Our store house at the office doesn't have a great selection, but ..." He shrugged. "Anyway, you can take a shower if you want, or rest—you must be exhausted. I'll make dinner in a little bit."

"You told me I have choices to make before we left the FBI office. What choices are those? And what about Wilhelm?"

"Right. So you have to decide what you want to do with your life going forward." Martin scratched his head. "We're always looking for people to join Project Elysium—several former Jumpers have worked with us, but not all. You can go and work on the *Hawaiian Sun* if you want, or you can go home to Germany."

"I have nothing in Germany. Not anymore …"

"That's not quite true." Martin opened his duffel bag and pulled out a file folder, then passed it to Fredrick. "Open it."

Fredrick did as instructed, flipping through some documents and finding a couple of photos. "That's the house I grew up in."

"Wilhelm has it in a trust for you. It's yours. Also, in the trust is some money—not a lot, but enough to help you out, should you want to go home."

"He did this for me?" Fredrick looked up at Martin. His heart both sank and lifted at the same time. Why would Wilhelm have done any of this when he didn't have to?

Maybe he did love me and this is his way of showing it.

"Wilhelm cared a great deal for you, from everything I've heard."

Fredrick ran a hand over the image.

My home. I have a home.

"Keep the file. You'll need the paperwork, but you can worry about that all later. Germany is still your home. You might like it—it's nothing like what the Nazis had done to it. Germany's economy is in the top ten in the world. It's also Federal parliamentary republic and is one of the strongest members of the EU. With a high Human Rights Index score," he huffed. "They are higher than the US."

"What's the Human Rights Index?"

Martin scratched his head. "It's a matrix that basically keeps track of people's civil liberties. You want your country to have a high score, and now Germany does."

"So it's good?"

Martin nodded.

Fredrick inhaled. Martin wasn't wrong—Germany had been his home once and it might be nice to see a free and safe Germany, or to see what his home is like now.

Thank you, Wilhelm.

"We'll help you as best we can," Martin continued. "You should now have an active Deutsche Bank account and they're overnighting you a credit card. We'll have to go to the office tomorrow so you can sign everything, and we'll scan the documents to send over to them. I wanted to have it all today, but—oh ..." Martin shifted through his duffel again and pulled out an envelope to hand over to Fredrick. "Inside you'll find a German driver's license and all your work visa Information. I wasn't able to get your passport before we left the *Hawaiian Sun*, but I can have one of the team pick up your belongings and mine tomorrow when the airship arrives here in Honolulu."

Fredrick glanced at the paperwork in the envelope, then placed the folder on the table. "I need to think. I'm going to take a shower."

"Sure. I'll pull together something for us to eat."

Driver's license. German bank account. Credit card. It's all so unbelievable. Now what am I supposed to do?

• • •

After Fredrick's shower, he decided to lay down to hopefully clear his mind. The vocals of a woman's voice echoed from the living space. He followed the music and saw Martin's head bopping up and down in time with the song as he sang along with the music.

"What's this?" Fredrick asked, trying to bite away his grin. He wouldn't lie, observing Martin move to the music reminded him of their dance at the Captain's Gala.

At least I have some wonderful memories.

Martin froze, dropping something from his hand. The clatter revealed the item to be something metal. He quickly wiped his hands and tapped his smartphone next to him, ending the music. "Sorry. I hope the music didn't bother you."

"No, but what was it?"

Martin watched him a moment. "Um ... *I will Always Love you*, by Whitney Houston. She was an incredible singer, and the song is considered to be one of the best love songs ever written."

"The music is lovely," Fredrick commented. He caught a whiff of the prepared food and was transported to his childhood home, his mother standing by the table calling him and his brother, sister, and father to come eat.

Martin cleared his throat. "I like her. Anyway, dinner's ready if you want to have a seat."

Was he embarrassed by his singing and me walking in on him?

He couldn't help but beam as he sat at the small kitchen table. There was a plate of mashed potatoes, carrots, and pickled beets lying next to two knachwurst with a dollop of mustard on the side.

"I hope you like it." Martin sat across the table.

The scents of the sausage and the potatoes continued their pleasant assault on Fredrick's nose, and he couldn't help but lick his lips as he salivated. He huffed out a laugh. "This looks like something my mom would have put together for us, when I was still at home."

"I assumed a taste from home might be appreciated." Martin wiped his hands on his towel as he set it on the table next to him.

Fredrick glanced up from the plate of food. "Why are you being so nice to me?" He had a lot of time to think and he wanted to understand what part Martin played in all this.

This couldn't be how he treats everyone. Can it? Maybe I'm only a case. Maybe that's all I ever was. But I want to know.

Martin inhaled. "Because ..." His gaze dropped as he studied his plate of slowly cooling food.

"Because why?"

"Fredrick, I had to evaluate you before I took you off the ship." Martin glanced around the kitchen. "I had to get—"

"Why not take me when I first arrived?" Fredrick's voice grew in volume as he interrupted Martin. Allowing him on the airship in the first place seemed foolhardy.

"We've been wrong in the past." Martin sighed. "It doesn't happen often anymore, but it does happen and the cleanup can be a nightmare. I had to be sure."

"You've been wrong?"

"We're not perfect, and despite us believing you were our target, we couldn't be sure. We didn't have any photos to work from—only a sketch that Wilhelm had made." Martin dug out his phone to show Fredrick the drawing. "See?"

The image on the screen was big enough that Fredrick noticed how much the drawing looked like him. Maybe a touch more flattering than how he appeared, but there was no question that was him.

Martin put the phone away. "You did a good job of blending in. I wasn't a hundred percent certain, even after we had brunch. I didn't know for sure until Hilo, when you went to the Hilo Coin Trove."

"You followed me—well, us?"

"Yes."

"Wow, everything you said and did was all for show?" Fredrick barked louder than he wanted, his heart pounding in his chest and head. "All a lie? Poor Mr. Kakoa."

"Mr. Kakoa's fine. Once I knew where you were going, I had my tech team tap into his security cameras so I could watch your exchange from the ship. That's when I knew."

A shudder ran through Fredrick's body. He had been spied on, and so had Uncle Billie. That wasn't right. None of this was right. "I can't believe you did that."

"Would you've preferred we burst into the shop and arrested everyone?" Martin's brows rose. "Taken you, Leo, and Mr. Kakoa in for questioning? I don't think Leo or Uncle Billie would thank you." He took a deep breath and exhaled before he spoke again. "A large part of my job requires discretion. We find using a scalpel better than using a dagger."

There was a logic to what Martin told him, and he couldn't fault the man for being as discrete as he had been, but still. The man was a liar.

Or is he only doing his job? One he doesn't seem happy with at the moment.

Fredrick's stomach rumbled and he took a bite of his food. "It's good."

"Thank you." Martin had yet to pick up his fork.

He took a couple more bites of his meal, enough to subside the ache in his gut. "If I'm understanding, everything about our interactions was a fabrication so you might learn about me. See if I'm whom you believed me to be."

Martin's gaze moved around the room instead of Fredrick. "No. Look, I like you. The more time I spent with you, the more I ..." He ran a hand over his chin. "We're not supposed to get attached. When we danced, you felt amazing. I should've taken you off in Hilo, but I couldn't. I tried to stay away from you, but ..." He met Fredrick's gaze. "And I ... look ... I'm sorry."

"You like me?" Fredrick asked, surprised by the confession.

"Couldn't you tell?" Martin snorted. "I followed you around like a lost puppy. Yes, some of it was to ensure you weren't messing things up, or causing trouble, but you were with Leo so I doubted that would be an issue. You know, you weren't the only one who *enjoyed* our dance at the Captain's Gala."

Fredrick bit away a smile. He shouldn't be smiling, but it was good to know that not everything about Martin was a lie—plus, he appreciated the flattery. "What do we … what do I do now?"

Martin shook his head. "I can't make that choice for you. After tomorrow, someone else will take over your case and I'll head home, to San Jose."

"You're leaving?" Fredrick stomach did somersaults. Yes, he was sore with Martin, but he didn't want him to leave. They were only recently getting to know each other. "Didn't you say you're here to help me?"

"I am, but only until tomorrow." Martin frowned. "While you were in the shower, I checked in with my boss. She wasn't happy I didn't take you off before we left Hilo, and they think I'm getting entangled."

Fredrick eyed Martin. "Are you? Are you getting entangled with me?"

"What do you think?" Martin picked up his fork and slowly chewed his way through the meal.

"I see." Fredrick returned to his plate of food. "And this is our last dinner together?"

"Look, Fredrick, you're a great guy, and whatever you decide to do, you'll be fine." Martin glanced across the table meeting Fredrick's gaze. "I have no doubt you'll adjust to this new time and your new life."

"Can't I go with you?" The words fell out faster than Fredrick could stop them. His face and neck warmed at once.

"That … look, even if you decided to work for us, I couldn't have you working with me." Martin broke off his gaze with Fredrick. "It'd be too difficult."

Martin was probably correct. He needed to live his own life. "Can I return to the *Hawaiian Sun*? At least there I know people and have a job."

"Don't you want to go to Germany?"

"Not right now … I think I need to get used to things first before going home. Plus, I like the *Hawaiian Sun* and everyone there."

"Is that what you want?"

What I want and what I can have are two different things—something I'm used to growing up when I did.

Fredrick scanned the cozy house. There was a lot he could do with a small place like this, maybe turn the space into a home—their home—but that wasn't to be. "It's the only option that makes sense. Can I do that?"

Martin leaned forward in his chair. "We'd need a reason for me to have released you. And I'm sure no one has bought into the whole you being sick thing."

Not if he knew Leo or the others. The story was rubbish even as Martin suggested it, and they all knew it.

"No," Fredrick agreed. This wasn't like on the *Hindenburg* when he and Wilhelm were simply going to run away. Back in the 1930s, vanishing would have been a lot easier.

What would Wilhelm do?

"I think I have an idea." Fredrick smiled as he took another bite of his meal.

This might work.

23

LEO PACED BACK AND FORTH in his cabin, the slight scent of his woodsy cologne stinging his nose. He fanned his shirt as he continued to wear a path in the cabin's floor. The flight to Honolulu had been smooth, but he couldn't sleep. He glanced at the empty bunk—he was filled with worry over Fredrick. He thought a hot shower would help.

It didn't.

What was happening to Fredrick? Was he in some dark cell? Would Detective Masson be able to help, or find anything out? Glancing out the small cabin's window, he couldn't see much; just the blues of the ocean, he assumed. He would have loved to have been on the bridge again, watching the mooring, but he couldn't bring himself to go. His nerves and state of mind wouldn't have allowed him to focus.

Luckily, today was a big port day. Everyone went into Honolulu. He had given Ollie a full day off, and let his team know he'd be manning the lounge for him. There was work that needed to be done, but ... he would've loved to have shown Fredrick the city. Diamond Head, or even the North Shore.

His worry was cut off with a ding of his phone. It was a message from Barron.

Heard from Det. Masson this morning. Can I meet you in the club?

Leo tapped out a response, then checked his reflection in the mirror. He dabbed at his eyes—other than slight puffiness, they didn't look too bad. He slipped on his jacket, then checked the mini fridge. He had some fruit and a quarter of a loaf of bread. He quickly shook his head; he'd grab something in the club.

David always made enough.

Fussing around the lounge, Leo couldn't keep himself still. He cleaned the buffet counter and the glass shields, tidied the tables and chairs, and even dusted the rail by the viewing windows. Unlike the Hilo and Kahului landing fields, the Honolulu zeppelin mooring docks where adjacent to, but not incorporated with, the airport. This provided a location to house and repair a zeppelin if need be. And they had a lot more space for everything. The downside was they were farther away from the tourist locations, and the only view this side of the zep had was of the military base, and some of the mountain.

He glanced at his cell, checking the time.

No one will be here for another thirty minutes. Where's Barron?

As if on cue, there was a knock on the club's door. Leo rushed over to the lounge's etched stained-glass double doors, he glanced through the image of the *Hawaiian Sun* blurring out the figure on the opposite side. He opened the door to greet Barron with a big hug and kiss. "Babe, thank Christ." Barron wore tan linen shorts, brown shoes and a light gray shirt, opened at the top to show off the chain Leo got him.

Handsome as always.

"Good morning to you, too." Barron stepped back to study Leo. "Did you sleep at all last night?" He sniffed the air around Leo. "Is that the cologne I bought you?"

"Off and on." He ignored the comment about the scent as he sat down. "Well, what did Elijah's mom have to say?"

Barron sank heavily into his seat. "Nothing good, I'm afraid."

Leo massaged his forehead. "Okay."

"Did you know that Fredrick's ex went missing in Germany, William—no, Wilhelm?"

Leo would need more than aspirin to fight off his growing headache. "He mentioned that he thought Wilhelm died ... but they can't believe he had anything to do with it. He wouldn't have been allowed to leave Germany if he was a suspect. Hell, they probably would have seized his passport."

Barron shrugged. "Which is what Sara Masson told us, but ..."

"But the FBI has him in custody ..." Leo rubbed his temples again.

"And that's all she was able to find out, since it's an open investigation involving a German citizen. She mentioned something about an organization, that I can't pronounce, in Germany that's working with the FBI on this." He sank back against the chair.

"Well ... fuck."

"I'm going to ask—"

Leo knew the question and answered before Barron finished. "There's no way Fredrick had anything to do with this guy's disappearance ..." His expression dropped into what he knew was a frown.

"What?" Barron shifted forward.

Leo ran a hand over his face and through his hair. "Fredrick mentioned he caught the guy cheating on him."

"Hell's bells." Barron's head dropped, meeting his risen hands.

"And this is why rumors are messed up."

"You can't deny it gives him a pretty good motive." Barron pinched the bridge of his nose.

"There's no way." Leo refused to let any more worry or dread infiltrate his thoughts. "I refuse to believe any of this."

Barron wiped his mouth and chin, keeping quiet.

"Babe, you can't honestly think ...?" Leo's gaze bore into Barron.

"Leo, what do you know about this guy?"

"I know he passed our background check. I know he has all his paperwork in order. I know that every 'i' was dotted and 't' was crossed. There is no way Fredrick is that kind of person."

"Okay, I believe you." He took and squeezed Leo's hand for emphasis. "And honestly, given all my interactions with Fredrick, I think he's a good guy too, but you never know. I'm only worried about you, cause you bunk with him and you work so close. And you're risking everything to look into what happened."

Leo's head bobbed up and down in the affirmative. He understood, but that put him in a good place to be a judge of Fredrick's character. "What else did Detective Masson say?"

"Not much. She said she'd check out more today, but given the situation, she doesn't think she'd find anything else out."

Leo frowned, his frustration building. "I bet Elijah's going to have a field day with all this."

Barron shook his head. "I don't think so. He seemed pretty upset about all this, especially after the scene he made during the tea service. Believe it or not, he doesn't think Fredrick would do anything of that sort ..." He clucked his tongue. "He actually told me I was being overly dramatic."

"Pot to kettle." Leo smirked.

"Right." Barron kissed Leo's hand. "It's too bad about the two of you. I think in other circumstances, you might be friends."

"Hey, none of that was on me."

"Oh, babe, trust me, I know." Barron kissed Leo's hand one more time. "Elijah, when he's not being nasty, can be a decent person. Sometimes you have to dig deeper to find the good is all."

Leo glanced around the club. His team, sans Oliver, would arrive soon enough for their morning check in. "Do you think we'll ever know what happened? With Fredrick, I mean?"

Barron sighed. "Honestly, I don't think so. Do you want me to stick around today? You have to work, but I can hang out here in the club. You know, be here if you need someone?"

Leo stood. "That's sweet, babe, but no. As the Captain likes to remind us, we have an illusion and fantasy to keep up for the guests. I can't do that with you here, as much as I'd love it." He pulled Barron up and kissed him. "Go out with your friends and enjoy Honolulu, but if you hear something more, call me. Okay?"

"Absolutely."

They shared another kiss, this one deeper. Leo pulled Barron in as close as possible, feeling both their hearts beat. The door clicked and they glanced toward the door to watch Aurora enter. "Did I interrupt something?" She eyed the two of them.

"No." Leo huffed out a laugh. "We wanted to talk and Mr. Masson was in the cabin so I had Barron meet me here."

"In fact, I need to get back." Barron kissed Leo on the cheek. "Our group wants to go out to the Aulani for a spa day. Elijah signed us up for a day pass. Should be ... interesting."

"Oh, that sounds nice." Aurora patted her hair, ensuring her bun was in place. "I'm only slightly jealous. Make sure to have a drink in the 'Ōlelo Room for me."

Barron smirked. "You'd think. I'm sure Elijah has some ulterior motive."

Leo laughed.

"Don't laugh. If I'm not back later, it means I've been kidnapped by Chip and Dale." Barron squeezed Leo's hand. "Have a good day, okay? I'll see you later. If you need me, give me a call."

Leo's lips pinched together as he gave a firm nod. "Thanks, babe." He sighed as Barron's hand slipped out of his. With one more glance, Barron smiled as he made his way to the door.

"I like him," Aurora announced to Leo after the door closed.

"He's a good guy." Leo's heart fluttered. "Part of why I love him."

•   •   •

Fredrick stuffed his duffel in the back of the car, hints of the ocean making its way to his nose. He loved the smell of the sea, and how the forest smelled after a rainstorm. The neighborhood was silent now, but that wasn't the case before sunrise. A loud rumble like thunder, or revving of what he imagined to be a jet engine, pulled him from the dream of his family back in Germany. The noise from the vehicle must have woken up the local dogs, because a choir of barking started and didn't stop until he and Martin were ready to leave.

"Sorry about all the noise this morning." Martin opened the door behind the driver's seat. "I hope it didn't bother you."

"No. It was fine. I was awake." He didn't need to complain, or make Martin feel bad.

Martin shook his head. "While you were packing, I got a call from the office. They got a call from a detective in San Jose, asking about you. Do you know a Detective Sara Masson?"

Fredrick thought for a moment before shaking his head. "No; the only Masson I've heard of is one of the guests—Mr. Elijah Masson, he's a friend of Barron's, Mr. Hillchild."

"The bigger guy with the perfect brown hair?" Martin asked. "Had a flare for dramatics?"

"Yes," Fredrick agreed, checking his pockets for his watch and billfold. He wanted to ensure he didn't misplace his new ID. "Why?"

Martin couldn't hold in his laugh. "Seems like Leo called in some favors."

"What do you mean?" Fredrick asked as he crossed the back of the car, meeting Martin by the driver's side as he spoke.

"I think your plan is going to work." Martin beamed at him.

Fredrick glanced around and didn't see anyone watching them. He leaned in and kissed Martin, the soft feeling sending a bolt of energy through him. He inhaled the scent that was all Martin's, a mix of the soft soap from the shower, the fruity shampoo he had used, and the warm spice scent of his aftershave. The kiss faded and he stepped back.

I will never forget the smell or this moment now.

"What was that for?" The grin on Martin's face stretched from ear to ear.

"I may never see you again, and I wanted to thank you properly."

"Thank you." Martin's neck and face pinkened. "We should get you back to the airship by noon. We still need to stop by the office and take care of your banking paperwork."

"Right." Fredrick felt his pocket for his wallet again, he had a lot of cash with him and wasn't sure what to do with it. "Are the banks better in this time?"

Martin's brows narrowed. "Yes ... since the Great Depression and a few other incidents. Any money you put in the bank is protected up to a certain amount. I believe it's €100,000 per depositor in Germany and here in the US it's $250,000. You definitely want to put your money there. It's a lot easier to access your funds these days, and a lot of people don't even carry cash anymore."

"As long as I can get my money out and it won't go away." The memory of the failed banks in Germany and how expensive everything got rushed to Fredrick's mind.

I don't want to have something like that happen again, especially since I'll be on my own.

"You'll want to talk to the bank in Germany about getting a debit card, something that you can use here in the States. It'll take time, but in the meantime, you can use cash as well as your credit card. Since you're going to be here in the US for a while, you might want to open up a US Bank account. Something your hero, Leo, can assist you with," Martin suggested. "How much did you end up with from the Hilo Coin Trove, if I can ask?"

Fredrick lowered his voice. "About $7,300, and I was supposed to put it all in the safe in our room ..."

"How much do you have with you right now?"

"$5,000." The words were barely audible but the look on Martin's face told him he heard him.

Martin's head quickly moved up and down. "You're gonna want to put most of that in the bank. You never want to be out with that kind of cash. It's not safe."

"I wasn't expecting to be off the ship when you met me in the club yesterday. I planned on going into town and buying several items. I didn't know how much I would need with me."

"Crap, yeah, okay," Martin stammered. "I get it, but you're gonna want a debit card. It's like cash and a lot safer to use."

"Okay."

Martin pulled out his phone. "We should head out. You have everything?"

Fredrick felt his pockets again. Everything was there; the files Martin gave him were in the duffel bag, and his German ID was safe in his billfold along with his cash. "I think so."

24

L EO GLANCED AT THE STACK of cards they'd received for Fredrick, various notes wishing him well and a speedy recovery. There was no such thing as a secret on a zep like this. None of the guests or crew knew the truth, but it still warmed his heart to see the outpour of support for his crewmate.

The time on his computer said it was slightly after noon, and the morning in Honolulu had been predictably quiet. It gave him time to review the excursion data for Nawiliwili. He also noted that the Hoomaha Spa would be offering Club-level guests a 25% discount on the remainder of the trip—*they must be under their target for the trip.*

He switched screens to check his emails. Tammy had sent him a message to see how he was doing, and to check if he needed anything. He shook his head and scanned his email folders. He would need to think about a new Butler to replace Fredrick. His guts moaned as his mood and stomach dropped. In theory, they can get someone temporarily, in case Fredrick came back. The scents from the lunch buffet tickled his nose. David was a sorcerer when it came to his culinary prowess.

Nuwa's stomach grumbled, catching Leo by surprise, and he chuckled.

"That man is going to be the death of my waistline," Nuwa commented, glancing at the parade of trays being put in their warming stations.

"You and me both," Leo confirmed as he patted his belly. "Why don't you go grab yourself something since no one's around."

"You don't have to tell me twice." She stood, pulling off her glasses to give them a quick clean. "You want anything?"

"Sure." Leo sniffed the air to catch the glorious aromas making his mouth water. "But don't go full hog."

Nuwa laughed as she headed over to the buffet to chat up the dining team putting out the food.

Leo frowned back at his terminal. The back end of the trip wasn't any easier than the front half of the trip—they would need to plan for escorting the club guests off the ship, ensuring their luggage was ready and waiting. He would need to speak with Tammy and verify that the room attendants would have everything the night before. Almost as if on cue, his radio beeped. He picked up the device. "Go for Leo."

"Leo, can you join me in my office please?" Tammy's voice was tight.

"I'm on my way," he responded as Nuwa appeared with two plates of food.

"Everything okay?" She put his plate down in front of him, containing a couple of tea sandwiches and some fruit.

"Not sure." He grabbed a sandwich and a grape. "I need to go meet Tammy. Call me if you need anything."

Leo finished off his smoked salmon and cream cheese sandwich and grape as he departed the club. He stopped and turned back to glower at the etched image of the *Hawaiian Sun. What new drama do you have in store for me today?* His phone beeped, and he pulled it out to see the reminder he set to ensure he knew when the guests returned for afternoon tea.

Nuwa should be fine.

He greeted each guest he passed on his way to Tammy's cabin. Luckily, there weren't many, but he knew they would be heading for the club. *I hope this doesn't take long. I'm not in the mood.* Instead of waiting for the elevator, he took the stairs to the Prominade deck, figuring the exercise would do him some good, especially since he spent most of the morning at the desk. He arrived at Tammy's office and knocked.

"Enter," Tammy's voice called out.

He opened the door and stepped inside. "What the …" Sitting on the sofa were Fredrick and Mr. Shaw.

"Close the door, please," Captain Monroe directed.

Leo closed the door behind him. "What's going on?" The words fell from his mouth.

Martin stood, holding a manila envelope in his hands. "Thank you for joining us."

"Now, will you please explain?" Captain Monroe's tone was tight and there was none of her typical pleasant nature.

Clearly, I'm not the only one not happy to see the Special Agent again.

Leo ignored Martin and focused on Fredrick. "Are you okay?"

"I'm fine," Fredrick responded.

Martin cleared this throat. "I think it would be best if Fredrick explained."

Leo continued to examine Fredrick to ensure they hadn't hurt him, though nothing stood out. Fredrick was dressed in jeans and a polo shirt, not the clothing that Fredrick and Leo bought the day of Fredrick's arrival.

Where'd these clothes come from? Where's his uniform?

•   •   •

The butterflies in Fredrick's stomach felt as if they were going to explode from his body. Was he ready to do this? Would this even work? If it didn't work, he supposed he could work with Martin, but the idea of espionage had no appeal for him.

In general, he hated lying, but he didn't see another option—the truth would cause too many questions, and he didn't think the news would be well-received. *No, this is for the best.* Fredrick cleared his throat and wiped the damp from his hands onto his jeans. "First, I want to apologize for any trouble I may have caused."

"You didn't cause any trouble," Leo reminded him. "Well, not much."

Fredrick forced a smile to his lips. "Anyway, remember when I told you about my ex, Wilhelm?" He focused on Leo; he didn't think he could stand looking at the others as he went through all this.

"Yeah, you told me you caught him cheating on you."

Fredrick's head moved up and down. "And that something happened to him, and I assumed he may be dead."

"What?" Captain Monroe barked out, stepping forward.

"How did this get missed?" Tammy glanced between both the Captain and Leo.

"So that's why you took Fredrick." Captain Monroe shook her head. "Jesus Christ, what a clusterfuck ..."

Martin had been right. You give people enough bits of information and they'll create the story. The goal today was to have the Captain, Ms. Lam, and Leo create the story that he and Martin needed to explain all this away. Martin had schooled him on staying quiet and only answering questions that came to him. This would allow him to share as much of the truth as possible without outright lying.

"You needed to question him?" Leo asked. His hand moved to his left temple as he started to rub. "Well, clearly he didn't do anything. I can't believe how you screwed this all up, and for what?"

"Mr. Asher, there was a dead man and we needed to ensure that Mr. Rudolf wasn't involved." Martin's tone was polite but firm.

Leo huffed out a short tight chuckle. "And I bet he never lost his luggage, did he? I bet you intercepted it ... you bastard."

"Wait," Captain Monroe called all their attention to her, "why's he here? What're we supposed to do now?"

Fredrick's stomach sank deeper. Maybe they wouldn't want him. He did cause a lot of trouble and no one needed the kind of mess Fredrick brought with him. And he was still lying to them—he wasn't telling them that he was from an alternate 1937 and the man he had been involved with appeared in 1942 and died in 2004.

I know I wouldn't believe any of this, if I hadn't been through it.

"Fredrick's free to go, so we brought him back." Martin held out the envelope he brought with him. "Inside you'll find a letter from the Consulate General of Germany in San Francisco, and from my office, ensuring Fredrick is cleared and there will be no trouble should you allow him to return to his job, which I hope you will, Captain."

Captain Monroe rubbed her forehead. "Jesus. Do you have any idea how messed up this is? I don't like these kind of—of—shenanigans happening on my zeppelin."

"And for that I apologize." Martin lowered his head. "We should have taken him off in Hilo—"

"No," Tammy interjected. "You should have picked him up at the airport with his luggage. He shouldn't have ever gotten on the *Hawaiian Sun*."

Leo raised his hands. "Well, now, I mean … okay … I understand things are messed up, but if I'm understanding this correctly, Fredrick wasn't involved and he's cleared of everything. Right?"

"Correct," Martin agreed. "And again, I apologize. After this, I'm leaving for the mainland. You won't see me again. I've also sent a copy of my report to United AirShips Corporate, so they'll have a record."

"Good." Tammy's eyes were wide. "I can assure you, if you were on my team and you screwed up like this, you'd never work on a zeppelin again."

"Understood." Martin's tone remained quiet and passive.

This is the most lifeless I've seen him. He plays his part well.

"It wasn't all—" Fredrick started to defend Martin, unwilling to let him be their punching bag, but the Captain raised her hand to stop him.

"Don't say anything. Don't speak."

Fredrick closed his mouth. He hated how this was all working out. Martin wasn't a villain—he was a good man and helped Fredrick. He was here to ensure all their safety.

Das ist so beschissen.

Leo rubbed his mouth. "Okay, so, legally, there's no reason why Fredrick can't continue, is there?"

"Leo." Tammy rubbed her forehead as she let out a hard exhale.

"Hear me out," Leo started. "Until the unfortunate incident in Kahului, Fredrick has been an excellent hire and a good worker. The guests like him. In fact, we've gotten at least seven different notes from guests who heard Fredrick was unwell, not to mention his crewmates asked me about how he's doing."

"Seven?" Tammy asked.

Wow! That's kind of everyone. Fredrick bit at the joy that wanted to burst from his lips as his heart lightened at the news. *People here really are amazing.*

"That was as of this morning, but I'm sure there'll be more. I even got a note from the Montgomery-Clarks asking if they might be able to do something for him. And we all know how well connected they are." Leo glanced over at Fredrick. "I told you people were going to be impressed with you on this trip."

Fredrick couldn't believe that people he barely knew were wishing him well. Hearing all this helped lessen the bitter sting of witnessing their treatment of Martin.

I wish I could tell them the truth.

Captain Monroe sat down in the chair nearest her, lacing her fingers together in front of her face as she took several breaths. The room fell silent as everyone watched her. In short order, she spoke, "The only people who know what happened are my First Officer, the Doctor, and those in this room."

"As far as I know." Tammy nodded.

Leo cleared his throat. "Mr. Hillchild, Barron, and Mr. Masson both know. I may have asked Mr. Masson to contact his mother, who's a Detective in San Jose—"

"You did what?" Captain Monroe's voice barreled out of her. "I may not have specifically instructed you to keep this confidential, but I assumed you wouldn't need to be told. This is not how an officer on my ship acts."

"Yes, Captain." Leo sunk at the dressing down.

Fredrick was powerless to say or do anything, no matter how much he appreciated all that Leo did for him. To speak up for him now would only make the Captain's ire that much worse ... for all of them.

"Captain, about that." Martin had hints of a grin dancing around his lips. "Detective Masson's been contacted and informed of the situation. You won't hear from her again."

"Well, isn't that lovely for Detective Masson." Captain Monroe narrowed her gaze on Leo. "Is there anyone else? Maybe one of the crew in laundry services? Or did you perhaps say something to Dapper Dave or Krystal Chandelier?"

"I ... I couldn't—"

Captain Monroe raised her hand to Leo and turned to Fredrick. "This is not how I run my airship. This is not how we do things in the United AirShips Family. For over ninety years, we've never had a situation like this, and in all my years as a Captain, I've never dealt with a state of affairs this screwed up. I've had people pass away, we've had rough air, we've had lift malfunctions, we've had outbreaks of illness, but never ... never have I had one of my crew investigated and cleared of a potential homicide. And to be asked to let said crew member return to the ship, as if nothing happened ... No." She shook her head.

Fredrick's stomach dropped.

"Captain Monroe—"

"I'm not finished, Mr. Shaw." She glared at him as if daring him to speak. "I'm not in a position to punish a person for mistakes made by someone else, especially someone like you, Mr. Shaw." She inhaled. "Leo. Tammy. I trust your judgement. Although, at this moment, I'm questioning whether having faith in Leo is wise."

"Captain, I know Leo may have made a mistake, but you and I know he's one of the best."

The Captain remained silent but gave a sharp nod in Tammy's direction.

Perhaps I shouldn't have dismissed going home to Germany so quickly.

Tammy faced Leo. "Well?"

Leo inhaled. Clearly his frustration and annoyance wouldn't help anyone right now. "I agree with the Captain. I don't like the idea of punishing someone for something that wasn't their fault. If Fredrick would like to return, I'm all for it."

"Thank you," Fredrick murmured, all his lips and body would allow him to say at the moment.

Leo continued. "As for the other matter, I hope, Captain, you'll regain your faith in me."

Captain Monroe faced the ceiling. "I'll have to clear this with HR at Corporate. And I hope, for all our sakes, every 'i' is dotted and every 't' is crossed, Agent Shaw." She returned her gaze to those assembled. "With this being Fredrick's first contract with us, I want a full thirty-day follow up and a sixty-day review. I want to ensure that ... that"— she waved her hand toward Martin—"this sort of thing doesn't happen again."

"Very good, Captain." Leo's tone softened and his shoulders appeared more relaxed.

"And I want Tammy to sit in the meetings," The Captain added.

"Yes, ma'am," Leo acknowledged.

"We'll need to get him cleared medically." Tammy rubbed her neck and shoulder. "So he can return to work."

Captain Monroe focused on Fredrick. "Meaning, Mr. Rudolf, before you return to your duties, you're going to have a conversation with Dr. Young. She's even less pleased than I am with how this all went down. Prepare yourself, young man." The Captain stood. "Mr. Asher."

Leo stood at attention.

"I'm not happy with you speaking to Mr. Hilchild or Mr. Masson. There is a level of discretion we need to keep with our guests. They pay a lot of money for the fantasy we create. I trust we won't need to take this any further than a verbal reprimand?"

"Understood, Captain," Leo responded. "And thank you, ma'am."

She squeezed Leo's arm. "That said, it shows a lot of character to how far you are willing to go for your crewmates, and I only wish everyone had your kind of dedication to their team."

Leo didn't speak, but the pleased expression blooming across his face told them everything they needed.

The Captain faced Martin. "And as for you, Mr. Shaw, if I could ban you from ever flying on my airship again, I would, but since your bosses far outrank mine, I doubt I have that luxury. Still, I trust that our paths won't cross again any time soon."

Martin stood up. "I understand, Captain. For what it's worth, I believe you're making the right choice in allowing Fredrick, Mr. Rudolf, to continue his contract with you and your ship. He's an amazing man and I'm pleased to have gotten to know him despite the circumstances." He looked at Fredrick. "Mr. Rudolf, I wish you nothing but the best."

Fredrick's heart sank as he took Martin's hand. "Thank you … I hope … well … I'd like …"

This can't be goodbye. I don't want you to go. I need … What do I need?

"I should go." Martin removed his hand from Fredrick's, then faced Tammy and Leo. "I hope you both understand that I was only doing my job, and even in the FBI, things don't always go to plan."

Tammy huffed with an abrupt nod, while Leo's lips pinched together as he remained silent.

Fredrick caught a final whiff of the ocean, and its familiar warmth enhancing Martin's scent, as he passed by and slipped out the cabin door, vanishing from the airship and probably disappearing from Fredrick's life.

Goodbye.

25

L EO SAT WITH BATED BREATH as the door closed behind Martin. None of what happened made any difference—all his worry had evaporated once he saw Fredrick. Even knowing the Captain was upset with him didn't matter. She would hopefully get over it since she was reasonable and understanding.

Leo rushed over to Fredrick, hugging him, the stress in his neck and shoulders vanishing. "Are you okay? I mean, really? They didn't hurt you, did they?" There was no hiding his worry for Fredrick, and they were safely behind closed doors, so none of the guests would see him hug his coworker.

My friend.

Fredrick smiled, patting Leo's back. "I'm fine. Thank you."

Captain Monroe cleared her throat, and Leo and Fredrick stepped away from each other. "Mr. Asher, if you'll take your new hire to medical, I'd like to get him cleared by the doctor and returned to his duties at once." Her expression hadn't changed much since Martin left, and Leo wasn't quite sure what to make of it. "There aren't any other surprises we need to look out for, Mr. Rudolf, are there?"

"No, Captain." Fredrick's stance stiffened as he extended a firm nod of his head.

"Good." She turned toward Tammy. "Never a dull moment, eh, Head Steward?"

Tammy huffed out a laugh. "No, Captain."

"Now, I have a ship to run. I'm assuming I can trust the three of you to clean up the rest of this mess." She didn't wait for an answer as she left the cabin.

"Jesus." Leo's body relaxed as the door closed. "I never believed we'd see you again." He collapsed into a chair, resting his hands on the conference table. "What did they ask you? What happened to your ex?"

Fredrick's mouth pinched together. "He died, but it was … natural. Nothing bad."

"Oh, Fredrick … I'm sorry. I know we have guests to tend to and duties to perform, but if there's anything we can do—" Tammy was cut off.

"No," Fredrick shot the small word out. "I mean, no, thank you. I'm sorry, it's all a bit of a shock."

Leo couldn't imagine going through everything that Fredrick has been through in the last week. He had a million questions but none that would be appropriate to ask right now. "I bet. Well, at least you got all your stuff."

"Yes." Fredrick ran a hand over his shirt. "I'm glad to have my new clothes again."

Leo pulled out his phone to check the time. "Look, I know there's a lot happening, but let's get you down to see the doctor and get you to work. I wish I had the ability to give you time to relax a bit, but …"

"No. I'd rather be busy." Fredrick shifted from foot to foot. "All the time with Martin left me alone with my thoughts, and I could use the distraction." He picked up a duffel bag Leo hadn't noticed until now. "If we can stop and drop this off, that would be great."

"Yes. Of course." Leo stood and adjusted his uniform jacket. "Being busy can help."

"We're glad to have you." Tammy's cheeks rose in a smile.

"Tammy, can you let Nuwa know I'm gonna be a bit longer?"

Tammy moved over to one of her coat hooks to grab her uniform jacket. "Go take care of Fredrick and I'll head up to the lounge."

"Thanks." Leo beamed. "We won't be long. Well, I hope we won't, but you never know with Dr. Young."

Leo opened the door for Fredrick and they made their way out of Tammy's cabin. Fredrick tugged the duffel over his shoulder. "I didn't picture you for a duffel kind of guy," Leo commented as they made their way to their quarters.

"I guess I'm used to having simple, easy to use items."

They made quick work of the stairs, as more of the guests were coming from their day out in Honolulu. Most of the folks would stay out for dinner and some of the night excursions, but a fair number would return to the ship and take advantage of the free food.

I don't blame them, with the price they pay for this cruise.

"Did you get any sleep?" Leo opened the door to their cabin.

Fredrick tossed his duffel on his bed. "Yes, but I'll be glad to sleep here again. There's something about the hum of the ship and how we move through the air."

"Agreed." Leo exited into the hall. "Let's get you to the doc." Leo moved them into the crew corridor. They arrived at the gallery on Deck A and Leo waved to the security team manning the zep's gangway. They crossed the gallery and Leo opened the door to the medical center. "I hope this goes smoothly."

"Me as well." Fredrick walked through the door Leo held open.

The space wasn't as grand as some of the larger zeps, but there was still enough capacity to assist a large number of people should the need ever arise. There was a small reception/lobby area with multiple chairs and a small table. Ahead of them was a hall with a couple of doors leading to the exam rooms. To their right was another hall with a nurses' area, doctor's office, x-ray facility, pharmacy, and laboratory. The zep even boasted a decontamination room.

Leo had only been here a couple times: once when he sprained his wrist, and the second time he got headbutted by a kid in the groin. That was a pain he wouldn't wish on anyone. On the plus side, the injury led to him finding out about his retrograde ejaculation and sterility. He shuddered at the memory. They assumed his condition may be trauma from the accident with the kid, and they ended up referring him to his own doctor in San Jose for more testing.

What a nightmare.

"Hey, Sunil," Leo greeted the man sitting at the reception station. "Is Dr. Young around?"

"Oh, hiya." Sunil beamed up from behind his monitor. "Welcome back, Fredrick. I heard you caught a nasty bug. You here to get cleared?"

"Yes." Fredrick glanced around the space.

"Let me guess, not as nice as the *Hindenburg*," Leo teased as he followed Fredrick's gaze around the facility. He'd heard that the *Hindenburg*'s medical facility rivaled some of the large ocean cruise ships.

Not something people want to think about when they are on vacation, but are happy to have when they need it.

Fredrick laughed.

"Ah, good." Dr. Young appeared from her office. "The Captain radioed to expect you." She wore her officer's duty uniform sans stethoscope. Her face was neutral showing off her clear dark complexion, high cheekbones, and black hair up in a neat bun.

Dr. Young had replaced Dr. Kepferle a few years ago when the medical practitioner retired. The new doctor didn't take long to make the medical facility her own, requesting additional equipment and adding a Nurse Practitioner to her team. The upgrades gave her a strong medical crew. Leo was pleased they didn't need to use the medical facility too often, maybe a couple times a trip. Luckily the injuries were mostly from slips and falls and minor cuts. However, they had their fair share of heart attacks and strokes.

"How're you doing, Leo?" Dr. Young asked by way of greeting.

"I'm good, thanks, doc." Leo forced a grin to his lips. He hated going to the doctor—they seemed to always find something wrong.

"Excellent." Dr. Young gestured toward Fredrick. "Fredrick, please come with me. You don't need to stick around, Mr. Asher," The doctor added.

"Okay. Thanks, Doc." Leo turned to Fredrick. "Once you're cleared, get changed and come on up to the lounge. We can use the help, and I'd like to get us all back to normal."

"Thank you. Leo." The words flowed gently out of Fredrick's mouth. "I appreciate everything you've done for me."

Leo squeezed Fredrick's arm as he exhaled. He made his way out of the medical center and pulled out his radio. "Tammy, I'm on my way up to the club."

•   •   •

Fredrick watched the door close as Leo left him in the hands of Dr. Young and the rest of the medical staff. He had never seen a medical facility like this. Leo didn't bring him here on the tour, and thankfully he didn't have any reason to come down here, until now. This area seemed like a luxury of space and weight that couldn't be afforded; however, as he had to remind himself, it'd been ninety years since he last saw an airship.

He stiffened his shoulders and followed the doctor to one of the rooms. Once in the room, he noted how similar it looked to the medical facility at Martin's building. There was a bed and a roller cart, but also more advanced equipment, if that was even possible. He couldn't fathom what all these gadgets were used for.

"I bet you hoped you wouldn't have to see a space like this," The doctor commented as she pointed to the bed. "Have a seat."

Fredrick swallowed hard and sat on the edge of the bed. Unlike the one in Honolulu, it felt more like an authentic bed, one someone might sleep on if need be.

Dr. Young didn't say a word as she studied him. The weight of her stare became unbearable; she ultimately spoke, breaking the tension. "I don't approve of lying, and I don't enjoy being used as a means of subterfuge." Her arms crossed over her chest.

"I apologize." The words were barely a whisper.

"I understand you didn't have much to do with any of what happened, but you are the crux of what transpired, so I'm asking, is there anything else I need to know about what happened? Or is this incident the end of it?"

Fredrick's face warmed, and he couldn't meet the doctor's eyes. There was so much that happened to him and now he was lying to the doctor. Well, a lie of omission is still a lie.

What would happen if I said something? She'd lock me up.

She cleared her throat. "I see. Is there anything that will put you or the rest of the crew in medical danger? I assume that is a fair question to ask."

"No." Fredrick shook his head. "No, there's nothing that I know of that will cause anyone any medical conditions."

She frowned. "Well, that's something, I suppose. Did they hurt you? Did they do anything to you?"

Fredrick absently rubbed his shoulder.

The doctor pulled on some gloves. "Take off your shirt."

"What?"

"Take off your shirt, and let me see what they did to your shoulder. If they hurt you, I want to make notes and take photos if need be. You rubbed your shoulder, so I want to see what's wrong."

"Nothing." Fredrick shuddered. "They … they had a doctor check me out, and since I couldn't remember my vaccination status, they updated some of my shots."

"So, your tetanus, flu and COVID?" she asked.

"Yes." He pulled off his polo shirt to allow the doctor to see his shoulder. "I got other shots before I came here, but I don't remember them all."

"Well, that's good." She checked his arm. "Is this sore?"

He winced where she rubbed. "Yes."

"You'll be tender a bit longer. The combos aren't fun." She checked his other arm and ran a hand along his collarbone, then rubbed his neck. "Is this sore?"

"No."

"Good." She pulled a stethoscope out of one of the built-in drawers. "I knew I should have grabbed mine." She moved behind Fredrick. "This will be a bit chilly." The cold metal instantly caused Fredrick to shiver. "Take a breath for me."

Fredrick inhaled. She moved the metal part touching him. "Again." Fredrick inhaled a second time. "Sounds good." She moved the metal to his lower back. "Breathe." He did as instructed. "Last one." She relocated the metal piece. He took a deep breath.

She stepped away, draping the stethoscope around her neck and pulled off her gloves, then tossed them in a bin. "You can put on your shirt. You seem fine to me. I don't think I need to do a full exam; however, I'm surprised they gave you the shots."

Fredrick shrugged. "I did as they told me. I didn't think questioning them was a good idea."

"Fair. Well, given you had to deal with the FBI and a potential murder charge, you seem in good shape to me, and I know none of that was any fun." Her expression softened. "Also, I'm sorry about your loss. That can't be easy."

Fredrick understood she meant Wilhelm. "At least I know what happened to him now."

"I suppose that's something. Well, I see no reason to hold you up, I don't see any bruises and you seem in overall good spirits. Mostly I wanted to get my eyes on you and meet the man I was covering for."

"I can get to work now?" Fredrick tugged on his shirt adjusting it as he sat there.

"Unless you want me to tell Leo and Tammy that you need a few days to recover from your experience ... call it a mental health break."

"No." Fredrick shook his head. "I'd like to get to my duties. Makes me feel normal."

The doctor chuckled. "I can relate to that. Listen"—her voice and tone continued in a way that reminded him of a parent talking with a hurt child—"coming and working on a new zeppelin is stressful enough, then getting accused of ... of ... foul play ..." She shuddered. "It can be too much. So, if you need anything, you come and see me, or Amanda, she's our NP—"

"NP?"

"The ship's Nurse Practitioner. I don't know about the *Hindenburg*, but we're staffed 24/7 so either me or Amanda will see you. Filipa, our other nurse, has a background in psychology and is a good listener if you need to talk. Okay?"

"Thank you." Fredrick pulled at the arms of his polo shirt. "I'll keep that in mind."

"Good," Dr. Young said. "You're all set?"

"I think so."

With a final nod, the doctor opened the exam room door and stepped out. Fredrick followed her to the front desk. There were two men sitting there, one holding his wrist.

"I told you not to put your hand there," the one man chastised.

"Well, how was I to—" The other person stopped, seeing the doctor and Fredrick arrive.

Sunil nodded to Dr. Young. "I was about to buzz you."

"Have a good day, Fredrick. Remember the offer stands."

"Thank you, doctor, I will." He tried not to focus on the two guests sitting in the lobby, but he wouldn't lie, he was intrigued as to what happened. Unfortunately, he didn't recognize them from any of his interaction with the club guests, so he doubted he would find out.

"I'm Dr. Young." The doctor started as she faced the two visitors. "How can I assist you ..."

Fredrick walked through the medical center's door and closed it behind him, then made his way to his cabin to change. Being on the *Hawaiian Sun* took away all his stress and he liked the doctor, she seemed nice. A bit tough and no nonsense, but still pleasant. And it was reassuring to know that he can at least go and talk to her or her staff, even if he couldn't tell them everything.

26

ALL THE WEIGHT Leo didn't know he was carrying since Fredrick got picked up by Agent Shaw vanished, and he could focus on his job. Yes, Fredrick was still with the doctor, but that was a mere formality. Leo scanned his messages and for the moment not seeing anything pop up, he peeked out the club's window to appreciate the limited view. *The Honolulu airfield doesn't have the same magic as the other airfields.*

Tammy left the moment he showed up; however, he was still able to jump into updating the schedule, this time returning Fredrick to where he had originally had him. The lounge picked up with guests as their day in Honolulu was ending. Margo, playing the piano, provided the lounge with a warm ambiance. They only had one more stop before they made their way to San Jose, and if he was being completely honest, he'd be glad to have this trip in his rearview mirror.

It hasn't been so bad. Barron and I are together again.

The click of the club's door caused him to turn and see who was entering. "Welcome," Leo greeted Fredrick as he strolled in.

His uniform was perfectly pressed, appearing as if nothing had ever been wrong. "Thank you. What do you need me to do?"

Leo chuckled. "The spot next to me is empty—how about you start there?"

Fredrick inhaled and walked to the workstation next to Leo, unbuttoning his uniform button as he sat down. He tapped on the computer to log into the system. "Feels like forever since I've been here."

"And yet it's only been a smidgen over twenty-four hours," Leo commented as he studied Fredrick. "You seem a lot more confident with the system."

"I think it's because I'm happy to be back ... it was ..." He didn't finish, but moved his head side to side as he continued to type.

"If it helps, I never did trust Martin." Leo's gentle voice was low enough so only the two of them heard. No need for the guests nearby to get an earful—he had no delusions about the gossip going on about Martin's sudden disappearance from the zep.

A frown pulled at Fredrick's lips. "He wasn't bad ..."

Leo leaned closer to Fredrick. "Seriously ... he was here to arrest you." He quickly pasted a grin on, meeting the eyes of a couple of guests who were close to them.

Fredrick sighed. "It wasn't like that. He's a good man, and felt bad for how things happened."

"He should. He almost cost you your job, and I got a verbal reprimand thanks to him." He tried not to huff. "I know the Captain still isn't a happy camper; she doesn't tolerate fools."

Fredrick's gaze dropped. "If there's anything I can do ..."

"Your job, and you're going to need to shine the rest of this trip and the next one." Leo patted Fredrick's arm. "Don't worry, though—we've got you."

"I appreciate that." Fredrick bit at his lower lip. "I know you're mad at Martin, and I understand why, but ..."

Leo's shoulders tensed.

"When I was with him, we got to talk and he ... well, he was the one that found out what happened to Wilhelm. If it wasn't for him ..."

"Wait. You mean to tell me, that if it wasn't for Martin—"

He cleared Fredrick. This whole time, Martin worked to help Fredrick, that's probably why he didn't take him in right away, wanted to ... Jesus, how can I be so wrong? And he got in trouble with his bosses for it.

"Why didn't you say something?"

"Would anything I said have mattered?"

"Yes ... well ... no," Leo stammered. "I ... I don't know. Well, crap. Now I feel like an ass."

"Don't." Fredrick's work expression returned to his face as three guests walked into the club. "Good afternoon," he greeted the group.

"Glad to see you, Fredrick," the guests' soft voices said.

Leo pulled himself together and managed to say, "Enjoy." Then, to Fredrick, "Thanks for the save."

Fredrick's real look appeared on his face, showcasing his dimples. "Anytime. What's on the schedule between now and the time we get to San Jose?"

Leo appreciated the change in topics. Fredrick gave him a lot to process. "Well, tonight"—he pulled up the schedule for the rest of the trip—"I was hoping to get to see the non-binary fashion show. Ainsley and Minh are going to be in it."

"Oh, fun."

"But with you here, not that I'm complaining, we have a bit of work to do." He smiled.

I don't care how getting Fredrick happened. I'm thrilled he's back.

"I know I keep apologizing for all the headaches this whole thing has caused, but no one would have ever done this for me. Well, maybe Wilhelm. Either way, it all means a lot to me and I don't want to mess up this opportunity." Fredrick adjusted the sleeves of his uniform's jacket.

"Hey, I'm trying to lighten the mood." Leo beamed, tapping Fredrick's arm. "I'm thrilled you're safe and sound. It wasn't the same without you."

"*Danke.*" Fredrick gave a slight nod of his head.

"Now, let's get to work."

Over the next hour, Leo updated Fredrick on the rest of the trip and the guest excursions planned for tomorrow. Nawiliwili was their final port of call and was the last chance for their guests to get off the zep and enjoy Hawaii. Typically, Hilo and Nawiliwili were the slowest days on board the zep, but there were a lot of folks who were signed up to take advantage of the deals provided by the spa, and Leo had a list of reminders for them to send out.

Once they got through the last port day, the rest of the trip was pretty much parties and events happening all over the zep, but luckily, nothing they were in charge of. In the evenings, the lounge would host Margo for the cocktails and dessert events. They would probably see an uptick in guests, but nothing they couldn't handle. He would be surprised if they had all 30 of their guests in the club, but people did enjoy their free booze and David's cooking.

Leo looked behind him out the window as the zep lifted off into the night sky. With a warm feeling of peace, he glanced over at Fredrick, who was typing up his notes from one of the guests for whom he had arranged a spa treatment. "I guess Javier got tired of buying coffee."

"Pardon?"

"Our elevator man, Javier. That liftoff was smooth." He pointed to the glass of water in front of him. "See? Almost level."

Fredrick leaned in and squinted. "I didn't even notice."

"Come on, let's check out our departure."

Fredrick buttoned his coat once he stood, and they moved to the windows. Leo loved the views as they took off, no matter where. Other than being in the cockpit, the lounge and the steakhouse had the best views on the whole zep. He and Fredrick weren't the only ones—almost everyone was taking up a spot by the windows to watch the zep leave Honolulu. The airfield grew smaller as more of the city came into view.

Now this is a great view.

"It's a beautiful place," Fredrick commented. "The mountains especially. Photos don't do it justice."

"Agreed." Leo pointed. "Check out Diamond Head."

"How long would it take us to get to Nawiliwili if we flew directly there?"

Leo glanced up toward the ceiling. "Oh … maybe … probably about an hour and a half, maybe two, depending on the weather."

Fredrick laughed. "It amazes me how we fly around in a giant circle for all that time."

"Well, we want people to enjoy their trip. Plus, there's no rush—I mean, our zep is part of the destination. You know?" Leo chuckled. "I've dreamed about getting married on a zep."

"Really?"

Leo shrugged. "You know, have the whole thing up on the deck …"

"That sounds lovely. I can't help but think about how in the past, people looked at airships as a way of transportation, and wanted to get to places as quickly as possible. Now ..." He raised a hand and waved it around. "Here we are."

"But even then, people enjoyed the experience; the fantasy and luxury," Leo mused. "It's not all about hurrying up. Otherwise, people'd take a plane and we'd be out of our jobs."

"Good point."

"Come on, enough daydreaming." Leo gestured to their desks. "Have you ever wondered what it must have been like to be on one of the old zeps, before the Second World War?"

"Colder, louder, not as spacious, and not as smooth," Fredrick explained without consideration.

"Sounds like you've been on one."

Fredrick's cheeks blushed. "I've heard the stories."

"Hello, Fredrick," Stan Clark greeted. "We're happy you're feeling better. The trip home wouldn't be the same without you."

"Thank you, Mr. Montgomery-Clark. I'm happy to be up and around. And I hope you enjoyed your time in Honolulu."

"Oh, yes, always," Stan said, beaming at Fredrick. "Do you mind helping me make dinner reservations for Larry and I at the steakhouse?"

"Absolutely." Fredrick tapped the keyboard. "Please remind me of your cabin number and when you'd like to dine?"

Leo watched a moment longer before turning to his monitor. He was beyond thrilled to have Fredrick where he belonged.

I wish there was something I might do for Martin. God, I feel awful.

•   •   •

By the time Leo, Nuwa, and Fredrick closed up the lounge for the night, it was 2245. Barron had stopped by earlier in the evening to let him know they'd be up at the deck party if he wanted to join. Given he hadn't had time to see Barron at all, since they had a full house the entire night, the invitation was all he needed.

He enjoyed seeing everyone chatting and laughing about their trip—some of the guests were already lamenting that their trip was ending. Leo would need to remind his team that once they left Nawiliwili, they should inform their guests about the current booking deals for another cruise. Leo made a note to find out from Tammy what special would be on offer to entice future bookings.

"Did you wanna go dancing up on deck, Fredrick?" Nuwa asked, fussing with her glasses. "I think Tomas and Aurora were going to head up there."

"Come dancing," Leo pleaded. "Barron told me he'd be up there with his friends."

At least Elijah and I have a truce. I hope it's still in place now that Fredrick's home.

"Oh—I don't—I mean—the Captain's Gala was the extent of my dancing." Fredrick glanced around the empty space as he stammered.

"Come on—or are you too sad that your dance partner got off in Honolulu?" Nuwa teased.

Leo's stomach dropped and Fredrick bit at his lower lip.

Oh, Nuwa ...

"No," Fredrick blurted out. "I mean, maybe, but given I'm still on the mend—"

"Oh, right." Nuwa's face and neck pinkened. "Yeah. Of course. I'm ... I'm such an idiot." Nuwa ran a hand through her hair. "I'm sorry."

"It's fine." Fredrick waved off the apology. "I think I'm going to have an early night." He smiled at them. "But you guys go. Have fun. Maybe tomorrow."

"Sounds good. You ready?" Nuwa smiled, the color lessening from her face. "I'm sure Dapper Dave and Krystal will have something crazy going on."

Leo's gaze bounced between Nuwa and Fredrick.

I doubt Fredrick needs me hovering over him. Plus, I want to see Barron.

"Absolutely." Leo's gaze landed on Fredrick. "But if you need me, you can use our room phone to call the bar and get me."

"Oh my goodness, don't be such a mom." Nuwa laughed.

"I'll be fine. Thank you." Fredrick yawned through his words as the three made their way to the club's exit.

Leo stepped aside, allowing Fredrick and Nuwa through. Once the double doors were shut, he ensured they were locked for the night.

"I'll see you tomorrow." Fredrick waved to Nuwa.

"Yep, enjoy your sleep." She waved as he moved to the crew-only door to head down to their deck.

"See you later."

"Have fun." Fredrick opened the door with his keycard.

"I'm glad he's back," Nuwa commented once the door closed. "I like him; he's a good guy."

"Yes. Yes, he is." Leo gestured in the direction of the elevators. "Let's go dance. I'm looking forward to seeing Barron—I missed him today."

"Oh, right. How's that going?"

"Good. I think." Leo beamed.

Everything and everyone seemed to be falling in place.

The Pali deck sparkled with twinkle lights, enhancing the inviting starry night. The warm tropical air seemed less so up on the deck, but that had more to do with the airflow from the zep's movement than anything else. Booze and cologne assaulted Leo's nose as they made their way deeper into the party. *Endless Summer* blasted through the DJ's sound system as Dapper Dave and Krystal Chandelier danced and hosted. Leo wasn't quite sure what they were up to tonight, since this was scheduled to be a dance party, but knowing them, they would find ways to interject themselves into the party.

To everyone's entertainment and enjoyment.

Leo greeted a few of the guests, and ensured his team enjoyed themselves while staying out of trouble. Given his staff, he wasn't worried. After getting a glass of club soda, he found Barron, Elijah, Ainsley, and Minh all dancing in a group off to the side, away from the hot tubs. The tubs overflowed with several men from the bear community, chatting and laughing.

Everyone always looks like they're having such a good time. I wonder how authentic their reactions are, or if it's for show?

Ainsley and Minh were in Ainsley's custom outfits. Tonight, Minh showed off a royal blue sparkly floor-length gown that opened at the collarbone like a vest, revealing his arms and a bit of his chest. Around his neck he wore a matching bowtie. Ainsley wore dress slacks and a matching vest, and under the vest they had on a white shirt. Both outfits were made of similar materials and colors, with the exception of Ainsley's white shirt, which still had a sparkle to it.

Elijah danced around, waving his hands in the air. His outfit wasn't nearly as put together as Ainsley's and Minh's. Clearly, Ainsley wasn't loaning him anything tonight. Or he chose this to wear. Barron wore shorts and a black tank top, showing off his arms and his white gold necklace.

Clearly they're having a great time. At least, I hope.

"Hey," Leo greeted the group, moving in next to Barron as he danced in time with the music.

"Hi, babe." Barron kissed Leo on the cheek. "Or should I not do that since you're in uniform?" He chuckled.

"It's fine."

"Does this mean we all get to kiss your cheek now?" Minh teased, making kissy noises.

"Leave him be," Ainsley admonished. "It's good to see you outside the lounge. I was sad you weren't at the NB fashion show."

"Sorry about that. With everything happening, it's hard to get to all the events." He gestured to Minh and Ainsley. "Are those the outfits you wore?"

"These? No, please." Ainsley shook their head. "I had my rainbow-colored, frilly dress, with pride-colored train and heels. And I put this one"—they indicated to Minh—"in a sequined rainbow-colored jumpsuit. We looked incredible."

"And you should have won," Barron chimed in as he took Leo's hands, continuing to dance.

Ainsley shrugged, holding Minh's hips as they moved together. "Didn't matter—we enjoyed ourselves."

"Well, we missed you." Elijah fanned himself. "Sounds like you had a busy night."

At least he's not scowling at me and is being pleasant.

"Yes. Having Fredrick back certainly helped." Leo shifted as he danced, allowing him to speak to Elijah.

"We're glad he's better." Minh leaned in closer to Ainsley as they continued to move in time with the music.

"Do they know what he had? Was it food poisoning?" Ainsley asked.

Clearly Elijah didn't say anything to them, which is good.

"You know he can't say anything, even if he does know." Elijah continued to move with the music. "Come on, let's leave these two love birds."

Leo took Elijah's arm. "Hey, thank you."

"I still don't like you." Elijah smiled and winked. "But you're welcome. I'm glad Fredrick's well; he's a good guy."

"Ah, do we detect a thaw in the ice?" Ainsley pointed between Leo and Elijah.

"Not likely." Elijah smirked but held Leo's gaze a bit longer and there was a twinkle of mischief in his eyes.

"Oh. Look, it's Quinn, Onyx, and Kendall." Ainsley pointed and moved Minh off to go chat with the other group.

"And I see my beefy friend has arrived. Byeeee." Elijah waved as he rushed off, greeting a tall bearish fellow, a bigger guy with a nicely trimmed beard, full head of brownish red hair, glasses, and an overall handsome face.

"I see someone found a friend."

"Fingers crossed, come on." Barron drank some of his cocktail as he and Leo walked away from the crowd of people.

Leo found them a spot that wasn't as loud and gave some privacy, near the closed spa and gym. He sipped his club soda. "Elijah stepped up."

"Like I've said, he can be a good guy when he wants to be." Barron put his drink on the table and sat down.

Leo pulled out a seat and scooted closer to Barron. "Well, he came through. I don't know if the call to his mother helped or not, but I appreciated it. Fredrick does as well."

"You told him."

"When he first arrived this afternoon, with Martin. It was this whole big thing." He took another sip of his drink.

Barron's lips pinched.

"What?"

"Nothing."

"No, it's something." Leo leaned in closer. "Tell me."

Barron inhaled. "I think you're being too hard on Martin."

"What? No, you misunderstand." Leo took Barron's hand. "Yes, I was pissed at the guy, but after talking to Fredrick—" He stopped, scanning their surroundings, and leaned in closer. "If it wasn't for Martin, I think they would have arrested Fredrick."

"Really?"

"According to Fredrick, part of why Martin didn't take him off the ship right away was he was trying to clear Fredrick. I don't know all the details, but ..." He shrugged.

"That makes sense. Look, I got to talk with Martin a lot. I watched him check out Fredrick. He wasn't only keeping an eye on him for his work, or trying to clear his name, or whatever. There was definitely attraction there. I think he likes Fredrick." He shook his head.

"Wait, you talked to him today? When he left?"

"He was upset. He didn't strike me as someone only doing a job." Barron raked a hand through his hair. "I mean, he was, but still. I said goodbye to him, you know, to be polite, and he stopped and shook my hand. He told me that he was sorry about the fuss and that if I didn't mind, to keep an eye on Fredrick. He gave me his business card and asked that if anything, anything at all happened to Fredrick, to call him and he would return in a heartbeat, no matter what."

"Wow." Leo finished his club soda, adjusting in his seat.

"Does that strike you as someone only doing their job?"

"No."

"I think he cares," Barron continued. "I don't believe any of this was easy on him. What else can explain how poorly things where handled?"

"You don't even want to get me started. But given everything, I think you're right." Some new song played over the speakers that he didn't recognize. As the beat played, the music shook his whole body. "It's not like we can do anything."

"Do you think Fredrick likes him?"

"You're kidding, right? Mister Doe Eyes?" Leo laughed. "Whenever Martin walked into the room, he lit up. And did you see them dancing?" Leo watched the people; the crowd was still thick with bodies as he glanced up at the sky. "I'm not a big believer in love at first sight, but I do think Fredrick and Martin have amazing chemistry, and I doubt we're the only ones who noticed."

The whole situation was a mess. *Why can't relationships be easy, like in the movies and on TV?*

"So, how do we fix this?" Leo met Barron's gaze.

Barron held up Martin's business card, a grin blooming across his lips.

"Oh, I like how you think." Leo leaned in and kissed Barron. *And who says there isn't magic to be found when you're on vacation.*

27

F REDRICK WAS HAPPY to be resting in his bunk, the hum of the engines a familiar relaxing noise—so much better than car engines and dogs barking. Knowing that there were others like him out there provided him a small sense of comfort. Other—what did Martin call them? *Jumpers*. He guessed that was as good of a name as any.

How many more jumpers were there? How many different places did they come from? And why was this world the place they all came to?

Maybe it's not.

He deliberated. Even Martin confirmed how little they understood about what happened to him, and that all they were able to do is ensure a smooth transition to this place. He also assumed they continued to study each event as they occurred, but Martin didn't mention anything about that. To Fredrick's mind, doing so only made sense. How challenging. They had to welcome people here with no way of returning them or figuring out if they were good people or not. He had an image of one of the leaders of the Reich being dropped here. A shudder ran down his spine—he wouldn't wish that on anyone.

But they existed here as well.

Learning about World War II, and knowing that the Nazis were defeated here, gave him hope for his world. They would probably be defeated there as well. Maybe only in the darkest of realities did they win. Fredrick couldn't imagine what a world like that would look like.

His mind shifted to Wilhelm and how happy he looked in the video. His old friend appeared to have had a good long life, so that was something. Still, his heart hurt knowing he wouldn't see Wilhelm again. Deep down, he hoped that maybe he might find him and they would be on the *Hindenburg*, in his world and his time.

Although this time isn't bad. And this time has Martin. Even if he's gone.

"And I'm alive here." He patted his chest. "I have a chance for a happy life like Wilhelm had."

Rolling over on his side, he called up images of Martin: his brown hair and hazel eyes, his pleasant looks, and the sensation of their kiss. A grin pulled at his lips as he remembered the wonderfully warm oceany scent of Martin. Would he ever get to see him again? He didn't know, but he hoped so. Maybe once they got to San Jose, he would ask Leo to help him find Martin.

The thoughts of Martin lulled Fredrick off to sleep. Images of the two of them together were a warm comfort.

Waking with a start, Fredrick glanced around the cabin. The heat from the fire still felt warm on his face. He had tugged at Wilhelm as they tried to escape the burning ship, but as the images cleared from his mind, he realized he hadn't been trying to save Wilhelm, but Martin instead. And they weren't on the *Hindenburg*, but on the *Hawaiian Sun*. Closing his eyes, he pushed the memory of the dream away from him.

Only a dream. It was only a dream. I'm fine.

He peeked over at the small clock Martin had gotten for him. It was a nice surprise he found when he unpacked his duffel bag. There wasn't a note, but there didn't need to be one. It was slightly before 0500 and Leo was still here. Didn't he have plans to assist in the landing of the ship at Nawiliwili? "Leo. Leo, it's almost 0500, shouldn't you be in the cockpit?" Fredrick asked, trying to wake Leo with his voice.

Leo didn't move and continued to breathe softly.

Fredrick tapped Leo's arm. "Leo, aren't you supposed to be in the cockpit today?"

Leo's eyes fluttered open. "What?" his voice rasped. "What's wrong? Mom?"

"We're landing in Nawiliwili and you're supposed to be in the cockpit. Aren't you?"

"Oh." Leo yawned and stretched. "No. I … I … No."

A pit opened in Fredrick's stomach as his heart dropped into it. "You missed your opportunity because of me." He shook his head. "No matter what I do, I keep messing things up for you."

"No." Leo pushed his feet over the edge of the bed, rubbing his eyes. "We were short-staffed, which happens, and I was scheduled to have a long day today, so I asked the Captain for a raincheck."

"Because of me."

"Fredrick, it's fine." Leo glanced around the room, pulling out his phone, tapping on the device; the glare from the machine filled their cabin with a bright white light. He pushed the side of the phone, the light turned off. He shook his head. "You didn't get out of bed for this, did you?"

"I had a nightmare." He huffed. "I saw the time and—"

"You figured I overslept." Leo ran a hand through his mussed hair. "Thank you. I should have said something last night, but I didn't think about it. Oof."

"This is all my fault." Fredrick fussed with his pajama bottoms.

"No, it's my fault. I should have said something last night, but I was excited to see Barron."

Everything that happened was all Fredrick's fault—his fault for jumping here, his fault for Wilhelm dying, and now his fault for keeping Leo from his dreams. "You shouldn't have let me return. I should have gone home to Germany."

"What?" Leo jumped down off the bunk, wearing just his bare chest and boxers. Fredrick took a step back, giving them space. He didn't understand why some people stood so close to each other, especially when they were all but naked.

Well, that's not true. It's like Leo's wearing a swimsuit.

"I should have stayed in Germany."

"No way! Fredrick, you belong here on the *Hawaiian Sun*. Everyone adores you." Leo touched Fredrick's arm. "I don't want to think of this place without you. I know you've only been here a short time, but—"

"But what about all the stuff with Martin?" Fredrick's words were harder than maybe they should have been, but Leo didn't know the whole story. "You don't understand."

Leo glanced around to all the corners of their cabin, his lips pinched tight. When he met Fredrick's gaze again, his expression softened. "I think I do. Look, I know I wasn't a big fan of Martin, but ... I'm not blind and I think there's a lot there. Do you like him?"

"I don't know him." Images of Martin filled his mind and a warmth moved throughout his body at the thoughts.

When I'm with him it feels so safe. I can't imagine being with anyone else. Not even Wilhelm.

"That doesn't change the fact, if you like him."

Fredrick bit at his lower lip.

Leo let out a long exhale. "Okay, well, it's way too early for this and we have to be on duty in a couple of hours."

"Yes." Fredrick shoulders stiffened. "Of course, I'm sorry to have woken you up."

"That's not what I mean. But there isn't much we can do about any of it right now."

"What do you mean?"

"There's always something to be done." Leo shook his head.

"What?"

"Never mind." Leo smirked. "Let's put a pin in this for now. I'd like to at least pretend at being able to get some more sleep before I have to officially get up for the day. What about you?"

Fredrick wasn't going to lie, he wasn't exactly jumping at the idea of getting up and starting his day this early. He wasn't sure he'd get any more sleep but he might as well lay down and try getting some rest. "I doubt I'll sleep."

Leo climbed on his bunk as Fredrick waited, then got into his own bunk. He closed his eyes and figured he would try to rest and see where his mind took him.

•   •   •

Fredrick massaged his temples. It was a mistake to have tried to get any additional rest. When he at long last dozed off, his alarm had blasted. All he wanted to do was sleep, and now here he sat, trying to work. "How could we have been wide awake at 0500 and now I can barely keep my eyes open?"

Leo sipped his tea. "I don't know, but we should have gotten up. This absolutely sucks. It's going to make for a long day." He yawned.

Fredrick stood up, trying to fight his own yawn. "I should clear and reset the lounge." His eyelids were as heavy as bricks and he couldn't sit anymore or he'd fall asleep. Moving would help him get through the day, like on the *Hindenburg*.

"Well, you two look great." Tomas smirked as he joined Fredrick and Leo at the guest services stations. "It must have been one hell of a party—sorry I missed it." He unbuttoned his uniform jacket. "Since the morning rush is over, I'm heading out, unless you want me to stay?"

"No." Leo waved a hand to dismiss him. "We'll see you this afternoon at tea."

"You got it." Tomas watched Fredrick move. "You sure you're feeling okay? You're not having a relapse, are you?"

"No." Fredrick's shoulders stiffened. "I didn't sleep well."

I need to pull myself together. I don't want there to be any reason for anyone to question my work performance.

"I've been there." Tomas pulled off his uniform jacket. "Well, maybe during your break, go and catch a catnap. That helps me most of the time."

"Thanks." Fredrick rebuttoned his uniform jacket after missing one of the buttons the first time around.

"See ya." Tomas waved.

"Wait." Leo frowned, typing on the computer. "Sorry, don't you have an in-room dining today?"

"That's tomorrow and I was going to have Nuwa work with me on that, if that's okay? It's a larger group and I think having the extra support's a good idea."

"Oh, right. Sorry. Yes, Nuwa's fine, I'll add it to her calendar."

"Well, despite it all, I'm happy you're here, Fredrick." Tomas beamed and walked toward the club's exit, his jacket draped over his shoulder. "Remember, try and get some additional rest when you can. We don't want you getting sick again." He looked Fredrick up and down. "Bye."

Fredrick made his way around the lounge, tidying up, moving chairs into place and ensuring the buffet of snacks, now replacing the morning continental breakfast, was properly displayed. It was busywork, but he needed the distraction not only from being exhausted but from his thoughts of Martin. He shouldn't have let him go, but how could he have made him stay? And going with him wasn't an option.

Verpassen.

As he finished making his rounds, before returning to his station, he poured himself a cup of coffee. He tried not to drink too much of the stuff, but on days like today he needed the boost.

Nothing compares to a good Berlin Coffee. That's something to go home for.

"I don't know how you drink that stuff." Leo sipped his tea, watching Fredrick return to their workstation, mug in hand.

"It's not near as good as the coffee in Berlin, but it'll do." Fredrick tasted the drink, enjoying the bold bitterness. He refused to muddy the drink with milk and sugar.

"Well, I'll stick to my green tea that gives me all the caffeine I need ... or can handle." He chuckled. "Oh, a request came in from Mr. and Mr. Montgomery-Clark. They asked to have a special in-room dinner tomorrow and asked for you."

"Oh, that's sweet. I like them." Even though technically they were younger than him, he seemed to understand them, how they sometimes appeared to not fully fit in with the younger crowd on the ship, how they were more reserved and more conservative in their manners, and how they reacted toward each other. Also, how he caught when they missed some reference to something contemporary.

At least I can blame it on the language barrier.

"Is there a special occasion?" Fredrick asked over his cup.

"I don't believe so. They usually like to have a couple of private dinners. They also enjoy working through the staff so they get to know them. Plus, I think Stan likes to have a fuss made over Larry." Leo smirked. "I've sent you all the details for you to review."

"*Wunderbar.*" Fredrick caught himself—he was definitely tired.

"They asked to have dinner at 1800. I think it'll be pretty straightforward—they're not requesting anything special, but I might have added a couple of notes for David to zhuzh it up a bit. Be your charming self, and if you need anything, we're here for you."

"After the tea service with Ollie, I think I'll be fine." Fredrick smiled. "I'll go over everything tomorrow and I'll check my serving gloves tonight. Should I have another person with me?"

"Nah, I don't think so."

A click caught Fredrick's attention, and he glanced over to the lounge doors as Barron walked in. "Good morning."

"Didn't you say you were going to town this morning, babe?" Leo greeted Barron with a kiss on the cheek.

"We are." Barron smiled at the kiss. "I wanted to come and see how Fredrick was doing, and let him know how happy I am that everything worked out."

Fredrick took another sip of his bitter drink, allowing the warmth to flow down his throat before putting it down. "Thank you, Mr. Hillchild. That's kind of you. Thank you for all you did as well. I appreciate it."

"Well, after Leo told me what happened I—well, Elijah and I couldn't sit by and do nothing. Even if the call didn't help much."

"Hey now," Leo countered, "I'm sure it helped plenty."

"The additional support didn't make me feel all alone." Fredrick stiffened his shoulders, remembering he was on duty and this wasn't a social visit. "Oh, would you like something to drink? A mimosa? There's a lovely Prosecco I'll throw in."

Barron laughed. "Um … I think—you know what, why not?" He sat down in the guest chair in front of Leo.

Fredrick stood and buttoned his jacket, heading off to the bar. It took him a moment as he figured Leo and Barron probably wanted privacy now that they were together again. *They make a handsome couple.*

He decided to take his time mixing the drink, adding more Prosecco than probably necessary. He also pulled out some of David's warm morning mix and put some in one of the wooden ramekins. He fussed with the drink and the snack, ensuring he had the serving tray and napkins nicely placed. Fredrick continued to dawdle around the bar, not wanting the drink to warm or go flat he picked up the service tray.

I think I've given them enough time.

"Babe, you sure?" he heard Leo ask in hushed tones.

"Yes." Barron sat taller as Fredrick turned the corner, coming into sight. "Oh, that looks great and you brought … is that some of David's morning mix? That stuff is like crack."

Fredrick wasn't sure what 'crack' was, but it must be something equally as delicious.

Whatever they were talking about, they didn't want me to know about.

"I hope you enjoy your mimosa with Prosecco." He placed the tray next to Barron.

"Nice presentation." Leo chuckled, his cheeks and neck a bright crimson.

"I figured I'd give you a minute."

"Thanks." Barron took the drink and finished it in one gulp. He grabbed a small handful of the snacks and popped them in his mouth. "Well, I'm off. Fredrick, if I don't see you later, have a great day." He stood and kissed Leo, "We still have our dinner plans for tonight?"

"It'll be later, but yes," Leo confirmed.

"Yay." Barron walked to the door and exited the lounge.

"That was ..." Fredrick's gaze narrowed.

"Oh, sorry about that. We ... well, you know ..." He cleared his throat.

Now he's being strange. What are they up to? Oh, I bet they're planning on being together.

Fredrick picked up the tray and empty glass. "You two are having dinner tonight?"

Leo faced his monitor and started typing away. "It'll be later, but yes."

Fredrick laughed. "Anything else planned? I can always see if I can bunk somewhere else for the night."

Dejan appeared from the kitchen pushing a trolley, and waved. "Morning."

Fredrick and Leo both responded to the greeting.

"Why Fredrick, you naughty boy." Leo's face grew even redder, but his voice remained low so only Fredrick heard. "I might see if I can work out something with him tomorrow night, but with the Captain still being a bit upset, I don't want to push things with either her or Tammy."

"You know Agent Shaw's cabin is vacant," Fredrick proposed. "And no one has to know."

Leo laughed, shaking his head. "What is this? Is our sweet innocent German Boy not so sweet or innocent?"

"I've caused a bit a mischief now and again." Fredrick took the tray, glass, and ramekin to the service area to clean without another word.

If he only knew.

28

L EO ADJUSTED THE SLEEVES on his dress shirt. It was nice to be out of his uniform for the night. Since he didn't need to wear a jacket, a bright mixed blue shirt with tan accents and fancy cuffs were in order for the evening.

Dinner with Barron would provide him with a long overdue distraction from how tired he had been all day. He would have to push through, especially since he wasn't about to pump himself with more caffeine. As it was, he worried about not being able to sleep.

With another look in the mirror, he checked his appearance. A short spray of cologne was the final touch. He loved the fresh scent. Always being mindful of not over doing like some people did, one spray was all.

And there we have it. As good as it's going to get.

He took in the empty cabin, grateful he and Fredrick were both studious about keeping a clean space. His last roommate could be a bit of a slob. Seeing both their bunks made up, and no clothing lying about, helped in giving him piece of mind. He always had a thing about messes; he couldn't go to bed, or go out and enjoy himself, knowing chaos waited for him.

Leo focused on Fredrick's bunk and shook his head. The poor guy had a rough go. Now that his situation was starting to improve, there was still one bit of a mess outstanding: Martin. But what could he and Barron do? Barron loved playing matchmaker, and once he got an idea in his head, he wouldn't let it go. Still, with everything that happened between Martin and Fredrick, what kind of havoc awaited them as they got involved?

We'll see what he has planned tonight, since we weren't able to talk today. Maybe he'll have changed his mind.

He checked himself in the mirror one more time. Either way, he was ready for dinner and Fredrick was out with some of the team. And who knew? He might meet someone new to occupy his time. People were always hooking up, crew and guests alike, so Fredrick might get lucky.

He moved to the door and headed up to meet Barron. At Barron's cabin, he knocked, excited to see him. The door opened and his handsome man greeted him with a simple kiss.

"Hey babe." He stepped closer. "You look amazing."

"Thanks, so do you." Barron wore gray dress pants, a pink pinstriped long-sleeve shirt with black belt, and black dress shoes. "Maybe we should blow off dinner and go straight for dessert?"

Barron laughed as he adjusted his collar, his necklace sparkling in the light. "I don't think Elijah would appreciate that."

"No, probably not, and given we're in a good place, I don't want to mess that up."

"Good call. Shall we?"

"Absolutely."

"I've been looking forward to this all day."

Leo tugged at his cuffs. It was always an odd feeling walking past the lounge's doors. The etched glass windows always beckoned him to go in. He knew Aurora would have everything under control so he could enjoy his night off.

They arrived at the steakhouse's lobby and were quickly seated. David came over to greet them and let them know they were in for a treat tonight.

That man is not only a brilliant chef, but incredible at guest relations. I hope the company treats him well. I'd hate for us to lose him.

Once David left, their waiter, Dejan, came over to present the dinner menu and took their drink orders. Luckily, Barron and Leo had dined here often enough that they saved Dejan from going over the whole spiel.

After Dejan returned with their bread service, wine that Barron ordered, and club soda for Leo, they sat and relaxed, enjoying their meal and their time together in relative privacy.

Barron held up his glass of wine. "To us."

"To us." They clinked glasses. Leo took a sip of his club soda—he had decided against wine, since he didn't need any help relaxing. "When you showed up on the zep, I was so frustrated and hurt, and now sitting here with you at dinner, I'm glad you did. I missed you."

"I'm glad we're both here." Barron sipped his wine. "But I'll be glad to get home." He returned his glass to the table.

"Really? Why?"

Barron leaned in, checking around him. "So we can have some much overdue sexy time."

Leo laughed.

Good to know we're both on the same page.

"What? I've missed you." Barron sat back, his smile slightly dipping.

"Well, I won't lie," Leo took Barron's hand in his. "I'm looking forward to having you to myself ... you know, Fredrick and I were talking, and Martin's cabin is empty for the rest of the trip."

"Interesting." The grin on Barron's face grew. "But I don't want to get you in trouble. We can wait."

Again, glad we're on the same page.

"Well, I was thinking about that today." Leo took a sip of his club soda. "I can always see about an upgrade for Elijah because of all his help. You wouldn't need to share the bedroom, and we can have your steward make up the beds to king-sized."

"But Ainsley and Minh would still be there in the living room ..."

"True, but still, I might ask Tammy. Elijah was a lot of help and the room is vacant. Plus, I think it'd go a long way at keeping us on our good footing."

"Well, I'm sure he'd like it. You know the guy we saw him rush over to, Glenn? Well, he's gotten to know him quite well, and I'm sure they'd like some actual privacy instead of ... well, whatever they're doing now to get together."

"I wish we had single cabins." Leo's brows furrowed. "They're trying them out on the Southern Sun. Not many, I think only ten or twelve, but still ..."

"I wouldn't complain," Barron said as Dejan arrived with their first course.

"The chef's tasting menu," Dejan recited as he placed the two plates. "Tonight, we're starting off with Chef David's"—he was sure to pronounce the French accents in David's name—"take on the classic lobster roll. Enjoy." He refilled Barron's wine glass and Leo's glass of club soda.

"Well, this looks and smells amazing." Barron adjusted his plate as he inhaled.

Leo picked up his fork, ready to dig in. "Oh, I have no doubt. We should be in for a big treat tonight."

They worked their way through their dinner, each of the courses building on the last. None of the courses were too large, each planned for maximum enjoyment and not to fill you up, but Barron and Leo chatted about how they weren't sure they'd be able to eat dessert. As Dejan's Assistant Waiter dropped off their chocolate soufflés, Barron chuckled. "There is no way I'm missing out on this."

"And I thought the Wagyu was epic." Leo picked up his spoon.

Barron leaned forward. "I want to let you know, after we talked this morning, I called Martin's office."

"Really?" Leo had mixed feelings, but knowing all Martin had done to help Fredrick, if there was a chance, how could he be against helping? He paused before digging into his luscious warm dessert. "Let me ask—don't you think this whole thing has been ... well, messy? I mean, it's all a bit bizarre."

Barron rolled his glass in his hands. "Life's strange. Think of all the BS we've been through. If I didn't come here, what would you have done?"

Leo frowned, knowing the answer.

"Look, babe ... there's been something picking at me since I saw them dancing together. It's like they were made for each other. I can't explain any better." He laughed. "Elijah thinks I'm crazy."

"Well, I don't think you're crazy. Hopeless romantic, sure, but never crazy. And I'm glad for it."

"Ah, I knew there was a reason I loved you." Barron took a bite of his soufflé.

Leo beamed at the comment. He didn't think he would ever get tired of hearing Barron say he loved him, and he didn't believe he'd ever get weary of saying the same. "I love you too."

Barron's face brightened. He picked at his soufflé again, taking another bite. "Oh man, this is worth every minute I'm going to have to spend in the gym tomorrow."

Leo didn't argue as he continued to enjoy the chocolaty wonder before him. Despite his reservations, he was pleased Barron tried to contact Martin. The attempt would give them more time to figure out what to do. And better yet, they put the ball firmly in Martin's court. "What'd he say?"

"Nothing. I got transferred through voicemail hell. I left him a message." He shook his head. "It's stupid. I told him that despite all that happened, if he had feelings for Fredrick, he was an idiot for not doing something and letting things end the way they did."

"Well, honestly, what can he do?" Leo sipped at his club soda, giving his palate a break.

Barron shrugged. "What would you do?"

Leo deliberated a moment. "Honestly, I'd wonder why some random guy I met on a zeppelin cruise was getting all up in my business."

"And after that?"

"I don't know." Leo took another bite of his soufflé. "Probably have a think about everything that happened, and decide if the gains were worth the potential cost."

For all we know, Martin might lose his job over this ... and that was quite the cost.

"Well, hopefully Martin will figure it out, as will Fredrick." Barron finished off his soufflé. "Everyone has their own story about love and romance."

"True." Leo glanced around the dining room, taking in all the people. Each one of them had their own narrative, and for the couples, they had their story about how they met. Whatever their tale and whatever their cost was, they were all here together now, so that was something. "You know, life isn't like some Disney movie. Not everyone gets a happy ending, no matter what they want or dream of."

"True, but we can all hope for that chance at a happily ever after." Barron smiled, giving Leo a wink.

"God, you're a hopeless romantic."

"Get it right, I'm a hopeful romantic."

Leo chuckled before finishing off his soufflé, then placed his spoon next to the empty plate, taking Barron's words to heart. *One can dream.*

29

W HATEVER FREDRICK ASSUMED he knew about the final days of traveling on an airship quickly changed. The day after Nawiliwili hadn't been too bad; the ship was busy and there was always something to do or someone who needed assistance. The schedule was very much like on the first full day in the air; however, on the last day, not only did they have to provide the level of service the guests had grown to expect, but they had to prepare for the next day's debarkation, meaning they had to ensure all the club-level guests had everything they needed to get off the airship with ease. Bags would need to be picked up and sent to meet the guests as they were escorted to the club lounge at Moffett Airfield in San Jose. They could enjoy additional refreshments while they waited for ground transportation, or, if they parked on site, they could get to where their vehicles had been parked for the trip. This location also gave them a dedicated way out to the freeway.

A level of convenience and service that I wouldn't have dreamed of.

On the final night of the trip, the Lani Club held the Aloha Reception, thanking the guests for joining the *Hawaiian Sun* on her trip to the Islands. Leo referred to the reception as the 'kiss goodbye'.

The gathering did overlap the final drag performance of the ship, which some of the guests preferred to see. Fredrick couldn't blame them—from everything he heard from the rest of the crew, this performance was the event to see, given that the queens and kings went all out for the last night.

Ah, well. Next time.

Fredrick appreciated the concept of the reception, but given all the extra duties, was the additional event necessary? The soirée was one more thing Fredrick and the other butlers had to manage. But when all was said and done, the event provided for a nice night and an opportunity for each of the team to say a proper goodbye to the guests they had served over the last ten days.

By the time Fredrick got to his cabin, he was ready to hit his bunk.

The cabin door opened as Leo eased into their shared space. "Not going to party the night away?"

Fredrick shook his head as he pulled on a pair of shorts. "No. With everyone leaving in the morning, I want to rest up."

Leo pulled off his uniform jacket and hung it up. "Well, what did you think of your first cruise?" He snorted. "I suppose I should ask you that tomorrow when we're in San Jose."

Fredrick pondered the question as he pulled off his shirt. "Given all that happened …"

"Hey, I know this hasn't been the easiest first trip for you, but I hope overall you're enjoying your work. And honestly, so far all the guest feedback has been positive."

"I am." Fredrick pulled one of his black tank tops from the shelf, draping it over the desk chair. "The work and the guests are amazing, and this ship … fantastic."

"But …"

"It's stupid, but I miss Martin. I know, I know, but he was kind, funny, and handsome." Fredrick's cheeks warmed as he pulled off his undershirt.

"Well, you never know." Leo unbuttoned and unzipped his dress pants. "Stranger things have happened in the air." He let his pants drop to the floor and stepped out of them, before picking them up to hang.

Fredrick laughed. "Agreed." He slipped on his tank top. "I think I'm going to go take a shower. Hopefully the hot water will help relax my body and my mind." He grabbed his towel, draping it around his neck as he pushed on his sandals.

"Okay." Leo started taking off his shirt. "I've got some work to do for tomorrow, but I may hit the hay."

"I'll be quiet when I return."

"No worries." Leo turned toward his cupboard, standing in nothing but his multicolored briefs that hugged his posterior nice and tight, also providing a bright contrast to his tannish flesh tones making his physique stand out even more. Fredrick glanced away as Leo hung his duty uniform.

•   •   •

Fredrick was glad he took a shower before bed. His breakfast wasn't as rushed as the meal might have been, but considering the marathon Fredrick and the others had ahead of them today, he certainly appreciated having some time to recover before the guests arrived for the next trip. Now they were stationed in the club ready to help their guests off the ship.

Fredrick waited as Leo assigned passengers to crew. "Fredrick," Leo called. "I believe Sandra, Teresa, Marco, and Rick are ready to depart the ship."

"Of course." Fredrick moved over to greet the foursome. They had been a highlight this trip—all the guests were lovely, but these four … well, he supposed everyone had their favorites. "Did you enjoy your trip?"

"*Wir hatten eine wundervolle Zeit. Danke schön.*" Sandra beamed, her German music to Fredrick's ears.

Fredrick smiled as his native language washed over him.

"Hey! None of that." Marco waved a hand in their direction.

"Yeah, if you're going to talk about how sexy I am, at least do it in English," Rick teased as Fredrick ushered them to the terminal lounge where their luggage was waiting.

"Oh, Fredrick, don't you listen to them," Teresa instructed as they moved through the busy airship. "They're being catty."

Fredrick laughed. "I'll call the lift."

"We've been taking the stairs this whole trip trying to counterbalance all the wonderful food we've been eating," Marco announced. "We're not waiting for the elevator. Especially today."

"Are you sure?" Fredrick asked.

"Stairs are perfectly fine." Sandra started walking to the staircase.

Fredrick wasn't going to argue. Taking the stairs would save them time as everyone seemed to want to take the elevators, especially considering some of the guests were walking their luggage off.

The group made their way to security as Fredrick took them through the Club Guest Security Check Point, and showed them to the lounge. Earlier, he had shadowed Aurora with their first guests so he knew what to do and where to go.

Honestly, this has been smooth. I don't know why I was worried.

The temporary Lani Club lounge, or simply 'the Lounge' as it was referred to at the airfield, was three times the size of the Lani Club and Lounge on the *Hawaiian Sun*, but not nearly as nice. Everything here appeared generic and not as well-maintained. There were restrooms and an area for snacks and drinks, and soft jazz played through the speaker system, giving the space life.

It reminded Fredrick of the Promenade on the *Hindenburg*—a big world map filled an entire wall and a bank of windows looked out on the airfield and at the giant airship. From here you could see both airships, should there be a second one moored. Under the map wall was a small buffet that had sodas and snacks that people might grab and go.

"Is there anything else I can assist you with?" Fredrick asked his group.

"Not unless you're going to let us take you with us," Marco proposed light-heartedly as a grin tugged at his cheeks.

"You've been an absolute dream." Teresa pulled over her backpack and plucked out an envelope. "This is something for you."

Leo told him this might happen. Not everyone offered the staff gratuities, but some of the guests provided bonuses. He heard this was commonplace on the ocean cruise ships, but not on the airships. Leo told him the lack of tipping had to do with their salaries not being reliant on gratuities, similar to flight attendants. "Thank you. I'm glad you had a good time." Fredrick took the envelope and quickly put it away as to not make an event of the gift.

"Here ya go, Freddy." Rick handed him an envelope as well. "I'd slip you my number if you'd call." He chuckled.

"Rick, you're such an ass." Marco shook his head.

"Part of why you married me." Rick snickered. "Seriously, thank you for everything you did for us this trip. We had a lovely time. And we're so glad that whatever you had didn't keep you down long."

"It was my pleasure." Fredrick beamed. "I hope we'll see you again soon."

"Same time next year." Sandra waved. "Now shoo. You have other people to take care of."

"Ja, meine Dame," Fredrick spoke in his best German, offering the group a slight bow before heading off to get his next group.

The rest of the morning had been much the same. All in all, he assisted four groups, and the only other tip came from the sweet older gay couple, the Montgomery-Clarks, though he was pretty sure they gave envelopes to all the Club staff. It was a nice gesture and Fredrick was grateful. Leo told him the tips were his, unless the guest asked that they be shared with all the Butlers. Usually if people did that, they would give the bonus to him or Aurora.

Fredrick dropped in one of the chairs when he returned from the last group. Nuwa, Ollie, and Tomas were all chatting about their tips and how they enjoyed the gay cruise because everyone was fun and generous.

"Well, you survived." Tomas glanced over at Fredrick.

"I'm so glad you weren't too sick." Ollie undid the top buttons of his jacket and shirt. "I didn't realize how good it was to have you until you were under the weather."

"And just think, we get to do the same trip again tomorrow," Nuwa announced, pulling off her glasses to give them a clean.

"Oof. And it's not even a specialty cruise ..." Tomas scanned the group. "What's the plan for tonight anyway? Did we want to go to Valley Fair or Santana Row? There's a new club downtown that I heard might be fun. Something for everyone."

"Not for me, mate." Ollie cracked his neck. "I have a date tonight with my missus. I've been looking forward to this night since we left."

"Missus?" Nuwa asked, her brows lifting above her glasses. "Since when?"

"I've been seeing her for a couple months. She texted me and asked if I was free tonight."

"Nice." Tomas slapped Ollie on the back. "Guess that means the cabin'll be all mine tonight." He rubbed his hands together.

Fredrick glanced over at Leo, who was on the phone at the workstation. "Is everything okay?"

Nuwa and Tomas glanced over to where Leo was working.

"We told you, he's a workaholic." Tomas smiled. "He seems to always be doing something. I tell you, that's why I'm happy with my job. The guests are great, and I don't have all his responsibility."

"Probably working something out with Aurora over at the lounge." Nuwa motioned in the direction of the club's guest station.

"You know, I didn't see Barron leave this morning." Fredrick clicked his fingernails together. "Is he okay?"

"He's alright." Ollie's English accent danced around his words. "He got off the ship first thing. His friends told me when I took them off the ship. Some new drama or something."

"I hope it doesn't mess up their plans for tonight."

I don't think I can handle any more mistakes that I might be responsible for.

"Nah, it'll be fine." Tomas commented. "They were making out before he left."

Ollie and Nuwa laughed.

"Well, that's good." Fredrick lightened and his muscles relaxed. Knowing they were happy brought him some joy.

"Speak of the devil," Tomas said as Leo walked over to the group, adjusting his uniform jacket.

Leo huffed and smiled. "Fredrick, you and I need to go and close out the lounge. I want you to get a feel for our closing procedures."

Fredrick stood. "Sure thing." He flattened his uniform jacket and dusted off his pants.

Leo glanced around at the rest of his team. "Once you finish with your closeout reports and review the guest list for embarkation tomorrow, the day is yours."

"Nice." Tomas stood.

"And don't forget to write your welcome cards and go over the upcoming excursion roster and see if any of your guests are signed up. Also, the spa is going to be running a special this next cruise. Their numbers were off and they want to see if they can do better this next trip."

"Cheers," Ollie said.

"I'm all set," Nuwa announced, adjusting her glasses.

"Of course you are." Leo chuckled and glanced at Fredrick. "Shall we? The sooner we finish up the sooner you get to enjoy your time off."

"Sounds good."

They made their way through the quieting airship. Now with most of the guests off the *Hawaiian Sun*, the cleaning and maintenance teams were out in full force, ensuring that everything was ready for their next round of guests. There was a certain kind of buzz in the air that reminded Fredrick of the turnovers on the *Hindenburg*. The crew can work and not worry about ruining the illusion for the customers.

We can almost relax on days like this.

They exited out of the ship and into the empty private lounge. "Aurora already left?"

"I figured you and I can handle this."

"What do we need to do?" Everything appeared to be cleaned up: there were no misplaced pieces of luggage, all the snacks and drinks had been removed, and even the music no longer played.

"We're waiting," Leo responded, pulling out his phone to type.

"I need to get one of those. They seem to come in handy."

"Especially when you're planning a bit of a surprise." Leo gestured to the entrance/exit.

"What?" Fredrick turned.

"Sorry." Barron turned the corner, wearing a simple pair of jeans and a green button-up short-sleeved shirt. "The Captain wasn't kidding about not letting—"

Fredrick's heart leaped and heat filled his face as his mouth opened. Following Barron was Martin, donned in black jeans and a powder blue long-sleeved shirt. In his hands was a bouquet of white roses. "Martin," Fredrick gasped.

"...Martin anywhere near her ship." Barron's sentence faded and he moved over to Leo.

"What are you doing here?" The words rushed from Fredrick's mouth as he crossed the gap between them, stopping short of jumping into his arms.

"I didn't like how things were left between us, and I got a call from Barron."

Fredrick turned toward Leo and Barron. "You called Martin?" His heart pounded all the way from his feet to the top of his head as his body buzzed with energy.

Barron shrugged. "Everyone deserves to have at least one Disney ending."

"Come on, Fairy Godmother." Leo took Barron's hand. "Let's give them some time to talk."

"But don't we have—"

Leo raised his hand, cutting off Fredrick. "Everything here is finished. You'll need to complete your closeout, but I think this is more urgent."

Fredrick wanted to rush over and hug and kiss them both, but there was a certain level of decorum that he always insisted on maintaining, even if his own body and mind screamed to the contrary.

"Thank you." Fredrick beamed at his friends before Leo and Barron headed back to the airship.

"I can't believe you're here." Fredrick's whole body tingled and was as light as the *Hawaiian Sun.* If he wasn't careful they would need to moor him to keep him on the ground. "I didn't think I'd see you again."

"I didn't think so either." Martin held out the flowers. "These are for you."

Fredrick laughed. "You remembered."

"How can I forget? They remind you of your family and that's a pretty powerful image."

Fredrick took the flowers and sniffed them. "I can't believe you're here. I can't believe any of this."

"I'm happy you're happy to see me." Martin moved to some of the seats and sat down.

Fredrick joined him. "So now what?" This was all fine and dandy but their reality still existed. "We leave tomorrow afternoon on another trip to Hawaii."

"But you'll be back, and we have tonight, if you're interested. Fredrick, I'd like to get to know you. I'd like to spend real time with you. I don't know where things will end up, but ..." He sat deeper in his seat. "Why is this so difficult?"

"I'm over a hundred and ten years old and I'm from a different Earth." Can any of this work? Was he fooling himself? What kind of future did they have? "Maybe this isn't such—"

"Fredrick," Martin cut him off. "Do you like me? Do you want to spend time with me?"

"I think so … I mean, yes, of course. I'm still dreaming about our dancing and being at that safehouse in Honolulu. Watching you leave the other day hurt, because I know all that you did for me. You let them treat you like some petulant child. I wanted to—I don't know. I was relieved and annoyed."

"But they came around. Barron and Leo arranged this for me. For us." He took Fredrick's cheek in his hand, turning his head to face him. "Do you like me?"

Fredrick laughed and leaned in, resting his head on Martin's shoulder. "I do, yes."

"Okay, finish what you need to finish today, change into your civvies, and go out with me. There're several places we can go, and be together, and get to know one another outside of this carefully crafted fantasy world." He waved his hand around.

"I'd like that." Fredrick's lips and heart rose. In this moment, he felt like he had a real shot at happiness. He didn't have to worry about being found out, or being a disappointment to anyone. He could ultimately live his life for himself. He could be the man he wanted to be and live in a world where that was possible. His past didn't matter. Where he came from wasn't important. Only what lay ahead of him, of them, held any importance now.

EPILOGUE

L EO PULLED AT HIS DRESS UNIFORM. It wasn't fitting right, and he looked stupid. His outfit was all wrong.

"No." He shook his head at the mirror. He made the right choice, and despite his misgivings at first, he knew all dreams might change. And his did. He inhaled, noting a piece of lint on his jacket and picking it off as a knock caught his attention. "Come in." Leo pulled out his lint roller and started running the device over his dress uniform again.

Fredrick strolled through the door, fully dressed in his formal uniform. "You look incredible."

"Did I make a mistake?" Leo asked, meeting Fredrick's gaze in the mirror instead of turning to face him. Leo's stomach was a jumble of nerves and he went from being freezing to burning up.

Maybe I should go to medical and have Dr. Young give me the once-over.

Fredrick crossed over to him, took the lint roller, and placed it on the table next to the mirror. He gently moved Leo so they faced each other and Fredrick adjusted Leo's tie. "Regarding?"

"All of this?" He took in Tammy's quarters. Today the space felt so different than all the other times he'd been here.

"No." Fredrick inhaled. "I know you wanted to be the Captain someday. I know that was your dream, but dreams change. I know my dreams changed." His face lit up as his dimples appeared. "Our lives change. Look at you now. Head Steward of the *Hawaiian Sun*— that's a big deal. Okay, you're not the Captain, but you're all but her equal. She flies the ship and you do everything else. You ensure the dream and the magic is real for all our guests. This is where your heart is. You know it and I know it."

Leo's heart slowed its pounding. The banging drum in his head slowly retreated. "Well, not my whole heart."

Fredrick smirked. "True." He stepped to the side of Leo, picking up the lint roller and running it over Leo's shoulders and down his back. "By the way, Ms. Lam made it here."

"But I thought—"

Fredrick put the lint roller back down. "Now. Are you ready?"

Leo inhaled and took one more look at the mirror. "Yes."

•   •   •

Fredrick arrived on the Pali deck with Leo, his friend jumpier than he had ever seen him, even more so than on the day he took the promotion to Head Steward. The more time Fredrick spent here on the *Hawaiian Sun*, the more this world became his home. He missed his former life sometimes, but this was where he belonged; the universe, Fates, or maybe the Angels knew what they were doing. His life before here seemed more like a bad dream.

Leo had been a grounding rod for him, so being here today with him, seeing how nervous Leo was, it was time for Fredrick to return the favor. Fredrick glanced over at Leo. "You good?"

Leo took a shaky breath.

"I'm going to take my seat. We're all here if you need us."

Leo took Fredrick's hand. "Thank you. You've been an amazing friend."

Fredrick's heart lifted at the comment. "As have you." He leaned in and gave Leo a hug before leaving him in the shadows to wait for his official entrance.

Fredrick took in all the people who were here for the event, including Mr. and Mrs. Asher at the front, and he knew them being here meant the world to Leo. Meeting Leo's parents and getting to know them over the years had been nice. They were incredible people and took him in without so much as a question. He wouldn't say they treated him like family, but they were kind and always treated him well.

They're as close to family as I have anymore. And I'm happy with that.

Fredrick quickly sat and his hand interlaced with Martin's.

"Is he all set?"

"I believe so," Fredrick answered.

"I bet you never figured you'd live to see the day when something like this happens," Martin whispered.

"I've arranged plenty of weddings on board this ship."

"True, but still." Martin rested his head on Fredrick's shoulder.

"Seeing two people who love one another, no matter their gender, getting married—no, I never imagined I'd see the day," Fredrick admitted. "And I bet you never considered the Captain would allow you back on her ship."

Martin ginned. "Fair, but here we are. Did you tell Leo about your wedding gift?"

"No. I figured I'd tell him later. He's always wanted to cruise on the *Hindenburg 2000*. I think between that, and letting him stay at my home in Seligenstadt, will be a nice surprise."

"I wish he didn't have to wait."

Fredrick shrugged. "I don't think he'll mind."

After Fredrick's first contract with the *Hawaiian Sun* ended, he took some time off and headed home to Germany. Seeing his hometown and the home that had been his parents' filled him with so much joy, he kicked himself for waiting so long. But sharing that adventure with Martin had made it all the more special and worth the delay.

Everything he discovered with Martin had been special, even when they fought and parted ways. The break in their relationship gave Fredrick time to learn more about himself and what he needed. When he and Martin met up seven months ago, he was ready for them to be together.

As much as I hated the time apart, it was the best thing for us.

As the music played, everyone turned and faced the rear of the deck, the ship's cover closed to protect from the cooler temperatures, though the sun still managed to keep the space comfortable.

•   •   •

"Hiya, babe." Leo inhaled. "Are you ready?"

"Ready or not." Barron beamed over at him as he laced his hand through Leo's arm. Barron wore a traditional groom's tuxedo with vintage white jacket, black bowtie, and black pants. The studs on his shirt sparkled from all the light, as did his cufflinks.

He looks so beautiful. I can't believe we're doing this.

"By the way, you look fantastic," Leo commented as they walked in time to the music down the aisle.

His team had done an amazing job. Every detail was in place: the white carpet they walked down, the alter with a mix of pastel colored roses. In fact, there were more flowers than Leo had ever seen. Even the seats along the aisle were adorned with flowers.

Standing under the alter, the Captain waited for them, smiling. Leo saw his family and Barron's family, and all their friends and coworkers. It wasn't an easy ask, but this trip was for them, for all of them. Almost everyone on the zep today and for the rest of the trip were there to celebrate him and Barron. There were a few guests not part of the wedding party, but that always happened with these special trips. It was going to be a challenge to keep from trying to be the boss, but the Captain and his department heads swore they would lock him and Barron in the cabin if need be.

They are a wonderful group.

Aurora had been an easy choice to move into the role of Concierge, and bringing Nuwa up to her assistant had been a decision he fully supported. At least now Leo was in a position to get them all the extra help he knew they needed. From all reports, Jun and Makena were both excellent at their jobs.

Leo caught sight of Elijah and his partner Glenn. The two met on Fredrick's first disastrous voyage with the company. Leo was continually amazed at how that one trip to Hawaii changed all their lives.

At least Elijah stopped treating me like a pariah.

Sitting next to Elijah and his beau were Minh and Ainsley. All four were dressed to impress, but they always looked amazing, especially with Ainsley's eye for fashion and talent with design. Leo's cheeks rose higher and higher as they passed each of their friends and family. He was greeted with warm smiles in return.

They arrived at the alter and stopped as the Captain began.

Here we go. I can't wait.

•   •   •

The ceremony had been beautiful and Fredrick was honored to have been there to see one of his good friends find happiness. He wished the world could always be like this, but that wasn't the case. Despite the beauty of the day and of the coming trip, there was still a world out there filled with awful people doing awful things.

But good will always overcome evil. It has to, or none of us would be here.

"What a wonderful ceremony," a male voice called out from behind Fredrick and Martin.

They turned, and Fredrick beamed. "It really was. Are you a friend of Barron's?" Fredrick didn't recognize the African-American man. He had short-trimmed black hair, and some of the brightest green eyes Fredrick had ever seen. The guy almost looked angelic.

"No, I'm here with a couple of my friends." He gestured to a man and woman. The gentleman wore gray slacks and a light-green dress shirt with the cuffs rolled up. He had blue eyes and chiseled features. Fredrick almost gasped at how beautiful the man was.

Next to the tall blond was a woman with long black hair and high cheekbones. Her almond-shaped brown eyes seemed to grin at him. She was gorgeous in her golden flowing gown. The three could be models with ease, and might very well be.

"I'm Tad," he introduced himself. "We heard about the wedding going on and I had to come up for a quick peek. I hope that's okay. We won't stay."

I wonder if Elijah's messing with us—some drama for the day?

With all the guests milling about eating and drinking, he couldn't be sure that only the wedding party was here, but the staff shouldn't have let any uninvited guests up the elevator.

"Oh, don't blame anyone for us popping up," Tad spoke with a gentle tone.

"Come on, Tad, time to go," the blond man called over.

"Coming, Destin."

Fredrick's ears perked up at the name. "Destin?"

Sounds a lot like destiny. How odd.

Tad chuckled. "I've seen that look before on a friend of mine when I introduced him to Destin. Anyway, you two make a good couple ... maybe ...? Enjoy. I'm sure we'll see you around." Tad rushed off to his friends and they vanished toward the lifts.

"They were—"

"Fricking sexy as hell," Martin finished.

"That too," Fredrick quipped as they turned to the party.

"It's funny, though," Martin continued. "I would swear I've seen them before, especially Tad. He looked so familiar."

Fredrick scanned the deck and all the people. "What a wonderful day. I couldn't be more pleased."

"You know," Martin started, putting his empty glass on the table next to them, "this might be us … someday."

Fredrick smirked as he sipped his glass of Prosecco. "Why, Mr. Shaw, are you proposing to me, here at a wedding of our friends?"

Martin laughed. "It depends on if you're saying yes."

"Well I'm not saying no, but today isn't about us." Fredrick took a heavier pull from his drink, his heart skipping a beat. Martin had been hinting and playing coy about marriage since they got together, and it only ramped up when Leo and Barron announced they were getting married. Martin's non-question question wasn't a surprise and he had considered the idea more and more these days.

Being here on the *Hawaiian Sun* he had been involved in making a lot of weddings happen. Part of him worried that if he said yes, something would happen and thrust him into a different place and time. The more time moved forward, the less those negative intrusive thoughts crept into his mind. This was his world. This was his home. This was his life. And standing next to him was his man, just like standing next to Leo was his husband.

And for today this is all that matters.

ACKNOWLEDGMENTS

As with all my novels, this book would not be possible without the support of my amazing publisher, editors, and incredible beta readers. A special thank you to those of you who helped me get all the fiddly details correct. And most importantly none of this would happen without those of you who pick up the book and read it. To you all, I say thank you.

ABOUT THE AUTHOR

M.D. Neu is an international award-winning inclusive queer Fiction Writer with a love for writing and travel. Living in the heart of Silicon Valley, and growing up around technology, he's always been fascinated with what could be. When M.D. Neu isn't writing, he works for a non-profit and travels with his biggest supporter and his harshest critic, Eric, his husband of twenty-plus years.

ALSO BY THE AUTHOR

A DRAGON FOR CHRISTMAS

M.D. Neu

Since Carmen was seven years old, she understood two things: she was going to be the strongest Dragon Keeper there ever was, and she was going to marry her best friend, Mattie.

THE REUNION

M.D. Neu

It's been 20 years since the quiet Midwestern town of Lakeview was struck by tragedy.

Available from Water Dragon Publishing in
hardcover, trade paperback, and digital editions
waterdragonpublishing.com

www.ingramcontent.com/pod-product-compliance
Lightning Source LLC
Chambersburg PA
CBHW021141310726
48971CB00002B/432